BY
VICKI LEWIS THOMPSON

MILLS
BOON

First published in Great Britain 2012
by Mills & Boon, an imprint of Harlequin (UK) Limited,
Eton House, 18-24 Paradise Road, Richmond, Surrey TW9 1SR

© Vicki Lewis Thompson 2011

ISBN: 978 0 263 89388 5
ebook ISBN: 978 1 408 96936 6

14-1012

Harlequin (UK) policy is to use papers that are natural, renewable and
recyclable products and made from wood grown in sustainable forests. The
logging and manufacturing processes conform to the legal environmental
regulations of the country of origin.

Printed and bound in Spain
by Blackprint CPI, Barcelona

Dear Reader,

Writing romance novels is my dream job. And when you're lucky enough to have a job like that, the years go by like greased lightning!

This is the sixth book in my SONS OF CHANCE series, and I'm grateful for all of you who visit the ranch through my stories. I love hearing from you! You can e-mail me through my website at www. vickilewisthompson.com. Please do!

And finally, thanks to all the readers who've helped make Blaze such a roaring success over the years. Here's to hot heroes and happily- ever-afters!

Yours,

Vicki

New York Times bestseller **Vicki Lewis Thompson**'s love affair with cowboys started with *The Lone Ranger*, continued through *Maverick*, and took a turn south of the border with *Zorro*. She views cowboys as the Western version of knights in shining armor—rugged men who value honor, honesty and hard work. Fortunately for her, she lives in the Arizona desert, where broad-shouldered, lean-hipped cowboys abound. Blessed with such an abundance of inspiration, she only hopes that she can do them justice. Visit her website at www.vickilewisthompson.com.

To my grandmother, Nellie Sharpe,
a die-hard baseball fan. Your legacy jumped two
generations to live on in your great-granddaughter
Audrey, who eagerly awaits that first crack
of the bat every spring.

Prologue

August 8, 1963
from the diary of Eleanor Chance

NOW THAT JONATHAN's seventeen and chasing after girls, I decided to find a hobby so I wouldn't be forever worrying about him. This summer I became a Chicago Cubs baseball fan! I figured that both Jonathan and my dear husband, Archie, would share in this new passion and we'd have some family togetherness listening to the games on the radio here at the Last Chance Ranch.

So much for that idea. Turns out neither of them have the slightest interest in the sport, but I love it! I don't care if my Cubbies don't win very often. They're historic, dating way back, and Wrigley Field is a piece of history, too. Besides, I like the team's name. Bear cubs are the cutest things ever, and I should know. Here in Jackson Hole we have bears aplenty.

I suppose I could have picked football or basketball, but I don't understand those rules as well. Baseball has always made sense to me. Hearing the crack of the bat sends a chill down my spine, especially in games like today! Ron Santo hit a home run in the bottom of the tenth to beat the L.A. Dodgers, which is amazing because the Cubs aren't doing so hot, as usual, and the Dodgers are leading the National League.

When I announced this thrilling victory at dinner tonight, Jonathan and Archie both smiled and said that was nice, but I could tell they don't give a flip. Too bad for them. They're missing some great entertainment. I've sent away for a Cubs baseball cap. I'm going to wear it, too.

1

LOGAN CARSWELL, FORMER catcher for the Chicago Cubs, had two surefire remedies for a troubled mind, and he couldn't use either one. Booze was out because he'd taken pain meds for his knee so he could dance at Alex Keller's wedding reception in Shoshone, Wyoming. As for the second method, he didn't know any of the women in this tiny town well enough.

Eventually, in spite of the meds, his knee began to bother him. Retreating to one of the Spirits and Spurs's well-worn bar stools, he swiveled to face the dance floor, where Alex was two-stepping with his bride, Tyler. Logan had known him ever since they were both kids living in the same Chicago neighborhood.

Alex had never had trouble getting girls, with his all-American blond good looks. Add to that his natural charisma behind a microphone, and he'd been able to pick and choose. Apparently he'd chosen Tyler, a dark-haired Italian beauty, or she'd chosen him.

Near as Logan could tell watching the happy couple on the dance floor, they were both quite pleased with the situation. Alex was obviously in love and seemed to have his life together at last. Logan should be so lucky. But he refused to allow his problems to cast a shadow over this celebration.

"Can I get you anything, Mr. Carswell?"

Logan swiveled back to the bar and concluded that luck hadn't totally deserted him. Of the two bartenders working the wedding reception, he'd drawn the girl instead of the guy.

He'd noticed her earlier. She wore her sun-streaked brown hair in a no-nonsense ponytail and didn't seem to go in for a lot of makeup. Her hazel eyes tilted up slightly at the corners, adding a touch of the exotic to her girl-next-door appeal.

From her enthusiasm and ready smile, he guessed she might be exactly his type—a born optimist. He could sure use a dose of optimism right now.

As he gazed at her, he realized she was looking right back with similar interest. He'd built a night of outstanding sex on less. But Shoshone was a folksy town, and one-night stands wouldn't go unnoticed around here the way they would in Chicago.

Still, he could flirt with her a little without doing any harm. He tipped back the Stetson that Alex had insisted he buy, along with the requisite jeans, boots and yoked shirt. "I think this is the part where the teetotalling stranger orders a sarsaparilla." He wished he could remember her name, but if someone had mentioned it, he'd forgotten.

She laughed. "Sorry. Don't have that. But the root beer is excellent."

"That'll do."

After placing a coaster decorated with a bucking bronco in front of him, she picked up a glass mug. Her nails were short and unpolished, her movements quick and efficient. "How do you like Shoshone so far?"

"Friendly place."

"We think so."

He grabbed the first conversational topic he could think of. "Is it true that this bar is haunted?"

"So they say. That's why it's called the Spirits and Spurs." She filled the mug to the top, and foam oozed over the lip. "Personally, I've never seen a ghost in here, but some claim they have."

Logan had never considered root beer foam erotic, but as it slid down the side of the mug, his balls tightened. Not much, but enough for him to register the sensation. Yes, a good romp in the hay with someone cute and personable like this bartender would be therapeutic, but he didn't give himself much chance of having that any time soon.

She allowed the foam to settle before putting the mug on the coaster. "I've never talked to a major league ballplayer before." She sounded fascinated by the prospect.

Oh, boy. If she had a fantasy image of him as some big celebrity, he needed to nip that in the bud. "I'm afraid you're not talking to one now, either. I'm out of the game."

She met his gaze with sympathy in her eyes. "I know. Alex mentioned it. He said if you were still playing, you wouldn't have been able to come to the wedding."

"Right." He managed a smile. "At least some good came out of it."

"Still, it can't be easy. But kudos to you for putting on a brave face for the party."

A knot loosened in his chest. Just kind words from a complete stranger, but they soothed him in a way he couldn't explain. "No, it's not." He rarely admitted that to anyone, because nobody liked a guy who felt sorry for himself. But after tonight, he'd probably never see her again, so letting down his guard was easier.

"Josie said you were a starting catcher for the Cubs."

That made him smile for real. This adorable bartender didn't follow the game, or she would have known that fact without getting the info from Josie, Alex's sister. Logan's injury had come while defending the plate against a rather spectacular slide into home, and the news clip had been replayed a lot last year.

"Yes, I was a catcher," he said. At least she wouldn't be pestering him for gossip about the big-name players. Sure, his ego took a small hit because she wasn't a fan, but all things considered, he counted it a good thing that she wasn't.

He decided to extend the friendliness. "So how long have you been tending bar?"

"Not long. I was the restaurant waitress until recently, when Josie asked me to start easing into her job so I'll be comfortable with it by the time her baby's born and she has to take time off."

"You seem comfortable with it now."

"Only because she sent me to a crash course in bartending."

Logan nodded. "I know all about those. When I was in the minors, I supplemented my income serving drinks."

"Yikes. You probably know more about this than I do!"

"Nah. It's been several years. Excuse me for not remembering, but what's your name?"

"Caro. Caro Davis."

"Karo like the syrup?"

"Caro like short for Carolyn. Josie started calling me that a while back, and I like it. I feel more like a Caro than a Carolyn, anyway."

He thought the shorter name suited her. "Is Josie a good boss?" Logan remembered Josie as a pesky little kid who was constantly tagging after him and Alex. He had a hard time imagining her as a wife and mother-to-be, let alone the proud owner of a cowboy bar in Wyoming. She'd married Jack Chance, the oldest of the three Chance brothers, and seemed blissfully happy living at the Last Chance Ranch, located about ten miles outside town.

Caro grinned at him. "As if I'd tell you if she wasn't. But she's great. She managed to promote me to this position without upsetting Tracy, who's a little young to take over Josie's job, or Steve, who's a new hire but knows bartending. Either of them could have resented me getting it. Josie handled it beautifully."

"Hey, Caro." The tall guy sharing bartending duties glanced her way. "Orders piling up down here."

"Be right there, Steve." She smiled at Logan. "Excuse me. Gotta do my job."

"You bet." He watched her walk away, ponytail bouncing. Damn, that smile of hers really cheered him up. He'd love to see more of it. He'd love to…no, he shouldn't start imagining how her perky self would react in bed. He shouldn't, but he did.

"Hey, Logan, don't be hitting on my best employee." Josie took the bar stool on his left and punched him playfully on the shoulder. She was more dressed up than he'd ever seen her, all blue satin and lace. Instead of braiding her hair in one strand down her back as she usually did, she'd created an upswept arrangement that made her look like a princess.

He winked at her. "Wouldn't dream of it."

"Yeah, right. You were sizing her up just now, and don't try to deny it."

"Just having some innocent fun." Thoughts weren't deeds, right? "By the way, you look terrific, Josie. This Jack character must be treating you right."

"Don't try to change the subject." But her gray eyes, so like Alex's, sparkled with obvious pleasure at the compliment. "Caro has enough on her plate without having you swoop in and dazzle her with your big-city ways."

"Big-city ways?" He pressed a hand to his heart. "You make me sound like an operator. I'm wounded."

"You know what I'm talking about, Logan. A guy can't live the life you have without picking up a boatload of polish and sophistication."

"Now that's more like it." He winked at her. "Thanks for the compliment, Josie."

"See, that sly wink is exactly what I'm talking about. And I can tell she's impressed with you."

"You think so?" His poor ego could take all the help it could get.

"Don't mess with her, okay?"

"I had no such plans." He'd already decided that getting cozy with a local girl would be a mistake. Now Josie was warning him off of this particular one, which was more than enough to cool his jets. He really wasn't here to cause more problems. He already had enough to handle, like what the hell to do with the rest of his life.

But he couldn't help being curious about the cute little bartender. "What did you mean when you said she has enough on her plate?"

"It wouldn't be my place to tell you."

"Man troubles?"

"No. Listen, take my word for it." Josie patted his arm. "Caro's become a close friend in addition to being an employee, so I can tell you with certainty that she doesn't have time for romance right now, and she especially doesn't have time for someone who will be gone in a couple of days."

"Is that when my guest privileges expire?"

She flushed. "Uh...no! You can certainly stay as long as you want. I just thought, with Alex and Tyler leaving on their honeymoon tomorrow, that you'd...well, you'd want to go back to Chicago."

She had no idea how much he dreaded going home. The

season was in the middle of its usual August frenzy, with billboards and TV ads reminding him every ten seconds that some guys were playing ball and he was not. He was thrilled to get away from the unspoken message that he was a washed up has-been at the tender age of thirty-two.

"Well, yeah, I need to get back eventually," he said. "But I've never spent time on a ranch, so I was thinking, as long as I'm out here, I'd like to play cowboy for a few days. Unless I'd be in the way."

"Of course not. We'd love to have you. Are you thinking about riding?"

He wasn't sure what he was thinking about, except that the Last Chance felt like a haven, and he could use one. "Riding would be great. I'll need a little instruction, but—"

"What about your knee?"

"It's my right knee that's dicey, and I vaguely remember you mount from the left, so I should be fine."

Josie smiled at him, understanding in her gray eyes. "You can stay as long as you want, Logan. Glad to have you."

"I appreciate it." More than she knew.

"But leave Caro alone."

"You've got it." And to emphasize his willingness to ignore the lovely bartender, he left his half-full root beer on the bar and held out his hand to Josie. "May I have this dance, Alex's little sis?"

"Might as well. Can't drink!"

"That's right, you're on the wagon for the next few months. I'll bet you're popular as a designated driver these days."

"I am, at that." As they arrived at the edge of the dance floor, she moved into his arms. "I must say, you picked up country dancing really fast for a guy raised in the city."

Logan guided her expertly into the crowd of two-stepping couples. "Thanks. Guess it's the athlete in me."

"Guess so." She twirled under his arm. "The Chance

brothers are famous for their dancing. You're not quite in their league, but given more practice, you could be."

Logan grinned. "See? I have the boots, the jeans, the hat and the dance moves. I'm halfway to becoming a cowboy already."

THE RUSH OF DRINK ORDERS finally slowed, but when Caro returned to check on Logan, he'd hit the dance floor with Josie. He'd left his unfinished root beer behind, though, which meant he might be back. She felt a little jolt of excitement as she remembered the way he'd looked at her with obvious interest.

And she'd looked right back. She had no business flirting with anyone right now, but those deep brown eyes temporarily made her forget her obligations. And that, she realized with a pang of guilt, was nice for a change. She just couldn't let it get out of hand.

Her grandma Bonnie, who had raised her, joyfully and without complaint, deserved all Caro's free time. Caro had been a baby when her parents divorced, and Bonnie had welcomed her daughter and granddaughter into her house. When Caro was twelve, her mother had died in a blizzard on her way home from work. Grandma Bonnie's strength had seen Caro through those dark days and taught her that a person had to be resilient to survive life's tragedies.

Her dad had started a new family by then, but Caro had never seriously considered living with him. She'd stayed with her grandma in the only home she'd ever known. Selling that beloved house so that she could afford assisted living in Jackson for the increasingly frail Bonnie had broken both their hearts.

Caro visited her grandmother every day in hopes she wouldn't feel abandoned, but she obviously wasn't happy with the move, necessary though it had been. For the first time since Caro had known her, Bonnie had lost her resilience and optimistic outlook. Caro had to be optimistic enough for both of them.

Lately Caro had done nothing but work and visit her grandma. No wonder she'd been bewitched by a heated glance. Besides, she'd been predisposed to find this ex-baseball player intriguing.

Alex had warned everyone to tread carefully around Logan, whose wicked knee injury had ended his career and the dream he'd cherished from the age of seven. He'd made it to the big leagues and then to the Cubs, the team he'd always wanted to play for. Now he was done.

Caro had never been able to resist a person in need of comfort, a trait she'd picked up from her grandma. Besides, Logan was gorgeous, the kind of gorgeous that made her think of hot nights on cool sheets. Good thing he'd be gone soon. Once Alex and Tyler left on their honeymoon, Logan would have no reason to stay.

She filled several orders while Logan whirled around the dance floor with Josie, but somehow, about the time he returned to his root beer, she happened to be standing at that end of the bar. She hadn't meant to.

Oh, shoot, yes she had. He was the most exotic man to come her way in quite a while. Mostly she dealt with cowboys. Logan might be wearing the outfit and dancing the two-step like a pro, but he was no cowboy.

Instead, he was a professional athlete from the big city. She didn't know much about baseball, but she knew Logan was hot.

He settled onto his stool and heaved a sigh. "That's challenging."

"But you do it well." The action of those tight buns on the dance floor had created a serious distraction from her bartending duties.

"Close enough for jazz." He took a long swallow of his root beer.

"What does that mean?"

He glanced up. "What?"

"Close enough for jazz. I've never heard that before."

"Sorry. It's something jazz musicians say, meaning that there's a lot of improv going on when they perform."

She felt a little bit like a hick, but she was fascinated, nevertheless. Besides, if she kept this conversation going, she'd have an excuse to gaze into those brown eyes. "Chicago's known for its jazz, I guess."

"It is. I don't suppose that's the kind of music you…"

"Not normally, but I'm always ready to learn something new." No, that statement wasn't strong enough. She *hungered* for something new, something different. She'd lived in Shoshone all her life. Travel had been a luxury she hadn't been able to afford beyond an occasional trip to Yellowstone.

But this man, who'd jetted around the country for years, represented adventure beyond her wildest dreams. She found that irresistible.

Picking up a bar rag, she began wiping up imaginary spills. "Shoshone must seem small to you after spending so much time in big cities."

"Actually, it's a nice break. I can see why Alex is so crazy about the place. The Grand Tetons are amazing."

"I agree. They are. But I'm sure the Chicago skyline is amazing, too, especially at night."

"It is," he said with a decided lack of enthusiasm.

Damn. She felt like an idiot. Of course he wouldn't want to talk about the wonders of Chicago and be reminded of losing the job he loved. "The Tetons are great, though. Wonderful for hiking. You should—" She groaned as she realized she'd made a mess of this discussion. "But you have a bad knee. You know what? I should just shut up."

He laughed. "It's okay. I forget about my knee all the time, until I stay on it too long and it lets me know."

"Can you ride? Because you could take a horse up into the mountains, if it wouldn't be too strenuous." She'd bet he would look terrific mounted on a horse. Yum.

"I'll have to brush up on my riding skills, but I've been thinking about that. Do you ride?"

"I know how, but lately I haven't had the time." She refused to allow herself to be resentful of her grandma, but still, a trail ride with Logan would have been fun.

"Caro." Steve, looking pale, appeared at her elbow. His short buzz cut was dark with sweat. The room was warm, but not that warm. "I hate to do this to you, but my stomach's going wonky. Feels like food poisoning. I must have eaten something bad earlier today. In any case, I gotta go home."

She put her hand to her own tummy, which had immediately rolled in sympathy. "That's terrible. Don't worry about the bar. Just go home and get better."

"Thanks. I can take your shift tomorrow if you want."

"Only if you're well enough. Get out of here, cowboy." She sucked in a deep breath as Steve opened the hinged bar top and headed toward the back door. She'd counted on him to get her through this first big event, but she could manage, especially if the party started to wind down soon.

But Murphy's Law was working against her. The minute Steve left, the band took a break and wedding guests swarmed the bar in search of drinks. Fighting down panic, she squared her shoulders and grabbed an order pad. No way could she keep all those drinks in her head.

"You handle the beer and wine. I'll mix the drinks."

She looked up from the order pad and discovered Logan had joined her behind the bar and was already reaching for a couple of martini glasses.

"No, you shouldn't." She put a hand on his shoulder—his

very warm, very muscled shoulder. Instantly, that heat spread through her body. Whew. "You're a guest. I'm sure Josie could—"

"She's the sister of the groom. She shouldn't have to work tonight. Besides, I want to." He set the glasses on the counter and gave her a quick glance before picking up a bottle of vodka. "It feels great to be useful for a change."

She couldn't argue with that reasoning. Didn't really want to, actually. If helping her would make him feel better about his lot in life, even for an hour or so, then she couldn't deny him that. And she'd get the benefit of working side by side with the hottest guy in Shoshone.

"Okay, then," she said. "But only until it slows down."

"Right." He picked up a martini shaker, flipped it high in the air and caught it behind his back.

Someone in the crowd whistled.

Logan winked at Caro. "You know, I'd forgotten how much I used to love this job."

Oh, baby. He was positively delicious, and Caro was the lucky girl who got to co-bartend with him for an hour or so. She would never wish ill on anyone, but in that moment, she was really glad that Steve had ended up with food poisoning.

2

BEFORE JUMPING IN TO help Caro, Logan had spent a couple seconds weighing the pros and cons. Josie had asked him to stay away from Caro, but then again, Josie hadn't anticipated Steve getting sick. Logan had seen the panic in Caro's eyes when the band had stopped playing and the surge toward the bar had commenced.

Finally, deciding Josie shouldn't have to worry about working tonight, and surely she'd rather have happy customers than obsess about Caro and Logan working together, he'd swung into action. He couldn't pretend it was a selfless act. He'd told Caro the absolute truth—doing something useful felt fantastic.

And yeah, the idea of being Caro's heroic savior for an hour or so was very appealing. The looks she gave him generated a sexual buzz he hadn't felt in quite a while, and he was enjoying the hell out of that.

He promised himself that once the rush subsided, he'd retreat to the other side of the bar. Somehow, the rush never let up. Part of that could be his fault, because he hadn't been able to resist showing off a little. Besides juggling the martini shaker, he'd built a few flaming drinks, which caused folks to order more so they could watch the process.

And damn, he was having a good time. He was also

impressing the girl. He'd caught her staring a few times, although she didn't allow herself to be distracted from her work. For two people who'd never bartended together before, they managed with a minimum of bumping into each other.

That was a good thing, because whenever he accidentally brushed up against her, he registered exactly how soft and curvy she was. That message went straight to his groin.

She also smelled of lemons, which might be her perfume or might be the lemons she'd been cutting before he took over the cocktail part of the bar duties. Whatever the reason, the scent fit her personality, which was fresh, bright, and sexy as hell.

Once in a while his knee gave him a twinge, but then he'd take his weight off his right leg and be okay again. He was grateful for that, because the party showed no signs of letting up, even after Alex and Tyler left in a shower of birdseed. One o'clock came and went. Most bars closed then, but this one was owned by the sister of the groom, and she didn't seem ready to kick people out.

Caro slipped past him holding two brimming mugs of beer. "I'm worried about your knee," she said.

"Don't be." He garnished a cosmo. "I'm fine."

"I'm not sure I believe you."

"Working back here is a hell of a lot easier than dancing." He delivered the cosmo and came back with a couple dirty glasses. "Besides, I'm enjoying the company." He probably shouldn't have said that, but it wasn't as if he planned to ask her out.

"Me, too." She sent him a dazzling smile.

That made him feel good, probably too good. He wondered what she had going on in her life that kept her from dating. She seemed like someone who was worth getting to know, on many levels, but they were too busy for him to ask any questions.

Around two, the crowd finally began to thin, and Josie came to sit at the bar.

"Can I get you something?" Logan asked.

"No, thanks, but I owe you a huge debt for filling in tonight. I hope you haven't stressed your knee."

"I'm fine."

"I'd forgotten you used to tend bar, but Alex reminded me after he saw you back here flipping martini shakers around."

"I had fun." Working in close proximity with Caro had been ninety percent of that fun, but he'd keep that fact to himself.

"I could tell. Anyway, we're all about to head back to the ranch, and most everyone else is ready to call it a night, too. Or technically, I guess we have to call it a morning."

Logan took stock of the remaining dirty glasses, popcorn baskets and crumpled napkins lining the bar and grouped on the tables. "It was some party, Josie."

"It was. Alex and Tyler deserved a blowout, so I'm glad we did it up right. When you're ready, I'll give you a ride back, along with my slightly toasted husband."

Logan gestured around the room. "Do we need to take care of the final cleanup?"

"We probably should, at that." Josie straightened her shoulders. "You're right. I don't want to leave this for the morning crew."

"Or you can let Caro and me handle it." He made the suggestion casually, but there was nothing casual about his intentions. He wanted to be alone with the lovely Caro Davis.

"I can do it, Logan," Caro said immediately. "No worries. Go home and rest your knee."

"My knee's fine." Logan started gathering glasses. "I want to stay and help get this cleaned up. It won't take long."

Jack Chance wandered over and hooked an arm around Josie. "Ready to take off?"

"Not quite," Josie said. "I really need to—"

"No, you don't," Caro said. "Go home, Josie."

"I hate to leave you with this." She surveyed the room. "It's too bad that Steve—"

"Well, he isn't here," Logan said, "and I'd really like to help out. Besides, maybe one of the fabled ghosts will show up."

"It could happen." Josie looked perfectly serious. "I've often seen them after a bash like this."

"Ghosts or no ghosts," Jack said, "I need to get my pregnant wife home. I have a suggestion. Let Logan stay and help, and then he can crash at Grandma Judy's."

Josie turned to him. "I'm not sure about that, Jack. Do you think your grandmother will—"

"She'll love the idea. She's always complaining that nobody uses her guest room. Let me borrow your pen, Caro." He picked up a napkin from a stack on the bar and sketched a quick map for Logan. "Here's where she lives. When we drop her off we'll make sure she leaves a key under the mat. The guest room is down the hall to your right."

Josie took one last look at the debris left by the wedding guests and sighed. "Okay. There's probably some fatal flaw in that plan, but I'm too tired to think of anything better, and I do hate to leave Caro alone with this huge mess."

"And the ghosts." Logan tucked the napkin with the map into his pocket, and did his best to sound nonchalant when he felt anything but. He wondered if Caro was anticipating some alone time as much as he was.

"And the ghosts," Josie said with a smile.

"Thanks, Logan." Jack stuck out his hand and the two men shook. "I'll drive in tomorrow morning and pick you up."

"Sounds good."

"Josie said you'd like to stay on for a few more days and do some riding."

"I'd like that, but I'm a little rusty."

"Anybody with your athletic ability shouldn't have any trouble." Jack touched the brim of his hat with two fingers. "See you tomorrow."

"That was very gallant of you," Caro said as the last of the wedding guests disappeared out the front door. "You must be exhausted."

He turned to her. "No more so than you, I'll bet." He took note of the wisps of hair that had escaped her ponytail and now curled around the nape of her neck. Any lipstick she might have applied earlier in the evening was gone. She looked infinitely kissable.

Her hazel eyes were bright, as if she might be feeling some of the same excitement he was. "Yes, but I'm paid to do this. You're not."

"You want to know something really sad? Getting paid isn't an issue for me anymore. I've invested a good chunk of the money I earned while playing with the Cubs, and unless I start buying yachts and staying in hotels that charge several grand a night, I won't ever have to work again." That was all true, but he might have said it to impress her. Hell, sure he had.

It obviously did, because her eyes widened. "But that's not sad, that's *wonderful.*"

Her honest reaction demanded honesty in return. "You would think so, wouldn't you? But in reality, it's kind of depressing. I have no reason to go out and hustle anymore."

"You could do all sorts of volunteer things, take charge of some cause or other, travel—"

"I could, and I probably will look into a charitable cause, but I'm not much of an administrator. That doesn't get me excited. Helping people, yeah, I'd like that. But the thought of being the one in charge gives me hives." He hadn't meant to discuss this, but talking to someone who had no vested interest in his future seemed to loosen his tongue.

"What a fascinating problem to have, deciding what to do with money and free time." She walked over to the wall and put her hand on a bank of switches.

"I suppose it sounds lame to call that a problem."

"Not if you're used to being busy. Get ready. Bright lights."

He blinked. In the glare from the overhead lights the mess looked even worse. "This would be more fun with the lights off."

She glanced over her shoulder, a definite invitation in her eyes. "That's true of a lot of things."

He met her gaze. He knew that look, and instantly his cock responded. Okay then. "Oh, I don't know. Sometimes I like to see what I'm doing."

She turned back to him with a seductive smile. "Is that when you're not very sure of yourself?"

"On the contrary." Lust was quickly obliterating the memory of any warnings Josie had given him. "The more confident I am, the more light I want on the subject." He paused. "How about you?"

She swallowed, and her cheeks grew pink. "Personally, I like to retain a little mystery."

"That can be exciting, too." He'd instinctively drifted closer. If he kissed her now, they wouldn't get any cleaning done.

As if realizing the same thing, Caro cleared her throat and glanced away. "It's getting late." Pulling a plastic bin from under the counter, she lifted the hinged lid of the bar. "I'll clear if you'll wipe up after me."

He followed her out through the opening and got a grip on the bin. "I'll clear and you wipe up. You're the brains of this operation. I'm just the muscle."

Her laugh had a breathless quality that told him she was

very aware of the sparks flying between them. She let him have the bin. "If that makes you happy, knock yourself out. I'll get a damp towel. Just know that I can balance a full tray of drinks on one hand, so I'm no wimpy girl."

"So you're the brains *and* the muscle." He loaded glasses, popcorn baskets and used napkins into the bin while she followed behind and wiped off the tables. "How am I supposed to impress a girl who has everything?"

"Those flaming drinks were pretty darned impressive. I know you don't need a job, but I'll bet Josie would love to hire you. Oh, wait. You might take my job, and unlike you, I need the money, so forget that idea."

She'd just handed him a golden opportunity to ask why Josie had said she was off-limits. He cleared the last table and headed back toward the bar. "So how come you don't have time to go riding these days?"

"My grandmother's in assisted living, and whenever I'm not working, I visit her."

"You mean, every day?" Logan thought of his two grandmothers, plus two grandfathers, all living back in Chicago. His folks and his younger brother, Jeff, lived there, too. He saw his grandparents maybe six or seven times a year. He didn't see any of his relatives daily.

"Yes, I go every day. But I'm sure you don't want to hear about this."

"Yes, I do. Come back into the kitchen while I stack the dishwasher, and tell me about it."

"It's not all that interesting. You go on. I'll start putting up the chairs."

He rested the bin against the counter. "Why don't you want to tell me?"

"Because it's boring." She picked up a chair and turned it upside down on a table, and followed that with another chair, and another.

"I don't think so."

"I do." She stacked chairs in rapid succession. "I love my grandmother more than anyone in the world, but there are times when worrying about her is a real buzzkill." She paused, her hand on the back of a chair. Then she turned to him with a stricken expression. "Did I just say that? I must be a horrible person to say something like that."

He smiled gently. "Not a horrible person. Just a person who needs to get out more. And I don't mean to the assisted living facility."

She shook her head. "I can't. She knows my schedule, and she expects me to come whenever I'm not working. I need to be there for her. I *want* to be there for her."

"That's pretty intense. Can't you back off from that a little bit?"

"Eventually I hope to, once she's back to her usual sunny self. These first few months have been rough on her. I had to move her out of her house and sell it to pay for this place, because she needs constant medical supervision. It was the only answer."

Josie might be annoyed, but Logan thought of his next move as a good deed. "Didn't Steve say he'd take your next shift?"

"He did, but he might not feel up to it."

"Then again, he might. When is it?"

"Three to eleven, but he looked pretty sick to me."

"If it's food poisoning, he could be over it by tomorrow. And if he can take your shift, then you could go riding with me at the Last Chance. Your grandmother would never know." He would explain to Josie that her best employee was about to blow a gasket if she didn't get some recreation into her routine. Surely Josie would understand.

Caro hesitated. "I have to admit that sounds nice."

"Of course it does. Taking a trail ride was your suggestion in the first place."

"Josie and Jack have told me anytime I want to come out and ride, I'm more than welcome."

"There you go." His excitement grew as he imagined spending hours with her out on the trail. No doubt he'd end up saddle sore, but it would be worth it to watch her soaking up the sunshine and fresh air. And maybe a long trail ride could turn into a private little... But he didn't want to get ahead of himself.

"Now I'm really hoping Steve recovers."

"Me, too." Logan was prepared to find another replacement if Steve was still on the disabled list. He'd plead Caro's case to Josie and see what could be done. "Now let's finish cleaning so you can go home and get some sleep." He tossed that last part out on purpose, to see if she had any plan to linger around...with him.

"Okay." She started stacking chairs on tables again. "Fortunately, I don't have to go far. Josie's renting me her old apartment upstairs."

That info flashed in neon lights in his hormone-soaked brain. So her bedroom was right over their heads. "That's convenient." He picked up the bin full of glasses and headed into the kitchen.

As he loaded the commercial dishwasher, he fought with his conscience. He'd pictured some time alone, maybe a few kisses, some fondling. *But her bedroom was right upstairs.*

He probably shouldn't go there, even if he could work it so nobody ever had to know but the two of them. Then again, she might have mentioned it on purpose, hoping he'd take the hint. She might not have time for a relationship, but was there anything wrong with some good old-fashioned sex?

He sighed. Josie had specifically requested that he put on the brakes, and he was considering flooring it. She was obviously protective of Caro, and Logan admired that. But should Josie be the one to decide what happened between Caro and him? Or should she be allowed to choose for herself?

So much hinged on Caro's attitude. After spending several hours working with her, he saw her as upbeat and levelheaded, not the sort of woman who would expect one fun night together meant wedding bells.

He started the dishwasher and walked back out into the bar, where Caro wielded a push broom with gusto. The rapid motion made her breasts quiver under her red checked Western shirt. From her complete concentration, someone might conclude that the fate of the world rested on getting every last bit of debris off the floor.

Logan had always admired hustle, but he knew she must be tired. "I'd be glad to finish that up if there's something else you need to do to close the place down."

"Not really." She kept sweeping, her gaze focused intently on the job, her fingers clenched around the broom handle. "As you noticed, it was an open bar tonight, which was Josie and Jack's gift to the happy couple, so I don't have to tally any receipts."

"Want me to take out the trash?"

She shook her head and kept working. "It's better to put it out in the morning. Once in a while we have bears come through at night." She looked up. "We're basically done, Logan. Thanks so much. You can head on over to Judy's place if you want." She put her head down and continued to sweep as if her life depended on it.

"Trying to get rid of me?"

She stopped in midsweep and gazed at him. "No, but I'll bet you're exhausted."

"Funniest thing, but I'm not particularly sleepy."

"Oh." She started sweeping again, but her motions were

slower. "Then if you don't mind getting the small broom and that long-handled dustpan, I'd appreciate it."

"I can do that." He found them over in a corner and began gathering up the piles she'd made and dumping everything into a plastic-lined trash can.

"Logan, do you have a girlfriend?"

He almost choked on his answer. "No." He could think of only one reason for that question. He cleared his throat so he could elaborate as he continued to scoop up trash. "I was dating someone, but it turned out she wasn't crazy about going out with an ex-baseball player."

"Ouch."

He glanced over at Caro. "Actually, it was one of the good things about leaving the game. She had a chance to show her true colors." He paused. "Do you have a boyfriend?" From Josie's comments, he was fairly sure she didn't, but he might as well make certain.

She leaned on the broom. "I used to. Curtis got tired of me not being available because of my grandma. We broke up about six months ago." She took a deep breath. "Quite obviously, I'm not girlfriend material at the moment. There's no room in my life for a man."

Logan nodded, as if they were discussing the weather. "I understand completely."

"But…"

"Yes?" Dear God, he hoped this conversation was leading where he thought it was.

She opened her mouth, and then closed it again. When she finally spoke, the words came out in a rush. "Would you be interested in coming up for a nightcap?" Her cheeks were pink but her gaze was steady.

His heart thudded in anticipation, but he wanted to be sure this was what she really wanted. "You must be tired."

Her hazel eyes grew dark and her breathing quickened. "Not that tired."

Dear God, she wanted him in her bed. Only a fool would pass up a chance like this, and Logan was no fool. "Then yes. Yes, I would love a nightcap."

3

CARO COULDN'T QUITE believe she'd just invited Logan Carswell, big league baseball star, up to her apartment. Even more
unbelievable, he'd accepted. Eagerly. She'd acted on pure
instinct, and apparently her instincts were on target. They
wanted each other.

The old nightcap routine was as transparent as ever. He had
to know as well as she did why they were going up there. And
unless Logan walked around with condoms in his wallet, he
needed to make a trip into the Spirits and Spurs men's room.
After Curtis had dumped her, she'd taken the remaining condoms out of the medicine cabinet and cut them up with a pair
of scissors as part of some silly ritual to proclaim her new
celibacy.

Once Logan left town, whenever that turned out to be,
she'd be celibate again, at least until her grandmother regained
her former spirit. But opportunity had pounded on the door
in the person of Logan Carswell, wounded athlete. Caro was
more than ready to give up her mental chastity belt and embrace that opportunity to have a little fun.

Logan dumped one final dustpan's worth in the trash. "Is
that it?"

"Yes." Her heart raced. "I'll put the brooms away in the
kitchen if you'll…" She found herself unable to finish the

sentence. Inviting him up to her place on the flimsy pretext of a nightcap was one thing. Telling him to patronize the vending machine in the men's room was a whole new level of chutzpah.

"If I'll what?" He met her gaze. "Oh." Understanding registered in his brown eyes. "Guess I'll just duck into the bathroom for a minute."

"Okay." Her cheeks felt warm with embarrassment as she grabbed both brooms and the long-handled dustpan. She fumbled and dropped the push broom. The handle banged against the floor.

Before she could retrieve it, Logan reached for it in one fluid motion and held it toward her. "Here you go."

"Thanks. I'll be right back." What a doofus she must seem to a guy with his sophistication. Here she was, dropping brooms and sending him after condoms. She wondered if the women in Chicago always had supplies on hand before they impulsively asked someone up for a nightcap. Probably.

Well, she was a small-town girl from Shoshone. Besides, she'd been pissed at Curtis, and cutting up the condoms had seemed justified at the time. She'd wanted to destroy something, and that had been the best target for her anger.

Logan hadn't returned by the time she walked back into the bar. Her hands trembled slightly as she pulled her keys out of her pocket and locked the back door. Then she doused all the lights except for the soft ones that Josie left on for security purposes, although crime was unlikely in Shoshone.

The dim light helped calm her a little, but if Logan didn't come out soon, she was seriously going to lose her nerve. She'd almost made up her mind to cancel the plan when she heard the door to the men's room open. Then she heard it swing shut again.

She gulped. It was put up or shut up time.

He walked toward her. "Seen any ghosts yet?"

"Nope." She wondered how many condoms he'd bought and if that was what had taken him so long, but she wasn't about to ask.

"What kind of ghosts are they supposed to be?"

"Cowboy ghosts, of course." She could barely hear herself speak over the thundering of her heart in her ears. "Have you heard of the old song 'Ghost Riders in the Sky'?"

"Yeah, I think so."

"They call these guys 'ghost drinkers in the bar.'"

He laughed. "I like that. I almost wish one would show up, but not enough to hang around waiting."

So he wanted to get on with it. Gulp. "Like I said, I've never seen one myself." Her chest felt as if somebody had tightened a cinch around it. She'd never done anything like this before. Usually she got to know someone over a period of weeks or months before she progressed to this step.

But if she wanted Logan, and she did, then she had to woman up and direct him to her apartment. "We'll have to g-go outside," she said. "The s-stairs to my apartment are on the outside of the building." Damn. She *never* stuttered.

"Caro." He laid a gentle hand on her arm.

"What?" She whirled to face him, nearly stabbing him in the chest with her keys.

He rubbed her arm. "You don't have to go through with this if it makes you nervous."

"But I want to." And now that he'd touched her—on purpose, and not accidentally while they'd been working together—she *really* wanted to. Nervous though she might be, she yearned for him in a way that was shocking in its intensity.

His voice dropped to a soft murmur. "You're sure?"

Her answer came from some deeply buried part of herself, one that she'd never allowed to surface. "Kiss me and you'll find out how sure I am."

"Good idea." His grip tightened on her arm and he guided her forward while he cupped the back of her head with his other hand, fingers spread.

She stopped breathing, stopped thinking, stopped noticing anything but his mouth as he drew her closer. He had a beautiful mouth, sculpted enough to be masculine, full enough to be sensual. She closed her eyes and trembled in anticipation.

"I've wanted to do this all night." His breath was warm on her lips. He brushed her mouth with his. "You're shaking."

"I know."

His lips stroked over hers again. "It'll be okay."

"I know."

Then he settled in, and it was more than okay.

His kiss was velvet and sleek, rich and luxurious, slow and sweet. He savored her mouth as if tasting expensive brandy served in a crystal goblet. She had never felt so cherished.

Her keys clattered to the floor as she took his head in her hands. She wanted more. She wanted everything. Angling her mouth over his, she invited him deeper. He accepted the invitation with a firm thrust of his tongue.

Yes. She whimpered and he pulled her in close, sliding his arm around her waist and pressing her against his very hard, very aroused body as he continued to kiss the living daylights out of her.

Dear heaven, he really was a professional athlete, with all the toned muscles that job required. She'd known that intellectually, but experiencing it physically was more exciting than she'd imagined. She stroked his supple back, his broad shoulders, his tight buns.

With a groan he lifted his head and gazed down at her in the dusky light. His voice was hoarse. "You've convinced me. Let's go."

She struggled to breathe.

Releasing her, he scooped up her keys as if fielding a

baseball, and put them in her hand. "If we don't get out of here right now, we'll never make it up there."

"Then let's go." She moved toward the front door on unsteady legs. As she opened it, she thought she heard soft laughter coming from somewhere behind her. She turned. "What's so funny?"

"Nothing."

"Didn't you laugh just now?"

"No. I thought it was the door hinge."

She paused, playing the sound over again in her head. "Guess so." It hadn't been a door hinge, but she wasn't going to go ghost-hunting tonight. She had more important things on her mind.

SMALL-TOWN GIRLS PACKED a sensual punch, Logan concluded as he fought to stay cool while climbing the narrow set of stairs behind Caro. Her hot little body sang a siren's song with every creak of the steps. He swore steam was coming off her denim-clad fanny.

Although he hadn't indulged himself with a woman recently, in the past he'd been involved with sophisticates who dressed in expensive lingerie, women who were into sex toys and flavored body paint. Not a single one had turned him on the way Caro had with her blushing request for vending-machine condoms.

When she'd invited him to kiss her, he'd gone up in flames. Where had she learned to talk like that? When she paired her down-home cuteness with sex-kitten suggestions, she became an irresistible combo of sweetness and sin that made him wild for her.

He'd bought three condoms, and those had been hard-won. Despite a few whacks with his fist, the machine hadn't wanted to cooperate. He'd finally decided three would do. He still wanted to end the night in Grandma Judy's guest room, for appearance's sake.

Now he wondered if three would be enough, after all. He might not be able to force himself to leave before dawn, and he was a real fan of sex in the morning.

Caro reached the landing and seemed to have lost her jitters, because she opened the door without fumbling. He took the last two steps in one leap and followed her inside, his heart hammering and his johnson aching.

She hit a switch beside the door and a floor lamp in one corner illuminated a small living room on the right and a tiny kitchen on the left. Both were spotless, with cozy touches like gingham curtains at the kitchen window and colorful throw pillows on the leather sofa.

As he clicked the lock on the front door, she turned to him. "I could offer—"

"Just you." He tossed his hat like a Frisbee toward the sofa. He didn't look to see if it had landed as he pulled her into his arms. "Offer yourself, and I'll be a happy man."

"I can do that." Sliding out of his arms, she backed toward the hallway. "Follow me."

"You've got it."

"First, the shirts." She took hold of her lapels and pulled. Snaps popped like cap guns, and the cotton bra covering her pert breasts didn't fool him in the least. She might not be wearing something obviously sexy, but he saw the fire in her hazel eyes. She was a volcano ready to erupt.

He was so busy looking at what her open shirt revealed that he didn't follow orders.

"Your shirt, Logan."

He sure as hell didn't want to hold up the program. He wrenched open his shirt, shrugged out of it and tossed it to the floor as he continued down the hall.

At the doorway to her bedroom, she reached for another

switch, and lamps on twin nightstands winked on. "You said you liked light."

"I do." He gestured toward her bra. "Are you going to take that off, or shall I?"

She backed into the room with a soft smile. "I will." She reached behind her back to unhook it. "You've had a long night."

"Wouldn't trade it for the world." He started to unbuckle his belt, but his hands stilled as she slipped off her bra. She might prefer cotton, but breasts as full and perfect as hers deserved designer silk. Her wine-colored nipples puckered under his gaze.

His fingers flexed and he took a step closer. "I want—"

"And you'll have." She backed to the other side of the small room, putting the bed between them. "But I can take off my clothes faster than you can." She waved at him. "Continue with what you were doing."

He had to laugh. She was the most logical little sexy thing he'd ever come across. He had to admit she was right, especially when it came to dealing with belts and boots.

He tried to be quick about it, he really did. He managed to pull off his boots, but after that, she became a major distraction. When she leaned down to take hers off, her breasts quivered enticingly.

Then she began to wiggle out of her jeans, causing more breast shimmy. The soft denim caught on the elastic of her panties and they came off along with the jeans. She stood naked before him, and that required his undivided attention.

As she pulled the scrunchie from her ponytail and shook her hair free, she glanced over and caught him staring. "You're still mostly dressed."

He swallowed. "And you're not." He'd suspected she'd be fine to look at, but hadn't realized she'd look *this* fine. Maybe country living made a woman's skin glow like that.

Or maybe—and this was an ego-boosting thought—she was flushed with desire for him.

In any case, she was radiant, as if someone had buffed her body until it gleamed with rosy good health. He stood mesmerized, his glance traveling over the wonders he longed to touch, to taste, to lose himself in. No body piercings for this woman. No Brazilian wax, either. A neat triangle of light brown curls awaited him.

She cleared her throat, which snapped him out of his daze long enough to get rid of his jeans and his knit boxers. He had to work both of them over an erection that felt bigger than the Hancock Building. He was gratified when she sucked in a breath. Nice to be noticed.

She'd stood still while he looked, so he afforded her the same privilege. This was the first time—and maybe the last time—they would see each other without clothes. They should make it count.

He wished he was in better physical shape, but his knee had kept him from the full workouts he was used to. Her breathing picked up as she studied him, though, and he kind of thought she liked what she saw. Her gaze lingered on the purple scar where he'd had knee surgery.

Surgery hadn't put him back in the game, but at least he could walk without hobbling. In fact, he could dance for short stretches, a fact he'd proven tonight. He'd told himself to be grateful for that much.

"Looks painful," she said.

"It is, and I'm not talking about my knee."

Her mouth tilted in a smile. "Cute."

"I prefer the term *impressive*."

She laughed and flung back the covers, which included a colorful patchwork quilt. "Are you fishing for compliments, Carswell?"

"Yes."

"Then let me just say that UPS would likely slap a surcharge on that package of yours." She climbed into bed and stretched out, facing him. "Gonna deliver it?"

"Yeah." He was really starting to like her, and that could be a problem. He might want to remind himself, beginning now, that this was only temporary. "Special delivery, overnight male."

4

Caro was proud of herself for keeping the tone light. She'd never had a one-night stand, and this was shaping up to be her first try at it. If so, she wanted to make sure the mood was carefree and playful, not intense and sordid.

So far, so good. Logan was following her lead, and as he climbed into her bed, she told herself not to mentally record this moment and think it was significant, because it wasn't. Yes, his body was incredible. He was the most muscular guy she'd ever seen naked, not counting marble statues or issues of *Playgirl*.

He was so ripped that she felt a little intimidated, as if she were about to take a ride on a monster roller coaster and wasn't sure if she'd chicken out before it began. Could she keep up with all that energy and power? She was willing to try.

Her body was more than willing. From her first glimpse of his spectacular endowments, moisture had collected between her thighs and her womb had contracted. Natural instinct had taken over, demanding that she join with him in the most basic way.

So she'd take this wild ride, but she'd better not get used to having a hard body in her bed. She'd look into his sexy eyes, which reminded her of dark chocolate, but wouldn't set that shade of brown as her new standard. His mouth not only looked sensual, she knew from experience that it felt even better. Still, she couldn't get attached to his kisses, either.

What was about to happen between them was an unexpected gift, a moment stolen from each of their regularly scheduled lives.

Then he looked into her eyes, and she was caught by surprise at the warmth and caring in his gaze. When he touched her, all her promises to stay objective shattered. He could have grabbed her. With all their banter, he would have been justified in rolling her onto her back and having his way with her.

Instead, he skimmed the tips of his fingers over her cheek with such tenderness that her throat tightened.

"I want you so much I can barely stand it," he said. "But before this gets hot and heavy, and I can guarantee it will, I wanted to say…thank you."

She swallowed the lump in her throat. "Shouldn't I be thanking you? I'm sure you can get girls by snapping your fingers. I'm the one who's in a sexual wasteland."

He smiled. "I've been in a wasteland of my own making, bogged down in self-pity. This…" He paused to sweep his hand over the bed. "This feels as if you just tossed me a lifeline."

"I'd say 'anytime,' but we both know that's not possible."

He cupped her face with one hand. "So let's make the most of right now." But his kiss was slow and easy, as if they had all the time in the world. Leisurely, he combed his fingers through her hair and nibbled his way from her mouth to the curve of her neck. "You smell like lemons."

"Homemade lemon juice hair spray." She shivered as he ran his tongue along her collarbone.

"Love it." His virile body was inches from hers, yet his mouth and fingertips were the only contact points between them.

Tension wound tight within her. She tamped it down,

fighting for the kind of control he seemed to have. In an attempt to mirror his restraint, she slid her fingers across his lightly furred chest. She'd meant to keep her caress as soft as his, but oh, the muscles on this man!

She flattened her palm against the most magnificent pecs she'd ever touched. Her breath caught as she absorbed the heat and power, and imagined his body poised over hers.

The ache that had been building ever since he'd first kissed her threatened to overwhelm her good manners. She was fast approaching the point where she was liable to move her hand lower, latch on to the object of her desire and demand that he use it immediately. That would not be classy.

"Logan?" She heard the desperate note in her voice and couldn't do anything about it.

"Uh-huh."

"Um, do you know where your condoms are?"

"Yes." He sounded amused.

"I don't mean to rush you, but…"

He chuckled softly, his breath warm against her shoulder. "Caro, I didn't want to rush *you*. I'm not a small guy, and I didn't want to hurt you because you weren't ready."

"I'm beyond ready, Logan. Rushing sounds like a wonderful idea."

He raised his head, his dark eyes sparkling with lust and laughter. "Yes, ma'am."

"Thank you." She curled her hands into fists and squirmed with impatience as he rolled to the far side of the bed, snatched up his jeans and rummaged in the pocket. The sound of ripping foil was music to her ears.

When he came back, he was ready for action. "No more foreplay, then?"

She shook her head and held out her arms. "Main event, please."

"God, Caro." He moved over her, his breathing ragged.

"You are some kind of woman." Bracing himself on one arm, he reached between her thighs. "But I still need to make sure you're—"

"Logan." She squeezed her eyes shut and arched off the bed as his probing fingers nearly made her come. She'd never wanted a man so much that she was dizzy with anticipation.

He groaned softly. "You weren't kidding."

"No." She opened her eyes and met his gaze as she cupped his firm bottom. "Now."

"With pleasure." He thrust forward and gasped. "God, that feels good."

Good didn't begin to cover what she was feeling. Pressing her fingers into the muscles of his backside, she closed her eyes again. The rightness of this connection stunned her. She'd imagined that sex with Logan would be nice, but she hadn't counted on this…perfection.

He leaned down and brushed his mouth against hers. "You okay?"

"Fabulous," she murmured.

"You're so still."

She looked up at him. "I'm just…" Overjoyed? Ecstatic? No, she couldn't say that.

"Don't worry. I'll go slow. Let you get used to me." He eased back and slid forward in a gentle motion.

That was all it took. She gasped as the first spasm hit.

His eyes widened. "Caro? Are you…?"

"Yes…*yessss.*" A powerful orgasm arced through her, leaving her shuddering and breathless.

His voice was low and intense. "Okay, then." His buttocks flexed beneath her fingers as he began a steady rhythm that urged her quivering body to tighten once again. He gazed down at her, his dark eyes gleaming with purpose. "I think you're used to me."

"Uh-huh." Her breath caught as he shifted his angle to penetrate even deeper.

He paused and gulped for air. "Still okay?"

"Mmm." She wrapped her legs around him, opening herself in complete surrender. "Don't…"

He frowned in obvious concern. "Don't?"

"Don't stop." She smiled up at him.

"Caro, you're…" He dragged in more air. "Amazing."

Logan's movements took on new authority as his forceful thrusts propelled them forward. Gradually he increased the pace, urging both of them toward the brink.

Caro abandoned herself to his rhythm as they rocked faster, and faster still, and then…heat flooded through her, brilliant, golden and intense. Through the haze of her climax she heard him cry out, and he surged forward. She absorbed his orgasmic shudders with a laugh of pure delight.

This had been an outstanding idea.

LOGAN FELT THE RIPPLE of laughter caress his happy penis. He'd never had any woman laugh at the end of sex with him, but was beginning to understand that Caro was unique. Once he had enough breath in his lungs to form a sentence, he nuzzled her ear. "Do you usually laugh after sex?"

She laughed again. "No."

"Should I be honored or insulted?"

"Honored, for sure. I couldn't help it. I'm so happy."

He raised his head and peered down at her. Sure enough, she looked content. Her eyes sparkled and her skin was flushed with obvious pleasure. He'd like to claim credit for that, but he had a hunch Caro was pretty easy to please. Still, she had said she didn't usually laugh.

"So what brought on this happy laughter?"

She stroked his back. "Well, because I've never invited a

man I just met into my bed, I wasn't absolutely sure it would work out well. But it did, didn't it?"

"That's an understatement." He loved the way she touched him—not too light and not too heavy. Not everyone was good at that.

"See? We took a chance on each other and had a terrific time. We even managed a mutual climax, and that doesn't always happen, especially the first time with someone."

"That's true." She was adorable—and that tug at his heart should serve as a warning to be careful. But he wouldn't have much luck distancing himself while he was this close to her sweet, sunny self. He'd work on the distancing thing later, maybe on the plane ride home.

In the meantime, he planned to soak up as much of this *therapy* as he could, and give her some in return. "I'd have to say that was the best first-time sex I've ever had."

"Me, too. Hands down. Which is a good thing, because we needed to get it right the first time, all things considered."

"Yeah, not much time to practice." But he was willing to work in whatever practice they could. She ought to have some input on that plan, though. "Especially if you want to get some sleep before morning comes."

She switched from stroking his back to fondling his chest. "Are you sleepy?"

He wondered if she'd ever studied massage. Her touch was magic. "I asked you first."

"All right, then I'll be honest. I want to come at least once more before morning does. That is, if you have another condom available."

He grinned. "I have two more."

"Excellent."

"I would have bought more than that, but the machine wasn't very cooperative."

"It probably needs maintenance. I'll bet nobody would

report it to Josie or me. A guy might tell Steve, but it's not like some cowboy would come up to me and say the condom machine is malfunctioning. It's kind of a prob—"

He cut her off with a quick kiss. "Let's not worry about it. I have two more, and if you'll direct me to your bathroom…"

"Across the hall."

He eased away from her and left the bed. "Be right back." The moment he put his weight on his right leg, pain sliced through his knee. Without meaning to, he sucked in a breath.

"Is it your knee?"

Thank God his back was to her and she couldn't see his grimace of pain. "It's fine." He did his best not to hobble out of the room.

"I don't believe you," she called after him. "You're limping."

"I'll make a believer of you when I come back," he said over his shoulder. "It was just a twinge, that's all." His knee ached like a son of a bitch, but he would never admit it. He had a couple of hours with this woman, and he damned well wasn't going to be treated like some kind of cripple during that time.

He'd thought any position, including the missionary one, would be okay by now. Apparently not, especially after dancing and tending bar for hours. He'd been so blissed out by what was going on with his cock that he hadn't noticed he was stressing his knee at the same time.

Oh, well. He'd stress it again if necessary, because he wasn't about to put limits on his sexual positions. Talk about a wussy attitude. He wouldn't baby himself, and he didn't want her to baby him, either. It was only one night, and he'd enjoy the hell out of it.

He flipped on the light in her miniscule bathroom and tried not to bump his knee against anything while maneuvering in the limited space. He wasn't used to small spaces. His condo in Chicago had a bathroom three times this size.

Yet he'd much rather be here. The bathroom was decorated in the same cozy country style as the rest of the place, with red gingham curtains at the tiny window and an old oak bucket serving as a wastebasket. The scent of lemons reminded him that Caro had mentioned using homemade lemon juice hair spray.

He wasn't a big fan of hair spray, but lemon juice sounded better than the other gunk women put on their hair. She must not use much of it, because her hair slid through his fingers like silk. Everything about her was silky and smooth, in fact. She'd been wet, ready, and a perfect fit, as if her body had been created specifically for him to enjoy.

He'd had some good sex in his life, but, as she'd said, never this good this soon. Maybe that first time had been a fluke, and the next episode wouldn't deliver such a rush. He was ready to find out. Disposing of the condom, he massaged his knee for a few seconds before turning out the light and crossing the hall.

She'd propped a couple pillows against the oak headboard and was sitting up. The multicolored quilt covered her lap, but her breasts were bare. "I took the condoms out of your jeans pocket and put them on the nightstand. I hope you don't mind."

"Does it look as if I mind?" One glimpse of her waiting for him, condoms at the ready, and he was hard.

She glanced at his package and smiled. "No, not really. That's a very gratifying reaction."

"It's a perfectly natural reaction with a woman as sexy as you are." He walked over to the bed.

"I've never thought of myself as particularly sexy."

"Unconscious sexiness is the most potent kind." He tossed back the quilt and started to climb into bed with her.

"Don't get in like that. You're putting pressure on your knee."

He'd forgotten and put his right knee on the mattress, because he was used to getting in bed that way. Yeah, it hurt, but he would ignore it. Nobody was going to treat him like an invalid.

"I saw that flash of pain in your eyes, Logan. You can't fool me."

"Be quiet, Caro." On all fours, he leaned toward her, his mouth seeking hers.

She ducked out of his reach. "You're a crazy man. And I'm not kissing you again until you're flat on your back and off that knee."

"That's totally unnecessary. I'm fine." He cupped the back of her head, his grip gentle but firm. "And I'm desperate to kiss you, so hold still."

"Have it your way."

"Thank you." He lowered his mouth to hers.

She kissed him back, but while he was savoring the lush wonders of her mouth, she got both hands around his dick and instituted the kind of sweet torture that would bring him to climax in no time.

He lifted his lips a fraction from hers. "Stop that or I'll come."

"Agree to lie on your back for me and I'll stop."

"No need to be on my back, Caro." He clenched his jaw as his balls tightened and his orgasm threatened.

She toyed with the sensitive tip of his penis and used the gathering moisture to lubricate the surface. "Maybe you're afraid to let a woman be on top, where she has more control."

"It's not that." He could overpower her and make her stop, but he would never use superior strength to exert his will on a woman.

"I think you have control issues."

"I will any second if you keep that up."

"Logan, do you really want to waste precious time arguing about this?"

When she put it that way, so logically, he had no sensible response. It was a silly argument, after all. He lifted his head and looked into her eyes. "No, I don't. You win."

She stopped stroking him. "That's better."

"On one condition."

"Which is?"

"That you don't mention my knee again while we're sharing this bed."

"Why not? You need to be careful of your knee. Alex told me all about the injury, and if you aren't careful, you might—"

"Let me worry about that, okay? It's bad enough that I'm out of baseball because of my knee, without having my sex life impacted, too."

She nodded. "I see your point."

He stretched out flat on the bed. "Then I'm all yours."

5

IF ONLY HE COULD BE all hers. Caro banished that thought the
minute it popped into her head. No need to be greedy about
this. She had far more now than she'd had a few hours ago.

And what she had, for the time being, was one spectacular
man stretched out in her bed. He was all muscle and magic
to her, this man who could catch a ninety-eight-mile-an-hour
fastball. Once she got a minute to herself, she'd use the computer in Josie's office to look up his stats and see if any clips
were available.

But that was for later. For now, she took the package he so
graciously handed her, ripped it open and rolled the condom
lovingly onto his very large, very erect penis. He trembled
as she did that, and his massive chest heaved.

She'd thought about exploring him a little more before
putting on the condom, but she didn't think he'd last through
what she had in mind. Her very presence seemed to get him
hot, and that surprised her. The guys she'd known had required more obvious turn-ons, like a generous display of
cleavage or a skirt slit to midthigh.

She'd been told more than once that she was too whole-
some to be sexy. Logan's comment about her unconscious
sexuality would stay with her for a long, long time. He was
good for her, and she wanted to be good for him, too. Thank

God he'd agreed to a position that wouldn't put pressure on his knee.

She'd keep her promise not to mention that again, because she, of all people, understood when someone didn't like being reminded of an infirmity. Grandma Bonnie *hated* admitting she wasn't as capable as she'd once been. Logan's bad knee seemed like a minor problem in the grand scheme of things, but Caro wasn't the pro ballplayer who had lost his career because of that knee.

"You're driving me bat-shit crazy, taking so long with that condom." He propped himself on his elbows to glare at her. "I hope you know that."

"So you *do* have control issues."

"Yeah." He flopped back to the mattress. "I feel like I'm going to come any second, and in my world, the woman gets to come first. I'm not sure that's going to happen."

"Is there anything I can do to make your world a better place?"

He turned his head to gaze at her and his dark eyes smoldered. "As a matter of fact, there is." He caught her hand and tugged on it. "Straddle me."

"I thought that was the idea."

"Not like that." He patted his breastbone. "Up here."

"Oh." Her heart raced.

"Chicken?"

"I've never…"

"Never?"

"Well, of course I've…I mean, naturally, I've tried…but not like that."

His smile was wicked. "You'd be in control."

She doubted it. She suspected that once he began, she'd lose control very quickly.

He tugged on her hand again. "Are we going to waste time arguing about sexual positions?"

"I—"

"We're having a secret rendezvous, one that nobody ever has to know about." His voice grew husky. "You can do whatever you want, Caro. Anything at all."

"Then I want to turn out the lights."

"And spoil all my fun? Don't do that. Please."

"Logan…"

"I've wanted to taste you ever since you stripped down on the other side of the bed and I saw those caramel curls."

"You already know. You were there."

"My cock was there. I couldn't see, couldn't savor. Let me do that."

She was on fire, and she wasn't sure if the heat came from embarrassment or raging excitement. He was pushing her boundaries…and she *liked* it. He was right. They were indulging in a secret rendezvous, and if she ever wanted to be wild, this was the perfect time.

"Come on, Caro," he said softly. "Let me find out how sweet you really are."

As if drawn by the magnetic pull of his eyes, she moved toward him.

"Swing your leg over," he coaxed. "That's it. Scoot up. A little more…come to me…" He slid both hands under her bottom and then…

She gasped at the first contact with his hot mouth. Lying on her back with her thighs open was one thing, but this felt decadent, as if she were demanding it, as if she had him at her mercy, and he had no choice but to…oh, dear heaven. He had a choice and was making it, with gusto.

Trembling, she balanced by bracing her hands above his head. Gradually, she realized the whimpering sounds were hers, and the moans were hers, and the lusty cries of delight… were hers. She came once, in a shower of vibrating color, and when she tried to pull away, he held her fast and made her come again. As the contractions overtook her, she threw back her head and screamed in ecstasy.

She might have imagined that she'd have control with Logan flat on his back, but she was so wrong. While still in the grip of her second orgasm, she felt herself being bench-pressed up and back. Without quite knowing how she got there, she slid effortlessly down his rigid penis until they were locked together, a perfect fit once again.

"Got anything left for me?" He stroked her breasts and spanned her waist with both hands.

"Yes." Energized by the connection, the fullness of him deep inside her, she spread her palms on his chest. Her fingers flexed as she absorbed the warmth, the shiver of his muscles, his rapid heartbeat. "Yes."

And she began to ride him, slowly at first, and faster as he caught the rhythm and responded, his hips lifting in time with her downward strokes. They both began to pant, and the room filled with the liquid sounds of bodies pumping and straining toward the ultimate completion. Once again, they found it together, in a frenzy of rapid thrusts and mingled cries.

Caro slumped against him, boneless, unable to imagine moving, let alone leaving this bed. She realized that moment would arrive eventually, but she shoved that reality aside as she lay on Logan's sweat-slicked chest and listened to the wild beat of his heart.

He rubbed her back, his caress a soothing counterpart to the passion they'd shared. As sanity returned, she wondered where they would go from here. The first time had been amazing, but the second time had obliterated all her benchmarks. Whether that was good or bad, she wasn't sure. All she knew was that Logan had forever raised the bar and there was no use pretending she would ever be satisfied with less.

LOGAN HAD ALWAYS BELIEVED that great sex should wind down slowly, with lots of cuddling and touching to maintain the mood. But because the lights were still on in Caro's little bedroom, he could easily see his watch. He purposely hadn't taken it off.

Sadly, his watch indicated that he had to get the hell out of Caro's apartment and over to Grandma Judy's if he expected to pull off this caper. Being discovered in Caro's bed would be bad for him, but potentially worse for her. He could leave town and the gossip. She couldn't.

He wrapped his arms around her, as if he could somehow soften the announcement. "I have to go."

She sighed. "I know."

"If I leave now, I might be able to sneak into Grandma Judy's house and convince her and everyone else that I've been there longer than I actually have."

"I know that, too." She didn't move.

This was for Caro's own good, but he didn't think she'd appreciate hearing that sentiment. He'd never much liked being told that. He needed her cooperation, though. Condoms could be tricky things, especially with the woman on top.

"Just so you know, I'm going to make sure we go riding today." He hoped that would help. It wasn't as if this was the last they'd ever see of each other.

Her breath was warm on his chest. "How can you guarantee we'll go riding if Steve is still sick?"

"There must be someone else who can fill in."

"Normally Tracy would, but she's in Cheyenne for a girlfriend's wedding. We'd better hope that Steve gets well. That would be the best scenario."

"It would, but I'm prepared to make a case to Josie that you need the time off, somehow. I would probably be more convincing if I can get over to Grandma Judy's without anybody knowing I've been hanging out in your bedroom for a couple of hours."

"Right." She carefully rolled onto her side of the bed. Then she reached for the patchwork quilt and pulled it over her as she gazed at him. "Just know that if the ride doesn't work out, it's okay. We've had a terrific time, better than I even could have imagined. That's plenty."

"You'll get that ride." As he left the bed and headed into her bathroom, his heart ached for her. She was already preparing herself for disappointment. No matter what, she'd make the best of things.

Damn it, he wanted to treat her to an afternoon of riding, a carefree time in which she wouldn't have to be serving customers or taking care of her grandmother. Once he returned to Chicago, she'd go back to that routine, but while he was here, he wanted to execute a small jail break.

Walking back into her room, he discovered her standing by her closet and shoving her arms into a white terry robe.

"You don't have to see me out."

She sent him a smile. "Of course I do. I invited you up here, so the least I can do is see you to the door."

He walked over and took her by the shoulders. "Your invitation was the best thing that's happened to me in a long time."

"Good. It was a two-way street, though. I obviously needed a…" She flushed.

"A lover," he murmured, and kissed her softly on the mouth. Her lips tempted him, but he forced himself to draw back. "I feel lucky to have been in the right place at the right time."

"Me, too. Listen, can I get you anything? A soft drink? Coffee? I feel as if I shouldn't just send you off into the night without something."

"You're sending me off with something." He pulled on his jeans and sat down on the edge of the bed to deal with his socks and boots. "I feel a lot more like a man than I did a few hours ago."

"You're kidding, right?"

He pulled on a boot and glanced up. "No. Not even slightly."

"I don't get it."

He focused on putting on the other boot, because it was easier to confess these things when he wasn't looking at her. "I don't know who I am anymore, Caro, or what my future is. But for these couple of hours, I've forgotten all that. I was simply a guy who could make a woman happy. You have no idea what that means to me."

He sensed that she'd moved over to stand beside him. He felt her body heat, but even more, he felt her caring heart envelop him. He looked up, and sure enough, she gazed at him with more empathy than he'd felt from anyone in these long months.

"I wish I could help," she said.

"You already have." He stood and cupped her face in both hands and brushed his thumbs over her cheeks. "But as I'm sure you know, being the intelligent, logical person you are, this is an inside job. You've given me a chance to shift focus off myself. Maybe I can build on that and climb out of this funk I'm in."

"I hope so, Logan. I truly hope so."

"Which is why you need to come riding with me tomorrow. Show this city boy the majesty of the scenery. It will help both of us."

She smiled. "I like that. Win-win."

"Exactly." He dropped a quick kiss on her lips. "But in order to foster that plan, I need to find my shirt and get the hell out of here before the town, or worse yet, Grandma Judy, wakes up." He headed down the hall and scooped up the shirt he found crumpled on the floor.

"Yes, you do." She followed him, and retrieved his hat from the couch as he fastened the snaps. "You look good in cowboy clothes."

"It's all an act." He finished snapping the shirt and tucked it into his jeans. "Clothes don't make the man, or in this case, the cowboy. I'm still a city slicker at heart."

She handed him his hat. "That's what Alex used to say. Now look at him."

"Yeah, but he had a skill the Last Chance needed. They could use a marketing director. I can't think of any reason they'd want a washed-up baseball player."

"Now that's the kind of phrase you need to banish from your vocabulary, immediately." She put her hands on her hips and attempted a ferocious frown.

He had to laugh. She was so not the frowning type. "You're right. That's very negative on my part."

"It sure is. I've promised not to mention a certain condition of yours, but you have to promise to stop referring to yourself as a failure."

His laughter faded. "But the thing is, I *have* failed. You can blow sunshine up my ass all day, but it doesn't change the fact that I'm no longer fit for my chosen career."

"So choose another one."

Anger nibbled at his mellow mood. "Easy for you to say."

"But it's the only way to move forward."

"I suppose so, but can you begin to imagine what it's like to focus on a dream for twenty-five years, and then have it destroyed?" He heard the bitterness in his voice and winced. This was not the time or place.

"No. Truthfully, I can't." She looked contrite. "I'm sure it's terrible, and you have a right to be angry that your life didn't work out the way you'd hoped."

He sighed and rubbed the back of his neck. "But I don't

have a right to spray negativity all over the place, just because I have no idea where I'll go from here."

"Didn't you ever think about what you'd do once you retired from baseball?"

"Not really." He gazed at her and realized he'd needed to meet this woman for many reasons, and this was one of them. "Nobody else has had the guts to ask me that question, you know. Everybody—my agent, my teammates, my family, my friends—they all tiptoed around the subject. I think they knew the answer and didn't want to bring it up."

"Well, no wonder you're so upset! You don't have a plan B!"

"No." Which made him look pretty damned stupid. But baseball players were a superstitious lot, and he was no exception. On some level he'd thought planning for his retirement might hasten it, and he couldn't imagine being happy doing anything besides playing ball. Secretly, he'd hoped to go on record as the oldest catcher in baseball history. What a joke.

"We'll talk about it during our horseback ride this afternoon," she said. "I'm great at coming up with a plan B."

He couldn't imagine how a small-town bartender would be able to figure out a new career path for a washed-up…no, a *former* pro baseball player, but he didn't want to insult her. "Thanks. I'll take all the help I can get."

"You're humoring me. You don't think I'll be able to help you think of something."

"All right, no, I don't, but I appreciate that you're willing to try, considering I'm just a stranger passing through."

She smiled at him. "Technically, that's what you are, but you don't feel like a stranger to me."

He closed the gap between them and latched on to the lapels of her bathrobe to draw her close. "Good, because you don't feel like a stranger to me, either. But if I don't get out of here, the whole world will know how familiar we've become." He kissed her, a down-and-dirty quick maneuver that involved tongues, but was over before it could progress to heavy breathing.

Even so, he felt his johnson respond and he backed away from her before he was tempted to kiss her again. "How soon can you drive out to the ranch this afternoon?"

She took a deep breath, as if she had to rein herself in, too. "I'll be home from Jackson around two. Assuming Steve takes my shift, I can be at the ranch before two-thirty."

"If Steve doesn't take it, I'll make sure Josie has it covered, so just come on out there."

"All right."

"I'll look forward to it." Ha. He'd be counting the seconds.

"Me, too."

"Okay, I'm really leaving." He backed toward the door.

She stood with her hands clasped in front of her, as if determined to stay in that one spot until he was out of her apartment. "See you this afternoon."

"You'll be there, no matter what, right? Because I *will* get that shift covered for you."

"I'll be there."

He groaned. "I don't want to leave you."

Unclasping her hands, she made shooing motions. "Get out of here, cowboy."

"I'm not a cowboy."

"You never know. That could be part of your plan B."

"Hell—I wish I didn't have to go, but I do, so…I'm outta here." With a supreme act of will, he opened the door, walked out and closed it behind him.

A cool breeze leeched the heat from his body and he shivered. Watching his step in the dim light, he descended the narrow stairs to the darkened street below. Caro was so warm, so full of sunshine. The afternoon seemed very far away.

6

CARO HURRIED TO THE window and watched Logan go down the stairs. He was favoring his right knee, and she battled guilt because she hadn't thought about his injury when they'd first had sex. Of course he wouldn't mention it, macho guy that he was. He had to be more careful.

She should take him to the assisted living facility and show him what real infirmity looked like. Maybe then he'd understand that carelessness now would mean depending on a wheelchair when he was eighty. He might also realize how lucky he was to be healthy in every other way, with only a bum knee to worry about.

Plus he had financial security, and he was, in her unbiased opinion, incredibly handsome. All in all, he was a fortunate man. He wasn't thinking like that right now, though. But she'd never had a single-minded drive to accomplish something like becoming a nationally known sports star, so maybe she couldn't relate properly to his angst.

She watched him cross the street and head off toward Grandma Judy's house. If Jack hadn't come up with that alternative, Logan might have been obligated to go back to the ranch instead of staying to help her. Caro owed Jack a debt of gratitude.

She wouldn't tell him so, because he'd mention it to Josie,

who might start worrying about Caro ending up with a broken heart. It would be like Josie to be protective. She'd helped, both with a truck and emotional support, during the difficult time of moving Grandma Bonnie from her little house in Shoshone into assisted living. She'd also offered this apartment at a very reasonable rate, when selling the house had meant Caro no longer had a place to live.

But Caro wasn't some delicate flower who couldn't handle a brief love affair without wilting. She'd accept whatever Logan could offer and be grateful. What woman worth her salt wouldn't? Logan was a fantasy guy who'd delivered everything that gorgeous body of his promised.

Mmm. She savored her memories of his hands, his mouth, his hard...ahem. There was no way she'd be able to sleep now that she'd reminded herself of the stupendous orgasms she'd enjoyed compliments of Mr. Carswell.

Hurrying back to the bedroom, she picked up her shirt and dressed quickly. Then she descended the stairs, keys in hand, and went into the bar. She wanted to find some information on Logan's career on the internet, and she couldn't very well surf the web on Josie's computer during working hours, or somebody would get suspicious.

As she opened the door, she heard what sounded like a soft chuckle, a very male chuckle.

A shiver traveled up her spine. "Who's there?"

No answer.

Her first instinct was to turn on every light in the place, but an early riser somewhere in the neighborhood might notice that all the lights were on at four forty-five in the morning, and report it to Josie. Caro didn't want to have to explain. So she waited, heart pounding, until her eyes adjusted to the muted glow coming from the lights under the bar.

Straining to see, she finally concluded that the room was empty. Maybe the door hinge was to blame, as Logan had suggested earlier. She moved the door back and forth, and the hinges squeaked a little, but they sounded nothing like the laughter she'd heard—twice.

But there had been nothing threatening about the laughter. The person, or the spirit of a departed person, had seemed mildly amused. Taking a deep breath, Caro decided to forget about it. Josie swore ghosts visited the bar, and Morgan, Gabe Chance's wife, said she'd seen one last summer. They'd both insisted the spirits were friendly and Caro had nothing to fear.

She walked into the office and closed the door before turning on the light. The blinds were already pulled down, so no one outside the building would know she was in here. After booting up the computer, she settled into Josie's desk chair and proceeded to look Logan Carswell up on Google.

An hour later, she checked the digital clock at the bottom of the screen and reluctantly turned off the computer. If she planned to drive to Jackson this morning, she needed a shower and lots of strong coffee. But she'd learned quite a bit about Logan, and now their time together in her apartment seemed even more surreal.

She had trouble reconciling her image of a very naked, very ardent Logan with the intense guy crouched behind home plate wearing a catcher's mask, chest protector and kneepads. Surely she hadn't just made love to that man? Yet her sexually satisfied body indicated she had.

She'd watched a few clips of him playing ball, and he'd always reacted with precision, whether he was behind the plate or up to bat. Most of all she'd noticed his intense focus, a trait he'd no doubt honed in the years he'd spent training and practicing. She understood his anger a lot better and wished she hadn't flippantly told him to "get a new career." Anyone that dedicated couldn't be expected to switch gears immediately.

She'd also watched the incident that had ruined his knee,

although seeing it made her stomach twist. He'd thrown off his mask to make the play, so his expression of agony was right there, front and center. Caro wanted to hate the player that had collided with him, but that wasn't fair. They were both simply doing what they'd been paid to do.

Moving away from the computer, she turned off the light and locked up after herself. No ghostly laughter greeted her, but then again, it was light outside, time for all self-respecting ghosts to go back to wherever they came from. She hurried up the stairs, grateful that no one was around to notice. She was terrible at making up stories.

If she wondered whether her sexual adventures with Logan had been real, she had only to walk into her bedroom and gaze at the rumpled sheets to know that he'd been there, loving the daylights out of her. Talk about a peak experience. She'd never forget a moment of what they'd shared as long as she lived.

She hoped to see him again today, but she wouldn't count on it. All things concerning Logan had to be wonderful surprises, not sweet certainties. If that time in her bed was all they ever had, she'd consider herself blessed.

After a long and reviving shower and two cups of coffee, she felt a little more fit for company, namely Grandma Bonnie's. As she was about to head out the door, her cell phone rang.

Her first thought was always about her grandmother, one of the few people who called her regularly, and the person whose welfare most concerned her.

Instead it was Josie. "Logan came to talk with me this morning," she said. "He seems to think you're headed for burnout if you don't get the afternoon off."

Warmth spread through Caro. Logan was watching out for her, and that was a great feeling. "He might be exaggerating a little." She crossed her fingers. "If you need me to work my shift this afternoon, I'll be happy to do that."

"Actually, I contacted Steve to see how he's faring after his stomach problems last night. He seems fine, and he's volunteered to take your shift."

"Thank you, Josie. I admit a break would be terrific."

"So you and Logan are going riding this afternoon?"

Excitement bubbled in her veins. She managed to sound reserved even as she mentally turned cartwheels at the prospect. "Yes, if that's okay."

"Sure, that's fine. I've wanted to get you out here to ride, but you've been so busy. It promises to be a beautiful day, and we'll saddle up a couple of cooperative horses for you and Logan. If I know Mary Lou, she'll insist on fixing you some snacks to take along."

It took Caro a moment to remember that Mary Lou was the cook at the Last Chance. "I'd hate for her to go to any trouble."

"No worries. She'd be upset if I didn't let her do that. You probably don't remember seeing her, but she was at the reception last night, and she noticed that you were working extra hard. She'll want to treat you right."

"Well, then, that sounds fabulous. Thank you, Josie."

"Don't thank me. Thank Logan. He's the one who brought it to my attention that all you do is work and visit your grandma."

Caro groaned. "Please don't think I was complaining to him. I have a wonderful situation. I love working for you, and I love my grandmother. I would never—"

"Relax, Caro. He emphasized that you weren't complaining, that you're the most positive person he's ever met. But I think he has a point. I realize that your grandma needs a lot of emotional support while she's in this transition period, but she'll think you're working. You should grab the chance to have some fun while you can."

"Okay. I just didn't want you to think I bent Logan's ear about how sad my life is, because it's not."

"I don't think that at all. Anyway, I don't know if I'll be around or not, so if I don't see you, have a wonderful ride. Here's Logan. He wanted to double-check something with you."

Caro's pulse kicked up a notch as Logan came on the line, his tone casual, as if he hadn't had to tear himself away from her a few hours ago. "So it's all set."

"Yes. Thank you."

"My pleasure."

She remembered the last time she'd heard him say that, and a zing of awareness made her tingle all over.

"Listen," he continued, "as long as you're coming out here, you might as well stay for dinner. Sarah suggested it."

"How nice of her." Caro had always admired Sarah Chance, who'd raised three fine sons and had handled her husband's sudden death two years ago with courage and grace. She was another woman who understood the meaning of resilience.

"Then you'll stay for dinner?"

"I'd love to." She made a mental note to bring lipstick along on the trail ride, in case he kissed it all off. It wouldn't be classy to appear at dinner looking as if she'd spent the afternoon making out with Logan. But she hoped she would end up doing exactly that.

"Great. I'll see you around two-thirty, then."

"I'm looking forward to it."

His voice lowered a notch. "Me, too. 'Bye, Caro."

His tone sent shivers up her spine, but she wasn't sure he should have taken the chance on Josie overhearing. He'd put a wealth of meaning into those last four words. Yes, she would definitely take lipstick along.

LOGAN HANDED THE CELL phone back to Josie. "Thanks for arranging this for her." His plan was working perfectly.

Josie had shown up to search for an old wooden cradle Jack remembered being stored in the barn. Spotting Josie's truck, Logan had gone down to the barn and offered to help find the cradle. During the search he'd mentioned Caro getting time off, and Josie had been glad to arrange it.

She tucked the phone back in her jeans pocket. "Happy to." She gazed around the barn. "I know that cradle has to be here. I can't imagine anyone pitching it out. Let's try the tack room." She started in that direction. "Did Caro tell you about her grandmother?"

"She did, and she tried very hard not to sound stressed about her schedule, but she is."

"I know she is, but I didn't think of this solution of getting somebody to take her shift. Good idea. Before the move into assisted living, her grandmother was a really cheerful sort, not needy at all, but now she asks Caro for her schedule and expects a visit whenever Caro's off work."

"Isn't that a little unreasonable?"

Josie surveyed the tack room, where saddles and bridles hung from hooks lining the walls, and saddle blankets were stacked in a large bin in the corner. "I suppose, but this is a woman who's lived in the same little house in Shoshone most of her life, and who had Caro living with her for the past twenty-some years. My guess is she's suffering from separation anxiety."

"Don't those assisted living places have counselors to deal with that?"

"I'm sure they do, but counseling isn't an instant fix for people in their eighties. Or anyone, for that matter." Josie glanced up into the rafters. "There it is! Somebody put it up there for safekeeping."

Logan gazed where she was pointing and spotted the cradle

balanced on two beams. He also saw dust and cobwebs, but maybe the cradle would look great once it was cleaned up. "I'll get it." He pulled a wooden stool over and climbed up on it.

"Be careful, Logan. I don't want you reinjuring your knee."

"I won't." He wished he could do that *Men in Black* trick and erase everyone's memory of his knee problem. He was sick of having people worry about whether his knee could withstand whatever activity he'd chosen to do.

He brought the cradle down in a shower of dust that made them both sneeze. "That's been up there a hell of a long time." He placed it gently on the floor, but anyone could see that a simple cleanup wouldn't do the trick. Something had been gnawing on the wood, and the cradle listed to one side. It didn't smell very good, and although Logan was no expert on bat shit, he thought that might explain the odor.

"It's a mess, isn't it?" Josie sounded distressed.

"I'm afraid so. I wouldn't trust my baby in that thing. Sorry, Josie."

"Jack said that supposedly his grandpa Archie built this for Jonathan. But then Diana, Jack's mother, didn't want to use it. I guess it got shoved into the rafters and ignored."

"Maybe you need to buy a new cradle."

"But I like it, Logan. Look at how he cut that heart pattern out of the head and footboards. You're not going to find that just anywhere." She glanced at him. "Could you fix it? I remember you were always building things back in high school. When you weren't on the baseball field, you were in wood shop."

Logan studied the cradle. "It's been a long time." But her comment reminded him of the satisfaction he'd felt whenever he finished a woodworking project. He'd abandoned that interest in favor of baseball, but he remembered with fondness the smell of fresh lumber.

"I'm thinking you could salvage some of it and make a new piece for the parts where the critters, whatever they were, chewed on it," she told him.

"I'd rather start over and use this as a pattern."

Josie shoved her hands in the back pockets of her jeans while she considered that. "It won't be the cradle Archie built."

"No, but it won't have bat shit on it, either. And I'm not sure those stains would ever come off."

Josie glanced at him. "I don't want my kid in a cradle with bat shit stains on it."

"I don't blame you."

"Could you really build a replica?"

He crouched down, which made him wince at the pressure on his knee, but he needed to get a closer look. The cradle was finely made, and he hated to think of all that work ending up in the trash. But it was ruined, and he could create something that would look just like it and smell a hell of a lot better. "Yeah, I think so. I'll need tools."

"Let me call Jack." Pulling her phone from her pocket, she punched in a speed-dial number. "It's been a trick getting everyone to use cell phones. It's not the cowboy way, apparently. But I think we're converting people gradually. Jack loves his phone now."

Logan no longer loved his. He'd deliberately left it in his room in the ranch house, because now that he wasn't a baseball star, nobody called. He used to be on a dozen people's speed dials, but no more. His lack of calls was so depressing that he tended not to carry it at all.

While Josie consulted with Jack about the availability of carpenter tools, Logan hunkered down and began to deconstruct the cradle. The more he thought about the project, the more he liked it. When he left the Last Chance in the next week or so, he'd be leaving behind something he'd made, something that might become the heirloom this cradle was supposed to be.

Josie got off the phone. "Jack says Archie's old tools are all packed away in a box. He thinks Sarah can locate them. Jonathan didn't have much aptitude for carpentry, I guess."

"Was he Sarah's husband, the guy who died?"

"Yes, and the only son of Archie and Nelsie—Eleanor. Jack and his brothers weren't interested in carpentry, either, so the tools have gone unused ever since Archie died."

Logan felt a little as if he might be intruding on Chance family history. "Are you sure it's okay if I use them?"

"Positive. Jack said if you can make a replica of that old cradle for our baby, he'll be eternally grateful, because, to quote him, 'I sure as hell can't do it.'"

"Then let's go find Sarah and see if she knows where those tools are. I might as well get started."

"All right." Josie headed out of the tack room. "How long do you think it'll take you?"

"I have no idea."

"Will you be able to stay until you finish it?"

Logan's first thought was that this cradle project might give him the excuse he needed to hang around longer. "I think I can manage to stay until it's done." And in the process, he'd get to see more of Caro. He wasn't remotely ready to give her up yet.

7

A COMBINATION OF ADRENALINE and caffeine fueled Caro's morning with Grandma Bonnie. More than once her grandmother asked her why she was so perky, and she blamed it on one too many cups of coffee. That was true, as far as it went.

She'd had enough coffee to float a battleship by the time she drove out to the Last Chance. She was determined not to fall asleep while riding her horse, or worse yet, while in a clinch with Logan.

Although she didn't know the ranch well, she'd been there for Josie and Jack's wedding the previous October. The double ceremony had included Jack's brother Nick and his bride, Dominique. Technically, Jack and Nick were half brothers, but there was nothing halfway about the relationship.

Caro knew some of the story from local gossip, but during one of the trips to Jackson to check out assisted living facilities, Josie had explained the whole convoluted situation. Jonathan Chance was the father of all three brothers, but each had a different mother.

Jack's mother, Diana, had left the ranch when Jack was four, never to return. A despondent Jonathan had taken up with a free spirit named Nicole for a while. She'd left Wyoming and later died unexpectedly. Baby Nick had arrived in the company of a lawyer who'd said Nicole had named Jonathan as the father and guardian.

By that time, Jonathan had remarried, and Sarah Chance was pregnant with Gabe, Jonathan's third son. Sarah had proceeded to raise all three boys as her own, and Caro suspected each of them would give his life for her.

Almost two years ago, Jonathan had died in a rollover, a tragic end to a true love story. Now Sarah shared the job of running the ranch with her three sons. Caro had always been in awe of the woman, but after hearing Josie's version of the family's history, Caro had elevated Sarah to sainthood.

The ranch buildings lay at the end of a long, unpaved road. As Caro's ancient truck bounced over the ruts, she remembered something else Josie had mentioned. Jonathan had left the road unpaved to discourage casual visitors. Sarah and his sons had continued to honor that wish. Caro hoped her shocks would hold up under the assault.

Considering the poor condition of the road, the house and outbuildings were surprisingly luxurious. Caro wasn't sure where to park, so she pulled into the gravel drive that circled in front of the main house. She could always move her truck down by the barn if necessary.

The two-story ranch house was immense, an expanded version of a log cabin. In the center stood a boxlike structure that was obviously the heart of the house. Two wings stretched out from there, each of them canted forward, like arms reaching to embrace a weary traveler.

A covered front porch ran the entire length of the house, and rockers sat quietly spaced along the porch as if anticipating a time when the family would have the leisure to sit and contemplate the view. That view, Caro noted as she climbed down from her truck and reacquainted herself with it, was spectacular.

The house faced the Grand Tetons in all their majesty.

Even now, in mid-August, snow clung to the jagged peaks. She stood for a moment and admired it before putting on her hat, a summer straw that she'd picked up a few years ago, back when she'd still had time to take trail rides from the local stable.

"Hey, Caro."

At the sound of Logan's voice, she spun in the direction of the barn, a hip-roofed structure that looked as if it belonged on a postcard. "Should I move my truck down by the barn?" She noticed two horses had been saddled and tied to the hitching post.

"Your truck's fine where it is." He walked to meet her, but kept a safe distance between them. "I'm glad you're here." His stance was casual, but his eyes, shaded by his tan Stetson, glowed with a banked fire.

Her heart thumped heavily in her chest. It could be all the caffeine she'd consumed today, but she figured it was probably the man. "It's good to see you again, Logan."

"You have no idea how good it is to see you, Caro." He studied her with such intensity that she began to tremble. "Love the hat."

"It's old."

"Looks great on you, though. I like the ponytail you wear at work, but I like your hair down like this even better. It reminds me of…well, never mind."

"I know what it reminds you of." She longed to reach for him, but that would be a bad idea. "We should probably get going, huh?"

"Yeah." He cleared his throat. "But first I want to show you something. It's in the barn."

"Sure." She fell into step beside him as they walked to the building.

"How's your grandmother?"

"She wanted to know why I'm so perky today."

He choked on a laugh. "And what did you tell her?"

"I said I'd been drinking espresso."

"Have you?"

"Yes. I didn't get any sleep last night, for some reason."

"Not even after I left?"

"No. I looked you up on Google instead."

He stopped and turned to stare at her. "You did what?"

"I looked you up on the web. I learned a lot."

His expression was unreadable. "Ancient history, I'm afraid."

"Maybe so, but I want to apologize for so breezily suggesting you find another career. You were brilliant. I understand why you can't just move on to something else. It's not that easy."

He took a deep breath. "It may not be easy, but it's the right idea. I haven't slept, either, and I've guzzled coffee, too, so my mind is probably hopped up on caffeine. But I do know that you were absolutely right to say that."

"I was arrogant to say that."

"I'd call it practical, and I apologize for being irritated. The door has closed behind me. Time to find a new door."

She met his gaze. Obviously he was making progress in his thinking, and she didn't want to wreck that. "Any ideas?"

"Not a single one." He smiled at her. "But you promised to help me come up with a plan B once we got out on the trail."

"Now that I've seen all that stuff on the internet about you, I don't think I'm qualified. It won't be easy coming up with something that absorbs your attention like that. And I know nothing about sports."

"Doesn't matter. I have to start somewhere, and I can't think of a better person to brainstorm with than you. But before we leave, I have to show you what I'm working on. It's kind of cool." He turned and started back down the pathway to the barn.

Whatever this new project was, she was encouraged by his enthusiasm. That attitude was a huge improvement over describing himself as a washed-up baseball player. Maybe he'd get lucky and this project would lead to something bigger, something he could latch on to.

A dog lay on either side of the barn doors. The one on the left had short hair and was tan and white, with a snub nose and pointed ears. The one on the right was all black, with long curly hair and floppy ears.

"Meet Butch and Sundance." Logan pointed to the left and right. "Guys, this is Caro, a most excellent lady of my acquaintance."

The dogs lumbered to their feet and came toward her for some attention. She crouched down and petted both at once. "I'd forgotten how much I love dogs. My grandmother is allergic to animals, so I couldn't have any while I lived with her."

"Knowing Josie, she'd be willing to let you have a dog in your apartment."

Caro gave each dog one last scratch and stood. "It wouldn't be fair. I'm either working or driving to Jackson. Dogs need someone who can take them out for walks, throw balls for them, keep them company." She glanced at him. "I don't have room for a dog in my life, any more than I have room for a man."

"At least the man wouldn't need you to play fetch with him."

She laughed. "No, but he'd want me to play other games, no doubt."

"Yes, he would." His eyes gleamed with wicked intent. "Come on, let me show you this real quick, and then we'll ride off into the sunset." He ushered her into the cool interior of the barn, which smelled of hay, manure and leather.

She rather liked the combination, but then, she was a

country girl. She wondered if Logan simply tolerated it for the time being.

"I don't have an elaborate workbench." He gestured toward one of the stalls, which had been swept clean. "But Jack helped me put something together so I could tackle this job. Take a look."

She peered into the stall, which had been recently modified, judging from the sawdust and the scent of cut lumber. A waist-high shelf spanned the end of the stall and a pegboard loaded with various tools hung above it. Under the shelf lay pieces of what must have been an old cradle. Judging from the newly cut sections on the workbench, Logan was in the process of creating a replacement.

She was surprised. His complete dedication to baseball didn't seem to have left room for a hobby. "You didn't mention that you were a carpenter."

"I wouldn't go that far. I like working with wood, and I did a fair bit of it when I was in high school, but after that I abandoned woodworking completely to concentrate on baseball. Fortunately, the techniques I learned in shop class are coming back to me."

"You are a man of many talents."

He gave her a lazy grin. "Thanks. Care to elaborate?"

"Not here." She lowered her voice. "Anybody could come in."

"You have a point. Emmett Sterling, the foreman, will show up any minute to adjust your stirrups before we ride out. He's already fixed mine, but you need to mount up before he can adjust yours. I wouldn't pretend to know how to do it."

"It's not that hard."

Logan laughed softly. "Maybe not yet, but it will be soon."

"Logan…"

"Couldn't resist. I love making you blush. Anyway, you've seen what I'm doing, so now we can leave."

"Hang on a minute." She wanted to explore this new side of him a little more before they left the barn and got sidetracked by…well, obviously, sex. "I assume you're making a cradle for Josie and Jack's baby, and using the old one as a guide."

"That's right."

"Where did the old one come from?"

"It should have been an heirloom." Logan crouched down and picked up one of the sections that had a cutout of a heart in it. "Jack's grandfather Archie built it for Jack's dad, Jonathan. But Jonathan's first wife, Diana, didn't use it for Jack when he was born. Instead it got shoved up in the rafters above the tack room, and has been there ever since."

"What a shame." She noticed he winced a little when he crouched down, but she wasn't about to mention it.

"It is a shame. Archie put a lot of loving care into making this. I hope I can do the project justice."

"I'm sure you can." Caro almost said what she was thinking—that maybe Logan could consider making furniture, at least until he figured out what else he might want to do with his time. But the solution seemed too simplistic. She didn't know anything about that field, and it had nothing in common with a high-profile job like baseball.

Of course, if Logan put his name on the furniture, it could become a high-profile venture. He might not like that idea, though. He didn't strike her as the kind of guy who would enjoy trading on a reputation for past accomplishments.

"I can see the wheels going around," Logan said.

"Just thinking about the cradle."

"You wouldn't be thinking that my future is in cradle making, would you?"

She looked into his eyes. "Okay, I did for a minute there. Not just cradles, but other stuff. I don't suppose that's the answer, though."

"No, it's not. I don't see myself peddling furniture I've made. I have a certain amount of skill, but I'm no master craftsman. I'd be embarrassed to charge money for making something."

"But you said you don't need money."

"I don't, but I'm not going to build furniture and pass it out to strangers on the street for free, either."

"Of course not."

"The thing is, if I make something that's a labor of love, like Archie did with the cradle, that's a joy. Mass production for customers I don't know doesn't appeal to me."

She nodded. "Totally understandable."

"But for the record, I'm not going to shoot down everything you come up with, so don't stop thinking, okay?"

"I won't. I like solving problems."

"Well, here's one." He lowered his voice. "How fast can we ride out of here and find a secluded spot so I can get you naked?"

She felt as if he'd shoved her under a heat lamp and sucked all the air out of her lungs. She gasped.

"Sorry." His grin was positively wicked. "Was that too direct?"

She had only enough breath for a single-syllable response. "No."

"It's so tempting to tease you. You're as pink as the inside of a ripe watermelon."

She wouldn't be surprised, considering the heat pouring through her.

"Anyway, I figure we've spent enough time looking at my woodworking project. Let's move on to more important things." He touched the small of her back lightly, a signal to move out of the stall and back to the barn entrance.

That brief contact was enough to dampen her panties. She gulped. "Okay."

As he walked beside her, he pulled a piece of paper from his jeans pocket and continued to keep his voice to a low murmur. "Josie drew me a quick sketch of the trails we can take. I'm not a great rider, but I should be able to stay on the horse long enough to find us some privacy."

"All right." She sounded like robot woman, but putting one foot in front of the other took all her concentration as she fought the urge to drag him back into the stall and strip him down.

"They put me up on Destiny, because he's easy, but I've been warned if we don't tie him well when we have our, uh…" He coughed. "Our *snack* that Mary Lou fixed, then he'll go back home."

"That wouldn't be so good."

"Actually, riding double sounds kind of fun."

"Have you ever done it?"

"Nope, but I'm picturing you in front of me, and I get an excellent image."

That made her smile. If he thought two people could have comfortable sex on a saddle, he was sadly mistaken, and neither of them were accomplished enough to ride bareback and have sex at the same time. Still, it was a fun fantasy.

They emerged from the barn, and the bright sunlight curbed her raging libido somewhat. Besides, Emmett would be along anytime now to adjust her stirrups and she didn't want the foreman to pick up on any sexual vibes zinging between her and Logan. She walked toward the horses standing patiently tied to the hitching post.

"That's Destiny." Logan pointed toward a brown-and-white paint with a white blaze down his nose. "The one you'll be riding is Cookies and Cream, or Cici for short. She's a mare, but Destiny's no longer in the mating game, so we shouldn't have any trouble with these two."

"I can probably adjust the stirrups myself." Caro walked

around Destiny and approached her chocolate-colored mare. She was a pretty thing, with a white mane and tail. "Hello, Cici." Caro rubbed her velvety neck. "Thanks for taking me out today."

"Or you can tell me what to do once you're up there." Logan came to stand beside her. "I watched Emmett, but I want to make sure I don't screw it up."

"All right. I'll—"

"You two ready to head out?" A square-jawed cowboy came around the corner of the barn before Caro had a chance to mount up. His mustache was mostly gray and his face was lined, but his manner was that of a much younger man. He touched the brim of his hat in a courtly gesture. "Nice to see you out here, Caro."

"Thank you, Mr. Sterling."

"Ah, call me Emmett. Everyone does. I don't get into the Spirits and Spurs very often, but I was there last night for the reception. You did a great job."

"Thanks, but I wouldn't have if Logan hadn't helped me out."

"I know." Emmett glanced over at Logan. "I saw the juggling act. Impressive."

Logan shrugged. "It's pretty easy."

"It is if you've been a top-notch catcher for years. It's too bad Nelsie isn't still around. She was a devoted Cubs fan."

"She was Archie's wife, right?"

"Yep. She started following the Cubs in the sixties, and she kept up with them until the day she died. I'll bet Sarah still has the Cubs cap Nelsie used to wear all the time. And now here's an actual Cubs player staying at the Last Chance. She would have been thrilled about that."

"That's quite a coincidence." Caro decided to say something before Logan cut in with some nonsense about not being a player anymore. "Why did she follow the Cubs?"

"Sarah has her old diary. In it she says that she picked them because they were a historic team, one of the oldest in the game. Nelsie gravitated toward anything with history attached to it."

"That's one of the things I loved about playing for them," Logan said quietly. "Being part of all that history."

Caro heard the sorrow buried in his comment, and she wished they were alone so she could wrap him in her arms and give him comfort.

Emmett put a hand on Logan's shoulder. "Didn't mean to bring up a sore subject, son."

"Hey, no worries." Logan smiled at the foreman. "I'm glad you told me about Nelsie. It makes me feel more like a part of the ranch, to know my team was her favorite."

"Well, good, then. Now let's get Caro mounted up so you two can explore the ranch. It's a pretty day for it."

Caro climbed aboard and Emmett busied himself adjusting her stirrups. In no time they were headed away from the ranch on a trail that crossed a meadow filled with wildflowers. Logan had the map, so he led.

That suited Caro just fine. She could ogle his tight buns all she wanted, because there was no rearview mirror on a horse, so he'd never know.

Then he turned to look back at her. "Checking me out, Caro?"

"Would I do that?"

"I sure as hell hope so, considering my plans for the afternoon."

"I see." Her body tightened deliciously. Rocking along on a warm leather saddle didn't hurt matters, either.

"That grove of trees seems damned far away. How do I shift this horse into high gear? It's been a while since I've done this."

"Are you sure you want high gear?"

"Okay, maybe not. I don't want to fall off. But meandering down the trail at a snail's pace is not working for me."

She laughed. "You're supposed to be enjoying the scenery."

"All the scenery I want to enjoy is currently covered up."

"Carswell, you have a one-track mind."

"So I've been told."

She considered that his ability to be very single-minded, which was probably what had made him an excellent ball-player, also would explain why he was such a fantastic lover.

"Seriously, Caro, what signals do I give this animal so he'll move out? Do I kick him or cluck at him or what?"

"You nudge with your heels, but the next level up after walking is trotting. In my experience, it's hard to sit a trot unless you've practiced."

"So what if I skip that level and go to the next one?"

"You think you're ready to canter? How long has it been since you were on a horse?"

"Three or four years. Some buddies and I went to a dude ranch in Colorado for a couple of days."

"And before that?"

"There was no before that. That was my first and only time on a horse."

"Hmm." She thought about his knee and what sort of damage he could do if he came off the animal. "We'd better walk."

"To hell with that." He dug both heels into Destiny's ribs, and the horse broke into a trot. Logan began to bounce in the saddle. "This sucks!"

"Told you." Caro trotted behind him, but she'd had enough practice to keep from bouncing.

"Next gear, then." Logan kicked again and Destiny moved into a canter. "Better!" He jostled around some, but then settled in. "*Much* better!"

She watched in amazement as he transformed from awkward city boy on a horse to someone who could almost pass for a cowboy. Apparently that's what the gift of natural coordination could do for a person.

He was an incredible guy, the kind of man who'd be easy to fall for. She wouldn't, of course, because that would set up the perfect scenario for heartbreak. Caro was one hundred percent against heartbreak.

Logan cantered ahead of her, taunting her with his broad shoulders and tight buns. He must have been feeling really confident, because he turned in the saddle to grin at her.

As she opened her mouth to warn him that he shouldn't get cocky, Destiny shied at something on the trail. The horse crow-hopped, and Logan sailed off into a patch of wildflowers. Caro pulled Cici to a stop and leaped off; heart pounding, she prayed he hadn't landed on his knee.

8

LOGAN'S FIRST THOUGHT as his butt left the saddle was that this was no way to impress a woman. And sadly, he had hoped to impress Caro with his newfound cowboy skills. He'd seen right away that a trot wasn't going to accomplish it, but the canter had shown real promise until Destiny veered in one direction and he veered in the other.

His second thought was for his knee. He'd had a lot of experience falling during his baseball career, and in this instance he didn't have to worry about where the ball was or how other players might be impacting the situation. Twisting his body as he fell, he managed to land on his backside, which was the part that could take the most punishment.

He hit with a jolt that made his teeth click together, but fortunately, his tongue wasn't in the way. He lay there a second or two, flexing everything to make sure he hadn't broken a vital body part. Other than the fact that his butt hurt a little, he seemed to be in decent shape.

"Logan!" The stalks of wildflowers surrounding him rustled and then Caro dropped to her knees by his side. "Oh, my God. Are you okay?"

"Yes, other than feeling like a damned fool. Where are the horses?"

She glanced up. "Cici's right over there, eating flowers.

Destiny's…getting away! Stay here. I'll be right back." She jumped to her feet.

Logan sat up in time to watch her leap on Cici and trot off to retrieve his homeward-bound mount. Then he carefully got to his feet, only to find his knee was no worse than it had been. At least he wasn't totally without luck.

Meanwhile Caro, the heroine of the hour, caught up with Destiny and grabbed his reins. As Logan dusted off the seat of his pants, noting that he felt at least one good-size bruise forming there, she rode up, leading his mount. So much for impressing the woman he hoped to have sex with.

"I got him. Emmett needs to train him out of that bad habit." She gazed down at Logan. "How are you doing?"

"My pride is shredded, but other than that, I'm fine."

"You have a purple flower in your hair."

He leaned on the only thing he had left, his sense of humor. "Does it look good on me?"

She cocked her head to one side. "I think red's more your color."

"Then I'll ditch it." Combing his fingers through his hair, he dislodged the flower, plus a few pieces of grass.

"Where's your hat?"

"Somewhere in the area, I suppose." He glanced around and finally spied it upside down about ten feet away, among the prairie grass and wildflowers. He went after it, dusted it off and settled it on his head. "Time to mount up."

She handed him Destiny's reins. "We can go back, if you want."

He climbed back up and settled gingerly into the saddle. "I'll leave that up to you. Are you still interested in a guy who falls off his horse and ends up with flowers in his hair?"

"Yes."

He glanced at her and discovered she was smiling. "You are?"

"Absolutely. Some guys I know wouldn't have been able to handle being humiliated like that."

He laughed. "Humiliated?"

"Well, yeah. You were thrown from your horse while you were trying to show off for me, and then I had to recapture that horse so you wouldn't be on foot. Some men would deal with that by retreating to their man cave to nurse their damaged egos."

"Then I guess those guys have never dropped the ball for what would have been a game-winning out in the World Series. Try being humiliated in front of millions on national TV. This is chicken feed compared to that."

"Then lead the way to the trees, Mr. Carswell. But maybe we should walk the horses."

"Don't worry. I'm all about walking. In fact, I'm letting you lead."

"But you have the map."

"We don't need a map. We aren't going any farther than that line of trees." He wasn't going to admit that his backside probably couldn't take more riding than that. But he could think of one thing that would make all his aches and pains disappear.

"Okay, I'll go first then." She pointed Cici down the trail and gave her a nudge.

Destiny fell in behind the mare, and Logan realized that from this angle he could watch Caro's cute fanny in the saddle and contemplate the joys he might find at the end of the trail. As an added bonus, she wouldn't be able to observe him shifting around as he tried to find a comfortable spot that didn't press on his bruised behind.

She'd already decided he shouldn't have sex that put pressure on his knees. If she thought he couldn't lie on his back without pain, they'd be even more limited in their choice of positions. Sometimes she was too caring for his own good.

"I've been thinking about that cradle you're making," she said. "Do you suppose Josie would like a baby quilt to go with it?"

"Why, do you have one?"

"I have some quilt squares and I could make one that size. I've been wondering what to give her for the baby, but for some reason I didn't think of that."

"You're a quilter?"

"I haven't sewn for months, but yes, I'm a quilter. My grandmother taught me how."

"Did you make the one on your bed?"

"Yep."

"Nice." He would always treasure the image of her sitting up in bed with the quilt over her lap. He liked knowing she'd made it. "I suppose you don't have time to do that these days."

"I don't, but I would create the time if I thought it was important enough. But I don't know what I'd do with the quilts. I have enough for myself and for Grandma Bonnie. She said the same thing when she stopped quilting. After you've given one to each of the people you know and love, what do you do with the excess?"

"Sell them?"

"Maybe, but I'm not sure I'd want to mass-produce them for strangers, any more than you'd want to mass-produce furniture."

"I get that." He thought about the problem. "But do you enjoy making them?"

"I do. I love finding interesting scraps of fabric, and some of the patterns are breathtaking. There's real satisfaction in putting together a quilt that will keep someone warm and be beautiful at the same time."

"I used to feel that way about woodworking. I made things that looked good but served a function."

"But then you run out of people to give them to."

"I know." But he had a sudden picture of a home filled with his furniture and her quilts. A home made for a family, something he hadn't allowed himself to think about while he was totally focused on baseball.

He wasn't focused on baseball now. Did that mean he was ready for a wife and family? No. He needed to find a purpose in life before he brought another person into his. Being a husband and father was an appealing possibility, more so now than ever, but it wasn't enough to fill his days.

"How far into the trees do you want to ride?"

He glanced around in surprise. Looking back down the trail, he could see that they'd entered the stand of trees some time ago. Apparently he'd been thinking so hard about quilts and furniture and families that he hadn't noticed.

"Here." He caught sight of a little glen to the right. "Over in that clearing."

"All right." Caro guided Cici off the trail, and the horse's hooves crunched on leaves and twigs that had fallen to the forest floor. As Caro dismounted, her denim jeans stretched tight across her bottom.

Logan forgot all about families and furniture, although he wouldn't mind having a fluffy quilt right now to spread on the ground. He steered Destiny toward a sturdy-looking tree and climbed down. "I'm tying this horse up good and tight."

"Glad to hear it." Caro secured Cici's reins around a leafy branch, then walked toward him. "Got snacks?"

He turned. He hadn't meant to grab her, but he must have, because her hat fell off and she squealed as he pulled her into his arms. "I've been waiting so long," he offered by way of apology, before he crushed her to him and claimed her mouth.

Somewhere in the middle of that hot kiss he lost his hat, too. He barely noticed as they began undressing each other with frantic movements and labored breathing. Soon his shirt was on the ground, along with her shirt and bra.

"Blanket?" she asked between kisses.

"Tablecloth." He fondled her breasts. He'd wanted a blanket but hadn't figured out how to take one along without arousing suspicion.

"Never mind." She unbuckled his belt and unzipped his jeans.

Once she had her hands on his cock, he went a little crazy. He wasn't a back-her-up-against-a-tree kind of guy, but that's exactly what he did. A large pine was handy, and he leaned her against it as he fumbled for the condom in his pocket— while she caressed him with those clever hands of hers until he had to beg her to stop.

"Don't you like it?" she asked in a breathless whisper.

"I love it. But I want to be inside you when I come." He snapped the condom into place and slid both hands under her bare bottom. He wasn't sure exactly when she'd kicked off her boots and jeans, but they were lying next to the tree instead of covering her body, and for that he was grateful. "Put your hands on my shoulders, and when I lift you, wrap your legs around my waist."

"You can hold me up?"

"I can bench-press two hundred pounds. Do you weigh more than that?"

She scowled at him.

"I can hold you up." He leaned forward and nibbled at her mouth. "Open for me, Caro. Let me in." He boosted her to the level of his waiting cock, and she spread her thighs and wound her legs around him.

One thrust and he was golden. She'd paved the way for him with enough moisture to make that slide easy and smooth. Once he was locked in tight, he sighed with pleasure. "Perfect."

"Yeah...." She leaned her head against the tree trunk.

"Arch your back. I don't want you to get scratched up."

She looked into his eyes with a sultry expression. "As if I care."

"I care. Arch your back. Move your hips toward…*me*." He sucked in a breath when she thrust her pelvis more forcefully against his. The contact was intense enough to nearly make him explode.

She ran her tongue over her lips. "How's that?"

"Incredible. I could come right now, just looking at you."

"I think I could, too." She contracted her muscles around him.

His penis twitched in response. He gripped her satiny bottom, squeezing gently. "Keep doing that and I won't have to move at all."

"That would be cool, if we could just—" she tightened her muscles again "—do this."

"We can. I'm close."

Her breathing was shallow. "Me, too."

"I love it when you come. Your eyes get dark, and then I feel you squeeze me…like that…do it again…yeah …" He was slowly losing his mind, and yet they were barely moving. No thrusting, no pumping, no gymnastics, and yet his climax edged closer each time she squeezed his penis.

Then she began to improvise. Taking one hand from his shoulder, she reached down and massaged his balls. "How's that?"

He groaned with pleasure.

She toyed with him some more until he began to quiver. "Not much longer."

She transferred her attention to her clit, caressing herself with slow circles of her finger.

"I like that, too," he murmured. "You're holding me tighter and tighter."

"Because I'm …" She moaned softly. "I'm coming… I'm—"

Her contractions rolled over his cock, coaxing him, taunting him, until he also came in a rush, jerking with the force of it, and throwing back his head with a low cry of ecstasy.

Legs braced, he somehow managed to stay upright and hold on to her as their tremors gradually subsided. Slowly, he brought his head forward again and met her gaze. She seemed as dazed as he was. Exciting as this had been, they both needed a bed in which to recover, but he didn't have one. He had a tablecloth and a couple of saddle blankets.

It would have to do. "Can you stand here for just a little while?"

Her smile was lopsided. "Maybe."

He gently lowered her feet to the ground and reached for his shirt. Draping it around her shoulders, he gave her a quick kiss. "Wait here. I won't take long."

Picking up his jeans, he disposed of the condom by wrapping it in his handkerchief. After that he approached the two saddled horses. Although he knew next to nothing about saddles, the cinch seemed no more complicated than a belt.

And he was a man on a mission, determined to provide for his lover. In a relatively short time he'd pulled off both saddles and placed the blankets on the ground with the side that had touched the horses on the bottom.

Then he pulled the red-and-white-checker tablecloth out of the saddlebag containing the snacks. He thought they needed rest more than food right now. The makeshift bed finished, he returned for Caro and led her to the tree-shaded bower he'd prepared.

She didn't question or protest as he drew her down with him. After some maneuvering, they were settled on the nubby blankets, Caro lying with her back to him and her knees drawn up, Logan curled protectively around her.

Last of all he spread the tablecloth over both of them, stretched out his arm and urged her to use it as a pillow. She must have been too exhausted to argue, because she cuddled against him and fell fast asleep. Wrapping an arm around her waist, he held Caro close.

As he drifted off to sleep, Logan realized he'd never been happier in his life.

9

CARO WOKE UP TO THE SOUND of birds chirping in the branches over her head. For a moment she was totally disoriented and couldn't imagine where she was. Then she felt Logan's arm around her and his warm body pressed against her back.

Oh, yes. She'd ridden out here with this hunky, conflicted man and they'd been so desperate for sex that they'd done it up against a pine tree. She'd never been that wild and crazy with a guy, but Logan seemed to bring out all her hidden fantasies. No wonder. The arm draped around her was beautifully sculpted, and the rest of his body was the same.

But her reaction to him was about more than his physical attributes. He needed her. Through example, Grandma Bonnie had taught her the joy and satisfaction of being there for a person in need.

Logan was going through a dark period in his life, and he needed someone to help him deal with his demons. She could help. She'd never lost a career, but she'd lost her mother at the tender age of twelve.

She didn't kid herself that this was a lasting attraction. He'd figure out his next steps and be on his way. She would have served her purpose, that of being a bridge over troubled waters. She was okay with that.

Or mostly okay. The longer she was with him, the more

she began to dream. But he wasn't for her, and she knew it. He'd find a career that would put him in the limelight again, and he wouldn't find that career in Shoshone, Wyoming.

He nuzzled the back of her neck. "You awake?"

"Uh-huh."

"That was the last condom, I hate to say. I couldn't come up with a way to get more without causing a stir in the community. Something tells me that if I drove into town and bought a box, the word would be out before I was halfway back to the Last Chance turnoff."

"You're probably right. The only secretive way to get them is in the men's room at the Spirits and Spurs, and we know that machine is completely unreliable."

"Do you have the three-to-eleven shift tomorrow night?"

"Yes."

"Think I'll have to come by for a beer…and a few condoms from the machine."

She sighed. "Nice idea, but if you stay after closing, we might as well put up a billboard announcing that we're shacking up."

"Yeah, you're right. And ultimately, you're the one who'll have to deal with the gossip after I leave."

He was right, but the more Caro thought about it, the more she was ready to stand up for her right to have sex with Logan if she wanted to. She was a big girl. "You know what? I don't care about gossip."

"You don't?"

"People may suspect something's going on, anyway. Let's get it out in the open. I'll give Josie the courtesy of telling her tonight. I'll let her know that you and I want to spend quality time with each other, and neither of us is looking at it as a long-term commitment. I know she worries that I'll get hurt."

His arm tightened around her. "So do I."

"You can only hurt me if I allow it." She was glad they

were having this conversation when she wasn't looking at him. She'd have an easier time convincing him—and herself—if they weren't face-to-face.

"And you won't allow it."

"No. I'll let Josie know I'm going into this with my eyes wide open, and that I know you're destined for greater things than a quiet existence in Shoshone, Wyoming. She should be fine with it."

"I hope so."

"I'll make sure she is. The bottom line is, we can do whatever we want, as long as I don't ignore my obligations to Josie or Grandma Bonnie."

"Are you going to Jackson in the morning?"

"Yes—I always do."

"Let me go with you."

"Why would you want to?" Caro remembered how she'd thought about taking him so he could appreciate his own good fortune in comparison. She was a little surprised that he would suggest it himself, though.

"You're helping me with my problems and I'd like to help you with yours. Maybe if I met your grandmother, I'd have some ideas about how she might adjust to her new circumstances." He paused. "She's had the rug pulled out from under her, and I know what that feels like."

"True. I'd love for you to go." Caro hesitated. "If you come with me, would you be willing to tell everyone who you are? The residents would be so excited, especially some of the men."

His breath was warm on her shoulder. "I can do that. For you."

"You'd rather not, though."

"No, it's fine. If it would make those folks happy, then it's a small thing. The more I'm with you, the less the end of my career matters to me."

She squeezed his arm. "Good. Maybe the pain is fading a little bit."

"It fades totally when I'm deep inside you."

She smiled. "Don't be saying such things when we're out of condoms."

"You're right. Sorry about that." He released her and sat up. "We should get back. It won't be long until dinner."

Immediately she missed the warmth and closeness of lying on the blankets with him. It wasn't a particularly comfortable bed, but she'd cherish their time here. She sat up, too, and combed her hair back from her face. "I must look like a mess."

"Nope, you look terrific. But your lipstick is all gone."

"I brought more."

"Smart girl."

"Thanks. I try to plan ahead." Feeling slightly shy, she tucked the tablecloth around her as she stood. Logan didn't seem to have any problem walking around naked, but then he'd spent the past fifteen or twenty years in communal showers with the rest of the jocks.

He began pulling on his clothes. "I think Josie and Jack are supposed to be at dinner, so that will give you a chance to inform Josie about us, if you still want to."

"I do." Caro lifted her chin. Let the gossip begin. Logan needed her, and she needed him, at least for the short term. He would be here only a little while, and she hated the idea of wasting that precious time because she was worried about wagging tongues.

"You're absolutely sure you're okay with being open about our arrangement?"

"This kind of secret won't last long in Shoshone, so it's either be open or stop. I choose option A."

He grinned. "I like a woman who has her priorities straight." He fastened the snaps on his shirt.

"Can't help it. You're pretty potent, Carswell."

"I am? That's nice to hear." He tucked in his shirttail.

"It's true. I've never let any man have sex with me up against a tree."

"For the record, I've never had sex with a woman up against a tree, either." He buckled his belt and looked up. "It's a total first for me."

"Really?"

His grin was quick. "Really. And I'd appreciate it if you'd put some clothes on while I saddle up the horses. Otherwise I'm liable to suggest we find ways to have fun without a condom. I can think of a couple already."

So could she, and her body began to hum. "You're going to saddle up the horses?"

"Sure. Blanket, saddle, cinch. How tough can it be?"

She could just let him do it and find out for himself. If Destiny puffed out his belly when the cinch was being tightened, Logan would end up on the ground when the cinch became loose and the saddle rotated.

But she wasn't the type of person to let that happen to any greenhorn, let alone someone who already had a bad knee and a sore behind. "Once you tighten the cinch, wait until the horse lets out a breath, and tighten it some more. Put your knee against their ribs if you have to." She caught herself before saying *use your good knee.* "They'll try to fool you by swelling up with air."

He glanced at her as he adjusted his hat. "Thanks for the tip."

"You're welcome." She was struck by how much more comfortable Logan looked in those clothes than he had when she'd first met him. He even wore his hat with more confidence. "You're liable to turn into a cowboy yet." She waited for him to contradict her.

Instead he smiled. "Funny, but I think I could, at that. I survived falling off a horse, which has to be one of the tests."

"It is. And you climbed right back on, like any true cowboy would."

"Well, I was motivated to get into the woods ASAP." He waggled his eyebrows at her and she laughed. "But I guess what I'm trying to say is that I like this riding business. Too bad my home owners association won't let me keep a horse in my condo."

"It's not exactly cowboy country back there, is it?"

"Nope. Now get dressed. I'm going to show how proficient I am at saddling these two hay burners."

"Now you're even talking like a cowboy." She watched him work as she pulled on her clothes, and his movements weren't as smooth as a seasoned rider's would be, but he got the job done, making sure the cinches were tight around each of the horse's bellies.

When he finished, he turned to her with a boyish grin of pride. "How's that?"

"Excellent." She finger-combed her hair and dug in her pocket for her lipstick.

"Hang on. Don't do that yet." He walked over and drew her into his arms. "One more for the road."

"You want to kiss me?"

"Yes."

"But you know we can't have sex."

"Yes. So what?"

She gazed up at him and wondered if he realized the significance of that. A kiss that was part of foreplay was purely sexual. A kiss that wasn't foreplay was... She didn't want to put a name on what it was.

"Don't you want me to kiss you?"

"I do." And she didn't want to put a name on the yearning in her heart, either.

"Good, because I intend to." But when he leaned down to kiss her, his hat bumped against hers. "Now that's inconvenient."

"There's a trick to it." Her heart melted a little more the longer she was in his arms. "Tilt your hat back a little. Then I'll lean one way and you lean the opposite way. It's how a cowboy kisses a cowgirl."

"Is that so?" Angling his head, he followed her directions. When his lips almost touched hers, he paused. "Any more kissing tips I need to know?"

"No." Emotion flowed through her, warm and sweet. "You've mastered the rest of it."

"Not even close. But fortunately, I love to practice." His mouth found hers.

His kiss was familiar now, and she welcomed the velvet heat of it with heat of her own. Passion was there, as it had been from the beginning, but…this kiss was about more than passion. It brimmed over with joy and with caring and… She blocked the next word that came to her in a soft, seductive whisper.

But the word, and the feelings it brought with it, crept around the edges of her barricade. She couldn't ignore the way he was kissing her, because it was different from the other times. Whether he'd admitted it to himself or not, he cherished her.

And that could blossom into something neither of them were prepared to handle. Her heart aching, she pulled back. "If we keep this up, we'll be up against a tree in no time," she said.

It was an excuse. She wasn't worried that he'd back her against a tree and rip her clothes off. He hadn't telegraphed that kind of wild urgency this time. She was worried about something far more significant.

He cleared his throat. "Thanks for teaching me how to kiss like a cowboy."

"You're welcome." She brushed a piece of grass off her sleeve. "You handled it like a pro."

"I'm not so sure. I think we need to try it again."

She looked into his eyes. "Better not." She hoped he'd get the message without having to discuss it. Once they gave voice to the possibility that they might be falling for each other, it would become the elephant in the room and ruin whatever time they had left.

"Okay." He sounded reluctant, but he released her. "You're the boss."

She glanced up through the trees at the angle of the sun. "Besides, it's getting late."

"We didn't eat Mary Lou's snacks. I don't know her well, but I don't think she'd take kindly to us rejecting her food."

"What is it?"

"I don't know. Let's look." He walked over to Destiny and opened the saddlebag. "Six cookies. Four chocolate chip and two oatmeal and raisin. Plus a couple small bottles of water. She probably won't care if we drink the water or not. She didn't bottle it personally."

Caro laughed. "Chocolate chip is my favorite."

"Mine, too."

"So let's eat those and leave the oatmeal cookies for the birds."

"All right." He brought the plastic Ziploc bag over to where she stood under the shade of a tree. "Bon appétit."

She smiled at him as she took a cookie from the open bag he extended to her. "Here's another tip. Cowboys don't speak French."

"I don't speak it, either." He bit into a cookie. "That's about all I know, but I'll strike it from my vocabulary while I'm home on the range where the deer and the antelope play."

"Wise plan."

"So what would a cowboy say?"

"Oh, maybe 'tuck in' or if they were feeling long-winded, they might say 'let's tie on the old feedbag.'"

Logan gazed at her. "Chocolate chip." He touched the corner of his mouth.

"Here?" She wiped her face with the tip of her finger.

His eyes darkened. "No, here." He reached over and brushed the crumb away. "And here." He touched the other side of her mouth. "And…God, Caro…" Dropping the bag of cookies to the ground, he swept her back into his arms.

Both their hats fell off as his lips came down on hers with no thought given to angle or technique. His mouth was hungry, the thrust of his tongue possessive. He kissed her until they were both breathless.

Then he released her and stood back, his chest heaving. "Sorry, but I needed that. You're the most adorable chocolate chip cookie eater I've ever met."

She drew a shaky breath. "Thank you. That's not something a girl hears every day."

"I suppose not. But I actually want to thank you—for being here, for generously giving of yourself with no thought of getting anything in return."

He was falling for her. And she was falling for him, too, damn it. She'd been so involved with her grandmother that she'd forgotten what it was like to be desired by a wonderful man. He inspired a vision of a fuller, more satisfying life.

But he wasn't the man to give her that life. She attempted to get them both back on safer ground. "I get something in return. Orgasms."

"Yes, but—"

"Logan, we really need to start back. If you'll scatter the oatmeal cookies around for the birds, I'll put on my lipstick."

He gazed at her for a moment longer. "Yeah, it's getting late."

Too late, she thought as she somehow managed to put on lipstick with a hand that shook. She'd been determined to keep an emotional distance between them, but it was too late.

10

As they rode back to the ranch, Logan felt as if a hive of bees had taken up residence in his brain. In his baseball career he'd always been able to think strategically, both on the field and when planning various career moves. But ever since learning that his playing days were over, he'd lost that ability, or so it seemed.

He certainly wasn't being sensible about Caro. She was supposed to be a diversion, a safe haven for a few nights while he tried to figure out what to do with his life. Good sex—and she certainly represented that—had always been a way for him to relax and forget his problems. Good sex had never *become* the problem.

Okay, he admitted to himself, it wasn't the good sex that was a problem. It was the woman herself. He liked her way too much, and he wasn't in a position to like somebody too much, especially a woman who belonged, in all senses of the word, in Wyoming.

Even if he asked her to go back to Chicago with him, she wouldn't. Her grandmother was here, and so were her roots. She liked living in Shoshone, liked her job, liked to ride horses and spend time outdoors. He could tell that from the way she'd perked up the minute they'd headed down the trail.

So what the hell was he doing, courting her? It was an old-fashioned word, but it fit his behavior. He found himself complimenting her and kissing her for no reason. Actually, he did know the reason, and he should be worried about it.

The sad part was, he couldn't seem to help himself, couldn't seem to control his emotions when it came to Caro. He'd always been a very self-disciplined person with his eye on the prize. Now there was no prize to keep an eye on—except her, and she was completely out of reach.

Well, unless he wanted to go into the furniture business in Shoshone. Oh, yeah, that sounded like a barrel of fun. See what former Cubs star Logan Carswell is doing now? He's building furniture and selling it out of a little storefront in Shoshone, Wyoming. Pitiful.

But he'd be near Caro, and that almost made him consider it. Almost. But he couldn't imagine how a little furniture business would be enough for him. So he sold a few pieces and kept busy building more. So what? It didn't compare to making the game-winning out against the hometown rival Chicago White Sox.

His life used to matter, and now it didn't. Oh, sure, it mattered to his family and his friends, but not to the world in general. He used to thrill people with a good performance behind the plate. But now he didn't know what his role was supposed to be, and that was no time to fall head over heels for a woman. He couldn't trust his own feelings.

By the time they arrived at the barn, Emmett and the hands were busy feeding the horses. Both Caro and Logan offered to help unsaddle and brush Destiny and Cici, but Emmett seemed to think they were both needed up at the house.

"Big doings," Emmett said. "Sarah has a visitor, a guy who plans to buy some horses. He's also a baseball fan, so he's eager to meet you. Sarah asked me to send you both up to the house when you arrived."

Logan groaned inwardly. Just what he didn't need, some rabid fan who would want to talk about the joys of baseball. He could handle the old folks at the assisted living facility, maybe because their glory days were behind them, too. Other than that, though, he had no interest in reliving old plays.

But he knew Sarah would be happy about the prospect of more sales. Alex's PR must be paying off, and Logan would be an ungracious guest if he didn't try to humor this man. So he'd put on his best manners and be pleasant.

"I need to at least wash up a little," Caro said.

Emmett nodded. "Will the sink at the end of the barn do?"

"Sure."

"I'll come with you." Logan walked beside her, down the aisle between stalls where horses were munching away. It was a cozy atmosphere and he wished he could stay here instead of going up to the main house to socialize with whoever this man was.

As Caro washed her hands at the sink, she glanced at Logan. "You don't look especially happy."

"It's okay. You know I don't relish talking baseball, but if Sarah needs me to because this is a good customer, I'll do it."

"You're a good guy, Logan." Caro moved away from the sink to give him room while she dried her hands on a paper towel.

"Not really." He lowered his voice. "A good guy wouldn't be trying to find more ways to get into your bed."

"I didn't say you were a saint." She moved closer to him. "But you're good…and good in bed."

He chuckled. "You're not so bad yourself, Miss Davis."

One of the hands walked by, so they didn't say anything more until they were on their way up to the house. Sure enough, a shiny black king cab sat in the drive behind Caro's old pickup.

"Still planning to talk with Josie?" Logan asked.

"Yes."

"Then I guess you might want to mention that I'm following you home tonight."

She looked over at him. "You are?"

"Of course I am. Once you've said something to Josie, you won't be able to get rid of me. I'll spend the night with you and then we'll drive into Jackson together in the morning. Besides seeing your grandmother, we'll stop at a drugstore so I don't have to manhandle the condom machine at the Spirits and Spurs anymore."

She smiled at him. "I see you have it all worked out."

"I have the next twenty-four hours worked out. Beyond that, I'm still struggling."

"I didn't provide you with a plan B like I promised, did I? I was thinking about that while we rode home. How do you feel about becoming a sportscaster?"

He sighed.

"That sigh says it all. You don't want to."

He paused at the bottom of the steps and turned to her. "It's just that so many ex-players go into broadcasting. I don't know if I have the personality for it, either. Alex does, but he's not an athlete. Some combination of Alex's talent behind a microphone and my sports knowledge would be terrific, but we happen to be two different people."

"I think you'd be good at it. You obviously know the game and the players. And you'd look great on camera."

"Why, thank you, ma'am. You're probably biased, but I'll take that vote of confidence that I'm photogenic."

"It's not bias. I saw your picture dozens of times on the internet. The camera loves you."

"Yes, but would I love it back?" He shook his head. "It's a thought, and I shouldn't dismiss it. I know my agent is exploring that possibility. He wants me to capitalize on whatever fame I've achieved."

"And you should. You've worked hard for it."

He wondered if he'd ever met somebody so unselfish. Some women who had a wealthy man paying attention to them would be trying to convince him to settle down with them and make their lives easier. Logan was virtually certain that his money made no difference whatsoever to Caro. She just sincerely wanted him to be happy.

"I promise to think about the TV angle more seriously," he said. "It makes sense. I just have to get used to the idea."

"You'd be terrific. If you end up doing that, I might have to start watching sports on television."

Now there was a depressing thought—him stuck in a broadcast booth somewhere and Caro in Shoshone watching him on TV. It was a realistic scenario, but that didn't mean he had to like it. "Come on, gorgeous. Let's go inside and make nice with the man who's buying Last Chance ponies. Then we'll reward ourselves with some quality time under your homemade quilt."

"That sounds wonderful, but I just thought of something. If you're going to spend all that time with me, when are you going to work on Josie and Jack's cradle?"

"While you're tending bar, I'll come back here and work. It shouldn't take me that long, anyway. Besides, the longer I spend on the cradle, the longer I can stay at the ranch."

"Nice."

"Yeah, I agree." But he was no fool. He knew the longer he stayed at the ranch the deeper he'd get into this relationship. He should probably set a limit on his time here by booking a flight out. A smart man would do that.

Lately, though, he hadn't been acting very smart.

CARO FELT A LITTLE MUSSED and underdressed to be a dinner guest at the Last Chance, especially with a horse buyer in attendance. But she told herself that nobody would be paying attention to her, anyway. Logan would be the man of the hour.

She knew he would rise to the occasion. She'd seen him in action behind the bar, juggling martini shakers. He might not think he was a showman, but he had the makings of one.

He could be anything he wanted, really. He had the intelligence and coordination to master whatever he set out to do. She just hoped that whatever it was, he loved doing it. He deserved to be happy in his work.

As they walked into the living room of the ranch house, she admired the casual elegance of the place. Large Navajo rugs hung on the walls, and a wooden staircase spiraled up to the second floor. The furniture was large and leather, befitting a ranch. It was grouped in front of an immense rock fireplace, although no fire burned there on this warm August afternoon.

Sarah sat in one of the brown leather armchairs, and a tall, gray-haired man wearing a white cowboy shirt and obviously new jeans sat in a chair across the round coffee table from her. She held a glass of red wine, and he was drinking what looked like Scotch on the rocks.

Both she and the man stood when Caro and Logan walked in.

"There you are!" Sarah put down her glass and came forward. "Caro Davis and Logan Carswell, let me introduce Peter Beckett." She gestured to the man behind her.

He set down his drink and walked toward them. "Miss Davis, Mr. Carswell, it's a pleasure." He shook Caro's hand first, and then Logan's.

Caro appreciated that, considering how the guy's eyes lit up when he saw Logan. Next to him, she could fade into the background easily, so at least Peter Beckett had manners. He was nice looking, too, with kind blue eyes and a wonderful smile.

She'd guess he was probably in his sixties, and obviously very prosperous. His boots appeared to be custom made and his watch looked as if he could use it to contact James Bond if necessary. She hoped he'd bought a lot of horses and given the ranch a hunk of his money in return.

"What can I get each of you to drink?" Sarah hurried over to the liquor cabinet. "I have wine, beer, bourbon, Scotch, brandy…"

"Whatever wine you're having is fine with me," Caro said. She hoped wine wouldn't make her too loopy considering how little sleep and food she'd had today. She thought of the cookies she and Logan had scattered for the birds, and wished she'd eaten more of them.

"I'll take a beer, whatever kind you have," Logan said.

Sarah opened a door in the cabinet to reveal a small refrigerator. "Bud, then."

"That works."

"Go ahead and sit down. Have some chips and salsa."

Caro took her cue and positioned herself on the leather sofa near the chips. So long as she ate those, she shouldn't embarrass herself with one glass of wine.

Logan sat next to her, but not so close that anyone would think they were a couple. He turned toward Sarah's guest, who'd remained standing. "So, Mr. Beckett, do you live nearby?"

"Not too far away. About thirty miles. I have a place outside of Jackson. And call me Peter."

"Peter came to the open house we had in June," Sarah said as she brought over Caro's wine and Logan's beer, along with a couple cocktail napkins. "He didn't buy anything then, but I think he's ready to now."

"Absolutely." The man waited until Sarah was seated before levering his tall frame into the chair opposite her. "But that's not the only reason I'm here."

"Oh?" Logan took a sip of his beer.

Caro felt him tense and knew he was afraid that he was the other draw.

Peter swirled the ice cubes in his glass. "I'm trying to talk Sarah into going along with a new venture of mine."

"And I'm still thinking about it," Sarah said. "Peter's involved with a program to help troubled teens, boys mostly, and now that I have so much empty space in this big house, he's asked if I'd take some in and help provide a work experience for them."

"Of course, I'd pay for the privilege," Peter said. "My investments have worked out well and I can afford to underwrite this program. I thought about creating a ranch from scratch on the land I own, but here's one ready-made."

Logan gazed at Sarah. He'd been here only a few days, but he could see what a big change this would be. "So what do you think, Sarah?"

"Well, Archie and Nelsie named this place the Last Chance because it was their last chance to make a go of things during the Depression. That's been sort of a mantra around here ever since. This would be in keeping with that idea. I have to consult the boys, of course. I'll talk to Jack and Josie tonight when they come to dinner."

"But this place is so beautiful," Caro said. "I'd worry that the kids might—"

"They'd sign a contract before they ever set foot on the property," Peter said. "Coming here would be an incredible privilege, and one step out of line would mean the end of their stay. I've seen it work in other places."

"And I raised three active boys here." Sarah sipped her wine. "There's nothing delicate about this house. And we had a runaway teen girl here for a few years. Roni's married and off on the NASCAR circuit now, but she was trying to hot-wire one of the trucks when we asked her to stay. It's not like we don't have a precedent for this."

"It could be really great." Peter leaned forward, his glass held loosely between his big hands. "On top of that, when I heard you were here for a visit, Logan, I had another brainstorm."

Logan put down his beer. "What's that?"

"I know you're not playing anymore."

"No—no, I'm not."

Caro hoped she was the only one who heard the emotional undertones in that answer, emotion that Logan tried so desperately to conceal. She held her breath, not sure what was coming next.

"I'm sure you have plans, lots of irons in the fire."

"A few."

Caro wanted desperately to touch Logan, to give him support as he braved this through. "I'm certain the TV networks will want him," she said. "He'd make a great sportscaster."

"Yes, he would." Peter nodded. "And if you go that route, Logan, you probably can't do what I have in mind."

"Which is?"

"I'd love to have you help run the program each summer. Kids love their sports idols, and you would be worshipped by the boys. You could do team building with them. If Sarah agreed, we could lay out a ball field in one of the meadows. You'd be a tremendous asset to the program. Of course, I doubt I could pay what the networks could pay."

Logan picked up his beer but didn't drink. "I appreciate the offer, and money isn't really the issue, but—"

"You have other plans," Peter said. "More exciting plans. I understand completely. It was just a thought."

"It's not only that. You'd also want me to be a positive psychological influence on those kids and I'm not sure I would be."

"Nonsense. Of course you would. You've achieved so much, and I know you had to have a great deal of self-discipline to do that. You could pass that on to them."

Logan shook his head. "I don't know that I could. Your plan's a good one, but I'm not a guy who could inspire anyone right now."

Peter gazed at him in silence for several seconds. "It's too soon. I can see that now. Forgive an old guy for rushing his swing. I'm so excited about the project that I barrel ahead even when I should go slow." He shrugged. "Besides, I still have to talk this lovely lady and her three sons into going along with my zany plan."

"It's not zany," Sarah said, her cheeks pink. "I think Archie and Nelsie would have loved the idea."

Caro couldn't say for sure about that, because she hadn't known the two people who'd created the Last Chance Ranch. But Peter Beckett's project gave her a new perspective. Logan had turned down his offer, but mostly because his self-confidence wasn't in the best shape right now.

But he was improving in that area. She'd seen progress in the short time she'd been a part of his life. For the first time since laying eyes on Logan, Caro nursed a tiny flame of hope that he might not be out of reach, after all.

_11_

LOGAN HAD BEEN RELUCTANT to lay himself bare like that, but somebody with Peter Beckett's good heart deserved the truth and not some trumped-up excuse. He'd expected Beckett would want to talk baseball. He'd been unprepared for a job offer.

As the four of them sat in the living room talking about Beckett's plans for the program, Logan was glad he'd refused the offer. Maybe someday he'd feel that he was qualified to guide young kids, but not now, or in the near future. He was having enough trouble figuring out his own life, let alone helping some teenagers figure out theirs.

Jack and Josie arrived and were told about the project. Josie was immediately enthusiastic, while Jack, typically for him, apparently, was more reserved. The group moved from the living room down the hallway, through the large dining room that seated all the hands during lunch, and into the small family dining room.

"The kids could eat in the big room with the hands during lunch," Josie said as they took their seats at the table. "And then they could gather here for dinner."

"What about family dinners on Friday nights?" Jack asked. "When we have the whole family here, we fill the place."

"I know exactly what we'll do." Sarah's eyes were bright

as she looked over at Peter, seated to her left. "Friday nights will be an old-fashioned cowboy cookout down by the bunk-house with the hands. I'm sure Watkins can handle that."

"Indeed, he could." The ranch's cook came through the door with platters of ribs. "And that would get him out of my hair for the time being."

Jack laughed. "Come on, Mary Lou. We all know you don't mind having Watkins around all that much."

Mary Lou rolled her eyes. "Depends. Sometimes he's a royal pain in the patoot."

Logan had talked a couple of times with the stocky wrangler, who sported an impressive handlebar mustache worthy of vintage baseball players. Logan had also heard the rumors that Watkins and Mary Lou were pretty tight. In fact, Watkins had been known to make regular nighttime visits to Mary Lou's apartment, located right off the kitchen.

"In any case," Sarah said, "we could put Watkins in charge of a cookout, which would free up the family dining room on Friday nights. I really like Peter's whole concept. I hope Nick and Gabe do, too."

Jack cleared his throat. "Hang on a minute, Mom. I haven't said I was in favor."

"Aren't you?"

Jack looked over at Peter. "I'd need to see some figures." Then he turned back to Sarah. "And what about Emmett's daughter, Emily? She's renting one of the upstairs bedrooms right now."

"Yes, she is, but unless I'm misreading the signs, she and Clay Whitaker will be married before next summer. She'll have moved out by then."

Jack picked up his fork. "We'd have to change the bedroom furniture, maybe put up some bunks." He glanced at Logan. "Built-ins make the most sense. If this is going to fly, we sure could use your carpentry skills."

"Well, I—"

"I'm afraid Logan's got other plans," Peter said.

Logan wasn't ready to be a project leader, but the bunk beds sounded like a fun thing to do, and he didn't want Peter speaking for him, either. "Depending on when you need them, I might be able to help with the bunks." He looked at Caro. Yes, he might have to return to Chicago soon, but the prospect of a future trip sounded good to him. Her quick smile told him she thought so, too, and his heart warmed.

"Excellent." Sarah beamed at Peter. "See how this is coming together?"

Logan thought something else might be coming together. According to Alex, Sarah had been a widow for almost two years, and Logan thought she was showing more than a friendly interest in Peter.

"So what does Mrs. Beckett think of the idea?" Josie asked.

Logan used his napkin to hide a smile. Count on Josie to cut to the chase.

"I'm sure she'd have loved the idea," Peter said. "She passed away three years ago."

Everybody around the table murmured their regrets, but glances darted with new interest to Sarah and Peter. It would be entertaining to stick around and see how this all turned out. Logan began to see the Last Chance as a continuing story, one that would never quite end, unlike his baseball career. He had to admit he was drawn to that aspect.

But he had more immediate concerns. Through some jockeying, Caro had arranged to sit next to Josie. Now they had their heads together, and Logan knew exactly what, or who, they were talking about. Josie kept looking at him, and he had to pretend not to notice.

Gradually the meal came to an end. Coffee and dessert were served and consumed. Chairs scraped back, and goodbyes started to circulate.

Logan glanced across the table at Caro, and she gave him a carefully disguised thumbs-up. Joy rushed through him and he fought the urge to suggest leaving immediately. Instead he lingered, waiting for the dining room to empty out.

Finally Josie made it around to his side of the table. "I've had an interesting conversation with Caro," she said in a low voice.

"And?"

"Just so you know, if you cause that girl any distress whatsoever, you'll answer to me."

He nodded. "Understood."

"She thinks you hung the moon, but I know better."

"Do you have to be so hard on me, Josie?"

"Not if you'll stick around and build cradles and bunk beds."

"That's not what you'd call a career path."

"No, but it beats wallowing in self-pity."

His gaze snapped to hers. "Is that what you think I'm doing?"

"I hope not, Logan. I sincerely hope not, both for your sake and Caro's." She patted him on the shoulder. "Be good to her. She's a special person."

"I know." His response was automatic, but he was still stuck on her "wallowing in self-pity" remark. That sounded a whole lot worse than trying to get his bearings, or searching for a new direction.

He was still considering that when Caro came to stand beside him.

"I think we're cleared to leave," she said. "Whatever vehicle you're borrowing, you should get it now if you're planning to follow me home."

"Caro, do you think I'm wallowing in self-pity?"

"Who told you that?"

"Josie."

Caro's response was a little slow in coming. "Well, don't forget that she's pregnant and hormonal."

"Right." But Caro hadn't really answered his question. Maybe she and everyone else on the ranch thought he *was* wallowing in self-pity. God, he hoped not. That was the last thing in the world he'd want to do.

The first thing, though, was to obtain a set of keys. He approached Jack. "Is there a truck I can drive for the time being?"

"Yeah. Josie already mentioned that you wanted to follow Caro into town tonight. Take the green Chevy. The keys are on the second hook from the right on the board hanging by the door."

"Thanks, Jack."

"Don't mention it. By the way, I spent a lot of nights in that apartment myself. There are shades tucked up under the valance of the curtains. I'd use them if I were you."

"Duly noted."

"And make sure they're all the way down, because they tend to flip back up a couple of inches and you'd be surprised what people can see."

"Good to know."

"Oh, and one other thing. The kitchen table isn't as sturdy as it looks."

CARO DROVE THROUGH THE night with the windows down and the radio up. Country tunes serenaded her as she kept checking her rearview mirror. She knew Logan was following her, but still she got a thrill every time she looked back and saw the headlights of his borrowed green Chevy truck.

Despite herself, she was entranced by the notion of the Last Chance Ranch. Until now, she hadn't heard how it got its name, and the optimism of that concept fit right in with her philosophy.

She understood why Sarah would be interested in Peter Beckett's idea. It blended perfectly with the ranch's mission. Selfishly, Caro wanted Logan to be interested in it, too.

But he wasn't, and he might never be. Once again she had to remind herself that she was welcoming him into her bed for the short term, and not because she thought he'd change his mind and stay forever. Josie had made it clear that Logan had always been very ambitious, and she predicted he'd eventually take a job in sports broadcasting because that was the kind of high-profile life he was used to.

Caro had listened carefully. Josie had known Logan ever since he was a neighbor kid in Chicago. The only person in Shoshone who would know Logan any better was Alex, and Alex was on his honeymoon and not due back for another week.

Still, Caro sensed there was more to Logan than pure ambition. He'd used ambition to get him to the big leagues, but that hadn't lasted. Maybe now he was ready to hook up with something less glamorous yet more likely to give him satisfaction for the rest of his life.

Caro thought this project of Peter's could be it, but she wasn't going to say so and risk poisoning the well. It was a decision that would have to come from Logan in his own time. It might never come.

Privately, though, Caro had decided to offer her services to the project, assuming that the Chance brothers gave it their stamp of approval. Initially, she could make quilts for all the bunk beds. A colorful quilt on each bed, handmade with love, might be the welcome that some of those kids needed.

But if the program ever expanded to include girls, she could teach them to quilt. She'd be willing to teach the boys, too, but teenaged boys living in cowboy country and searching for their identity might not go for quilting lessons. They might have girlfriends or mothers who would like one, though.

In any case, Caro wanted to be part of the Last Chance legacy. She hadn't appreciated that history before tonight. Up until now, the ranch had simply been the place where Josie lived now that she was married to Jack Chance. Sure, it was a landmark, but one that Caro had taken for granted the whole time she was growing up in Shoshone.

She approached the town limits and slowed down. It wasn't much of a town, really—two intersecting roads with one stop-light. When she reached the light, it turned red, as it usually did whenever a single vehicle arrived at the intersection of the highway and Main Street, no matter which direction they were traveling.

The Spirits and Spurs sat across the intersection. A person turning right on Main would pass all the major businesses, including a bank, a post office, a feed store, a small grocery and an ice cream parlor.

Elmer Crookshanks's gas station was across the intersection on the left. Last year Jack Chance had accused Elmer of rigging the light so that people had to stop and take notice of his gas station. Elmer had denied it, and the light continued to turn red more than seemed necessary, considering the lack of traffic.

It was a funky little town, and Caro loved it. Yes, she hoped to travel and see other places, but her heart would always be here. Now that she knew more about the Last Chance, she was even prouder of her little corner of the world.

Behind her, the Chevy's engine rumbled. She imagined Logan sitting in the driver's seat, waiting impatiently for the light to turn green so they could both cross the intersection. He might not know what he wanted out of life, but he knew what he wanted when it came to her, at least for the immediate future. Being desired with that kind of intensity was a thrill she'd never forget.

The light turned and she drove through the intersection,

with the Chevy right on her tail. She barely had time to park, pick up her hat from the seat and climb out of her truck before Logan was there, dragging her close. He must have left his hat in the truck, because he was no longer wearing it.

"That was the longest damned dinner and the longest damned drive and the longest damned red light." He kissed her quick and hard. "I'm so pumped I could carry you up those stairs, bad knee or not."

Heat sluiced through her veins. "But we have to go into the bar first."

He squeezed his eyes shut. "Right. How could I forget? Got your keys? I'd rather not parade through the bar itself if we can go in through the back."

"Right here." She held them up.

"Then lead me to the condom machine." Wrapping an arm around her waist, he guided her in the direction of the back door.

"If it doesn't work, I'll come in with you and see what I can do."

"That won't look right."

"Judging from the empty parking lot, the bar's not crowded right now, anyway. Nobody would notice." As they reached the back door she quickly unlocked it and stepped into Josie's office, which was also locked this time of night.

"But a guy should be able to obtain his own condoms." Logan walked in behind her. "Hey, it's dark in here." He slipped an arm around her waist and drew her back against him. Beneath his jeans he was ready for action. "Maybe we don't have to go upstairs, after all."

She couldn't resist nestling against him, but her words were as stern as she could manage, considering her level of excitement. "We're not having sex in Josie's office."

He pulled back her hair and kissed the curve of her neck

while he cupped her breast through the cotton of her shirt. "Or on your kitchen table, either."

"What?"

"Jack warned me it's not as sturdy as it looks." He raked his teeth gently over her skin as he fondled her breast. "I gather he and Josie found that out the hard way."

Caro moaned and leaned against him as she imagined making love on whatever available surface presented itself. "This is madness. We have to stop so you can get the condoms."

"I know." He continued to massage her breasts. "But I love touching you. I haven't been able to touch you for hours."

"I love touching you, too." She struggled for breath. "But... I'll be able to do that so much more...efficiently...once we're safely up in my apartment."

"You're so logical." He gave her one last squeeze before releasing her with obvious reluctance. "And so right. Give me a minute before you open that office door. I need to focus on some baseball stats."

She took a deep breath to compose herself. "I should go out and talk to Steve while you buy condoms. He might wonder what's going on if you come through the door of Josie's office all by yourself. Technically, you shouldn't have a key."

"In my current state, with all the blood drained south, I'm not sure I would have thought of that."

"I almost didn't. I was going to wait here in the dark until you came back." She walked over to Josie's desk and turned on the green glass lamp there. "Steve might wonder why we didn't turn on a light, too."

"Good thinking, once again." Logan heaved a sigh. "Okay, I've cataloged a list of every game-winning home run the previous season. I'm calmed down enough to walk out there."

"Want to stop for a drink?"

"*No.*"

"So I'll just say that we wanted to check to make sure he's doing all right. You should walk over to the bar with me, in fact, just to be friendly. For all he knows, you're headed back to the ranch and need to make a quick trip to the bathroom before you make that drive."

"Steve doesn't strike me as the dim-witted type. I doubt he'll think I'm going back to the ranch if I walk in from the office with you." His heated glance touched every part of her. "Especially if you have a couple of snaps undone on your shirt."

"I do?" She looked down and quickly fastened them. "When did you do that?"

"Just now, I guess. It was so automatic I didn't realize what I was doing."

"And I was so aroused I didn't notice that you'd done it." She met his gaze. "I think we'd better get ourselves upstairs, and fast, but we need to look casual doing it."

"Fine, but don't expect me to juggle any martini shakers."

She laughed as she moved toward the door. "I won't. But before you leave town, I want you to teach me how." She was proud of herself for tossing out a carefree line that included a mention of his inevitable leaving. More comments like that would help her stay focused on reality.

"I don't like thinking about that."

Then don't go. But she wouldn't say that, because he'd made his position clear when he'd turned down Peter Beckett's offer.

Her hand on the knob, she turned back to him. "But you should keep it in mind, Logan. You will be leaving." By the time she unlocked the door and walked into the bar, she was much more in control of herself.

If she intended to play this game, she needed to be.

12

LOGAN FOLLOWED CARO out of the office and tried like hell to look as if he had no sexual interest in her whatsoever. He kept his distance, and gave his best impression of a nonchalant cowboy saunter as they approached the bar.

The room was empty except for Steve, who seemed delighted to see them. "Business is slow," he said. "I guess everybody partied hardy last night and now they're staying home."

"That happens," Caro said. "So you're feeling better?"

"Way better." He grinned. "Rough night, but it was over fairly fast, so I think it was food poisoning, after all. Did you do something fun with the time off?"

"Sure did. Logan and I went riding." She kept her attention firmly on Steve.

Logan appreciated that. If she'd looked at him, they both would have been swamped with memories of their afternoon together, and no doubt it would have shown on their faces.

"Nice." Steve glanced at Logan. "Have you been on a horse much?"

"Nope. I came off of this one today, but I'm none the worse for wear."

"Didn't reinjure your knee, I hope."

"Fortunately not. Hey, if you two will excuse me, I need to head back to the men's room."

Steve's eyes didn't flicker. "You bet. I just cleaned it. Nothing else to do."

"Thanks." Logan wove his way through the tables to the tiny hallway that led to both bathrooms. He had cash in his pocket, and with luck, the condom machine would decide to dispense condoms tonight.

But after five minutes of fiddling with it, he was still empty-handed. Because the bar was deserted except for Steve and Caro, he couldn't risk banging on the sides of it the way he had before. He was forced to walk back out and over to the bar.

"Still no customers, huh?" He glanced around. "Seems like a waste to keep the place open. How soon would you normally close?" If he could get rid of Steve, then he could manhandle that condom machine. Or maybe there was a key to it somewhere. He'd take the thing apart, if necessary.

Steve checked the Budweiser clock on the wall. "Another half hour or so. But you're right. It is a waste. Unless you two care to order something? It's on the house."

"No, thanks." Logan controlled his impatience. "I really should be leaving." *And going upstairs with this delicious woman.* "I'm not the person in charge around here, but I can't believe Josie would care if you locked up early."

"No, she probably wouldn't." Caro either sensed there had been a problem with the condom machine or was simply going along with his suggestion. "I can't call to ask, because I'm sure she's asleep by now. Knowing Josie, I think she'd want us to use our own judgment. There are no customers to offset the utility bill, so let's lock up."

"Sounds good to me," Steve said. "If you'll turn around the sign on the door, Caro, I'll close out the register and be on my way."

She started for the front door, but turned back toward Steve. "You know what? I can take care of it. You've been sick, and although you may feel better, I'll bet you could use the extra sleep."

Logan could have kissed her. Well, he'd wanted to do that, anyway, but he really had the urge now that she was on the get-rid-of-Steve bandwagon. "Yeah, we can handle everything," Logan said. "Take off, buddy." *And I mean that sincerely.*

Steve glanced at Logan, and his eyes registered a lightbulb moment. "I do believe I'll take you up on that. I'll just head on out the back door, then." As he passed Logan, he lowered his voice. "Hope you didn't need the condom dispenser, 'cause it's empty."

"Oh."

"Nobody got more in, either. I checked."

"Oh."

"Good luck, buddy."

"Thanks." Well, damn. Not only were there no condoms, but good old Steve knew what was going on. Logan had predicted he'd figure it out, anyway. Josie also knew, and so did Jack, and word would spread from there. Soon the whole town would know that Logan and Caro were lovers.

Until this moment, Logan hadn't fully understood the consequences of that. The town would know, and then he'd leave. Although Caro had said she was going into this with her eyes wide open, was she, really?

He wondered if she'd considered that a certain percentage of those who knew would assume she'd been the plaything of a famous man and then been dumped when he was tired of her. He'd experienced firsthand the sour feeling pity left behind, and he didn't want that for Caro. Without thinking this through, he'd set her up in the victim role. And he didn't know how to fix it.

She came up behind him and wrapped both arms around his middle, mimicking the way he'd held her earlier when they were in Josie's office. "Am I guessing right that the condom machine is a problem?"

"According to Steve, it's empty and nobody ordered more. He checked."

"I see."

Logan took hold of her hands and eased out of her grip so he could turn and face her. "And I owe you an apology."

She laughed. "For failing to acquire condoms? That's not your fault."

"No, not that." He took her by the shoulders and kneaded them gently. "For failing to realize that when I leave, a lot of people in this town will assume you've been dumped, no matter what either of us say."

"I don't—"

"You can claim not to care, but you deal with the population of Shoshone almost every day. Are you prepared for the pitying looks? The veiled allusions to the guy who broke your heart? The cracks about sports stars who go through women the way other people go through a package of Twinkies?"

"Like Twinkies? Really?"

"Well, *I* don't, but plenty of guys do. I mean, yeah, I've had a few one-night stands in my life, but generally I—hell, this isn't about me. It's about you living in a small town where the word will now be out about…about us."

"I knew that when I decided to tell Josie," she said quietly.

"I wish you'd said something. I'm from the big city, where nobody cares unless it's juicy enough to make the tabloids. I didn't stop to think what bringing it out in the open with Josie would do to your…not your reputation, exactly, but you will get those who think you've been done wrong."

Her smile was soft. "Then I'll tell them I kicked you to the curb."

"I hope you do! I hope you tell them that I begged you to let me stay, but I had a ton of bad habits that you couldn't tolerate anymore. Say that." He squeezed her shoulders. "Promise me you'll trash my rep after I'm gone."

"I can't do that. You're coming back to build bunk beds. You don't want people snickering behind your back when you're buying screws and nails and lumber and stuff."

"You're not taking this seriously at all, are you?"

"No."

"You should."

"I should not." She reached up and pinched his cheek. "Because they won't pity me. You're like a rock star, Logan!"

"Oh, for God's sake. I am not."

"You are in this tiny burg. The women will envy me and want to know if you're as good in bed as you look like you would be. I'll just smile and let them eat their hearts out. The men will figure I must be hot stuff if I attracted the attention of a professional ballplayer, even for a few nights. Don't worry about me, okay?"

"I can't help it. This is uncharted territory for me, coming into a small town and getting involved with you. I feel as if I have to protect you."

"Well, you *do,* which brings us back to the condom issue."

"I wasn't talking about that kind of protection."

"I am."

"So are we driving to Jackson to find a twenty-four-hour pharmacy?"

"We could. Or…" She moved closer and rubbed her hand over the fly of his jeans. "We can get creative."

His happy cock leaped to immediate attention. "Like how?"

"The bar is loaded with all sorts of interesting items. You should know. You used to be a bartender."

As the possibilities slowly unfolded in his fevered brain,

his body tightened in anticipation. "Are you suggesting we grab a few supplies and take them upstairs?"

"We'll have to figure out a way to ring them up and pay for them, but, yes, that's exactly what I'm suggesting."

"Whipped cream?"

"For starters. And flavored liqueurs."

His johnson began to ache. "I'm in."

"I thought you might be. Let's go raid the pantry."

Fifteen minutes later they'd locked up the bar and climbed the stairs with their purchases.

"This could be messy," he said.

"I plan on it." She moved around the kitchen and living room, lowering shades.

"I don't want to get anything on that handmade quilt."

She braced one palm on the kitchen counter as she tugged off her boots. "That's why we're going to do it in here, instead." She glanced at him. "Are you planning to get naked or not?"

"I am." He pulled up a kitchen chair and sat down to take off his boots and socks. "But I have dibs on the first round. I have plans for the butterscotch schnapps and the cherries."

"I have plans for the whipped cream."

He paused in the act of pulling off his second boot as his penis responded to that statement by swelling with enthusiasm. "I can only imagine, and once you start licking whipped cream off my cock, it'll be all over. That's why I'm going first."

"But you're so slow." She flicked off her bra and shucked her panties before walking over to him. "I'm finished and you're still mostly dressed."

"So I see." Reaching for her, he pulled her down to his lap. "I'm still a city boy who's not used to boots and jeans."

"I'll help you." She straddled him, nudging her damp curls against the ridge of his fly.

"Much more of that kind of help, and you won't need the whipped cream." He spanned her waist and slid both hands up and around until he was cradling her breasts. "Mmm." He stroked his thumbs over her tight nipples. "I might not need the butterscotch schnapps, either. Lift up a little bit for me."

Putting her feet on the floor, she rose up so that her nipples were even with his lips. "Like this?"

"You read my mind." Slowly he drew in one firm tip and rolled it between his tongue and the roof of his mouth. They had all night this time, and he intended to make the most of it…or as much as he could without condoms.

So he would feast on the wonders of her body, with garnish and without. As he showered attention on her breasts, her breathing grew shallow and she began to quiver. She had such an erotic nature. She might give him credit for being good in bed, but she was the most responsive woman he'd ever been with.

Her fingers dug into his shoulders as he licked and massaged, nibbled and sucked. On impulse he reached between her thighs and rubbed his thumb over her clit. Just like that, she climaxed, arching her back and gasping his name.

Kissing his way upward to her lips, he lowered her to his lap.

If only he could lower her onto his cock, which strained against his jeans.

Logan feathered kisses over her parted lips. "You're easy to please, Miss Caro," he murmured.

"Not…" She gulped for air. "Not always."

"No?" He stroked her sleek backside as she sat on his jeans-clad thighs.

"You…turn me on."

"That's good news." Logically, he should want to believe she was like this with any man, because then it would be easier to let her go. But his possessive male instinct roared with pleasure knowing that her reaction to him was unique.

She took a shaky breath and looked into his eyes. "I want your shirt off."

"Then take it off."

Sliding both hands into the open neck, she yanked, and the snaps popped all the way down. "There." She flattened her palms against his bare chest. "I haven't spent nearly enough time touching you, either."

He hoped he could take it while she did. Her slow massage was sexy as hell, especially when she leaned down and began to play with his nipples. He had to admit they were more sensitive to her touch than to any woman's before her.

He moaned and shifted her weight so that she wasn't bearing down on his increasingly interested pride and joy. She was getting him riled up with nothing more than a chest massage and some attention from her hot little mouth. Incredible though it might seem, she might be able to make him come like that.

But he wouldn't allow it. When she reached for his belt buckle, he stopped her. "Not yet."

"But I want to—"

"I know, and you will." He lifted her off his lap and stood. "But first…" He glanced around the kitchen, planning his next move. The table was out, according to Jack. But the kitchen counter was fair game. He approved of the rounded edge on the laminate. That should suit his purposes nicely.

"Here." He circled her waist with his hands and placed her on the counter, thanking all those sessions in the gym for the upper-body strength that allowed him to do it without dropping her. That would have put a real dent in the mood.

As it was, she seemed sort of impressed that he could swing her around like that. She gazed at him in obvious anticipation. "What now?"

"Butterscotch schnapps time." He pulled the bottle out of the bag, along with a jar of long-stemmed maraschino cherries. "Lean back against the cabinets while I mix up a little something special."

Putting her hands behind her, she relaxed against the oak cabinets while she watched him.

"You said I could get creative, right?"

"Uh-huh." She ran her tongue over her lips.

He fished some cherries out of the jar and laid them in the lid. "Every time I made a buttery nipple for a customer, I wanted to make a real one."

"That's why you wanted—"

"The butterscotch schnapps. Yep." He opened the bottle. "Hold still." Tilting it, he allowed a little to drip on each breast.

She shivered. "Cold."

"That's because you're so hot." Lovingly, he smoothed the schnapps over her nipples. As they tightened into hard little nubs, she closed her eyes and whimpered. "That feels sinfully good."

"You're not garnished yet." Picking up a cherry, he tied the stem around her nipple.

She gasped. "What are you…ohhh, wow…" She closed her eyes again. "Funky. I like it."

"Not done yet." He tied the other one securely. And then he began to lick and nibble, both her and the cherries.

"Ahh, Logan…" She arched toward him, offering her breasts, squirming against the counter as he tugged at the end of the cherry stems. Tunneling her fingers through his hair, she gripped his scalp and began to breathe faster.

At last he closed his lips over both nipple and cherry, pulling them into his mouth and squeezing them against his tongue. By the time he moved to her other breast, she was writhing against the laminate.

"Logan, I want…could you please…"

With one final caress, he moved back and picked up the schnapps bottle. "Yes. Now. Just open up a little…." He nudged her thighs apart and dripped the liqueur onto her brown curls, where it slid down into the pink treasure hiding beneath.

She moaned and opened even more for him, all hesitation gone in the flood of her need. Her trust and surrender were complete, a gift he prayed he was worthy to receive.

Crouching down, he tasted butterscotch and woman, mixed into a heady brew that drove him insane. He would need some relief soon, but first…first he would give her this. He didn't rush, even as the pounding of his blood and the pressure on his cock, and yes, the tension in his knee, begged him to hurry.

Instead he started with gentle movements of his tongue and an easy suction. But gradually he bore down, pushing her harder as her cries grew in intensity. He held her hips to keep her right where he wanted her, right where he could… there, that was the spot.

Her thighs began to tremble as she let out her breath in one long wail and came, bathing his tongue in her release. He held her and kissed her drenched curls as she sank back to the counter.

Taking his head in both hands, she urged him upward. "That was…"

He gasped as pain jabbed his knee.

"Oh, Logan. Your—"

"Not a word." He looked into her eyes. "Not one word."

"All right." She met his gaze. "Thank you."

He smiled. "You're welcome."

"Now it's your turn."

13

CARO CONVINCED LOGAN to move into the bathroom, where they could rinse off in her tub shower. She knew it would be a tight fit for him in there, but she didn't think he'd fit any better on her kitchen counter. She lit a couple candles for atmosphere and brought the can of whipped cream as she led him into their new venue.

But it wasn't until she finally had him stripped down that she noticed the large bruise on his backside. "Yikes, Logan. You hit the ground really hard, didn't you?"

"And I don't want to hear anything about that, either. Next thing I know, you'll decide I'm too feeble for the whipped cream treatment. I'm a professional athlete. I can take it."

She slid her hands up his powerful chest. "You're one tough guy, huh?"

"Yes." His lips curved in a smile. "And don't ever forget it."

"I won't, but I'm putting my fluffy bath mat in the tub before you sit in there." She positioned the mat at the end of the tub. "Climb in, big boy."

"Is it pink?" He peered at it suspiciously in the flickering candlelight. "It looks pink."

"It's salmon. Besides, when I'm through with you, you won't care if it's purple with green and yellow spots."

That made him laugh, and he stepped into the tub. "No doubt."

Once he was in, she surveyed the situation. There wasn't much room left for her. He was a bigger guy than she'd realized. "Can you put one foot out on the floor?"

"Like this?" He accomplished it easily, by bending his knee and angling his leg outside the tub.

"Perfect." Now she had a spot right where she needed to be, facing his impressive package. Once she completed this maneuver, she'd never be able to mix a drink that involved whipped cream without thinking of Logan.

She started to ask him if he was comfortable, but that was a silly question. Of course he wasn't. He had a bruise the size of a saucer on his fanny. His knee probably still hurt from crouching down to give her an orgasm to end all orgasms. He was the walking wounded, but she intended to make him forget that, at least for a little while.

Stepping into the tub with the whipped cream can in one hand, she lowered herself carefully to her knees. "Hold still," she said, copying his words on purpose. As if she'd been able to hold still once he'd started smearing butterscotch schnapps on her nipples.

"I don't think I could move if I wanted to. Your tub has me in a hammerlock."

"Good. Then you can't get away." She put her finger on the nozzle of the can and pointed it at his gloriously erect penis.

"I have no desire to—ah! That's cold!"

"You won't be cold for long." She decorated him with whipped cream from tip to base, and he flinched with each sweep of the spray can.

"Am I supposed to like this?"

"You will in a minute." She set the can outside the tub, leaned forward and began to clean him up. Oh, yes, this was fun. He tried to maintain his cool, but soon he was breathing hard and twitching with every swipe of her tongue.

The combination of salt and sweet was delicious, and she was tempted to spray him again, except she didn't think he'd last through another coating of whipped cream. Whenever she glanced up, his eyes were squeezed shut and his jaw was tightly clenched. He was desperately struggling not to come.

That desperation aroused her, too, and she realized that must have happened to him while he'd treated her to his revised version of a buttery nipple. He had more self-control than any man she'd met, but she was about to destroy what little he had left.

After taking care of the last smears of whipped cream on his quivering penis, she closed her mouth over the tip and slid down, taking him as deep into her throat as she could. His answering groan was her reward. Hollowing her cheeks, she drew back, caressing him with her tongue as she moved upward.

His voice was strained. "Devil woman."

She released him and blew across the velvet tip. "Yeah. Want more?"

"Yes."

With a smile, she enveloped him in her warm mouth once again, and this time she reached down and cupped his tight balls. Some more suction, a gentle massage, and he was hers. With a hoarse cry, he erupted, and she took all that he had to give.

He lay there, his massive chest heaving in the aftermath of his orgasm. With one last swallow, she released him and sat back to survey her handiwork.

He opened heavy-lidded eyes. "That was incredible."

"Glad you liked it."

"Is it okay if I stay like this forever?"

"Sure." It was easy to say—they both knew he wouldn't.

But for now, she'd live for the moment, and this particular moment was pretty doggone wonderful.

LOGAN DIDN'T BELIEVE they'd both fit in the shower at the same time, let alone have room for him to give her another orgasm. But apparently they were both inventive and reasonably agile, because that's how it worked out. Afterward, they dried each other off, gave in to exhaustion and crawled under Caro's quilt to sleep until dawn.

Morning came with the cry of a hawk as it wheeled through the brilliant Wyoming sky. Logan pulled Caro close and couldn't remember the last time he'd felt this good.

She snuggled against him. "What time is it?"

Lifting his head, he was able to make out the numbers on the digital clock on her nightstand. "Eight."

"*Eight?* Seriously?"

"Unless your clock's on the blink, it's eight."

"We have to get a move on." She wiggled out of his arms and climbed out of bed. "Grandma Bonnie expects me there by nine every morning."

Logan thought Caro needed to break Grandma Bonnie of that habit, but it wasn't his place to say. He'd offered to go with her to Jackson, and he couldn't very well start off by criticizing her handling of her grandmother.

He swung his feet out of bed. "We'll pick up breakfast on the way."

"There are usually doughnuts and coffee in the visitor's lounge. She'll want to go there, especially if she thinks people will be excited about seeing you."

He wasn't used to making do with coffee and doughnuts, but he didn't mention that, either. After a lifetime of eating foods that would create the peak performance he required for his job, he was in the habit of eating a decent breakfast even though he was no longer playing ball. But if Caro needed to be there at nine, and that meant coffee and doughnuts were the easy solution, he'd put up with that for one morning.

"You take first shower," he said. "I left an overnight bag in the truck. I'll go get it."

She went into the bathroom and tossed his jeans out before turning on the water. "You'll need these if you're going down to your truck."

Putting on jeans without briefs was a trick, but he managed it with great care. The shower was already running by the time he went outside, barefoot and shirtless, and started slowly down the steps. His knee was stiff, but it usually was in the morning. Considering the workout he'd given it yesterday, it could have been worse.

Maybe sex was good therapy for his knee. He smiled at that as he walked gingerly over to the Chevy, his bare feet coming in contact with a few sharp rocks along the way. In his haste to be with Caro, he'd left the truck unlocked, with the keys dangling from the ignition. Not cool.

His overnight bag was still on the seat, though, along with his hat. He doubted the crime rate was particularly high in Shoshone, Wyoming.

A guy in a battered old sedan that was probably some shade of brown under all the grime pulled over and rolled down his window. "Everything okay?"

Logan gave him a wave. "Fine, thanks."

"Don't often see shirtless, barefoot cowboys out on the street."

"I suppose not." Logan didn't consider the parking lot exactly "the street," but he should have realized that coming out here wearing only his jeans would add to any rumors circulating about his relationship with Caro. He didn't mind being described as a cowboy, though.

"I'm Elmer Crookshanks," the guy said. "Run the gas station across the street. If you need gas, I'm your guy."

"Thanks. I'll remember that."

"You're that baseball fella, aren't you?"

"Yes."

"Staying with Caro, I see."

"Uh, no, not exactly." Now Logan really regretted not bringing his overnight bag up last night.

"If you say so. Well, gotta go open the station. You take care, now."

"You, too." Logan felt like banging his head on the roof of the truck. He might as well have put up a billboard announcing he was sleeping with Caro. Now every person who stopped to buy gas from that scrawny little guy would get the word—"that baseball fella" had been parading around minus his boots and shirt, which had to mean he was fooling around with one of the local girls, namely Caro. Shit.

Logan didn't say anything about Elmer while he and Caro got ready to go to Jackson. He would eventually, because she needed to know in case it came back to bite her later on. Caro insisted on driving, and he was sure relieved that she didn't need any gas from Elmer's station before they left.

She looked extremely pretty this morning, with her glossy hair swept up in the ponytail he'd found so perky when he'd first met her. She wore a moss-green tank top and khaki shorts. He supposed that was because today she wasn't required to be a bartender or a cowgirl. Instead she was a granddaughter.

Country music had been playing on the radio when she'd switched on the engine, but now she turned it off.

"I don't care if you'd like to listen to that," he said.

"I'd rather talk to you. What did Elmer Crookshanks have to say?"

"Weren't you in the shower?"

"I made it a fast one. Then I came out to see if you were

back, and when I looked out the window, there you were, trapped by old Elmer."

"Without my boots and shirt, which I think telegraphed what we've been up to."

She looked at him, wide-eyed. "You think that telegraphed whipped cream and butterscotch schnapps?"

"Maybe not *specifically* what we've been up to, smart-ass. I like to think the whipped cream and butterscotch schnapps will be our little secret for at least the next fifty or sixty years."

"Sorry. I've already contacted the *Enquirer* and they want my story. Gonna pay me big bucks, too."

"Don't bother. Elmer Crookshanks will have the whole thing leaked by sundown, and the *Enquirer* isn't interested unless they get an exclusive."

"There goes my retirement fund."

"Seriously, Caro, I'm sorry I ran down there half-dressed and practically announced to the world that I've been in your bed all night. I should have figured out a different plan."

"As I keep telling you, it will only raise my stature in this community if everyone knows I've had *S-E-X* with the great Logan Carswell. Relax."

"You're not going to tell anyone about the whipped cream and butterscotch schnapps, though, right?"

She grinned. "I don't know. What's it worth to you?"

"Caro!"

"No, I'm not telling that, for heaven's sake. That was private. But as for everyone figuring out that you spent the night in my apartment with me, I don't give a flip. It was worth it."

"You're one special woman, Caro."

She gave him a quick smile. "I'd have to be to snag a hunk of burning love like you for a few nights."

He reached over and gave her knee a squeeze.

"Watch it. We don't have condoms yet."

"I know. And you're driving. The last thing we need is a fender bender because I was distracting you." He settled back in his seat. "So what do you think about this Peter Beckett?"

"His project, or him in general?" She reached for a pair of aviator sunglasses on the dashboard and put them on.

"Both, I guess." Logan knew he should be enjoying the scenery out the window, but he was more interested in the scenery inside the truck. Caro looked hot in that outfit and the sexy shades made her look even hotter.

"His project sounds fabulous. I've heard of programs like that, where teenagers go stay somewhere they have space to move around, and can interact with animals. It's supposedly very good therapy for them."

"I can see how it would be. And there would be plenty of adult supervision, with all the hands around to ride herd on them. Emmett told me that mucking out stalls was great therapy."

"I'll bet it is. I haven't had much opportunity, but I can imagine that you get down to basics when you're shoveling horse poop."

"I should probably try it."

She glanced at him, but her expression was hidden behind her shades. "You probably should."

He couldn't help wondering what else she thought he should do, like maybe accept Beckett's offer. She hadn't said so, but if she was so high on the idea, she must be thinking he was a fool to pass it up.

"Do you think I should consider working with Beckett?"

"Not if you don't want to."

"It's not that I don't want to. It's that I don't think my head's in the right place to be a help to those kids."

She didn't respond.

"Caro?"

"I don't know whether I should say anything or not, Logan.

This is your life, and you have to come to these decisions on your own."

"You're right, and I will, but something's going on in your head. I can tell. I'd like to know your opinion."

"You might not like what I have to say."

"So what? Do you think I can't take it?" When she hesitated, he finally realized what was going on. "You don't think I can take it."

"Alex warned us that you would probably be a little…fragile."

Logan blew out a breath. "Fragile." The word felt bitter on his tongue. He might be struggling, but he was never *fragile*.

"Well, is that so wrong? You just said your head wasn't in a good place to help those kids! Isn't that the same thing?"

"No! It just means I don't feel qualified to give anybody advice on how to live their lives at the moment, because I don't know how I'm going to live mine. Eventually I'll figure it out, but I'm not there yet."

She took a deep breath. "If you would get into something like Beckett's program, I'll bet it would help you as much as it would help the kids."

"That's not what Beckett is looking—"

"You don't really know what he wants from you, because you didn't give him a chance to discuss it."

"He said he wanted someone the kids could look up to, a role model. I don't see how I can be that when I'm essentially out of work."

"Logan, don't you see? Those kids don't need some super-successful dude who's never had a real problem telling them how to live. I'm sure they'd prefer somebody they can relate to. You're coming back from a hard knock. They'll understand that. They might even teach *you* something about how to recover."

"Ah." Logan stared out the windshield, but he still wasn't

seeing the Wyoming countryside. Instead he saw his dad's face as he'd crouched down in front of him during a Little League game when Logan had just struck out, ending any hopes for the team's victory. He'd been eight years old, and close to tears.

His father had taken him firmly by the shoulders. *Never let them see you sweat, son.* His father's words had shaped Logan's entire career, his entire life, come to think of it. He'd had highs and lows during the past twenty-five years, but nobody, by God, had ever seen him sweat.

In effect, Caro was suggesting a complete one-eighty. She was asking him to show the world, or at least these teenagers, that he was vulnerable, that he could be hurt, that he *had* been hurt. He wasn't sure he could do that.

"I was afraid you wouldn't like it," she said.

"It's not that." He glanced over at her. "What you're saying might be great advice for somebody else. I don't know that it would work for me."

She shrugged. "No biggie. It was just an idea."

But he thought it was more than that. It was a way that he could be with her. Although she would never point it out, any idiot could see how taking Beckett's offer would mean Caro could be part of his life. But unfortunately, she had the wrong man for the job.

14

CARO DROPPED THE SUBJECT of Peter Beckett's project after that and spent the rest of the drive pointing out places of interest. At last they pulled into the parking area beside the assisted living facility, only a few minutes later than Caro normally arrived there.

"Looks like a nice place," Logan said.

"It's a beautiful place. As you can see, they nestled it in among some tall pines, without clear-cutting the property. There are shady walking paths for the residents who are ambulatory, and bird feeders by the windows of those who aren't. The décor is cheerful and the food's good. I just wish my grandmother liked it."

"How long has she been here?"

"Six months."

"And she's eighty...what?"

"Eighty-three. She lived in her house in Shoshone for almost sixty of those years. She and my grandfather rented it at first, and then scraped together the money for a down payment. He'd died by the time I moved in as a kid, but it was obvious the house contained many memories of him."

"So it's not hard to understand why she's resistant to this place."

"No." Caro gazed at the one-story building with its hanging

pots of petunias and rockers on the front porch. "I get it, which is why I come to visit her every day. I know physically she's much better off here, but mentally…" Caro sighed.

"What are her health issues?"

"Osteoporosis, for one. She's already had several small fractures and she has to use a walker because her balance is bad. And she's diabetic, and arthritic, and has a heart condition. You know. The usual."

"I don't know. My grandparents on both sides are doing pretty well, judging by that laundry list."

"Then you're lucky." She wasn't surprised that his relatives would be healthy, considering what a fine specimen he was. She'd bet that poor health was considered a weakness in his family. "We'd better go in. I'm sure she's sitting there waiting impatiently for me."

Caro opened her door, but Logan, despite his bum knee, managed to round the hood of the truck in record time. "Nice manners, Mr. Carswell."

"Good thing I have them, too. I learned right away that Sarah Chance is a stickler for manners. I wouldn't have lasted long in her house acting like a clod, no matter how famous I am."

Caro accepted his guiding hand as she climbed down from the truck. Touching him was such a pleasure. She would miss that. "Do you think Sarah has a little bit of a crush on Peter Beckett?"

"Looked like it to me." Logan gave her hand a squeeze before releasing it. Then he closed the driver's side door. "I wonder if anybody else picked up on it."

"Oh, I'm sure they did. Sarah might not be ready to admit it to herself, though. Jonathan Chance cast a long shadow in this area. She might think a romance would be disloyal to his memory."

"That would be too bad, especially if she's attracted to Beckett."

"I guess we'll just have to wait and see." Or Caro would. Logan's interest in the matter would probably disappear once he returned to Chicago.

She walked with him up to the glass double doors that opened onto the visitor's lounge. Sure enough, Grandma Bonnie sat in a wingback chair facing the entrance, her walker at her side. Her short white hair was perfectly styled, her makeup carefully applied, and her slacks and white blouse spotless. She'd always been fastidious.

Several other residents sat in the lounge, too. More casually dressed and quite chatty, they were gathered around a couple of card tables playing games. Grandma Bonnie had never shown any interest in joining them.

But she was certainly interested in Caro's companion. Her eyes widened behind her rimless glasses and she gave Logan the once-over. Then she glanced at Caro, her expression alarmed. She obviously thought this man represented a threat to her routine.

Caro hurried over, Logan by her side. "Grandma, I'd like to introduce Alex Keller's friend, Logan Carswell. He came from Chicago for the wedding." She hadn't rehearsed what to say after that.

"But why did he come to Pine Grove with you?" Bonnie immediately asked.

Logan stepped forward. "Until a few months ago, I was a catcher for the Chicago Cubs," he said in a voice loud enough to carry to the other residents. "Caro thought some of the folks here would like to talk a little baseball."

"You mean *Carolyn*. I hate that nickname she uses now."

"I'd like to talk baseball!" A bald guy with black-framed glasses left the table where he'd been playing cards. "Are you Logan Carswell, the guy who got hurt last season?"

"That's me."

"Logan Carswell!" A portly man hobbled over with the help of his cane. "Right here at Pine Grove! I need to find me something you can autograph! My grandson will be over the moon. Hell, *I'll* be over the moon. I need two things you can autograph. Wait here. I'll be back."

Caro watched in fascination as a crowd gathered around Logan. In addition to asking for autographs, they plied him with coffee and doughnuts.

"Here." A stout little lady shoved a paperback at him. "You can autograph this."

Logan looked perplexed. "But I didn't write it."

"Doesn't matter. You can still autograph it."

"But—it's a romance novel."

"And you look like a romance hero to me, so…" She waved a ballpoint pen in his direction. "Just put your John Henry on the inside. I don't know who you are, but everybody else seems to think you're important, so what the hey. You're cute, which is what I like about you."

Logan sent Caro a helpless look before signing the inside of the paperback.

Caro worked hard not to laugh. At least her grandmother couldn't be worried that she'd brought Logan here because he was her new boyfriend. She'd brought Pine Grove a trophy, obviously. Everyone was thrilled.

Except Grandma Bonnie.

"I still don't understand what he's doing here," she murmured to Caro. "The wedding's over, isn't it?"

"Yes, it's over. Alex and Tyler have left on their honeymoon."

"I'll bet they had the reception at the Spirits and Spurs. If I still lived in Shoshone, I could have gone to it."

Caro didn't want to let her get started down that conversational path. "Let me get some coffee and doughnuts for us, too."

"Okay, I guess."

Caro used her waitressing skills to balance the coffee, napkins and a couple of doughnuts. She set everything on a small table next to her grandmother's chair. "Exciting news, Grandma. A guy named Peter Beckett wants to set up a summer camp for troubled teens at the Last Chance Ranch."

"That's nice." Her grandmother seemed more interested in the doughnut selection.

"If they do it, they'll build bunks in the upstairs bedrooms, so I was thinking I might make some quilts this winter for the beds and donate them to the effort."

Grandma Bonnie frowned. "I don't know how you'll have time, what with your job and coming to see me."

"I may not, but I'd like to do it. I think it would be so homey and comforting for them to walk in and see those handmade quilts on the beds, don't you?"

Her grandmother's face softened. "There's nothing quite like the look of a handmade quilt on a bed."

"No." Caro waited to see if the seed she'd planted would take root. "There isn't."

"I might be able to make a quilt or two this winter."

Caro wanted to shout for joy. "Could you? That would be wonderful, Grandma."

"What you really need to do for those poor children is let them take the quilt home when they leave. Now *that* would be something special. Of course, then you'd need a lot more quilts...."

"I suppose so." Caro wasn't sure where this was going, but she let her grandmother take the lead.

"You know, there's a lot of card playing around here."

For one terrible moment, Caro thought Grandma Bonnie

was slipping into dementia, because the comment had no connection to the topic.

"When what these people could be doing, instead, is cutting out quilt squares. In fact, some of the ladies might know a thing or two about making quilts, and if they don't, I'll teach them." Bonnie glanced up at Caro, and for the first time in six months, there was a gleam in her eyes. "What do you think?"

"I think it's brilliant. I have to make sure this project is on, for sure, and the minute I know, we'll get started."

"You mean it might not happen?" Her grandmother's sparkle disappeared.

"I'm virtually sure it will happen." Caro mentally crossed her fingers behind her back. "In fact, I'm so sure, I'll bring in some supplies tomorrow when I come, and a few extra pairs of scissors, so you can get this show on the road."

"But if it might not be needed, then—"

"It will be. I'm positive. We'll get started tomorrow morning. You can alert whoever is going to help. Even the guys."

"Of course I'll tell those men! Why, your grandpa used to cut out squares for me all the time. He was good at it, too."

Caro glanced over to the crowd that still surrounded Logan, and realized he'd likely be busy for the rest of the time they stayed. She'd have to tear him away from his admirers when it was time to leave.

"He seems like a nice young man," Grandma Bonnie said. "If he didn't live in Chicago, you might want to date him."

Covering her astonishment that her grandmother would suggest she get involved with someone, Caro turned back to her. "Well, he does live in Chicago, so that takes care of that."

"I guess it does. Now, we need to make a list of what you're bringing tomorrow. I'm sure I gave you my box of fabric scraps, but you might have to buy some material. Look for a sale."

"If I'm going fabric shopping in the morning, I might have to show up a little later than usual."

"That's fine." Grandma Bonnie waved a hand as if it made no difference, something she never would have done before. "We'll need extra thread, and needles, and cotton batting." She glanced at Caro. "Why aren't you writing this down?"

"Uh, I have no idea." Maybe because she was too busy gloating over this amazing turnaround. She'd left her purse under the seat of the truck, so she had nothing to write on, either. "Let me find some paper and a pen." Once she obtained those from one of the attendants, she sat on the floor at Grandma Bonnie's feet and made the list.

They had so much fun planning the quilting project that she forgot the time, and when she finally looked at her watch, she jumped up. "Logan and I need to go, Grandma, or I'll be late for my shift."

"All right." Bonnie didn't look nearly as sad to see her leave as she had on past visits. "If I think of anything more for the list, I'll call you."

"You do that." Caro leaned down and kissed her on the cheek. "See you tomorrow." Then she raised her voice. "Logan, I'm afraid we have to leave."

A chorus of disappointed groans rose from Logan's new fans, but he extricated himself with a graciousness that he'd probably perfected over the years. Then he walked over to her grandmother and crouched down beside her chair. "I'm glad I got a chance to meet you," he said. "Sorry we didn't get to talk more."

"That's okay. You can come back tomorrow." She smiled at him.

"You bet. I'd be glad to. You take care, now." He touched her hand and walked quickly over to the entrance, where Caro waited for him. "We're outta here," he said quietly. Then he waved enthusiastically and called out goodbyes to the residents before turning and practically pushing Caro out the door.

"Was it terrible, then?" she asked, as they returned to the truck.

"Not terrible." He opened her door for her and helped her in. "I could use an insulin shot after all those doughnuts, but it was kind of nice to talk with everyone."

"I'm glad. I'll get you some proper food when we're back at the Spirits and Spurs."

"Fine, but I'm not leaving Jackson without a box of condoms, and by my calculations, we just barely have time to buy some and still get you back to the Spirits and Spurs for the start of your shift. I was getting worried that we hadn't left yet."

She laughed. "You really do focus on your stated goal, don't you?"

"That's why they used to pay me the big bucks." He closed her door and jogged around to the passenger side. "I'm not asking you to speed," he said as he got in and fastened his seat belt. "But I wouldn't mind having you push the limit a little so we can be assured of that trip to the pharmacy."

"No worries." She started the truck and backed out of the parking lot. "I've made this run every day for six months. I know exactly where we'll find a drugstore."

"Every day for six months is a lot of visits."

"Yes, but I had a breakthrough today. At least I hope it'll be a breakthrough. I'm in trouble if Beckett doesn't set up his summer camp, but I think he will, whether it's at the Last Chance or not. Anyway, I told my grandmother I wanted to make quilts for the bunk beds, and now she wants to help me with that. She's planning to rope other residents in, too."

"Hey, that's terrific! I saw you two with your heads together. Here I'd come with you intending to offer suggestions for handling her situation, and then I got swept into the other business. Good thing you didn't need me to help."

"Turns out I didn't, but don't minimize your contribution. You made a lot of people happy today. They'll talk about this for months. Oh, and you don't have to come back tomorrow. You've done your stint."

"You know, I probably do need to come back. Right before we had to leave, a couple of the guys told me about some die-hard baseball fans who are bedridden and couldn't make it out to the visitors' lounge. I need to go around the building and see those fellows." He sounded almost eager to do it.

"All right, but you'll have to hit the fabric store with me beforehand. I've promised to come armed with quilting supplies, and tomorrow morning will be my first chance to go shopping for them. You'll be bored stiff," Caro warned.

"I doubt it." He chuckled. "Watching you fondle bolts of fabric may make me stiff, but I won't be bored."

"You really do have a one-track mind." But his teasing was having an effect on her libido, and buying condoms had become a priority with her, too. Putting on the turn signal, she waited for traffic to clear, then swerved into the parking lot of a drugstore. "Here you are, hotshot."

He released his seat belt and opened the door. "I'll be right back. Keep your motor running."

"Mine or the truck's?"

He grinned. "Both."

15

THE NEXT FEW DAYS FELL into a routine that Logan knew couldn't last. But he put off the inevitable by procrastinating making plane reservations. Eventually he'd do that, but he was having too damned much fun to rush into it.

Hot nights in Caro's bed were followed by visits to Pine Grove, where Logan had become the highlight of the day for most of the residents. Some wanted to hear baseball stories, but some were interested in his rehab from the knee injury. Without really meaning to, he'd inspired quite a few to resume their exercise programs.

At a staffer's request, he'd drawn up progress charts, which attracted the interest of even more residents. The facility's director ordered a box of Cubs caps, and those who met their goals got one signed by Logan. Between the exercise programs and Caro's quilting project, Pine Grove buzzed with activity every morning.

During Caro's shifts at the Spirits and Spurs, Logan spent time at the ranch. He worked on the cradle, but he took it slow, because once it was finished, he really should leave for Chicago. So he took breaks from that project to saddle a horse and practice his riding skills.

He also asked one of the hands to show him some roping basics. At this point all he could lasso was a post located behind the barn specifically for roping practice. Before he left he planned to try his luck with a horse or a cow.

He'd just successfully roped the post for the third time one afternoon when Jack came around the corner of the barn and headed toward him. Logan flipped the loop off the post and coiled the rope. "Hey, Jack."

Jack nodded toward the rope. "Not bad for a greenhorn."

"Thanks. The post tried like hell to get away, but I was faster."

He grinned. "Anybody who can rope a runaway post can hang his hat at the Last Chance anytime. Listen, I wanted to ask you something."

"If it's about the cradle, I'm close to finishing."

"It's not about that, but the cradle looks good. Josie's looking forward to having it for the baby."

"So what's up?"

Jack took off his hat and combed his fingers through his hair. "We've decided to give Beckett's idea a try, which means we'll need the bunks." He gazed at Logan. "Were you serious about building them?"

"Yep. Totally serious." Logan couldn't help smiling. The project sounded like fun and would give him an excuse to come back here. More importantly, though, the Pine Grove quilt project now had a guaranteed purpose. Caro would be so excited.

"Good to hear. We need to figure out a time frame. It makes sense to get all the supplies before the first snow, but I suppose you'd have some leeway as to when you did the work because it'll be all inside."

"Let me take a look at my schedule," Logan said automatically, even though he had no schedule.

"Yeah, I know you must have obligations in Chicago. Josie asked me the other day if you had mentioned when you were heading back there."

"Soon." Logan was willing to bet Josie was worried about Caro's reaction to his departure, whenever that might be. "I wanted to make sure I finished the cradle first."

"Right." Jack didn't say what they both knew—that Logan could have finished the cradle days ago.

"Has Caro said anything to you about the quilts?"

"Oh, yeah, she told Josie all about that. Josie drove into town a little while ago to give Caro the good news that the Beckett project is a go. I was designated to get a final word on whether you planned to build the bunks."

"I do." Disappointment took a little of the shine off his good mood. He'd looked forward to telling Caro himself.

"Beckett's willing to pay you, by the way."

Logan frowned. "I don't want money for it."

"I didn't think you would, either. A tax write-off is probably better for someone in your bracket. Beckett's filing the paperwork to make this a nonprofit program, so our tax guy is working out whether we should charge him for the use of the ranch or claim it as a write-off."

"I guess it's good to consider all the angles." Logan's accountant would probably appreciate it if he'd be more conscious of such things. But he'd never been in the habit of thinking that way. He'd offered to build the bunks because he liked the work and wanted to help, not because he could write it off his taxes.

"Yeah, but bottom line, this will be a good thing for everyone, especially the kids."

"Yeah." Logan refused to feel guilty that he hadn't agreed to help next summer. The idea of helping those kids still made him nervous. Besides, he wanted to keep his options open. A network deal might come through, or maybe some offer he hadn't even considered.

Jack settled his hat back on his head. "Whenever you're

ready, we can take some measurements, decide how much lumber to buy."

"Tomorrow afternoon?" This afternoon was fading fast and Logan planned to drive into town soon. Caro would still be working, but sometimes he got behind the bar and helped out. He felt like doing that tonight.

"Sure, tomorrow works. See you then." Jack started to leave, but turned back with a sigh. "Josie made me promise to ask something else."

Logan tensed. "What's that?"

"She heard that you refused Beckett's offer to work with the kids next summer, and I totally understand that. But Josie wants to know if you've changed your mind."

"No, I'm afraid not."

"I told her you wouldn't have. Just because you're helping Caro with the folks at Pine Grove doesn't mean—"

"You know about that?"

"Buddy, whether you want to be or not, you're a celebrity around here. Plus, as you may have noticed, we're a small town. Word gets out—always."

Logan slowly nodded. "I'm beginning to see that. But you'll have to tell Josie I'm still not interested in Beckett's project, other than building the bunks."

"I'll tell her. See you tomorrow."

"Right." Logan stared after Jack as he walked away. Josie might not understand it, but Pine Grove and Beckett's project were entirely different animals.

The Pine Grove situation had dropped into Logan's lap, and nobody had expected anything from him. Whatever good came out of his visits was a bonus. Beckett's project would be loaded with expectations, ones that Logan couldn't or wouldn't meet because he wasn't willing to bare his battered soul to a bunch of teenagers.

But now that Jack had brought up Pine Grove, Logan

worried that Caro might be thinking the same thing as Josie. She could be. The two women were friends and they talked. He didn't doubt they talked about him. He'd told Caro that he got a kick out of working with the folks at Pine Grove.

Damn. He should probably discuss that with her and make sure she wasn't building castles in the air. His chest tightened as he felt a trap closing around him. Caro could be expecting too much of him. He wasn't the guy for Beckett's project, no matter what she might think.

Time to get out of Dodge. He'd make a plane reservation before he went into town to see her. These past few days had been great, but if they were giving Caro false hope that he'd be a camp counselor to those teenagers, he needed to stop immediately.

CARO FELT THE USUAL RUSH of pleasure when Logan walked into the Spirits and Spurs around dinnertime. She wondered if he realized how much he looked like a real cowboy these days. He seemed completely at home in his hat, boots, jeans and Western shirt. Even his walk seemed to have changed.

Or maybe it was wishful thinking on her part. When Josie had come in earlier to deliver her great news about Beckett's project, she'd commented on how settled Logan seemed recently. He was taking his time with the cradle, which Josie thought was a sign he was in no hurry to leave.

Both Caro and Josie were impressed with Logan's work out at Pine Grove. Josie had mentioned it to Beckett and told him not to give up on the possibility of having Logan on board. Caro had been afraid to put that thought into words, but after Josie's comments today, she had allowed a tiny ray of hope to shine.

Her life had definitely taken a positive turn. Grandma Bonnie was a different person now that she had quilts to make and workers to supervise. Her former optimism had resurfaced. That left Caro free to pursue her own future, which might, just might, include the tall man walking toward the bar.

"Hey there, little lady." He slid onto a stool and smiled at her.

"Hey, there, cowboy." She smiled back, happier than she'd been in a long, long time. "Did you hear that the Chances are going ahead with Beckett's project?"

"Jack told me. I'll bet you're doing cartwheels."

"I am. I called Grandma Bonnie and she's planning to step up the effort. She wants a backlog of quilts so that there's no question that each kid can take one home. She hasn't been this excited about anything in months."

"That's terrific."

"Did Jack talk to you about the bunks?"

"He did. We'll work out the details tomorrow."

"Good. I—whoops, excuse me. Customers. Be right back."

"Feed me a hamburger and I'll come back there and help you finish out your shift," he called after her.

"You've got a deal." She put in an order for a hamburger the way Logan liked it, with mushrooms and Monterrey Jack cheese. After delivering drinks to the two men at the other end of the bar, she filled a mug with root beer for Logan and set it in front of him. "Speaking of your carpentry skills, how's the cradle coming along?"

"Almost done."

It wasn't quite the answer she'd expected after Josie's claim that he was dragging his feet so he could hang around. But she told herself he might be finishing the cradle so he could start on the bunk beds. "I'd love to see it. Maybe we could skip Pine Grove in the morning and take a trail ride instead. My grandmother adores you, so she should be okay with that."

"Sounds good."

"Then let's plan on it." She hurried off to fill another drink order, but her thoughts remained fixed on Logan. Maybe it was her imagination that he didn't seem as enthusiastic about the trail ride as she would have thought he'd be.

Then again, he might really like going to Pine Grove, or he could feel that the residents would be disappointed if he didn't show up. They would be, but he couldn't be expected to keep up his daily visits. She decided to discuss it later, when they were alone.

That time alone, whether they were in her apartment or driving to Jackson, had become precious. The sex every night was amazing, but it turned out she liked his company even when they both had all their clothes on. She didn't dare put a label on what she felt for him, but it no longer fell into the category of friendship.

Business was brisk now that the regular customers had recovered from the wedding reception and had returned to their usual habit of stopping by for a beer or two. Once Logan finished his hamburger and joined her behind the bar, the usual requests came in for some martini shaker juggling or the flaming drinks he was now famous for.

Logan certainly spiced up her work life, too. Although she'd asked him to teach her to bartend the way he did, tossing things around and lighting various types of cocktails on fire, she didn't really want to learn. She'd rather have him do guest appearances.

But as much fun as she had working with him, she was glad when closing time arrived. Logan handled the cleanup duties while she closed the register. After several nights of doing it, they'd perfected the system so they were done quickly and could head up to her apartment.

She felt like celebrating tonight. Thanks to Peter Beckett, her grandmother had a new lease on life and Logan would be around at least until he'd finished those bunk beds for the kids. The longer he stayed, the more he seemed to like it here. That had to be a good thing.

Once they were in her apartment, he drew her into his arms, as he always did. But instead of kissing her hello, he gazed into her eyes. "We need to talk."

She laughed to hide her sudden case of jitters. "That sounds ominous."

"Sorry. Didn't mean to be dramatic, but something Jack said today has been on my mind, and I decided you and I need to be sure we're on the same page."

"Okay." That didn't improve her jitters. "How about something to drink while we talk?" She slipped out of his arms, walked over to the kitchen area and pulled some white wine out of the refrigerator. "I'd like to toast the Chances for agreeing to Peter Beckett's proposition."

"We can do that."

She wasn't imagining it. He'd lost that carefree attitude he'd had only hours ago when they'd been together. But she'd offered wine and she'd serve wine.

Taking two goblets from the cupboard, she opened the bottle and poured them each about half full. She had a feeling this wouldn't be as much of a celebration as she'd hoped. "Here you go." She walked over and held out his glass. "To Peter Beckett's project."

He touched his glass to hers. "To Peter Beckett's project. And that's what I want to discuss."

But not in a good way, she guessed. "What about it?"

"From what Jack said, I think Josie still hopes I'll be a part of it, mostly because of my visits to Pine Grove."

Caro shrugged in an effort to be nonchalant, but her heart beat faster. "She might."

"Caro, one doesn't have anything to do with the other. I might be helping the residents to exercise more, but I'm not expected to turn their lives around. What I've done there is a little blip on the facility's radar screen. Beckett wants a tsunami wave of inspiration out of me."

"Hmm." Neither of them had touched their wine, and she decided to drink some of hers. Maybe then she wouldn't lose her temper. The wine slid down her throat, but instead of calming her, it seemed to add fuel to her fire.

He gazed at her. "I take it you don't agree?"

"No, I don't." She took a deep breath. "But we've been over this. You see the job Beckett offered one way, and I see it another."

"Yeah, I know. You imagine that the kids and I would somehow bond and help each other heal, but as the adult in the equation, I don't think that's a fair—"

"Have you any idea how you've blossomed ever since you've been trekking out to Pine Grove with me? You're not dwelling on your own problems, because you're focused on theirs. Being around those old folks takes you right out of yourself."

"Maybe so, but I still think that handling kids is a whole other deal. They're so young and impressionable that what you say to them can leave a lasting imprint. Hell, half the time the old people don't even hear what I say."

She took a shot in the dark. She might be going down for the count, anyway, so why not? "Did someone say something to you when you were young and impressionable?" His expression told her she'd hit the mark. "Who was it?"

"My father. And that's my whole point. Quite likely these kids won't have a father figure in their lives, so I'm liable to be it. I'd be in a position of authority, compounded by the glamour of my baseball career. I hate to think what weight they'd give anything I'd say to them."

"But don't you see? You've been through that experience, so you *won't* repeat it with them. You can tell them how that statement, whatever it was, affected you, and why you won't do those things to them."

He shook his head. "Once again you're asking the impossible. I'm not made that way. I'm not about to reveal the innermost workings of my—"

"Why the hell not? What good is it to go through these things if you're not willing to share your experiences? Listen, if you don't work with those kids, somebody else will, and it might be a guy who doesn't have half the understanding that you've obtained the hard way."

He blew out a breath, walked over to her kitchen counter and set his untouched glass of wine on it. "I can't be the man you want me to be, Caro. It would be great if I could, but I can't."

Adrenaline surged through her system, leaving her shaking. "You mean you won't."

"I guess that's another way of putting it." His expression was bleak. "So I was right. You hoped that the Pine Grove experience would soften me up for Beckett's plan."

"No! You make it sound as if I orchestrated that. Let's not forget that it was your idea to go out to Pine Grove in the first place. I admit I wanted you to go, and discover that there are people a lot worse off than you, but the suggestion to visit came from you, not from me."

He nodded. "You're right, it did. I saw you drowning under the weight of your grandmother's needs, and I thought you deserved better. But as it turns out, Peter Beckett deserves the credit for saving you, not me."

"You deserve credit for caring. Peter Beckett has no idea that his project threw a lifeline to me and my grandmother. You do." She swallowed a lump in her throat. She was going to lose him, and she knew it. But then, he'd never been hers in the first place.

"I do care, and that's why I made a plane reservation today. I'm leaving day after tomorrow."

The statement hit her like a blow to the stomach. "So soon?"

"I would have made it earlier, but that was the soonest they had available."

She looked at him through a haze of misery. "Are you that eager to get away from me, then?"

"No. Leaving you will be one of the hardest things I've ever done. But I don't plan to stay here, Caro. We both knew that. The longer I stick around, the worse it will hurt you. I've been selfish to stay as long as I have."

She shook her head and fought back the tears. "Like I said, all you've done is beef up my reputation as a hot chick. A girl can't complain about that."

His smile was so incredibly sad. "You are a hot chick. If anyone doubts it, have them call me."

Desperate, she grasped at straws. "What about the bunk beds? What about building them?"

He hesitated, as if he hadn't thought of that. "I'll...I'll donate some money to hire a carpenter. I'm sure there are a bunch of them in the Jackson Hole area. It doesn't have to be me wielding the hammer."

"Guess not." Oh, but she'd counted on that more than he would ever know.

"All things considered, I think I should drive back to the ranch tonight."

"I don't." She was pathetic, but she'd take whatever she could get.

"I do." He walked toward her, kissed her on the cheek and headed for the door.

"A kiss on the *cheek*? Is that the way a major league ball-player ends things? That's the lamest breakup gesture I've ever seen, Carswell!" Yes, she was going a little crazy, and saying things she probably shouldn't, but then again, the love of her life had never walked out on her before.

He turned around and came back. "I'm going to miss you like hell, Caro Davis." Then he grabbed her and delivered a kiss that would have rocked her world if she hadn't been sobbing all through it.

Then he was gone, and she couldn't decide if she loved him so much she'd do anything to get him back, or hated him so much that she'd kill him if she had the chance. Either option would be a disaster, so she hoped he'd be in Chicago before she made up her mind.

16

LOGAN FELT LIKE SHIT. He was supposed to be a superior strategist on the field, but apparently off the field he was a total schmuck. He'd managed to take the most positive, optimistic woman he'd ever met and turn her into a sobbing wreck.

The memory of his parting with Caro haunted him as he finished up the cradle and packed to leave. He hadn't intended for their discussion to end with him dramatically stalking out the door, but once he'd realized how much he was hurting her, he hadn't seen an alternative. And as much as he wanted to talk to her again, that would only extend the misery, so he stayed away.

He also managed to avoid Josie and Jack, leaving the finished cradle on the workbench with a note. He had to borrow a suitcase from Sarah because he'd picked up so many pairs of jeans and Western shirts. He might never wear them again, but he took them, anyway.

He even went so far as to dress like a cowboy for the trip back to Chicago. Sarah drove him to the airport in Jackson, and it was a mostly silent trip. He wouldn't be coming back, so there wasn't much to say to each other. No doubt he'd let her down, but classy lady that she was, she took him to the airport, anyway.

In his jeans, white Western shirt, boots and hat, he wasn't

recognized as former Cubs catcher Logan Carswell as he stepped off the plane. He hadn't bothered to notify his family he was coming home, because he wasn't ready to discuss his recent trip with anybody. He took a cab back to his condo.

When he walked in, he hoped for a feeling of sanctuary and peace. Instead the condo just felt huge and sterile. He'd paid a professional to decorate the place, and she'd created a bachelor pad in black, white and gray, with a few touches of red. The furniture was modern, and the general effect, now that he looked at it with new eyes, was hideous.

He longed for gingham curtains and handmade quilts. He missed the noisy bar that smelled of smoke, beer and onions. Most of all, he missed Caro—her smile, her laughter, her ponytail that bounced when she walked.

But she was expensive. In order to have her, he'd have to sacrifice the image that he'd maintained of himself for twenty-five years. She didn't understand what she'd asked of him.

Soon after he carried his suitcase into his bedroom, which was no cozier than the rest of his condo, his home phone rang. His first thought was that it might be Caro, but then he remembered he'd never given her this number. When he picked up the receiver, his agent's name came up on the screen. He hesitated, and finally decided to answer.

"Where the hell have you been?" Derek sounded impatient, but that was par for the course with him. "I've been calling your cell all day, but all I got was your voice mail."

"I flew home today. Guess I forgot to turn my phone back on." He usually never forgot things like that, but he'd been a little distracted lately.

"Well, thank God you're back in town, because I have a fabulous deal for you. ESPN has offered a contract, and it's a good one. I think we can get them up a little more, but my advice is to take it once they bump the salary. They have big plans, and they're willing to put most of them in writing."

Logan realized he should be overjoyed with this news. Two weeks ago his career had been on the skids, but Derek had just found a way to put it back on track. Sometimes players became as well-known in the broadcast booth as on the field. This was a terrific break.

"I don't hear party horns and champagne corks in the background, Logan, old boy. Are you jet-lagged or what? This is *fabulous.* Most out-of-work players would give their right nut to have a deal like this. Do you read me?"

"Derek, it sounds great."

"Wow, try to contain your excitement, will you?"

"Sorry. I've spent the past week and a half in the boondocks." He felt disloyal saying that, but it was something Derek would understand. "I need some time to kick the shit off my boots. Then I'll be ready for—"

"You bought *boots?*"

"And a hat. It was a Western-themed wedding, so everyone was expected to dress the part."

"You can ditch all that now. You're going to be wearing ESPN polos and suits from this point on."

Logan had no intention of getting rid of the clothes he'd bought in Wyoming.

"So let me see if they'll go up some on the money, and then I'll get back to you."

"Sure, I guess." He heaved a sigh. "You know I don't need more money."

"*You* might not, but I do! My kid's decided to go to Harvard Law. That's gonna set me back. So let me wheel and deal. If they come up, are you in?"

He should be. Logic told him that he needed to take this deal while his name was still recognized. Another year or two, and they might forget who he was. It happened all the time.

"Let's see if they come up," Logan said. "Then we'll talk."

He was making no sense and he knew it. First he'd told Derek he didn't need the money, and now he wouldn't commit to the deal until he knew the bottom line.

Derek muttered something that sounded a lot like "temperamental sports stars," but his next words were cheerful and upbeat. "I'll get them up, Logan. Don't worry. I'll call you the minute I have a new offer."

"Thanks, Derek. You're working hard for me, and I appreciate that, man."

"I'm working hard for *us,* Logan. We're in this together, buddy."

No, they weren't, Logan thought as he disconnected the call. Oh, sure, there was a mutual financial benefit, but Logan had a different view of partnership after spending time with Caro. He clicked with her on so many levels.

They'd started off well, working together behind the bar without a hassle. Then…the sex. God, the sex. He'd never established such an instant rapport with any woman. Caro was the most perfect sexual partner he'd ever had.

But they complemented one another in other ways, too. He smiled as he remembered falling off during their trail ride. She'd come to his rescue by fetching his homeward-bound horse.

At Pine Grove, they'd worked in tandem, and because of their visits, the residents now had more reason to get up in the morning. They were making quilts and exercising with greater enthusiasm. Good things happened when Logan was with Caro.

Good things happened when he was with Caro. He stood in his silent apartment as that sentence bounced around his brain for several long seconds. *Good things happened when he was with Caro.*

How the hell had he missed that key point? She hadn't

actually said it, but he knew that if he accepted Beckett's proposition, she would be with him every step of the way.

Of course she hadn't said it. That wouldn't be her style. But if he asked her if she'd help him with the kids, she'd say yes. He knew that as surely as he knew that she loved him.

Yes, damn it, she *loved* him. He hadn't wanted to admit that she did, but he'd known it. And he loved her. Dear God, he was the biggest idiot of the century, because with Caro by his side, he could do anything. Her love would inspire him to be the man she believed he could be.

Without her, he would remain the out-of-work baseball player who never let anyone see him sweat. He might make it as a sportscaster or he might not. He might figure out how to be happy, but he wouldn't lay bets on it. With Caro around, it was a sure thing.

He glanced at his suitcase. Good thing he hadn't unpacked. He had another plane to catch.

THE PAST THREE NIGHTS the bar had been busy, but not overly so. Caro could have handled it alone, but Josie seemed determined to keep her company. Caro figured it was partly for moral support and partly to make sure Caro didn't accidentally poison the customers with some weird concoction.

Judging from everyone's concerned expressions when they looked at her, they expected her to crack under the strain. She'd be damned if she would. Logan had been right, though, and she'd been wrong. Instead of envying her for the fling she'd had, they pitied her for getting dumped at the end.

She'd thought about taking his suggestion and telling people she threw him out because of his bad hygiene and boring conversation. But Alex and Tyler were home from their honeymoon, and Caro didn't want to trash Alex's best friend with lies. Her real gripe about Logan—that he didn't love her enough—wasn't for public consumption.

He did love her, though. That last kiss had told her so. But not so much that he'd be willing to stay. That being the case, she was glad he was gone. She loved him enough that she'd follow him to the ends of the earth, even if it meant leaving Shoshone and Grandma Bonnie.

But he seemed to have a mild case of love, and that would never be enough for Caro. She required a full-blown, over-the-top, chronic case from a man.

"Caro, I think the mug's full."

She glanced down at the draft beer spilling over the top of the mug she'd been filling for a customer. Fortunately, it was running into the drainage area under the spigots, so it wasn't making a mess, but she was wasting beer.

She tilted the mug and dumped out a little more so she'd be able to wipe down the sides and hand it to the customer without slopping beer everywhere. "Sorry, Josie. You'd probably rather have me take the rest of the night off, but please don't. I'd rather be working than not."

"You're fine." Josie gave her a reassuring smile. "I've been there, kiddo, and staying busy is the best therapy there is. We can afford some spilled beer."

"Thanks." Caro swallowed a lump in her throat. Josie was the best. After delivering a few choice words concerning Mr. Logan Carswell, aka the Loser of the Century, she'd never mentioned him again. For that Caro was supremely grateful.

No point in talking it to death. Logan had made his choice, and that was the end of that. Alex hadn't brought up the subject, either, which Caro considered very wise. In Shoshone, Logan's popularity index had plummeted in the past three days.

Not so at Pine Grove, however, because none of those folks knew that Logan and Caro had been an item. They'd asked eagerly about him and had wanted to know when he'd be back.

She'd given them a vague answer because she couldn't bear to see their faces crumple with disappointment.

"Damn," Josie said under her breath. "I don't believe it."

"What?" Caro glanced up, and the glass she'd been holding slipped from her fingers and landed with a loud crack on the stainless steel counter.

Logan walked toward her, his expression tense.

Although Caro was speechless, Josie was not. "You have some nerve coming back, mister," she said. "There is not one thing you can say to excuse the way you treated my friend."

"I agree." Logan's voice was gruff with emotion. "I've behaved like an ass."

Josie nodded. "Well put. And unless you intend to grovel at her feet and beg her forgiveness, you can go right back out that door, because you're not welcome here."

"Josie!" Caro had never heard her talk that way to any customer, ever.

"Well, he's not. Logan and I go back a long way, but he's currently on my shit list. If I had a bouncer, I'd have him thrown out. Come to think of it, I could probably get a couple of cowboys to do it for me, gratis."

"Which is no more than I deserve," Logan said. "But I'm asking you to give me one minute to say something to Caro."

"Only if you say it while I'm standing right here. I no longer trust you not to make her cry."

By now Alex and Tyler had joined the curious crowd in the bar. Caro figured out that the newlyweds had probably driven to Jackson and picked Logan up at the airport. He couldn't have spent much time in Chicago if he was back this soon.

Her face felt hot with embarrassment. "Josie, maybe it would be better if Logan and I went—"

"Nope. I'm not letting him out of my sight." Josie looked at her watch. "Start talking, Logan. Make it fast and make it good. I'm timing you."

He swallowed and nodded in agreement before turning to Caro. "What my dad said that made such an impression on me was 'never let them see you sweat.' Well, I'm sweating now, and I don't care if you know it. I don't care if every damned person in the bar knows it."

Her heart squeezed. This had to be excruciating for him. But…sometimes excruciating was a good thing.

He cleared his throat. "I threw away a chance at happiness by leaving Shoshone and leaving you. I know forgiving me for treating you so horribly won't be easy, but I'm begging you to forgive me and let me come back."

Josie folded her arms. "That's a start. What else have you got?"

"A plan. I'm hoping Beckett can still use my services, because I can't think of a better job than working with kids at the Last Chance every summer. As for the winter, there's plenty to do at Pine Grove, and maybe Josie would consider letting me get behind the bar once in a while." He glanced at her. "Or not."

"I'll take it under advisement," Josie said. "Go on. There has to be more."

Logan ran a shaking hand over his face. "There is. Caro, I'd be the luckiest man on the planet if you'd consent to spend the rest of your life with me. With you by my side I can face anything. Including sweat."

Heart thudding, Caro opened her mouth to reply.

Josie got there first. "Are you talking about shacking up or marriage? Let's not have any of this vague language going on. Be precise, please."

Logan looked into Caro's eyes. Then he dropped to one knee. His bad knee. "Marriage," he said. "If you'll have me."

"Your knee! You shouldn't be—"

"You're probably right." He grimaced and staggered back to his feet. "But it seemed like the thing to do."

Josie nodded. "Nice gesture. Now what about kids?"

Caro stared at her. "You can't expect him to answer that in a crowd of people."

"Sure I can. He created this mess, so now he can clean it up. It's an important question. You're looking all dewy-eyed and gaga, so I'm afraid you'll say yes without finding out the important stuff."

"I'd love to have kids with you, Caro," Logan said. "If you want to."

She forgot all about the people standing around as she met his gaze. Her heart swelled with love for this brave man. "I do."

"That's great!" He beamed at her, and then his smile faded as he looked earnestly into her eyes. "I love you so much. Let me make you happy."

She didn't realize tears were running down her face until Josie glanced at her and threw up her hands. "See that? You made her cry, after all!"

Swiping at her cheeks, Caro forced words past her tight throat. "But these are good tears. I love you, too, Logan. And I can't think of a better life than being by your side, wherever you choose to be."

Joy glowed in the depths of his brown eyes. "I wouldn't ever ask you to leave Shoshone."

"You could, though." She sniffed. "You really could, Logan. It's not fair of me to expect you to stick around here, when you could—"

"I've already made that decision. ESPN wanted to hire me. I turned them down."

"You did?" Caro was beginning to believe in miracles.

"Yeah, I'm ready to leave those days in the past, where they belong. You're my future."

A sigh went up from the crowd. "That's beautiful," someone said.

Logan glanced over at Josie. "Is my time up yet?"

Josie was smiling. "It was up quite a while ago, but you were on a roll, so I gave you some overtime."

Caro looked at her. "Is there any chance that I could take my break, now?"

Josie laughed and hugged her. "Take the night off, kiddo. You've earned it. But if this big lug gives you any trouble, call me. I'll clean his clock, or better yet, get Jack to do it." She lifted the hinged portion of the bar and Caro ducked out.

As she walked toward Logan, she was aware that everyone continued to stand around watching the show. Logan would probably want to wait until they were alone before they sealed this moment with a kiss.

She took a deep breath as she reached him. "So, maybe we should—"

"I love you." Then he pulled her into his arms and kissed her thoroughly amid whoops and hollers from the crowd.

At last he released her and lifted his head. "Free drinks for everyone!" he called out. "I'm buying!"

The crowd surged around them, mobbing the bar.

Logan put his lips next to her ear. "Now's our chance to escape."

She struggled for breath. "But aren't you supposed to be buying?"

"I feel certain Josie will put it on my tab."

"So you want to go upstairs?"

"Uh-huh." He led her toward the door. "I've told you how much I love you, and now I want to show you."

She slipped out the door with him and nobody seemed to notice. Later, as they lay naked and sated from their lovemaking, she could still hear the party in full swing down below. "They're going to cost you a fortune."

"Nope. My fortune is right here." Moving over her again, he proceeded to show her how rich they were going to be for the rest of their lives.

Epilogue

JACK CHANCE COULDN'T imagine being happier. Until recently, his wife, Josie, had been a little bit on edge about Caro Davis, but that problem had been resolved last night when Logan had shown up and proposed.

Jack was glad of it. Josie had been threatening to take a hatchet to the cradle Logan had made, and Jack hated to see good carpentry ruined. He also hated to see his wife in a bad mood, and she'd been extremely cheerful when she'd arrived home after a long night at the bar.

As Jack sat in his dad's office the next morning, studying Beckett's plan in preparation for a discussion with the accountant, he smiled to himself. A cheerful Josie was a lusty Josie. They'd set the sheets on fire last night, and this morning Jack was thinking seriously of sending his wife flowers.

He'd have to order them from Jackson, but a motivated and well-paid florist should be able to deliver by dinnertime. That might earn Jack another roll in the hay tonight. He wasn't above a little bribery.

He was in the middle of checking the phone directory for a florist when Sarah walked into the office. "Someone's here to see you."

"Who?" He stood automatically. Sarah Chance had drilled manners into all three of her sons.

"His name's Wyatt Locke. Does that mean anything to you?"

Jack searched his memory. "No, but I'm not good with names. Did he say what it's about?"

"Just that it was private business. In fact, he's acting sort of...mysterious. I was sitting out on the porch with my coffee when he drove up in an SUV. He's not from around here, though. He asked for your dad, and when I said he'd passed away, this fellow seemed surprised. Then he asked for you."

"So where is he now?"

"I left him in the living room. Maybe I shouldn't have."

Jack rounded the desk and walked toward her. "I'm sure it's fine, Mom." He still got a kick out of the way her eyes sparkled when he called her that. A year ago he would have addressed her as Sarah, because of some stupid-ass idea that because he was her stepson, he didn't have the right to claim her as his mother.

"It probably is fine. I'll just go back to the porch and finish my coffee. If you need me, you know where I'll be."

"Thanks." He put his hands on her shoulders and leaned down to give her a kiss on the cheek. "By the way, I've been meaning to tell you that I approve of Peter Beckett."

She blinked. "You mean his project?"

"No, I don't mean his project. I've seen the way you look at him, and I just want you to know that I—"

"There's nothing to approve!" She flushed. "I don't know what you imagine you're seeing, but I'm simply being polite to the man. I was happily married to your father for almost thirty years, and I don't have any intention of—of..." Her face grew redder with each passing second.

Jack chuckled. "Then you might want to be a little less *polite,* because I think Peter has intentions."

"He most certainly does not. He's just being nice."

"Right." Still smiling, Jack gave her shoulders a squeeze.

"I guess I might as well see what this Wyatt Locke wants from me. Probably a donation to some cause or other."

"Could be. Just tell him we're putting all our financial support behind this teen program." Sarah headed back to her rocker on the front porch.

Making a mental note to order those flowers for Josie the minute this conversation was over, Jack walked into the living room. The visitor looked to be about the age of Jack's younger brothers, which put him under thirty. He was engrossed in examining the family photos arranged across the mantel, and didn't seem to be aware Jack had walked in.

Jack took a moment to try and place him, but nothing about the guy registered. He was at least Jack's height, and his sandy hair was cut short. Judging from his faded blue T-shirt, khaki shorts with extra pockets, and boots with some serious tread, he was a hiker.

"What can I do for you, Mr. Locke?"

The guy turned and his expression was difficult to read. He studied Jack for several seconds. "So you're Jack Chance."

"I take it we haven't met before?"

"Nope. I didn't even know you existed until a month ago."

Now there was a strange statement. Jack frowned. "Look, I don't mean to be rude, but I have a full schedule this morning, so could we please cut to the chase?"

Wyatt blew out a breath. "Sure. You might want to sit down while we have this conversation, however."

"I doubt there's any need for that." But uneasiness slithered up his spine.

"Up to you." Wyatt glanced at the ceiling. "Rafe is going to kill me for coming here, but I just thought…"

Impatience erased Jack's good manners. "Who the hell is Rafe? Could you just get to the point?"

Wyatt's eyes were a clear gray, almost silver, and he focused them intently on Jack. "Okay. Rafe is my twin brother.

We're from San Francisco, where our mother moved after she left Shoshone. She married Harlan Locke, who's our father."

Jack grabbed at the most salient piece of information in that barrage of words. "Your mother used to live here?"

"She used to live right here, as a matter of fact, in this house. Her name is Diana, and you look a hell of a lot like her. It startled me at first."

All the air left Jack's lungs. He stared at Wyatt. His mother had given birth again, and this time, apparently, she'd stuck around to raise her kids. All this time Jack had told himself that she'd left because she wasn't the motherly type. Apparently she was when she chose to be.

He'd thought he was over the pain of her abandonment. Between Sarah and Josie, he'd thought he'd healed. But Wyatt had just ripped that wound wide open. He swallowed. "Why are you here?"

"Mom and Dad got a divorce this year. I think he sensed that she was keeping some big secret from him, and he finally left in frustration. She got counseling and decided to tell us what she'd been hiding all these years. Turns out it was you."

Jack felt shaky, and wished he'd taken Wyatt's suggestion of sitting down. But he'd be damned if he'd do it now and show any weakness.

He cleared his throat. "So I'll ask again. Why are you here? If you expect me to roll out the red carpet, or give you a job, then I'm afraid you—"

"I don't want a damned thing. I guess Rafe was right, and this was a mistake. But I thought I should at least meet my half brother. Sorry to have taken up your time." He started for the door.

"Wait."

Wyatt glanced back, his stance wary.

"I need some time to get used to this."

Wyatt hesitated. "I suppose that's fair. Look, I don't want

you to think I came all this way just to lay this on you. I'm a wilderness guide. I took a bunch of folks on a trek through Yellowstone this past week."

Jack nodded. "I figured you for a hiker."

"And I figured you for a cowboy."

The mood lightened a little. Not much, but enough for Jack to consider this might not be totally bad news if Wyatt had a sense of humor. Jack admitted to being curious about these two guys. And Diana. He wouldn't call her his mother, but he wondered…lots of things.

He gazed at Wyatt. "So do you get down this way much?"

"It's my last trip to Wyoming this year, but I'll be back in June."

Jack let out his breath. That would give him plenty of time to get his head around this. "Maybe you could stop by when you come back."

"I'll think about it." Wyatt fixed that silver gaze on Jack. "You really do look like her. So does Rafe."

"So you're not identical twins?"

"Fraternal. He's four minutes older. People might not see much resemblance between you and me, but they'd know immediately you and Rafe were brothers. Doesn't matter, though. You'll probably never meet him. Well, so long, bro." Then he was gone.

Jack scrubbed his hands over his face. Hell of a way to start the day. At least he wouldn't have to think about the situation again until next June. Maybe Wyatt was so turned off that he wouldn't come back.

Jack wasn't sure whether he wanted him to or not.

* * * * *

The touch was sensual, the air around them turned electric…

"If it's okay, I'd like to move your panties so more skin shows…here." Jack touched the side of Melissa's hip. It was all she could do to stay in the pose. She wanted to arch up into his hand. She wanted him to flip her over and take her right there under the warm lights.

What on earth was happening? She was turning into a primal beast. *He* was turning her into one.

"Sure." She tried hard to sound as if men asked her to move her underwear out of their way so often she found it incredibly tedious. "No problem."

She had to close her eyes again, force herself calm. She wanted him to kiss her. Her mouth, her back, her thighs, everywhere.

Something was definitely working. Or getting worked up.

Click…click…click.

Melissa couldn't help it, she looked up at him, and caught his expression. Jack's eyes were dark and intense, his jaw set.

Kiss me, Jack. Touch me again. Make love to me.

Dear Reader,

As someone who hates pretty much every picture
I've ever taken or seen of myself, I've always thought
of photography as a mysterious and sexy art form.
So I loved the chance to explore Jack, the next hero in
my FRIENDS WITH BENEFITS miniseries, a man
who expresses himself better with images than words
—once he has the right model to inspire him.

That model is Melissa, who thinks she's got herself and
the world all figured out until she discovers the way
Jack sees her, and learns surprising truths about the
passionate woman she's always wanted to be.

I hope you enjoy reading about Seattle and the residents
of the Come to Your Senses building! Look for Demi's
story, *Feels So Right,* available in December 2012.

Cheers,

Isabel Sharpe

LIGHT ME UP

BY
ISABEL SHARPE

First published in Great Britain 2012
by Mills & Boon, an imprint of Harlequin (UK) Limited,
Eton House, 18-24 Paradise Road, Richmond, Surrey TW9 1SR

© Muna Shehadi Sill 2012

ISBN: 978 0 263 89388 5
ebook ISBN: 978 1 408 96937 3

14-1012

Harlequin (UK) policy is to use papers that are natural, renewable and recyclable products and made from wood grown in sustainable forests. The logging and manufacturing processes conform to the legal environmental regulations of the country of origin.

Printed and bound in Spain
by Blackprint CPI, Barcelona

Isabel Sharpe was not born pen in hand like so many of her fellow writers. After she quit work to stay home with her firstborn son and nearly went out of her mind, she started writing. After more than twenty novels for Mills & Boon—along with another son—Isabel is more than happy with her choice these days. She loves hearing from readers. Write to her at www.isabelsharpe.com.

This book is dedicated to two photographers:
Henk Joubert, friend and artist, whose brilliance
always inspires me, and Knox Gardner, whose
online picture of Seward Park and willingness
to help a total stranger did likewise.

1

"WHERE'RE YOU GO-ING, JA-ACK?"

The women's voices, raised in singsong teasing, carried easily from the propped-open bakery door, stopping Jack in midstride on his nervous trek down the hallway of the Come to Your Senses building. He and four friends from the University of Washington, Seattle, had bought the place a couple of years back and turned it into living quarters and places of business.

Two of those friends, Angela Loukas, owner of the bakery A Taste for All Pleasures, and Bonnie Fortuna, florist proprietor of Bonnie Blooms, were grinning at him, hands on their hips in identical poses. He was busted.

"Me?" He pointed to his chest, looking behind him as if he expected to see someone else, though at slightly past seven in the morning, the only business open in the building was the bakery. "You talkin' to *me*?"

"Off to take *pictures* of someone, are we?" Bonnie pointed to his camera and raised her eyebrows, a light-brown contrast to her dyed-red hair.

"Gee." Angela faked a look of confusion, plunking a finger on her cheek. "I wonder who?"

Jack rolled his eyes. He'd told Angela about the woman

way back in April when he'd first started taking photos of her practicing yoga in nearby Cal Anderson Park: an extraordinary woman, an immediate siren call to his photographer's instinct. He'd gotten to know her schedule and had taken picture after picture without her knowledge, obsessed on a level he didn't understand until the idea for a gallery show he'd been mulling over transformed from his original vision to one featuring this woman. Finally understanding what he wanted, he'd felt ready to approach her with an offer to model, and in a colossal demonstration of Murphy's Law, she didn't show up that day. Or the next or the next. May, June and July had been rainy and busy with graduations and weddings that kept the checks coming in. He might have lost track of the woman but he sure hadn't forgotten her, and hadn't stopped checking out the morning yoga class whenever he could spare the time. The vision for this series wouldn't leave him alone. He had to find her.

Then yesterday morning, the miracle.

"Tell me if you see this woman today you'll talk to her."

"For a raspberry muffin I'll tell you anything." He grinned at Angela, who made a sound of disgust and went behind her counter. Angela was a beautiful woman with thick chestnut hair, wide-set brown eyes and the warmest smile he'd ever seen. He adored her, thoroughly platonically.

Bonnie's arms were folded disapprovingly across her bright red tank top worn over a white-and-red polka-dot skirt. He and Bonnie had had a fling not long after graduation, a brief experiment neither regretted, which had then settled into solid friendship. Which meant Jack adored her, too, only slightly less platonically. "You should have talked to her yesterday when you finally saw her again."

"I was in my car on the phone with one client and on

my way to meeting another." He'd nearly driven off Denny Way when he saw the woman, for the first time in months, walking toward the park with her gym bag. For a split second he'd even calculated whether he could risk pulling over. "Leaping out of my car to ask for her phone number wouldn't have gone over so well."

"You *should* have talked to her last April." Angela handed him the muffin, fragrant and still warm.

"It's obvious why he didn't." Bonnie shook her head, tsk-tsking. "He's terrified of her."

Jack kept his features neutral as he slung the camera over his shoulder. Bonnie was dangerously close to a truth. Something about this woman had made him hesitant to contact her, a "something" he didn't care to examine closely. Fear wasn't Jack's operating mode, especially with women. "Yeah, she might beat me up."

He bit into the muffin, rich with a tart burst of fruit. Even his nervousness couldn't overcome the rapture of Angela's baking. "God, Angela, if Daniel hadn't already given you a promise ring, I would."

"Uh-huh." She smiled her pleasure, but whether at his compliment or the mention of her future fiancé, Jack wasn't sure. Daniel Flynn had walked into Angela's shop in early April, still grieving the death of his fiancée. In spite of some crazy vow he'd taken not to date anyone for two years, he'd succumbed in a very short time to Angela's beauty, sweetness and chocolate chunk cookies.

"Changing the *sub*-ject." Bonnie sang out her disdain. "If you don't find her today, stay in the park until you do. You're starting to piss us off."

"Seriously." Angela nodded. "Gossip around here is in a very sad state. We need you to goose it up."

"I don't owe either of you any—"

"Excuse me?" Bonnie was comically incredulous, green eyes wide with outrage. "Yes, you do."

"Absolutely, you do," Angela agreed. "What is *wrong* with you?"

Jack cracked up. The women were bright spots in his life. He was so happy Angela had found Daniel. Now if he could only find a way to yank their friend Seth's head out of his you-know-what long enough to realize he still loved Bonnie, and that she was perfect for him…. "If I see the woman again today I will make contact, I promise. Okay? Happy?"

"Ooh!" Bonnie clapped her hands. "Delirious."

"Ecstatic." Angela was beaming. "Then come back *immediately* and tell us what she says."

"I have an idea what she'll say." Jack took a leisurely bite of muffin and chewed, fueling the women's impatience. "Either 'Oh, your work sounds fascinating,' or 'Go away and die, you creepy stalker.'"

"Could go either way," Bonnie said. "Angela, what do you think?"

"She'll do it." Angela poured herself a cup of coffee from the pot on her counter. "No woman has ever been able to resist Jack Shea."

"Give me a break." He made a sound of derision, both uncomfortable with and proud of the reputation. Women did tend to respond to his interest, probably because intuition told them that beneath the predatory maneuvers, Jack liked and respected them. Not to mention they were put together with parts he really, really enjoyed.

If he dug deeper, he'd admit that when he was on the prowl, part of him was warily watching out for the connection that would make committing himself worth it. That part kept him from feeling like a typical guy out to get laid. Plus, he was discerning in his choices, never was with a woman only one night unless that's what she wanted, and always protected his health. So if there was such a thing as a nice-guy, responsible player, he'd like to think he was it.

"Thanks for the muffin. Amazing as always." Jack crumpled the paper and pushed it into the white domed trash can under the counter, then poured and tossed back a cup of water. "I'm off."

"Good luck, Jack." Angela crossed fingers on both hands.

"I hope she's there today." Bonnie gave him a brief, fierce hug. "You're an amazing photographer. I still can't get over the picture you took of me."

Jack grinned, remembering the titillation of seeing his former lover clad only in orchids. "You're beautiful, Bonnie. It was a pleasure."

He enjoyed her blushing smile, waved to the two women then pushed out of the building's front door onto the sunny sidewalk of East Olive Way. For a few seconds he stood quietly, breathing in early August air under the whimsical Come to Your Senses sign Bonnie had designed and painted. The friends had named the building because their businesses represented the five senses: Smell—Bonnie's floral shop, taste—Angela's bakery, sight—his photography studio, sound—Seth Blackstone's music studio, and touch—the rather mysterious Demi Anderson's physical therapy studio. Demi had bought the business from Caroline, their college friend who'd married and moved out of state. Demi didn't mix much with the rest of them, but no one could decide if she was shy or stuck-up, except Bonnie, who'd come down firmly on the side of stuck-up.

He turned right on Olive, then right on Tenth Avenue and entered the park, walking with deliberately unhurried steps to counter his urge to sprint. The class he'd seen the woman in started at 6:30 a.m. and went for an hour. Then his target went off to practice on her own, which was when he'd been photographing her, getting some amazing shots framed by branches in the foreground that had led to Angela and Bonnie's stalker-in-the-bushes accusations. They had a point. If Jack saw her today he'd have to play it cool. He was pretty sure saying, "Hi, I've been watching you for months, taking pictures without your knowledge, want to come up to my studio?" wouldn't cut it.

But photographing her without her knowledge had been addictive. Not everyone was comfortable in front of a camera, and she'd been beautiful, unselfconscious, serene and centered. If an earthquake hit the park—trees falling, people shrieking and scattering—he figured she'd go right on through the sun salute, pose after pose, chest and abdomen taking in breath and letting it out. He'd felt as if he were photographing an extension of nature rather than an individual human being. Talking to her could have ruined it all and brought an end to any possibility of her participation in his series.

As he approached the area where the class was held on Tuesdays, he could see students enjoying the clear soft air, colorful mats laid out on the grass, arms raised, bodies lowering slowly. Both eager and nervous, he scanned the figures, about a dozen of them today, looking for blond hair in a simple ponytail, a long neck, slender figure…

No. Damn it. He checked again more carefully.

Not here. Jack's stomach sank with disappointment. Yesterday he'd been so sure when he saw her that she must have resumed taking the class. He'd spent way too long pissing away time in April, stupidly taking for granted that she'd always be there, making excuses for not approaching her right then: his final vision for the project wasn't complete, there was somewhere else he had to be, she might turn him down if he didn't say the right thing, she might turn out to be nothing like the woman he envisioned.

So yes, he'd blown it last spring. But he sure as hell would like another chance. Because he had no idea what he'd do if he'd lost her.

Blood Pressure: Moderately Normal

"IT WAS OKAY." Melissa Weber adjusted her cell phone against her ear, moving her left shoulder in a tentative circle, monitoring the joint for pain. "Didn't hurt too much. I'm glad I took a few more days off from class, though."

"I *told* you." Her younger sister, Gretchen, sighed. "If it was up to you, you'd keep exercising until your rotator cuff snapped and your arm fell right off."

"And that would be bad?" Melissa giggled at her sister's exasperation, reveling in the clear flow of breath down to her diaphragm, the exultant loosening of her muscles that her yoga class made possible. The rest of the time she must pant like a dog and hold herself like a stretched rubber band.

"You could have injured yourself seriously."

"It was just an irritation this time." Melissa turned her face up to the sunshine, more precious than gold in Seattle, though August was generally dry and warm. Most likely this latest setback with her shoulder would have healed on its own, but Gretchen did have a point. Babying it short- ened recovery so Melissa only had to skip Tuesday's and Wednesday's yoga classes this week, not months of them as when she'd ignored the pain last spring. Then, she'd missed not only yoga, but her workouts in the pool and weight room and her dance and tennis lessons. Luckily she'd still been fine typing, because Au Bon Repas, the national cooks' supply company where she worked as a human resources specialist, had initiated a change in benefits, and she'd been crazy busy.

"Have you been checking your blood pressure every morning?"

"Yes, Sister Mommy." Melissa rolled her eyes, ambling through the park up to Broadway, where she'd turn north toward her car. She didn't generally amble; she strode. But yoga made all things non-type-A possible for her.

"And?"

"And I'm not dead yet." Melissa loved that Gretchen worried about her, and she also hated it. Finding out this young that she had high blood pressure was the worst thing that had happened since her mom died of cancer when Melissa was thirteen. "Slow down," Dr. Glazer had said. "Relax."

Slow down? Relax? What did those strange terms mean?

Melissa had been trying. She'd given up her French lessons, her ceramics class, her jazz-dance class and her astrobiology continuing-education class at the university. Which left her a life consisting of work and working out. Period. What kind of bland, empty existence was that? At least she could help organize Gretchen's end-of-the-month wedding, trying to keep her sister's expenses as low as possible. Gretchen was a great sister, friend and person, but planning was not her forte. To put it politely.

"Your blood pressure's gone down?"

"Yoga is my salvation. I hold on to that calm feeling for hours after class and even through the week. It's really helping."

It was sort of helping. The doctor had threatened medication if she didn't improve her numbers.

"You avoided the question."

Melissa sighed. "Gretchen, sometimes I wish you didn't

know me so well. No, I'm not much lower, but I'm work-ing on it. What's new with the wedding plans?"

The one topic sure to distract her sister from whatever Melissa didn't want to talk about. Gretchen and Ted had been inseparable since they were sixteen, which made Me-lissa very happy for her sister and utterly claustrophobic even thinking about it. The couple practically breathed in sync; it was amazing to watch them together. Mom and Dad had been like that, too, which was why Dad had gone into such a tailspin after his wife's death.

Melissa had dated here and there, but no guy seemed to hold her interest for long. She was happiest when she was learning and growing, and men didn't seem to be able to bring her that same stimulation.

Of course there was that *other* stimulation only men could bring, but given her experiences in that arena, she thought on balance a good class did more for her. Maybe she had a low sex drive. She hadn't been eager to compare notes with other women.

In any case, she was only twenty-five. She could take the next ten years to enjoy herself, if that's what she wanted, before she got herself tied down. Gretchen, how-ever, didn't have that long. When Ted asked her to marry him two weeks ago, no one had been surprised, but Me-lissa nearly blew a gasket when they announced the date. Who could plan a wedding in five weeks? Certainly not Gretchen and Ted. Big sister would have to try.

Breathing deeply, ambling along, listening to Gretchen ramble excitedly about her and Ted's plans—or rather their intentions not to plan—Melissa finally said goodbye to her sister at the corner of Broadway and Olive, by the Come to Your Senses building, home of the enticing A Taste for All Pleasures bakery. Most days she forced her-self to walk past, being an admitted control freak about her calorie intake, but today her stomach felt positively concave with hunger. Besides, she was working out again since her shoulder had healed, and needed those extra calories. Right?

Absolutely.

She mounted the steps to the building and went inside, then pushed open the bakery door, which triggered a familiar tune she couldn't place. A pretty woman about Melissa's age, maybe a couple of years older, was just putting out a tray of chocolate chip scones that smelled so amazing in a room already full of amazing smells that Melissa wanted to dive in and suck down a dozen of everything. Did the store do wedding cakes? Gretchen wanted to make her own, but last time she'd baked—a chocolate layer cake for Dad's birthday—Melissa, their father and Ted had pointedly turned the conversation to Olympic discuses, Frisbees, barbell weights, train wheels…until even Gretchen had broken down laughing.

The woman heard the chime, looked up at Melissa and did a startled double take.

"Oh. Hi, there. Hello." The woman was staring now. "What— Beautiful day, isn't it?"

"Yes." Melissa gestured to the bakery case, wondering if she'd turned orange or sprouted antennae. "I'll have one of the chocolate chip scones, please. And a cup of coffee. To go."

"Yes. Sure." Holding a square of waxed paper, the woman picked out a scone and put it into a white paper bag. "Anything else?"

"Well…" Melissa eyed a rack of perfectly domed cupcakes. Maybe instead of a traditional wedding cake, multiple tiers of cupcakes? She'd try them out. "One chocolate, one spice with buttercream and one yellow with strawberry frosting, please."

"Have you been here before?" The woman rang up the purchases, glancing at Melissa every few seconds. "You look awfully familiar."

"I've passed by on my way home, but haven't come in." She pointed in the direction of the park. "I've been taking an early yoga class at Cal Anderson."

The chestnut head shot up. "You take yoga in the park?"

"Uh. Yes." Melissa took a step back. This had officially become weird. "Why, is it dangerous?"

"No, no, no, of course not, I'm sorry." The woman offered her hand over the counter. "I'm Angela Loukas."

"Melissa." Something about Angela's eagerness made Melissa protective of her last name. You never knew. Angela could be a cult member who recruited yoga devotees and turned them to the devil.

A group of young mothers came in with kids and strollers, saving Melissa from having to come up with reasons not to sign a pledge to Satan. Angela hesitated, glancing between Melissa and the moms, then moved reluctantly away. "Nice to meet you, Melissa. The coffee is on the counter, help yourself. And…why don't you walk around the other businesses on the floor before you go? You'd enjoy…everyone. Especially at the end of the hall, there's—"

"Excuse me?" The mom of a fussy toddler broke in impatiently. "I'm sorry, but my child is about to lose it. Can we order?"

Melissa turned toward the coffee counter. Especially at the end of the hall there was what? She'd been planning to explore anyway, but Angela's suggestion had seemed oddly pointed. Maybe cult headquarters were down there?

Shrugging, she poured a cup of coffee and wandered out of the bakery, stopping to peer into the window of the business opposite, Bonnie Blooms. Beautiful shop, flowers everywhere, arranged in buckets at different levels, like a floral jungle.

Gretchen was in such sticker shock over florists' prices, she was ready to give up on flowers except for a bridal nosegay of daisies. As if! Melissa would check this place out. If the owner could produce a nice, relatively inexpensive bouquet, the shop might be a good candidate for her sister's limited-budget wedding.

She approached the counter and smiled at the shop's proprietor, whose red hair was set off dramatically by a yellow-and-black bumble-bee-striped minidress.

"Hi, there, can I help you?" The woman returned Melissa's smile, then blinked, looking surprised, then slightly puzzled.

Oh, no. Not her, too.

"I'd like a mixed bouquet—whatever you think looks nice."

"Okay. Sure." She hadn't stopped staring long enough to blink. "How much did you want to spend?"

"About twenty dollars."

"Coming right up." The woman backed toward a bucket to her left and was reaching for a rose, when her attention was caught by something across the hall, toward or in the bakery, Melissa couldn't see. The woman froze for a moment, eyebrows lifted, peeked back to find Melissa watching her and jerked her head away.

What the hell was going on in this place? "Is something wrong?"

"No. No. Sorry." She laughed nervously. "I…thought I knew you."

"Seems to be a lot of that going on around here."

"No, no." She shook her head as if to clear it. "I was mistaken. You, um, look like someone we used to know."

"We?"

"Angela." She gestured to Melissa's paper bag. "At the bakery. I'm Bonnie. We, uh, went to college with someone who looked freakily like you."

"Okay." That was more comforting than the devil-cult explanation, but Bonnie hadn't sounded quite convinced, so Melissa wasn't, either. "I went to Pacific University in Oregon."

"Definitely not you, then!" She laughed awkwardly. "Have a look around. I'll just be a minute."

"Sure." Melissa meandered through the shop, stopping to inhale over a blossom here and there, the soft fragrances enhancing her temporary inner peace. Really a lovely place. And Bonnie seemed pleasant and anxious to please, apart from the weird staring incident. Her talent remained to be seen.

"All set. Here you go."

"That was fast." Melissa returned to the counter and caught her breath. The bouquet surpassed her expectations. Hardly a skimpy bunch of carnations and baby's breath, the assortment was lush, full and gorgeously shaded with the burgundies and pinks of Peruvian lilies, a few exquisite roses and pale greenish-yellow tightly bunched flowers Melissa didn't recognize. If she had to guess how much it cost, she would have said twice what she'd asked to spend. "Oh, how beautiful."

"Enjoy it." Bonnie rang up the purchase, adding one of her cards to the bouquet. Only eighteen dollars and change. Gretchen could have herself a very talented florist here.

"Thank you." Melissa buried her face in the delicately scented blooms as she walked out, glancing farther down the hall then at her watch. She had about fifteen minutes before she'd need to get her car, drive to work, shower quickly in the company exercise room and deal with a rather fishy sexual harassment complaint. It was the third one from Bob Whatsisname in three years, as if he was really desperate to be sexually harassed and hadn't been able to get anyone to cooperate yet. But having finally stepped into Come to Your Senses after passing it so many times, she was curious to check out the building's other occupants.

Past the flower shop she came to a photography studio: Jack Shea. In his front window hung wedding pictures, anniversaries, graduation shots—the usual, but with a creativity that set them apart. A bride caught in profile descending a medieval-looking curving stone staircase, a graduate in mid–celebratory leap. Melissa lingered at the window, drawn to the images. Gretchen should definitely check him out, too, though he'd likely be too expensive.

She moved to the other side of the entrance and encountered a picture in a completely different style. Horrifying, disturbing, but also incredibly powerful, with a poignancy that kept her riveted for far longer than she could usually stand still. The photo was a close-up of a naked back on which a network of cracks had been superimposed, like those on asphalt or an eggshell, so that the skin looked as if it was scarred or about to disintegrate. Melissa stood for a long time absorbing the extraordinary concept and the strong emotions the image evoked.

It seemed hardly possible this work of art was by the same person who'd done the sweet celebration pictures opposite. Melissa peered curiously into the studio, unwilling to venture inside since she had to get to work. But she should at least pick up Jack Shea's card, even if he was out of their pathetic price range. Gretchen had been fine with the idea of passing out disposable cameras to the guests to take photos of the ceremony and reception. Melissa wanted her sister to have something better to frame.

She took a step inside, feeling as if she were trespassing, though a sign hung on the door said Open. Another step, her soft-soled sneakers making no noise. On one back wall hung more wedding, baby and family portraits. On the other, more of the artsy style, including the distant rear view of a lone figure on a pier staring out at the ocean beyond him, nothing but gray-blue sky, gray-blue water and his questioning solitude. Again, she was mesmerized, taking in the image for an endless moment, feeling called to something she couldn't name.

A noise from the back made her jump. Through the open doorway she saw a line of hanging prints, which seemed to be of—

The sound of a chair scraping across the floor distracted her. Was that Jack Shea? She felt unaccountably nervous, almost guilty, as if she'd been caught prying into his private life.

Footsteps approached. Melissa tried to picture him. The wedding images were so fresh and vibrant, full of hope— Jack would be a younger man. Except the depth and pain in the torso images pointed to more life experience than a young man would generally—

He appeared in the doorway.

Oh.

For a good five seconds they stared at each other.

Jack Shea, if this was Jack Shea, was not the weird, skinny young man she'd pictured, nor was he the bearded Bohemian child-of-the-sixties. This guy was…

Well, she'd just say her yoga-calm was in serious trouble.

Brown eyes, brown hair, nothing particularly thrilling to describe. But what he *did* for those brown eyes, which jumped straight into hers, and the brown hair, tousled sexily like a rock star's, set off all kinds of electrical reactions. Add to that broad shoulders straining the seams of a maroon T-shirt that showed off the solid planes of his chest and highlighted firm biceps and trim jeans-covered hips.

Yum. And wow. Melissa did not generally respond to men with quite this much...response.

As she stood there, her brain managed to resume the tiniest bit of functioning, enough to realize he was staring at her the way Bonnie and Angela had been staring— because Melissa looked like a college friend, or whatever the party line was. Not because he was overcome by her, too.

Darn it.

"Are you Jack Shea?"

"I am, yes." He laughed nervously, ran his hand over his head, which would explain the sexy tousle. "And you are— I mean, I think I've seen—"

"I know." She held up her hand. "I look like your college friend."

His eyes shot wider. "My what?"

Hmm. He obviously had no idea what she was talking about. "Bonnie and Angela told me about her?"

"Oh. Yes. Okay." He continued staring, clearly more rattled by whatever the hell she represented than Bonnie and Angela had been.

Unless...maybe that college friend did exist and had meant something to him?

Melissa's imagination went straight to a picture of Jack Shea passionately entwined with this woman who was apparently her twin. Which meant she was, in essence, picturing herself sleeping with him.

Good lord.

She made her body relax and smiled beatifically. "I was just passing by. Wondered if you had a card and a price list. My sister's getting married and hasn't settled on a photographer yet."

"Sure. When's her big day?" He reached under the counter and came up with a sheet, which she took, smiling her thanks. A smile that went on life support when she saw how high his prices were. As expected, but still disappointing.

"End of the month." Melissa nodded at his surprised expression. "I know, practically tomorrow in bride time. She and her fiancé wanted to do it simply and soon. They settled on the twenty-ninth."

He was already checking his BlackBerry. "Morning, afternoon or evening?"

"Oh, I'm not sure we can—" She waved the sheet Jack had given her, not wanting to admit he was out of her league.

"Just checking the date for you."

"You don't—" Melissa sighed. Easier to play along. "Late afternoon."

"I had a cancellation last week, so I could do that." He grinned at her, charming as hell, and quirked an eyebrow meaningfully. "In fact, I'd *love* to do that."

Ah. She'd just bet he would. It wouldn't surprise her if a majority of his clients were females who'd fallen for how much Jack would *love* to work with them, too.

"Okay. Good to know." She stepped back to leave, more disappointed than she cared to admit that a guy of his talent was free on Gretchen's wedding day and they couldn't use him. "We'll give you a call if—"

"What's your name?"

She stopped in surprise. Why did he want to know? Had Angela sent her to cult headquarters after all? "Sorry, but I really need to get—"

"You live around here?" He leaned against the counter, consummately casual.

She was immediately suspicious. Something wasn't right. "Not far. Listen, thanks for the—"

"I was wondering why I haven't seen you around more."

Oh, for heaven's sake. "Because I haven't *been* around more?"

He chuckled, watching her, the intensity of those brown eyes making it hard to maintain her calm—as if it wasn't hard enough anyway. "That would explain it."

Melissa looked pointedly at her watch. Whatever was going on in this building, she really didn't like being the only one who didn't know what it was. "I need to get to work. Thanks for the price sheet."

"Let me get you a brochure with more information." He looked under the counter and frowned. "Hang on, I'll get one from—"

"No, it's not necessary." She waved the sheet. "I've got this, it's all I need."

"I have more in back." He was already turning away.

"Seriously, don't bother."

He dismissed her with a wave. "It's no prob—"

"We can't afford you, Mr. Shea."

There. Embarrassing, but that would put an end to it and she could make her escape.

He turned back with a half smile, eyes warm. Very warm. "Call me Jack. And you are...?"

She sighed impatiently. "Melissa."

"Melissa." By now the eye-warmth was positively inappropriate. "I'm sure we can work something out...."

What the— Melissa drew in a sharp breath. Was her insta-crush messing with her brain, or was this guy about to teach Bob Whatsisname what real sexual harassment sounded like?

She drew herself up into her best attitude of icy disapproval. "What *kind* of 'something'?"

"Let me get the brochure. We can discuss it. Maybe over coffee."

Coffee! Melissa was flabbergasted. Never had her icy disapproval so totally failed her. Jack hadn't even noticed. In fact, he'd acted as if she was dying to take him up on whatever offer he flung at her. Good God, the arrogance. "You're asking me *out?*"

"Just to talk." He winked and disappeared into the back, leaving Melissa halfway to exploding her arteries with outrage. If he thought she was going to sleep with him so her sister could have him photograph her wedding at a discount, he had another think coming.

She was about to whirl around and stomp her way out when the door he'd pulled shut behind him swung slowly open. Behind it, the line of prints again caught her attention. Melissa stepped closer, frowning. Why did they seem—

She gasped. The bakery bag dropped from her hand.

Hanging from a wire were print after print after print of a woman dressed in different outfits, which meant they'd been taken on different days. A lot of different days. The woman was doing yoga. In Cal Anderson Park.

They were all pictures of Melissa.

2

Blood Pressure: High

WHAT THE—

Melissa put a hand to her chest to calm her breathing, not sure whether to be outraged or terrified, so she settled on both, heart pounding, ears buzzing.

With one glance, all that good yoga relaxation this morning was shot to hell. This was exactly the type of upset Dr. Glazer had cautioned her to avoid. But she didn't see any other way to react. Jack had been taking pictures of her—without her knowledge. And now he was being flirty with her and wanted her to have coffee with him. And he *really* seemed to want to photograph her sister's wedding. Was that what he did? Skulk around spying on women? Was he a sexual predator? Was Melissa in some kind of danger? Did he know where she lived? Should she run right now and call the police?

Shhh, breathe, Melissa. She picked up the bakery bag she'd dropped, and put it on the counter next to Gretchen's flowers. Then she set her gym bag down, stood in Mountain Pose and closed her eyes, forced her rigid shoulders to relax and took in a long, slow breath, letting it out the same way. She did it again and again—thank goodness he was taking a long time to find his stupid brochures—until she felt centered and stronger, and calm. Well…calmer.

Too soon to panic. Angela and Bonnie, both seemingly nice people, had obviously recognized Melissa from the pictures, and they hadn't looked anything more than surprised and intrigued by her presence. Neither of them had warned her away. In fact Angela must have been trying to send her down the hall to Jack. Maybe he just wanted pictures of someone doing yoga and figured out that Melissa practiced alone after class. She could have been a tree or a rock or a building that caught his artistic eye. The easiest explanation was often the right one. She'd confront him. Any creepy vibes and she'd go straight to the police.

"Sorry, had to open a new box. First I had to *find* a new box. Here's the brochure." Jack stepped into the room, did a double take behind him and shut the door firmly.

Yeah, too late, buddy.

"You know, I just remembered what I came in for." In spite of her struggle to sustain peaceful breathing, Melissa's voice came out high and harsh. "I'm looking for pictures of a woman."

His expression became wary. "Okay."

"More specifically, I'm interested in pictures of a woman doing yoga."

"Uh…" Jack began to look hunted.

"In fact, I'm looking for pictures of a woman doing yoga in Cal Anderson Park." Melissa pointed to the door he'd just closed. "About my height. And weight. With my coloring. And clothes."

"Uhhh…" He put his hands over his face, dragged them down and peeked at her over the tips of his fingers, his expression one of contrition. "I guess you saw them."

"I guess I did."

He swore under his breath.

"Busted?"

"I was going to explain over coffee." He sent her an I've-been-a-bad-boy look that he must know was adorable. She would remain unmoved until he proved himself innocent. And maybe even after that. "This must be a shock, Melissa."

"A shock?" She faked surprise. "No, no, not at all. Happens all the time. People spy on me and take pictures, oh, twice a week at least."

"No, it's not…" He shook his head, the hint of an embarrassed smile curving his masculine lips. "See, you were there and then I was, and then I, uh…"

Melissa scowled. Why did jerks always come in such fabulous packages? Her boss, Barbara, called them baby pools. Warm, inviting and totally shallow. Dive in and you'd get brain damage. Even her mother had warned her, one of the precious rounds of maternal advice she'd given Melissa before she died: really good-looking men— actually, Mom had said *people*—came first on their own priority lists, and thought they should come first on everyone else's, too. "And then you what?"

"See, I was thinking you'd be…" He scratched his head. "That is, I was *hoping* you'd be…"

"I'd be *what?*" If he didn't explain soon she was going to hurl her gym bag at his head.

"Oh, man." He held up both hands. "Can we start over?"

"Why did you take photos of me? Are you stalking me? Did someone *hire* you?" Melissa's voice cracked. The possibilities were awful.

"No. *No.*" His look of genuine concern caused a small bit of her anger to slip away, which made it easier to appear in control. "My interest was purely artistic. I swear."

Hmm. The simplest explanation… "Why didn't you ask my permission?"

"Honestly, I was going to."

"When were you going to?"

"Today, over coffee. Before that…" He wrinkled his nose apologetically. Another adorable-yet-masculine expression. He must practice in front of a mirror. "Thing is, the day I decided to approach you was the day you disappeared."

"Well." Melissa smacked her hand on the counter, uncomfortably aware he could be telling the truth. She'd stopped going to yoga for a few months because of her injury. But she wasn't ready to let him off the hook yet. "How's that for timing?"

"This isn't as bad as it seems."

Melissa arched an eyebrow. "How would you know how bad it seems?"

"I'm guessing you feel violated, vulnerable and afraid." He leaned both palms on the counter, which emphasized the broad sweep of his shoulders and back. His eyes were sincere, gaze unwavering.

Damn, he was good. Yes, she felt violated, vulnerable and afraid, and with her guard down on all three counts, he was creating an atmosphere of concerned intimacy.

Good thing she was on to him.

"Someone could have noticed you every day the way I did, watched you the same way I did." His voice was low, earnest. "But photography is a deliberate and permanent act, which is much more threatening."

Melissa had nothing to say. He'd nailed exactly how bad it was. "Why were you photographing me?"

Jack pushed back from the counter. "The camera loves you. You were irresistible to me."

He spoke matter-of-factly, photographer discussing his

subject, whereas Melissa had to hold herself statue-still and beg her circulatory system not to turn her face scarlet. "You could have asked."

"You might have told me to get lost."

"Yes." She folded her arms over her chest, wanting to appear tougher than she was feeling now that the worst of her outrage had abated. The way he looked at her, as if he could read her mind and see her naked at the same time, was making it very hard to feel she had the upper hand, which she damn well deserved in this situation. "But I would have liked the chance to choose. And to know what you wanted the pictures for."

"I show at the Unko Gallery." He reached for the pile of brochures he'd brought out and handed her one. "I was experimenting, working on a new idea, a way of photographing women. You had the look I wanted."

Melissa opened the brochure, wishing she could ask what look that was, but not willing to betray her interest. Was she the embodiment of every female fantasy he'd ever had? Or was she yet another trend-following Western capitalist pretending to understand yoga? Or was it something else entirely that only he could envision, and which she might not want to hear? Given some of the more disturbing shots in the shop, his ideas might not be that flattering.

Jack was indeed listed in the brochure, alongside a few prominently placed photographs, more of those odd, powerful images. Impressive. Melissa wasn't exactly an art maven, but even she'd heard of the Unko Gallery. Gretchen had taken her there once for a friend's opening party.

"Come have coffee with me, Melissa. Angela makes a really good cup."

"I just had one." She offered him back the brochure.

"Have one more?" He waved at her to keep the pamphlet. "Angela will chaperone."

"So I don't look like anyone you went to college with."

"Nope." He came out from behind the counter, broader, taller and closer without the protective barrier, leaving Melissa no idea what to do with her hands. "She and Bonnie must have recognized you from your pictures."

Melissa picked up her flowers and bakery bag. So far, she hadn't detected any creepy vibes, and she might have to entertain the fact that Jack was telling the truth. "You showed the photos around."

"I was excited about you." He still spoke offhandedly, but the eyes watching her were alert and focused.

Melissa glared at him suspiciously, again pleading with her blush mechanism for mercy. "Excited how?"

"Artistically. Of course." He grinned in a way that made it extremely difficult not to grin back. "Have coffee with me? A quick cup. I'd like to talk over what I hope to do with the pictures."

"Blackmail me?"

He laughed. "Not blackmail you. I promise."

"I need to get to work." Even she could hear her lack of conviction. Work would still be there half an hour from now. Melissa was always early, always thoroughly prepared to tackle her day. She was admittedly intrigued by this man and his work, and she wanted to see if he'd be open to negotiating a legitimate deal so she could afford him for Gretchen's wedding.

She and her sister hadn't grown up poor, but they hadn't been well off, either. Her father had imploded after their mom died; any ambition he might have had to get his PhD or pursue a principal's or administrative position had died with her. All he'd done since then was teach high school and watch TV. Melissa really wanted Gretchen to have a dream wedding, but without money growing on the family tree, it fell to her to make things happen, as it had so many times since her mom's death.

"One quick cup." She hoisted her gym bag briskly. "In the bakery. With a table between us. And Mace if you have any."

"Won't need it." His smile reached his eyes instantly. "Angela's better than Mace, she's stronger and faster. But really, I'm harmless."

Melissa had definite doubts about that.

They walked down the hall together and, in a moment worthy of farce, Melissa caught Bonnie doing a frantic double take at the sight of them, and then Angela doing the same when she and Jack came into the bakery.

"Oh. Hi." Angela glanced rapidly between them. "You two— Well. What can I get you?"

"Just coffee." Jack's voice came over Melissa's right shoulder; she was ridiculously conscious of his body close to hers. "This is Melissa."

"Yes." Angela nodded uncomfortably. "We met."

Melissa beamed at her, unable to resist a little torture. "I'm the college-friend look-alike."

"Oh…yes." She gestured desperately toward the other side of the shop. "Coffee's over there, help yourself, on the house, let me know if you want anything else."

Jack was laughing, a deep chuckle that was frankly delicious. "Angela, it's okay, she—"

"Hey, Angela." Bonnie sailed into the bakery and pretended to have just caught sight of them. "Oh! Hi, Jack. Hi, Melissa. Do you two know each other?"

"Melissa has seen the pictures. We're here to talk it out. Bonnie, go pot ferns. Angela, go bake a cake."

"Are you kidding me? Miss this conversation?" Bonnie sent Melissa a sly wink behind Jack's back. "Dish up the muffins, Angela. Front-row seats for the showdown are available."

"No." Jack took a threatening step toward Bonnie. "You are not staying—"

"Ooh, good *idea,* Bonnie." Angela threw Melissa a grin while Jack growled at Bonnie. "Chocolate chip, oatmeal cranberry, lemon blueberry…"

"Over my dead body."

"If that's necessary, sure, Jack." Angela bent down and started picking out muffins. "You don't mind if we're here, do you, Melissa?"

"Of course not." Melissa suppressed a giggle. Nice to see Jack wasn't always in control. It actually made him more appealing. "I'm happier in a crowd when I chat with my stalkers."

"Oh, me, *too.*" Bonnie plunked herself into a chair and patted the one beside her for Melissa, then pointed to the chair opposite and looked expectantly at Jack. "Sit."

Jack sat, glowering at all three of them. "Apparently I am outnumbered."

"Outnumbered, outclassed, outwitted and outmaneuvered." Bonnie rested her elbows on the table and her head on laced fingers. "Now, Melissa. First of all, let us reassure you about Jack."

"Yes. We must." Angela put a paper plate of divine-looking muffins on the table. "He might look and act like a complete creep—"

"Hey."

"—but he's a total sweetheart."

"And a very talented photographer," Bonnie added.

"I promise you are completely safe with him." Angela sat down and beamed at Jack.

"Absolutely." Bonnie nodded vigorously. She and Angela exchanged glances. Their confidence slipped. "Well… pretty safe."

"Yeah…" Angela bit her lip. "I'd say *more or less* safe."

"If you have people around."

"Hired to protect you."

"Who are armed."

Jack brought his hand down on the table, enough to make the muffins jump. His lips twitched. "Stop. Now. You are not helping."

"Of course we're helping." Angela turned to Bonnie in concern. "Aren't we?"

"Well…" Bonnie looked troubled. "Now that I think about it, we might not be. Melissa?"

"You are both helping. A lot." Melissa nodded her most gracious thanks. "It was pretty frightening seeing those pictures, but now, hearing from both of you that Jack is probably a sociopath…well, I feel a lot better."

Angela and Bonnie burst out laughing. Jack put his head in his hands and groaned. Melissa gave in and cracked up with the women, and for a few seconds, felt a sweet glow of belonging. Which was silly, since she didn't.

"All righty, then." Angela got up and pushed in her chair, smiling fondly at Jack. "Our work is done."

"We're outta here." Bonnie grabbed a blueberry muffin and kissed the top of Jack's head. "You'll do fine, Jack. Just be yourself. Or maybe…hmm. No, actually, if I were you I'd be someone else. Anyone, really."

"Yeah, thanks a hell of a lot. Both of you."

The women walked off giggling, Bonnie to her shop, Angela into the bakery kitchen, leaving silence and intimacy behind them.

Melissa clasped her hand around her mug so she wouldn't show her nervousness. "They are hilarious."

"Uh-huh." Jack didn't bother hiding his amusement. "And they knew exactly what they were doing."

"Trying to reassure me?"

"Did it work?"

Melissa shrugged. "Yes. I guess. Some."

"I'm glad to hear that, Melissa."

She moved uneasily. Something about Jack's deep voice saying her name was way more intimate than it should be, and she felt her guard go up again.

"How long have you known them?" Stupid question, but she needed words to break the tension.

"Five of us bought the building together. All graduates of UW Seattle, a few years ago. We get along, which is good, because launching businesses is not a job for sissies." He leaned back in the chair. "What do you do?"

Melissa jerked back to the conversation, having been calculating his age. Twenty-six? With his smooth confidence, she would have put him a few years older. "I'm a human-resources specialist at the corporate headquarters of Au Bon Repas, the kitchen-supply store. We do business all over the world."

"Oh, yeah, Angela's always drooling over your catalogs. You like what you do?"

"It's a good place to work, supportive and with a proactive corporate culture. Happy employees make our department's job easier. And I have a great boss." For some reason, though the phrases tumbled out in the usual way, they sounded stilted and overblown.

"Nice." He stretched his long legs to one side, hands folded across his tight abdomen. Her job recitation must have hit him as funny because he was smiling. Or maybe he was just thinking about how gorgeous he must look. She wished she could be totally immune. "What do you do for fun?"

Urgh. Melissa hated that question. It sounded vaguely suggestive, as if guys were hoping she'd say, *I like to get drunk, rip off my clothes and give blow jobs to strangers. Wanna go?*

"I'm pretty busy. I take a lot of classes. Dance and exercise and crafts classes, plus some courses at the university. I think if you're not learning, improving and trying new things, you might as well be six feet under." Melissa snapped her mouth shut. Again, she sounded robotic and puffed-up.

He leaned across the table toward her. Melissa held herself still, though her protective instinct told her to pull back. This close she could see the slight stubble around his jaw, the faint lines in his lips. She could tell herself he was an obvious player, bad news, not her type, anything she could think of, but the facts were simple: he was gorgeous and her body wanted to check his out. "I have something new you can try, Melissa."

Oh, lord. It took two attempts before she found her voice, and even then she only managed a tinge of cynicism. "Oh, really."

Jack folded his hands on the table, teasing charmer gone, an intensity in his gaze that sounded a loud you-could-be-in-trouble-here alarm. Usually it took Melissa time to overcome her reserve with men. Half an hour after meeting this guy she wanted to grab him and find out what his skin felt like. His hair. His mouth—

Melissa, honey, get yourself under control. Her boss, Barbara, would know what to say to calm her down. Melissa could practically hear her voice. *You shouldn't need a man to feel good about yourself. You shouldn't need a man at all.*

Exactly. Melissa hadn't needed one since she'd started

the process of finding herself, soon after graduation, and she didn't need one now.

"I saw you for the first time in April, practicing your poses after class. Immediately I knew I had to photograph you."

"Why?"

"One, because you're beautiful." He spoke with a low, slightly husky voice, a bedroom voice, except that his expression was distant, as if he were imagining her as part of his art, which effectively negated any feeling of seduction. Perversely, that made his words even more seductive, and Melissa finally lost the fight with her blush machine. "But also, because your body looks like it's part of nature when you're posing. You have an inner light, an incredible serenity, as if nothing could rattle you."

Spell broken. Melissa barely managed to stifle a snort. *Serenity?* Oh, my God. If they heard him say that, her doctor and everyone she knew would never stop laughing. "Jack, I don't think you quite have—"

"I was right." He blinked and resumed his focus on her. "My camera loves you. I captured everything about you that had already captured me."

"And you were planning to take more shots of me."

"Then you disappeared, but yes." He raised an eyebrow. "Here comes my sales pitch, you ready?"

Melissa glanced at her watch, buying time to think. Sales pitch. She'd been thrown by meeting Jack and seeing those pictures. She was still struggling with her attraction to him. Whatever he was going to ask from her now, she was not going to be able to give him a sane response. She'd do much better thinking first and talking to Barbara. Most likely he was going to ask to continue to photograph her. Could she trade him for a discount on her sister's wedding? How involved did she want to get with this man?

And wasn't that a loaded question.

"Can it wait? I need to get to work." She stood before she went soft and changed her mind.

He caught her forearm. "Meet me for a drink later?"

Melissa wasn't prepared for that one, or for his touch, or for him to get to his feet, too, which brought him even closer. She had to concentrate yet again on keeping her breath low and slow. Most men's persistence annoyed her. Why couldn't she summon irritation now when she needed it? "What's the nutshell version of your pitch?"

"I want you to model for my new series. The Unko Gallery has already shown interest. You're perfect for what I need."

He was still holding her arm, fingers squeezing, as if the tension was tough on him, too. Melissa's head whirled with reasons, pro and con. Dr. Glazer had warned her about adding more to her schedule, but it was ridiculously open these days after she'd dropped so many classes; she was too often at loose ends. And if modeling meant she could hire Jack for Gretchen's wedding…

Of course, she would have to pretend to be calm and serene around him for extended periods. That might kill her faster than her blood pressure.

"Look." She tugged her arm from his warm fingers, needing to put her scrambled thoughts in order. "For one thing, I've never modeled before. I didn't know you took the other pictures. I might be terrible at it when you're right there with the camera in my face."

"I doubt it. But we can test tonight, if you're free."

"I'm not free." She was not going to jump for a guy like this who probably had several women already leaping like kangaroos. Besides, she'd need at least twenty-four hours to regain her equilibrium.

"Tomorrow?"

Tomorrow was Friday. She used to have a pottery class at 5:30, but these days she'd be going home to read or meditate or something equally dull. Jack was anything but dull. "How long would this take?"

"An hour. Maybe two."

She was amazed. "For the series?"

"Oh, no." Jack shook his head, grinning. "I thought you meant the tests. The series would take longer."

"How much longer?"

He narrowed his eyes speculatively. She guessed he was figuring out what she wanted to hear. "Depends on how the pictures turn out, how the creative process evolves, whether I get the shots the way I want them."

Uh-huh. He wasn't risking specifics. If this only took a few hours, fine. She certainly couldn't spend any longer than that pretending she was serene.

"By the way, blatant bribery. If you'll agree to model for me, I can do your sister's wedding for nothing."

And there it was. She didn't even have to ask. A photographer of his talent would be an amazing gift to Ted and Gretchen. All Melissa had to do was…

Be around Jack. Alone with him for long stretches of time. He'd be posing her, touching her. She'd have to pretend none of it affected her.

Dangerous to her sanity and to her health. And so tempting. She needed to talk to Barbara. Her boss, mentor and stand-in mom had helped clear her head more times than Melissa could count, and had started her on a wonderful journey of self-awareness.

"Let me know what you decide." Jack held out his hand. "You can come by the studio after work tomorrow. Wear or bring black if you have it—something on the tight side for a good silhouette. We'll have a drink, talk it over, maybe take a few shots and see what we have."

"I'll give it some thought." Melissa shook his hand, proud of her ability to meet those killer brown eyes calmly with her insides still a mass of yes-please and no-thank-you confusion.

Give it *some* thought?

She could already tell that for the next day and a half she'd be thinking of little else.

3

BONNIE TURNED THE KEY, locking the front door of Bonnie Blooms. Her back ached. Her feet hurt. She had a crashing headache. Her parents had been right. She shouldn't have opened this store, she didn't have the experience. A pie-in-the-sky venture, launched on a wing and a prayer, and what other clichés could she use? Who ate pie in the sky anyway?

She was exhausted. Grinding through each day, hoping business would get better, putting on a good face for everyone. Wedding season always gave her a boost, and she'd painstakingly learned how to design a new funky website and blog page for the store with as much color and as many touches of humor as she could get away with while still appearing professional. Talk about a learning curve. She wasn't convinced the site was perfect, but it was better than the template-based one she'd started with.

Orders were dribbling in, both local and through the FTD network, but only dribbling. She was still in the hole more than she should be, still dipping into savings more than she wanted to. How could she get people and companies and organizations and agencies to buy more flowers? What did she have to offer that no other florist did?

Nothing. But Bonnie couldn't see that when she started this business. She'd been swept away by the can-do camaraderie of the other Come to Your Senses members, and had figured if they could do it, why couldn't she? She had as much passion as any of them. While other girls had been into ponies and princesses, Bonnie was designing gardens on paper, in the backyard space her parents put aside for her, and eventually took over the entire backyard when she proved to have more talent than her mother.

But that didn't make her a good businesswoman. She should have kept her job at Blossoms Dearie, making a steady, if small, paycheck.

Except then she wouldn't be part of this terrific fivesome. Well, foursome if you didn't count Demi, which Bonnie generally didn't. Not belonging to this crowd would be a terrible tragedy. She smiled, thinking of poor Jack's face when he'd finally found his beautiful Melissa and thought Bonnie and Angela were going to move in and ruin everything. That kind of teasing between people who knew each other so well, trusted and supported each other, teasing with genuine love at its heart—Bonnie couldn't get that from old Mrs. Blatter at Blossoms Dearie.

She shuddered at the thought of her tyrant former boss, and trudged past Jack's and Demi's studios to the elevator, pocketing her shop key. All hope was not lost. Something would work out, some marketing idea would kick in, some corporate account would materialize, her blog would catch on. Something. In the meantime, it was summer—Bonnie's favorite and most profitable season, Seattle's most beautiful—and denial was her friend.

On the second floor, she headed down the narrow hallway. She'd painted two twining lines of roses down either wall. When Seth and Jack felt their manhood threatened by the floral decor, she'd mischievously painted a line of tanks along the baseboard, guns aimed high, as if to blast the flowers into shreds of petal. They'd all had a good laugh. That was when they'd been a solid fivesome, when Caroline was still around.

Her key hit the apartment's lock at the exact moment her cell rang, as if the key had set it off. Bonnie hauled the phone out of her pocket and pushed inside, snapping on the foyer light.

Seth. A tingle of anticipation she could never quite control went through her. "Hi, there."

"Hey, someone sounds cranky. What's going on?"

"Long day." She wasn't in the mood for Seth. Or rather, she wasn't in the mood for their complicated relationship. Past lovers, now uneasy friends. Bonnie had come to terms with the fact that while she might never meet anyone who fitted her so well, Seth wasn't and might never be able to commit to a relationship.

"I just finished a song. I'd like to play it for you. Wanna come up?"

"I'm up already, just closed the store." Bonnie slumped against the wall. Yes, she wanted to see Seth if he'd take her in his arms, declare undying love and make all her problems go away. But being in Seth's arms had the unfortunate effect of creating many more problems than it solved. At least she'd figured out that much. Since they'd both lived at Come to Your Senses—nearly two years now—they'd been able to maintain a relatively peaceful and platonic truce. Though lately he'd been acting…odd.

"I'll feed you, too, and pour you a short or tall one of whatever you'd like. And…" Seth did a credible impression of a drum roll. The guy had talented lips. She should know. "For dessert I have mint chocolate chip ice cream."

Oooh, playing dirty now. Bonnie took a moment to consider. Her choice lay between morose, quiet loneliness here, and free food and drink with fun if slightly crazy-making company.

Sigh.

"Give me twenty minutes to rejuvenate and I'll be over."

"Cool." As always, he spoke as if he didn't care whether she came or not. Seth had a talent for making it seem he cared about nothing. Not the kind of thing you craved in a partner, though he'd had a hell of a childhood with an alcoholic father who hadn't exactly made loving support or emotional sharing the rule of the family.

Yes, Bonnie was learning.

"Seeya." She ended the call, slipped her phone back into her pocket. Seth had another talent, one she truly respected. He'd written music for some commercials and TV shows, sold a few songs and was in talks with a producer to score a movie soundtrack. He worked hard. Given that he had inherited enough family money to buy his own Hollywood movie studio, Bonnie respected him for that. If she had all that money in the bank, she'd be tempted to go on a tour of the world's most beautiful beaches and hone her lying-in-the-sun skills.

After showering and putting on a comfortable sundress of pale brown and sunshine-yellow, she felt more human. Only occasionally did she succumb to fear like this over her financial situation. Something would work out, she was convinced.

Down at the other end of the rose- and tank-strewn hallway, she knocked on Seth's door, and it opened immediately to the tall, model-gorgeous man whose fierce gray eyes seemed to glow in his face. Even now, after all the years of pain and exasperation he'd caused her, Bonnie got a fresh thrill every time she saw him.

Masochist.

"Hey, Bonnie. Come in, come in. Bar's open, buffet's

open. I made pot-sticker dumplings and bok choy with ginger and soy."

She groaned with pleasure. "You are a god among men."

"Well, *yeah*. What'll you drink with it?"

"Beer. Whatever you have."

"I have Tsingtao, imported from Shandong province, a brewery started by Germans in nineteen hundred and—".

"Psssht." She stopped him. "If it's got alcohol and bubbles, I'm in."

His grin turned him from tough-guy gorgeous to goofy farm boy—still gorgeous—a transformation that never ceased to charm her and, sigh, women everywhere. "It does, my little plum blossom."

Bonnie rolled her eyes and pushed past him into his combination apartment and studio. He was the only one of the Come to Your Senses occupants who didn't have commercial space on the first floor with public access, so the group had ceded him the largest unit, which had probably at one time been two apartments.

Seth closed the door and followed her toward the kitchen. "How was your day?"

"Not bad."

"Business blooming?"

She didn't want to talk about it, though Seth was the only person in whom she'd confided the extent of her financial troubles. "Not bad."

"Uh-huh. I'll get you that beer." He squeezed her shoulder as he strode to the refrigerator; in that touch she felt his sympathy and understanding. What a complicated and frustrating man. All that great empathy for some of her feelings, a huge block against others and an even bigger one when it came to understanding and processing his own.

"So what's this song you wrote?"

Seth pulled two beers from his state-of-the-art stainless refrigerator, popped off their tops and handed her one, then hit a button on his microwave, which started whirring. "Love song."

"Really." His songs tended to be about failed relationships, thwarted dreams and other forms of misery. Ironic for a man who had everything. "Happy love? Like, 'I love you and it's great'?"

"Yeah, like that."

Bonnie took a long swig from the bottle, maybe not the greatest way to soothe her suddenly agitated stomach. Had he met someone? She wasn't really excited to hear about how much he loved someone else. "How'd that happen?"

"A friend of mine was talking about marrying this girl he met after dating one disaster after another. He got me thinking."

Bonnie took another nervous swig, shorter this time since she'd skipped lunch. "Got you thinking about what?"

"About a song I could write." The microwave dinged and he moved toward it.

Bonnie shook her head. Trying to get Seth to talk about feelings…well, why the hell *was* she trying?

"Here you go." He handed her a heaping plate of dumplings and bok choy, steam releasing a fragrance that made Bonnie's stomach lurch with hunger instead of stress.

"All for me?"

"I ate earlier. Bring it in with you. And I'm not letting you leave until you finish it. You're skeletal."

"Yes, Daddy."

He shot her a scowl over his shoulder and headed for his studio. Bonnie followed, grinning, touched that he was worried about her. She had dropped weight. At first she was thrilled. Who didn't celebrate when pounds came off? But while her new body might be fine for a magazine shoot, she wasn't out to join the scary-thin crowd, and shouldn't lose any more.

"Now." Seth seated himself at his Bösendorfer grand, having put his beer carefully down on a nearby table. The piano and his extensive array of recording and sound-engineering equipment were the only things he was meticulous about. His bedroom and bathroom looked as if a fraternity had moved in and partied for two weeks.

He rubbed his hands on his long thighs, picked out a note or two, rubbed his legs again. He was nervous. Interesting. This drill was totally familiar for both of them. He loved playing his songs, she loved hearing them; they did this all the time. Bonnie had never seen him like this.

"Ready?"

"I'm ready." She stuffed a warm pot sticker, dripping soy sauce, vinegar and chili oil, into her mouth and groaned ecstatically. Seth's mom had been an incredible cook and passed along that passion to Seth, the youngest in a family of five boys and the only one who'd been interested. "No, wait, I can't listen right now. I'm having an orgasm."

"No, you're not."

She stabbed another dumpling with her fork and stuffed it into her mouth, moaned again. "Yesh, I am."

"Nope." He started playing a classical piece. "You're *much* louder than that."

Bonnie glared at him, sitting at the piano wearing an I-*know*-you look that made her lips twitch. Did he have to say stuff like that? "You're terrible."

"You need cheering up." He switched from the classical to a ragtime number, which he seamlessly fed into smooth jazz. She waited in delight until he wove in, as he invariably did, snippets of the *Flintstones* theme, "Happy Birthday" and "God Bless America," all improvised so skillfully into the melodic and rhythmic texture that if she hadn't heard him do this over and over again, she'd say it wasn't possible.

Talent was really, really sexy. As if Seth wasn't sexy enough on his own. Worse, he was staring intently at her, half his mind on what his fingers were doing, half on the impact he knew he was making.

Deliberately she shoved another dumpling into her mouth and followed it with a fourth, going for the unappealing chipmunk-cheek approach to keeping herself sane.

"What 'bout the shong?" She chewed noisily, and found it didn't help, because he was giving her that half smile that said she was adorable. Damn him.

"You're ready now?"

"I'm ready."

He nodded. Took his hands off the keys and rested them on his lap. Bonnie swallowed her dumpling. He was *really* nervous. What was that about?

"Here we go." Soft chords filled the room, then a clear high piano melody, slow and sweet, repeated lower, then dissolving into a gentle arpeggiated accompaniment with occasional rhythmic and harmonic twists that kept the song from settling into predictability. Bonnie put down her fork, heart swelling with pride at the beauty of the music. This tune felt different than anything he'd written, yet it was Seth all over.

He lifted his head, gazing out at a point beyond the piano, expression earnest, and the closest to vulnerable Seth ever got. His smooth, rich baritone filled the room.

You wash me with colors
Blues to take away the sadness
Green for drawing down the madness
Black for smoothing over rages

White for all the pages I've filled with you
Yellow takes the fear from me
Gold can keep you here with me
Red's for cinnamon-candy love
Burning hot and sweet
You wash me with so many colors
You make me feel complete.

He held the last note, let the chord under it die into silence. Bonnie swallowed convulsively, tears she hadn't been able to hold back spilling onto her cheeks.

If he turned and looked at her now, if he gave any indication he understood what the song was saying, not about them, but just about the love it was possible for two people to have, something he'd never acknowledged before, she was going to shatter all over his carpet. He'd be picking up bits of Bonnie for the rest of his life.

Maybe that's what he deserved.

He didn't look at her. He took his hands off the keys and put them in his lap.

"Beautiful, Seth."

"I hoped you'd like it." He cleared his throat, drew his finger across the keyboard without depressing notes enough for sound.

Bonnie wasn't sure what to say next. She felt as if she were walking on eggshells with this man who was so terrified of all the same emotions he'd just put down on paper. "You haven't written many romantic songs like that."

"Nope." His fingers turned restless, picked out a tune she didn't recognize.

"Your friend talking must have...I don't know, brought out something in you?" She laughed slightly hysterically. "I don't even know what I'm trying to say."

"Yes, you do, Bonnie."

Adrenaline bolted through her. He was right. She did. But she couldn't admit it out loud, and neither could he. They'd never get over their fears, either of them. Bonnie of being hurt, Seth of losing himself. It was such a poignant, frustrating and colossal waste.

She'd been looking at online dating sites—just looking for now. But more and more often she'd find herself thinking what she might like to say in her profile. After college she'd dated a couple of guys, friends of friends, but with Seth still firmly lodged in her heart, nothing had a chance of working out. Checking out dating services was a good sign, now, that she was really getting ready to burst free of the Seth-chains and find a relationship she could truly indulge, not one defined and bound by what it wasn't and couldn't ever be.

"I guess I wanted to know why you got so sentimental about love all of a sudden."

He wrinkled his nose, finally meeting her eyes with his sultry gray ones. "It's not all of a sudden, Bon. This is the first one I was happy with, though I still think it needs something. It's not quite there."

"Who else have you played—"

"No one's heard it but you." He spoke aggressively. She held her breath, waiting, but he didn't go on, not that she really thought he would.

Don't read anything into this, girl.

Too late. She could feel her eternally, relentlessly stupid hope rising yet again. Who was she kidding? Bonnie hadn't learned a bloody thing where Seth was concerned.

She pushed a dumpling across the plate, then gave up, appetite gone. "Well, I'm not a musician, but I think it's perfect."

"Thanks." He looked up, grinning that divinely goofy grin, and their eyes locked. Held.

Oh, Seth.

"Bonnie."

"Yeah?" She knew what was coming, she felt it. Please, God, give her the strength, courage and balls, if necessary, to slap him down.

"After all this time between us…"

"Yes?" That was the last time she was going to say "Yes" until she was back safely in her apartment having *not* just gotten laid again by the love of her life.

No, he was only her first love. There would be another man, at least one, and he'd be the real love of her life. She needed to repeat that concept over and over and over until she believed it.

"I want to tell you…" Seth got up from the piano bench, crossed over and knelt in front of her, put one gentle palm to either side of her face, gazing at her earnestly.

Bonnie took her hand off the plate in her lap because it was shaking so much her fork was rattling. *Don't do this. Not tonight.*

"I care for you a lot."

Oh, help.

"Seth, you know I care for you, too." She tried to keep the god-awful vulnerability out of her eyes and voice.

"You are a really great person. I just think… I want to say that…" His struggle was clearly painful, but she couldn't help him. She wouldn't. He took in a huge breath. "I'm…glad you're my friend."

What the—

Friend?

Friend?

For God's sake. She was suddenly and thoroughly furious. Lifting the plate, elbows out, which effectively removed his hands from her face, she shoveled in two dumplings at once, chewing viciously. "Yup. You 'n me, BFFs forever."

Seth sat back on his heels, looking frustrated. "I'm not good at this feelings crap. I just want you to know you're still…special to me."

This time Bonnie waited to speak until her mouth was empty.

"I know, Seth. We've been over that. We've been over that again and again and again. I get it. You are special to me, too." She put the plate on the table next to her chair and stood abruptly. "I really appreciate you sharing that song with me. It was wonderful. And I'm going to go now because I'm exhausted and it's been a long—"

"Bonnie." As he got to his feet she caught an all too rare glimpse of the bewildered boy who lived inside him, the one who was stomped down 24/7 by his father whenever he showed any sign of spirit or sensitivity. Whatever Seth had to say now, she didn't want to hear it unless he was finally admitting that he loved her and how about getting married? Since that wasn't going to happen…

"I've gotta go. Thanks for the dumplings. They were fantastic."

"Yeah. Sure." He nodded, stuffed his hands into his back pockets. "No problem."

Bonnie moved toward the door, sick to death of conversations over, under and around any solution to their stalemate. The past several months had brought back too many feelings and with them the problems she'd hoped were finally dead, or at least in permanent hibernation.

What a joke to have thought she could bear living so close to him, seeing him so often, being in these intimate situations time and time again.

If only the rest of her life were going well, and she didn't feel this undercurrent of neediness and fear that being with

Seth did so much to dispel. She had to stop looking to him for answers to problems only she could solve.

"Take care." She managed a bright smile at his door and gave him a brief hug, pulling away when his arms tried to hold her longer. She was proud of herself for leaving, keeping her feelings hidden, not showing him how close she'd been to teetering over the edge once more.

If only she hadn't said that same thing to herself so many, many times before....

4

Blood Pressure: Moderately High

"So…Mary Jo was constantly touching you and making suggestive remarks right in the sales department. But no other employees ever saw her doing this."

"Yeah. Uh-huh." Bob Whatsisname nodded. He was slouching in a chair in front of Melissa's desk, one of the most stunning men she'd ever seen, the kind that turned heads in the street. Her office was tiny, but since she often had to have confidential interviews, she did have four walls and a door. "I mean, yeah, she did, and no—no one saw."

"And after you asked her to stop…"

"She wouldn't."

Melissa sighed. "Bob, are you aware that this is your third sexual harassment complaint against store personnel in as many years? We could never prove the first two against Susan and Jess, and there has never been an employee who has been harassed even twice before you. We've transferred you both times in order to—"

"What does that have to do with anything?" He jutted his perfectly square jaw. "You think I'm making this up?"

"No, no, of course not." *Maybe.*

"Okay, tell you what. You come downstairs sometime incognito and watch. You'll see."

Melissa leaned back and scratched the bridge of her nose delicately with one finger, briefly considering using the middle one. "I don't think that would be the best use of my time."

"Well, how else are you going to believe me? No one ever sees it. But it happens."

Melissa sighed. She could certainly understand how some women might be tempted. Bob was not only handsome enough to stop traffic, but clearly spent every second of his free time working out. And wasn't that a life well lived? It was tempting to think this was more about him and his need to be wildly attractive to everyone than it was about any women needing to touch his manflesh. Melissa's boss, Barbara, knew Mary Jo, the woman he was accusing, and said she was happily married and the mother of two adorable kids. She couldn't imagine Mary Jo risking her job for a piece of male meat—Barbara's words, not Melissa's.

"Is there any chance that the women, in this case Mary Jo, are just being friendly and that you are misinterpreting—"

"How friendly do you have to be to clamp down on my ass and squeeze like it's a ripe melon?"

Melissa coughed so she wouldn't giggle. "Earlier you said she 'touched' you. But now it's 'clamp and squeeze'?"

She was doing everything possible not to laugh, thinking tragic thoughts, focusing on her new blood-pressure-friendly office decor: the Zen garden—a wooden box with sand raked in patterns among carefully placed stones; the metal figure of a cat stretching—the ultimate in luxuriant relaxation; her pictures—endless peaceful mountains, Gretchen and Ted, Mom and Dad....

All day she'd been having a terrible time calming down. The prospect of meeting Jack later had her in a state that would give her doctor apoplexy. She was doing the right thing for her sister's wedding. She just wished she knew what would be expected of her for these pictures, and how she'd be able to keep her physical reaction to Jack under control.

She'd get the chance to talk to Barbara soon; Barbara would be able to put this all in perspective.

"I don't know what words to use to describe what happened. I don't care." He was pouting now. "It just sucked. Like I'm burger meat or something."

"You're not burger meat, Bob." Well, there was a phrase she'd never imagined herself saying to anyone. "You're a valuable employee, one of our best salespeople. We will definitely take this seriously."

"Yeah. Good. Thanks. Thanks a lot. I'd hate to have to transfer again."

"I understand. Okay. So…" She stood up. He still sat there. She waited a beat. *Hello, Bob?* "Was there anything else?"

"I just want to say how you're really great." He grinned at her warmly, showing—of course—perfect white teeth.

"Oh. Thank you." She kept her voice brisk. Where was this going? "I appreciate that."

"I feel like I can come to you with anything."

"Absolutely." She smiled. *Okay, Bob, you can leave now. You're giving me the creeps.* "That's my job."

"Yeah. I guess. But you do it like you mean it. Not like most people."

"I do mean it." Most of the time. Not so much now. It was four o'clock. She was leaving to meet Jack in an hour. She wanted time to talk to Barbara. She wanted Bob to go away. She didn't think he was coming on to her, but he was definitely behaving oddly.

"Okay. Well." He rubbed his hands on his pants and stood up, extended a perfectly manicured hand for her to shake. "I gotta go."

"Enjoy your evening."

"You, too, Melissa." He threw her a grateful look and left the office.

Honestly. She had serious and legitimate problems to deal with: a manager who'd been with the company nearly two decades and was now suspected of having a substance-abuse problem, employees not getting along with their colleagues, the company struggling over the need to keep its most talented workers and at the same time cut back benefits to balance the budget. She did not want to spend this much time on Bob's melons. And yet the mess was in her lap now.

She gathered paperwork for her meeting with Barbara and headed around the corner to the bigwig offices on the west wall of the building, which faced Puget Sound. They were going to discuss Bob Whatsisname and a new hire for the store in Ann Arbor, but Melissa hoped they'd have a few extra minutes to talk about Jack.

"Knock knock?" She pushed open Barbara's door, ajar as usual.

"Hey, Melissa, come in." Barbara grinned her welcome, blond hair carefully arranged in waves to her shoulders, makeup perfect as always. Today she wore a blue suit that fitted her carefully preserved figure to perfection. She was one of those women whose age was impossible to pinpoint. Melissa would put her somewhere between fifty and sixty.

Barbara had taken a risk on Melissa, hiring her straight out of college, and Melissa had spent the past three years working her butt off so as not to disappoint her mentor.

As trust grew between them, their excellent professional relationship had gradually ventured into the personal. Barbara's husband had left her for a woman half her age, deciding out of the blue at fifty-five, right after retiring, that he wanted children. Through all that horror, Melissa had only seen Barbara in tears once—the day she and Frank decided he could take better care of their dog, Stuyvesant.

To say Melissa admired her boss was an understatement. Melissa had always felt like an alien in her family of passive peaceful personalities. In Barbara she'd found a woman much like herself, with strong attitudes and opinions, and a dedication to the goal of women being independent and self-sufficient.

Barbara had been instrumental in rescuing Melissa from a difficult time after graduation when she'd been in a bit of a panic, without a clear career path, feeling pressure to marry as her mother had done and many of her friends were doing. She firmly resisted, even though her then-boyfriend, Trevor, was a total sweetheart who would have been happy to settle down. Barbara had taken Melissa under her wing and shown her for the first time a basic truth more people needed to learn: it was never wrong to be the person you were.

"Hi, Barbara. How was the trip?" Barbara had been traveling most of the week, and had been swamped the day before, so they hadn't had much chance to talk.

"Long, tiring but productive. How are things with you?"

"Crazy week." She went over the Ann Arbor hire with Barbara, and brought her up to speed on Bob. "It's certainly possible he's telling the truth."

Barbara watched her keenly. "But you don't think so."

"I can't really call it, but something doesn't feel right."

"Go with that." Barbara tented her fingers. "Of course,

we have to get evidence and document our steps, but you can always trust your instinct. Let's get Mary Jo in here, see how Bob might have misunderstood. Maybe he's exaggerating or he's making it up, which gets my vote. He's one of our best salespeople, though, isn't he?"

Melissa nodded. "Two years running. People fall all over themselves to buy from him."

"Gorgeous, too, huh?"

"Unbelievable."

"They're always trouble. We'll keep on it and see what happens." She plunked her elbows on her desk. "So tell me how you've been doing on your new reduced schedule. Happy, relaxed, going crazy?"

"Yes." She grinned when Barbara laughed. "Though I do have an opportunity for something…different."

She outlined the situation, leaving out the part where she'd been awake half the night thinking about Jack and the other half dreaming about him, bizarre dreams that ran from arousing to disturbing.

Barbara listened, frowning more and more deeply. "I'm not loving the sound of this guy."

Melissa's stomach lurched. "He's…something."

"A manipulator. Is he attractive?"

She barely kept herself from shouting, *God, yes!* "Uh-huh."

"Your type?"

"Not in the slightest."

"Hmm." Barbara picked up a pencil. "But you think he's hot."

"He *is* hot. What I think is irrelevant."

She laughed. "Good one. So what's your feeling? Can he be trusted?"

"I don't know yet. His friends were great. I liked both of them and they obviously trust him."

"Men or women?"

"Both women."

Barbara dismissed Angela and Bonnie with a wave. "You don't know them, or what their agenda might be."

Agenda? She couldn't see Angela or Bonnie with agendas, but then Barbara was right. She knew nothing about either of them. "True."

"They could want you to model for Jack because he's been bugging them to do it, and it's a hellish procedure and they want him off their backs."

"Oh." Her leg started jiggling. "That's possible, yes."

"Or they could be in on some money-making scheme with him. Identity theft." She shook her head mournfully. "You really have no idea."

"No." She felt a churning in her chest, an overwhelming restlessness, and had to force her leg to be still.

Barbara shrugged. "Or it could all be completely legit. But you can't assume that."

"He says he shows at the Unko Gallery and that they're interested in whatever series he wants to use me for."

"*He* says."

"I saw the gallery brochure. Jack was in it."

"Hmm. That is impressive." Barbara frowned, as if she didn't like finding out Jack might be legit. "But it says nothing about his character."

Melissa released her hair from its clasp, put it back in. "I have to say, I was flattered he wanted to photograph me, but you're right, I have no idea what's really going on, or what he's after."

"Right." Barbara leaned back in her executive chair, tapping the pencil against her cheek. "One seldom does, though with men you can be sure they're after *one* thing anyway."

Melissa's leg started jiggling again; she was ashamed

of the thrill that had gone through her. "He won't be getting anything but pictures from me."

"Good for you. Once they get sex, they own you, or think they do."

"Ha." Melissa chewed at her lip. She wasn't sure she agreed with that one. Her father had adored her mother. Ted adored Gretchen. "Or you own them. Not sure which is worse."

"Good point. Unko is a positive sign, I have to say. But tonight I'd skip the drink and go right to the photo shoot. That way you send this guy a clear message up front that you're only in this for business."

"Yes. I will." Melissa stood, relieved to be moving. Barbara, as usual, had hit on the perfect solution. Melissa's brain had been muddled by her attraction to Jack. She'd approach their meeting tonight the way she did any other business meeting. She'd been attracted to men she worked with in the past. That didn't mean she had to fall apart around them.

"You were kind of hit by this guy, huh?"

Melissa took in a long breath, wanting to deny it. "A little rattled, yes."

"I can tell." Barbara pushed her chair back, got up and came around to perch on the other side of her desk. "You and I have come such a long way toward finding out who we are and what we want from our lives. When we're good and ready, we'll go looking for the romance we deserve. But neither of us is going to weaken and fall for someone just because he's conveniently around."

"Amen to that. If I wanted convenient, I could have married Trevor." She shuddered, thinking of what life with her college boyfriend would have been like. Get up. Go to work. Come home. Eat dinner. Watch TV. Go to bed.

Repeat. Like the life her father had. Melissa wanted so much more. With a man or without.

Barbara rose and put her hand on Melissa's shoulder, gazing earnestly into her face. "Tell me what your instinct says about him. I mean in man-woman terms."

Melissa couldn't look Barbara in the eye. Her instinct about Jack was as complex as her erotic and/or surreal dreams about him. Or as his pictures. Celebration to self-destruction. Love to loneliness. "Only that I should be careful."

"Ah." Barbara folded her arms across her chest, lips thinned in a disapproving line. "Then you should be, Melissa. Very, very careful."

"HEARD YOU FOUND HER." Seth walked into the upstairs apartment that the group had set aside to use as a common area. The five Come to Your Senses tenants divided the extra rent and contributed toward keeping the shared refrigerator and cupboards stocked with drinks and snack items. They'd furnished it in dorm-room chic, with salvaged and no-longer-wanted furniture. Seth helped himself to a beer and sat down on the worn sofa next to Jack's favorite chair, an old rust-colored wingback donated by Bonnie's grandmother. "You're seeing her tonight."

"News travels fast."

Seth laughed somewhat bitterly. "Dude, with Bonnie and Angela around, there is no such thing as privacy."

Jack nodded, surprised at his friend's irritation. Small group, good friends, close quarters, what did he expect? "Something bugging you?"

"Nah." Seth opened his beer, chugged down a few long swallows.

"Just being pissy for the fun of it, huh?"

"Sure." He drained his beer, crumpled the can. Something was definitely bugging him. Seth wasn't a big drinker. His dad had been, and that was all the excuse his son had needed to be the opposite. "So you're finally getting this girl in your studio."

"Yup." Jack knew better than to push. If Seth wanted to say anything he would, but it would take patience to get him to that point. Since Jack was meeting Melissa in fifteen minutes, Seth might be out of luck. Though, given that Bonnie had looked like a thunderstorm this morning, Jack would bet the two of them were frustrating the hell out of each other. Again. Jack wanted to give them both a wake-up smack. "We're trying out some test photos."

"Yeah? What's this series? Woman as corkscrew? Girl with dying monkey? Female as coffee table?"

Jack chuckled, because otherwise he'd get angry, too, and Seth was just throwing crap at him because he couldn't deal with his own. "Yeah, something like that."

"Seriously, man, what's this one about? You went looking for this woman for months. You've got to have a pretty good idea." He stood up and grabbed another beer. "You want one?"

"I'm fine." He rested his head back on the chair. "This series is different."

"Yeah? How?" Seth clearly just wanted to talk. Jack felt for him, but the guy was being a dope when he could just ask for help with his "Bonnie" issue. Yeah, easy for Jack to say. He wasn't exactly Mr. Share, either, something a lot of guys with deadbeat fathers probably had in common.

"I started out wanting to make a statement about how pop culture sexualizes women while society wants them to stay virgins."

Seth opened the second beer. "How would you show that?"

"In a couple of ways. One, a series of body parts. Separated from the whole, totally abstract. Chin, breast, ankle, as if they were separate bricks of a building. Woman as sum total of her parts. Then I'm thinking I'd move on to stories. Eve. Venus. Catherine the Great. Still don't have all the images nailed."

"At least you *know* what you want to do."

"Songwriting giving you trouble?"

"Fits."

Interesting. Jack had been around Seth when he was composing in college, and he'd never seen a less tortured creative process, which drove him crazy, because his own was all about torture. "What's the subject?"

"Love. Romance." Seth gulped half his second beer and sighed. "I don't even know why I'm trying to write this crap."

"Oh, come on." Seth could be incredibly dense. "I sure as hell do. Her name is Bo—"

"Don't start with me, man."

Jack shook his head. "Seriously, dude, for a smart guy…"

"Hi."

The two men turned in unison. Demi Anderson, the mysterious woman who'd taken over Caroline's massage studio, stood in the doorway. Dark hair pulled back in a simple ponytail, she was wearing her usual uniform of black shirt, black pants and an impenetrable expression. Jack thought she must be painfully shy. Bonnie thought she was a bitch. No one knew for sure since she kept to herself and interacted with the four of them in increments that revealed very little.

"Hey, Demi." Jack gestured her into the room. "Pull up an ugly chair."

"Can I get you a beer?" Seth half rose from the couch. Demi shook her head no. "Soda?"

"No, thanks. I was just wondering if one of you could help me."

"Sure." Jack stood and glanced at his watch. "If it's quick. I'm meeting someone downstairs in five minutes."

"I'm not doing anything," Seth said. "What do you need?"

"I had a new massage table delivered, too heavy for me to move by myself. Can you help me carry it into the studio?"

"Sure." Seth finished his beer and three-pointed it into the trash can across the room.

Show off.

"Thanks, I appreciate it." A rare smile lit her face, revealing a dimple in her right cheek. She should do that more often.

"So how come we never see you around?" Seth put his hands on his hips, towering over her. "You live with us, but you never hang out with us."

Oh, subtle, Seth.

Demi looked startled. "Uh. Well. I guess I'm just…"

"Don't listen to him." Jack moved toward her. "You do what's comfortable for you."

"It's nothing personal. But thanks, Jack." Demi seemed more at ease with him than the others, which his ego didn't mind at all. She was very attractive, very stylish and sexy. Not to mention that her body, which he'd had the happy occasion to see in a skin-tight jogging outfit a few times, was stunning.

If he hadn't met Melissa, he might be tempted to—

Jack nearly tripped over nothing on the carpet. What the *hell* was that? If Demi didn't live with them he'd be tempted to ask her out. That's all he should have been thinking. Melissa had nothing to do with this.

Feeling on edge, he followed Seth and Demi downstairs. Melissa had been popping into way too many of his thoughts recently. He did want her, and was pretty sure if she were forced to confess, she'd admit she wanted him, too, though she'd undoubtedly agree that acting on that desire was a bad idea. Which meant the two of them in his studio in close proximity, Melissa wearing some of the outfits—or non-outfits—he was considering, would be like gasoline and a lighted match working together to prevent fires.

He'd chosen her because she had that quality he was after, the serenity, the poise, the stillness that translated so well into photos. In person, though, she had an electric edge that fascinated him. He'd planned out some shots for her, but he had a feeling that until he got behind the lens with Melissa in front of it, he wouldn't know exactly what he'd get.

In the building's foyer, Seth and Demi were already busy hauling in a large box that looked more awkward than heavy, both laughing at something Seth had said, while Bonnie peered at them from her shop window.

Jack gritted his teeth. He should talk to Bonnie, get tougher than he had been, than any of them had been, and tell her Seth was not going to change, that it was time to abandon hope and rescue some kind of life for herself. She was too sweet, loving and sexual to be alone. Some lucky guy out there deserved all Bonnie had to give. She needed to make herself understand that Seth didn't.

"Jack?"

Melissa. Jack jerked away from Bonnie's painfully wistful expression, then told himself to chill. He didn't want to come across as eager as…he was. "Hey, Melissa, how's it going?"

She walked toward him, slender body wrapped in a sleeveless minidress, belted at the waist with a swath of the same silvery-gray fabric. On her feet were ballet-style flats with straps that wound up her ankle. Casual chic, and amazingly sexy. "I'm fine. How—"

"You certainly are." He shook her hand, noting the scent that arrived with her, herbal and fresh, maybe a touch of citrus. He'd caught it when she was standing near him the day before; smelling her again was incredibly intimate. He didn't want to think how tempted he'd feel with a drink or two in him. "You ready? There's a bar down the street that serves—"

"I'd like to skip the drink if it's okay with you." She was back to her usual calm today, no fear, no uncertainty, gaze direct and pure. He found himself missing her fluster. She'd been even more magnificent pissed at him. "I'd rather go straight to the picture-taking."

"Sure." That suited him fine. He was dying to get her on camera, dying to see where his planned shots would take him. He hadn't been this excited about a project in a long time. "Have you eaten? Do you want anything from Angela's before we start?"

"Oh." She slid a sideways glance into the shop. "Sure, that would be great. I am hungry."

He was hyperaware of her nearness as she followed him into the bakery, how she stood—strong and still— how her head came to his chin. He was also aware of how much he wanted to touch her. This was going to be a hell of a photo series. Good chemistry with his models tended to turn into good pictures.

Angela wasn't there, but he ordered two carrot muffins, two ginger cranberry scones and a couple of sodas from her student helper, Scott. With his piercings and jet-black hair he looked like a gang member, but was actually a nice and hardworking kid. A hardworking kid who couldn't take his eyes off Melissa, not that Jack could blame him.

"Does Angela make wedding cakes?" Melissa spoke beside him, shifting her fabric bag from one shoulder to the other. "Or would she arrange cupcakes on tiers like a cake for a wedding?"

"You can order either one." Scott handed Jack his bakery bag and cans of soda. "When's your wedding?"

"It's my sister's. End of the month. Can Angela do it that soon?"

"I'll have to check with her, but probably, yeah."

Jack grinned. "Angela can do anything. Your sister came to the right place."

"Oh." Melissa looked pained. "Actually it was my idea. She wanted to make her own cake. But since I'd like to eat some of it…"

Jack chuckled, at the same time wondering what the dynamic was between Melissa and her sister and why Melissa seemed to be doing all the wedding planning. "You can't go wrong with anything here."

"I found that out last night." She gestured to the cupcakes. "I tried three different kinds, just to taste, and nearly ate all of them."

Scott pushed an order form across the counter. "Fill this out. She'll let you know if there are any problems with the date."

She thanked him. Scott was still smiling like a smitten puppy as Jack escorted her out of the bakery, feeling ridiculously smug that she was with him. "How did you get stuck organizing your sister's wedding?"

"I wouldn't call it stuck."

"Most people would."

"I chose to do it. Gretchen is…" Melissa frowned. "She's not very demanding. I mean, she's sort of passive, takes the easy route even if it's not what she really wants.

I thought if I did it the way our mom would have, it would mean more to her."

"Would have? Your mom's gone?"

"When I was thirteen. Uterine cancer."

"I'm sorry." He was surprised by a rush of protectiveness. He knew what it was like to lose a parent, though his father hadn't died, just ditched the family and all his responsibilities. For a second he considered telling her that, to establish a connection, then stopped himself. Only a very few people particularly close to him knew about his dad. Melissa wasn't in that league.

"I want Gretchen to have a really beautiful wedding without breaking the bank, not something she and her fiancé cobble together last-minute. So wherever I can help, I'm helping. I was thinking of having Bonnie do the flowers, too. She's very talented and her prices are reasonable."

"She is. We also have a musician upstairs if she wants an original song, and a massage therapist if she gets bridal jitters. That's Seth and Demi. You saw them moving in the big box."

"Hey." Melissa turned to him, eyes alight, nearly making Jack drop the bakery bag. "You should advertise Come to Your Senses as a total wedding package."

"Not a bad idea." He recovered from his clumsiness and opened the door to his shop, ushered her in and through to his studio, annoyed by how much she unsettled him. His usual female targets were chatty women full of life and open sexuality. He responded instinctively to their energy and passion, knew how to handle them, how to tease, how far to go and when to pull back. Women like this, calm and utterly self-possessed, gave him no cues, no rules, no road map. Apparently he'd gotten too used to his standard operating procedure.

"Nice." She was standing in the center of the studio,

looking around, her silvery-gray dress the perfect complement to the black and white elements around her. The white canvas backdrop unrolled halfway across the floor, white walls and black equipment—tripods, umbrella lights for focus, soft boxes for more diffuse lighting. He watched her, wanting to capture her simply today, posed in front of the stark white background, bright lights exposing any potential flaws. Though if she had any, they were well hidden. "Where should I change?"

He pointed to the bathroom and fiddled unnecessarily with his equipment until she emerged minutes later wearing snug black capris and a clingy black top. "This outfit okay? You said black…"

"Fine." For today. She'd be wearing various different costumes in the final series. Many of which were almost not there.

"So." She stood, hands at her sides, body starkly silhouetted in front of the white backdrop. "How long have you been at this?"

"Photography? Since I was a kid taking pictures of my family, then for the school newspaper." He walked closer, focusing on her, his eyes as the lens, noting her lines, her angles, then reached for his trusty Nikon to let it do the same. "My heroes ranged from Walter Iooss, who shot for *Sports Illustrated,* to fine-art photographer Bill Brandt. I've always been interested in photographing people, which is good because people will pay to get their pictures taken. Objects not so much."

She'd been examining his wind machine, but at his last comment, she turned and smiled. *Click.* He got her. *Click.* And her startled expression. *Click.* And the beautiful, embarrassed laughter that followed.

He started circling her, taking more shots. Her laughter quieted. "Jack, I don't know what to do."

"Whatever you want."

"What I want is to sit down and have you point that thing at someone else."

"Whatever you want except that. Try some yoga? In very slow motion, half the speed you usually do it, maybe slower."

"Okay." She nodded, lips compressed, then took a deep breath and closed her eyes. Opening them, she began the sun salute, lifting her arms, swan-diving forward…

He photographed her, kid in a candy store, eager finally to get as close as he wanted, to capture all the shots he craved. He moved around her, thinking of his first set of images, waiting for his instinct to kick in and dissect her into parts and angles, textures and colors and shapes. He would pounce in that instant, on the pose, the perfect dis-embodiment of womanhood.

It didn't happen. He focused, shot, zoomed in and out, took a muffin, scone and soda break and tried again. He got the turn of her ankle, the curve of her hip, the deli-cate push of her collarbone, just the way he'd envisioned. But no matter how far he tried to remove himself, to keep the pictures cold, mechanical, it was always her, always Melissa. Not woman, not a study of the body, but Melis-sa's ankles, Melissa's hips, Melissa's collarbone, breasts, smooth cheeks, tempting lips.

He started to sweat. When he looked at the textures of her body and clothes, all he could think about was how much he wanted to touch them. The concepts in his mind were not about art, not about images, not about philoso-phy, sociology. They were all about…

Sex.

Photography was his craft, his art, his profession, one of the sacred aspects of his life in which he had absolute

confidence. Right now he felt like Don Juan in bed with
the woman of his dreams, not able to get it up.

Melissa had everything he needed for this series. She
was beautiful, alluring, and radiated spiritual calm. He had
to find some way to take pictures of her without spending every minute distracted by how much he wanted her.

Half an hour later he gave up, disappointed and frustrated. Since April he'd waited for this moment, convinced
Melissa was something special, that she'd bring to his camera exactly what he'd been looking for to launch this next
step of his career, an exhibit that would land him notice,
buyers and prestige. In short: success.

Now, as she stood at ease, watching him keenly, obviously able to sense his mood, Jack was horribly afraid
that he'd fail.

5

Blood Pressure: Moderately Normal

"Try this." Melissa handed her sister a carefully cut piece of one of Angela's chocolate cupcakes with raspberry frosting. They were sitting in the cozy kitchen of Gretchen and Ted's adorable house in the suburb of Ballard. The couple had scraped together a down payment from Ted's salary as a construction worker and Gretchen's as an administrative assistant for the phone company. "You will go nuts."

"Ooh, it looks gorgeous." Her sister took the fragment and popped it into her mouth. Her eyes closed. A rapturous expression spread over her face. "Oh, my God. Where did you get that and why did you only give me a little piece?"

"Because there are other flavors." She produced the bakery box from her lap and handed over a piece of a yellow chocolate chip cupcake with chocolate frosting. Then white cake with strawberry frosting. Then lemon with lemon buttercream. By that time her sister was reduced to moans of pleasure. "Not bad, huh?"

"Incredible." Gretchen blissfully licked frosting off her fingers. "You *have* to tell me where this place is."

"A Taste for All Pleasures in the Come to Your Senses

building on Capitol Hill, corner of Olive and Broadway. Here's Angela's card." She dug it out of the box and handed it over. "Three or four tiers of these would be perfect for your wedding cake. You and Ted can choose whatever kinds you want."

"Oh." Gretchen took off her glasses, without which she was half-blind, and polished them absently. "I was planning to make—"

"Wait." Melissa held up her hand, bursting with her news. "It gets better. There's a florist there, Bonnie Blooms. Those flowers I gave you? Guess how much they cost."

Gretchen put her glasses back on and turned to them, still blooming freshly on the butcher-block counter by her cheerfully curtained window three days later. "Forty? Forty-five?"

"Eighteen and change."

"Whoa!" Her narrow blue eyes shot wide. "You are kidding me."

"Nope." Melissa grinned triumphantly, nearly shaking with excitement. She felt like a fairy godmother. "You could get a bouquet for the ceremony and decorate the tables for next to nothing."

"Oh." Gretchen bit her lip. "But Ted and I were thinking we'd be fine with—"

"And." Melissa knew she was interrupting, but she couldn't wait to blab about her prize catch. "I got you a photographer."

"Melissa." Gretchen looked stricken. "I told you we were going to hand out disposable cameras and let people—"

"I know, but this is so much better."

Her sister folded her hands tightly on the colorful quilt-like tablecloth she'd sewn herself, looking close to tears.

"We're saving our money for the honeymoon. We can't afford a professional."

"This one you can. Know how much he charges?" Melissa held up her thumb and index finger in a circle. "Big fat zero."

"That's impossible. How did you manage that?"

"Simple." Melissa shrugged airily, enjoying every second of her surprise. "I'm trading him favors."

Gretchen gasped. "You're seeing someone? You didn't tell me!"

Melissa made an emphatic no-way gesture with both arms. "I'm not seeing him."

"Melissa." Gretchen looked as if she'd seen the devil himself. "If you are sleeping with some guy just to get me—"

"Ha!" This time she laughed outright. As if! "*No,* I'm not doing that, either."

She told Gretchen about the whole situation. Now that she had her reaction to Jack and her first modeling experience under control, neatly dissected by her and Barbara into manageable cause-and-effect emotions, it seemed silly she'd ever gotten so uptight about it.

"Oh, my gosh." Gretchen was shaking her head. "Wait until I tell Maureen that pictures of you will be at the Unko. She'll die."

"Who knows how far it will get. The important thing is, you've got your photographer. *And* your cake and flowers." She got up and hugged her sister. "I was so sure the perfect wedding couldn't be planned in five weeks. I am so happy to be wrong!"

Her sister hugged her back, then pulled away, her face not as wreathed in bliss as Melissa had hoped. "This is so great what you're trying to do for us. But…I don't want you to have to go to all this trouble."

Melissa waved her objections away. "It hasn't been any trouble, sweetie. I really wanted you to have the wedding of your dreams, the kind we talked about with Mom when we were girls, not some scraped-together mess. You both deserve so much better. And who knows, this might be the only Weber wedding, so we might as well do it up."

Gretchen scoffed as if the idea was beyond ridiculous. "Come on. You'll find someone. Look at you, you're gorgeous, talented, amazing. You haven't found anyone because you're burying yourself in too much activity and not enough dating."

"Marriage isn't what I want." Melissa's voice came out sharper than she'd intended. She made herself breathe, squeezing her sister's forearm in apology. "Not now anyway."

"So you say. I bet you—"

"Change my mind when I meet the right one, I know, I know. You and Dad always say that. But I'm different from you two."

"Okay. Well…" Gretchen's thin brows drew together; she twisted her mouth, the way she did when she was struggling with something she didn't want to say.

"What is it?" Melissa's knee started jiggling.

"This is wonderful, what you've done, Melissa. Really. But before I say anything, I should run it all past Ted…."

"Oh." Melissa was so taken aback her leg went still. What on earth would Ted find objectionable about a perfect wedding? In the next second, she had a duh! moment. Gretchen was no Bridezilla. She and Ted did everything together. Of course she'd want him to feel he had a say in their plans. "Absolutely. Take your time. Sort of take your time. Take a little tiny bit of time. We don't have much."

"I will." Gretchen smiled in relief. "He'll be back from his run soon. I'll talk to him."

"Perfect."

"Oh, let me show you my dress. It's nearly finished." Gretchen jumped up and disappeared into the family room where she kept her sewing machine. She and their mother had shared a passion for needlework skills. Melissa had taken a few courses in sewing and pottery and painting, but she didn't have that innate talent, and she definitely lacked the required patience.

Moments later Gretchen returned, proudly displaying the elegant silk sheath on a hanger, very nearly finished.

"It's so beautiful, Gretchen." Melissa rose from her chair and put a hand to her chest. The dress was gorgeous, simple lines with an off-the-shoulder neckline. Gretchen had embroidered earth tones onto floral lace appliques and sewed them around the hem and bodice. "My God, you're going to be a bride!"

"I know. I can hardly believe it." Gretchen gazed tenderly at the dress, probably imagining the look in Ted's eyes as he watched her walk down the makeshift aisle in their dad's backyard.

For one strange second, Melissa felt a pang of...what? Not envy, certainly. But something. Maybe the poignancy of realizing they were never going to be little girls together again.

She didn't much like the feeling, whatever it was. After admiring the dress for a little longer, she got busy putting the leftover cupcakes back in the box and taking plates and coffee mugs to the sink.

"I'm going over to Come to Your Senses this afternoon for my next *modeling* assignment." She rolled her eyes, but couldn't keep the grin off her face or the butterflies out of her chest. It was really exciting being part of a creative process. "Let me know when Ted gives his okay, and I can order the cake and flowers."

"Oh." Gretchen hung the dress carefully over the top of the door, her blissful expression gone. "Well...today might be too soon."

Melissa frowned, drumming her fingers on her thigh. How long would it take Ted to say yes? Granted, she and her sister were totally different, but even Gretchen had to realize they were playing with a fraction of the time needed to plan weddings, and it was a miracle that Melissa had landed Jack. They needed to sew up Bonnie and Angela, too. "Okay, but these people are really good. They're bound to be booked fast."

"Yes. Sure." Gretchen looked nervous, pulling at her blunt strawberry-blond bob, the same hairstyle she'd had since she was a girl. "Soon. I promise."

"Is something wrong, Gretch?" Melissa walked over and touched her sister's arm. "You guys aren't having trouble, are you?"

"No, no." Gretchen forced a laugh. "No, not at all, we can't wait to be married."

Melissa's mind whirled through other possibilities. "Oh, my God, is it money? I didn't say so, but all of this is my wedding gift to you. You won't have to pay for anything."

"Oh, Melissa." Gretchen's blue eyes filled with tears that didn't seem entirely happy. "That is so sweet. It's really...so sweet. Thank you."

"You're welcome." Melissa hugged her sister, feeling helpless that she couldn't fix whatever was bothering Gretchen. "Mom would have wanted you to have a beautiful wedding, and I do, too."

Gretchen's face went still until her lip started trembling. "I wish she could have known Ted."

Melissa grabbed a tissue from the box by the sink and handed it over. "I wish a lot of things had been different. But they weren't."

She spoke gently, but firmly. Gretchen tended to assume the victim role, and Melissa wished with all her heart she could get her to upgrade her attitude. She hated seeing her sister suffer.

"You're right." Gretchen wiped her eyes. "As usual."

Melissa paused as she gathered up her bag. For a second she thought she'd caught a bite in Gretchen's tone.

Impossible. Gretchen didn't have a bitchy bone in her body. "I have to go. Modeling calls."

Gretchen summoned a watery smile. "You go, sister. Give Gisele Bündchen a little competition."

"Ha! She's all but history." Melissa grinned and kissed her sister's damp cheek, heart aching for her sadness now and for the sadness they'd shared so young when they lost Mom. Maybe that was all that was bothering Gretchen. It would be completely understandable. At every crucial mother-daughter milestone they missed their sweet unflappable mom all the more, and there weren't many bigger occasions than a wedding. "I'll talk to you later, sweetie. Let me know as soon as Ted okays the cake and flowers."

She hugged her sister again at the door and headed for her car, glancing around the block of modest homes, suffering another pang at her sister's neat, settled life. Honestly. Melissa would go nuts with boredom if they traded places. Barbara would say the emotional jabs were vestiges of her old self, and that it was okay to acknowledge them before she pushed them away and kept looking forward.

On her way back into Seattle she felt her excitement rising—but not her anxiety. During their shoot on Friday, she'd kept herself firmly in check. As a result, whatever outrageous chemistry had blossomed between them on their first meeting had become manageable. Jack had seemed tense and grumpy photographing her. Who could go nuts for a tense grump? Not Melissa.

After he had finished they'd looked at the shots together. Melissa had been surprised and pleased. The photos weren't really even of her, just parts of her. Her ankle, for instance. Who could get all heated up about an ankle? Though with Jack's skill, her ankle had seemed a mysterious and fascinating place of shadows and angles. All of which went to show, reassuringly, that to Jack her body was simply art, and if she thought of it the same way, she'd remain in control of her emotions and reactions, and today's shoot would be nothing but fun. Calm fun. Goddess-of-Serenity fun, like playing dress-up with her personality.

Thanks be to Barbara, setting her firmly back on the right track. Melissa had done the rest herself.

She parked at her apartment and had a quick, light lunch so she wouldn't bloat or gurgle during their session. She kept the same clothes—khaki shorts and a scoop-necked green top—because Jack said he'd have something for her to change into. Would she be an Egyptian goddess? A kitchen wench? A stalk of celery? Who knew what was cooking in Jack's brilliant brain? Melissa would continue to learn and experience new things, that was the best part.

She walked over to Come to Your Senses, arms swinging. This month was Seattle's best, temperatures hovering around eighty, good breezes off Puget Sound, not much rain. August was good. Life was good. She bounded up the steps and down the building's long hall, waving at Bonnie as she passed. Didn't the woman ever take a day off?

"Hello?" Jack wasn't in his shop, which was officially closed Sundays, though he'd left the door unlocked for her. She walked through to the back. "Jack?"

No answer. Was he in the restroom? His studio door was ajar; she peeked inside. He was probably—

Oh, my lord.

Jack. Shirtless. Earbuds in his ears. Wires running down his bare chest.

What a chest. Wide shoulders, muscled body, not pumped to rigor mortis but definitely male.

Definitely.

She pulled her head back and collapsed against the wall, eyes closed, fanning herself. How was she supposed to regard Jack as nothing but a professional knowing he looked like *that* under his shirt?

Darn it. Melissa hadn't come here to be rattled again. She'd come here to be peaceful and in control and learn a lot about posing and photography and how artists create. So far all she'd learned was how wildly pecs and abs could turn her on when they were attached to a certain—

"Melissa?"

Gah! She stopped fanning abruptly. Her eyes flew open. "Jack. You scared me."

"Sorry. Feeling warm?"

"No, not particularly." She dared turn her head. He was wearing a shirt, thank God. And smirking like mad.

"You were fanning yourself…?"

The rodent. He'd been peeking.

"Oh. A bug was flying around my face. A fly or a gnat or something." She batted at an imaginary insect. "It was driving me crazy."

Somehow she managed to keep her face sincere and her blush at bay. Jack was going to make her an expert at controlling her circulatory system.

Doubt replaced his smirk. He might not be buying it completely, but he was no longer quite so sure about his chest-power.

"Come on in." He shook his head, a small smile on his sexy lips, and gestured into his studio. "I'm ready for you."

Good thing he hadn't said that when he was half-naked.

But all was not lost. He'd have her do yoga again and she could regroup and go all Zen and be fine. Last time Jack had been able to focus on pretty much every body part she had without being affected at all. Melissa could—and would—do the same. This was his job. She'd do hers, too.

"We'll work in here again today. I'll want to try some outdoor shots later on."

"Okay." She stood waiting in Mountain Pose in the middle of the room, almost totally calm. Getting there anyway. He had his back to her, fussing with a light.

"You'll need to take off your clothes."

Whah? The Mountain in her Pose suffered a catastrophic landslide. "I—"

"Keep your bra and panties on if you're more comfortable at first. And put this on." He turned, holding out a substantial length of silky material patterned like snakeskin.

"Um." Somehow she managed not to shriek. "Put it on how?"

"Drape it." He cocked his head, looking her up and down. "Over the parts you don't want to—"

"Right. I get it." She was about to grab it from him, whirl around and stomp out of the room, when she stopped herself. Grasping the soft, nearly transparent material, smiling with high-quality serenity, she turned and glided out of the studio—where the smile dropped and her body slumped.

She was going to have to be *naked* in front of him? Keep her bra and panties on *at first?* She put a hand to her thumping heart, face reddening. Even Dr. Glazer couldn't stay tranquil in this situation.

Jack had not mentioned the whole naked thing when he said she'd be posing for him. What was she supposed to do now? Go ahead and strip? Cancel the shoot? What about Gretchen's wedding?

Barbara's words came to her... *With men, you can be sure they're after one thing.*

She squeezed her eyes shut. Her brain jumped to supply an image of Jack making love to her on the studio floor, the snaky material tangled around them both. Oh, my...

Her eyes popped open.

No, no, no. That wasn't Jack's purpose. Nothing about their previous photo session had felt sexual. Nothing had felt that way today. He'd asked her to take her clothes off as if he was asking her to pass the salt. Matter-of-fact, no leering, nothing suggestive in his tone. For a flirt like Jack, that was saying a lot.

Models had gotten naked for generations of sculptors, painters and photographers. Jack wasn't shooting for *Playboy* here, but a respectable gallery exhibit. Melissa had seen the Unko brochure with his name in it. And the shots displayed in his shop were all in impeccable artistic taste, even if a bit unsettling.

So. No big deal, right?

Melissa chewed her lip. Sort of a big deal...

But she could do it. Not only could she, she'd act as if she wasn't the least bit anxious or titillated to be naked in front of him. And if she pulled this off, which she suspected she would through sheer stubborn pride and determination, she could line up with the other actresses on Oscar night and feel good about her chances.

Now...she just had to do it. Get naked. Or seminaked anyway. Wrap a flimsy bit of material around herself and walk back out there.

Oh, God.

She did it. Somehow. She took off her clothes, body shaking with tension, considered taking off her bra and panties just to show him, then decided she wasn't quite ready to, er, *show* him. Finally she wrapped the material over one shoulder and around herself, sort of a combo sari and toga.

There. That wasn't so bad.

Most important, before she went back in to face Jack, she took a minute for meditation, stretching tall, letting her body center and settle, clearing her mind as much as possible the way her yoga instructor had taught her. Her heartbeat slowed. Her muscles relaxed.

Ready.

Head high, she walked out of the bathroom and back into his studio without faltering, her stride smooth and even.

And the Oscar for Calmest Half-Naked Model goes to…

"Hey, you're back." He barely glanced at her, busy with his tripod. See? This was a photo shoot to him, this was work. This was not about her body except as it served his art. "Why don't you sit over there against the backdrop, whatever way is comfortable, and let me check the lighting."

"Sure." She sat gingerly on the white cloth, pulled smooth under and behind her, and pretended she was back in high school on stage, performing "Out of My Dreams" from *Oklahoma* for an adoring crowd of parents and families, not half-naked in front of a stranger.

"Good." He peered at the camera's display screen, adjusted the lighting and umbrellas around her, peered again, adjusted again, until he had the level he wanted, then moved back behind his tripod. "Okay, in this series you're Eve. Snakeskin scarf. I'll be using an apple later, pretty obvious. The poses will be superimposed on other images in the final print, so they might not make sense at first."

"Sure." Was she going to end up with cracks all over her? Ten feet underground? With worms crawling out of her she-didn't-even-want-to-think-about-it?

An hour later, she no longer cared. She'd been posed this way, that way, scarf wrapped this way, that way, the whole process routine and dull. Jack was distant, exacting and clearly frustrated. Was she doing something wrong? Didn't he know what he wanted?

"Let's take a break." Jaw set, he snapped off the lights and opened a small refrigerator she hadn't noticed before. "Beer? Water? Something to eat? Bathroom break?"

"Water, yes and yes." She stood stiffly, shook out her tired arms and legs. Lying in Upward-Facing Dog; sitting in Lotus; bending forward in Child's Pose. Apple on her head, apple in her hand being offered to the "snake" scarf in a weird twist that seemed oddly sexist, apple clenched in her jaw as if she were a suckling pig. Always keeping her face completely blank, devoid of emotion. Nothing satisfied him.

"Here you go." He tossed her a water, yanked the top off his and drank thirstily, hand on his hip. "Want an apple?"

"Uh." She grimaced, dragging on her shirt to cover herself. "Strangely, I've lost my taste for them."

He didn't smile. "Cheese and crackers?"

"That would hit the spot."

He grabbed a box of crackers from the top of the refrigerator and a plate of small squares of cheese from inside and started for the door. "Help yourself. I'll be back."

"Am I not working out?" Melissa spoke impulsively. If this was her fault, she'd back out now and find some other way to pay him for Gretchen's wedding.

"No." He barely turned. "You're fabulous."

Melissa watched him stride out of the room, not sure whether to believe him. Mysterious and complicated guy. From easy charmer to intense and grumpy *artiste*. She rotated her shoulders, the left one sore from holding poses. Whatever he was after, she hoped he'd figure it out.

Five cracker-and-cheese combos and one bottle of water later, she visited the restroom, put her clothes back on and wandered into his store, examined all of the pictures there and then the ones in various stages of completion in the back, glancing at her watch every few minutes.

Then she did it all again.

Finally, she gave up, cracked open a beer back in his studio and downed it while reading a photography magazine she barely understood.

Another beer later, also ingested too quickly, and the obvious question could no longer be ignored.

Was Jack coming back or had he ditched her?

6

JACK STOOD AMONG the trees in Cal Anderson Park, hands on his hips, breathing hard. He'd left the session with Melissa and stepped outside for a breath of fresh air to clear his head. Before he knew it, he was walking, striding then running down Broadway to get to the park, the place he'd photographed Melissa before.

Nothing was working. Nothing. This had never happened to him. Sure, he'd had shots that took some juggling, but it had always been a question of tiny elements, small changes that needed to be made physically, conceptually, visually, mentally. Never anything like this.

Melissa had done everything he'd asked except get completely naked. But every shot he took, every change he made took him farther from any result that satisfied him.

What the hell was he doing wrong?

A cool breeze blew a cloud over the sun, throwing the area into shadows, bringing him back to a day he'd photographed Melissa here, in similar light. She'd been radiant that day, her skin glowing gold and pink against the green around her.

Jack closed his eyes to bring her back, alive, sensual, an amazing contrast of focus, sensuality and vivid life.

Vivid life.

That's what was missing, what had drawn him to Melissa in the first place—the power of her life force, contained and controlled by the rigors of yoga. She was the perfect Eve, her feminine beauty, her stunning shape, her inner power. But he'd been fighting who she was and who Eve was by trying to stunt and twist both into roles and poses that suited neither.

He needed to let them both live and breathe, to be warm, female and natural, women tempting snake, tempting man, women resisting temptation, woman seeking temptation, woman giving in, gloriously and finally and rapturously...

Wait.

Melissa—warm, female, tempting. Was he out of his mind? He'd barely been able to keep himself from sexualizing her when he was photographing her ankles. To shoot her the way he wanted, he would have to come face to face with what this woman did to him. On a precipice now, looking over the cliff, he could stay where he was, turn back or gather himself for the leap.

Jack pulled the phone out of his pocket again and started walking back, determinedly dialing. He was not afraid of any woman, never had been, was not going to start now.

"Melissa, where are you?"

"Where am *I?*" She was understandably incredulous.

"Are you still in the studio?"

"For some reason. Where the hell are you?"

He grinned at her frank irritation. "Cal Anderson Park."

"Uh... Is there a yoga class you didn't bother mentioning?"

"I'll be back in five minutes. Can you wait?" He heard her sighing, and crossed his fingers. "The shoot will go differently when I get back. I've figured out the problem."

"What problem?"

"The problem photographing you."

"I'm not a model?"

"No, not that. Not your fault, it's mine. I wasn't letting you be you." He thought he heard her snorting, didn't blame her. "I wasn't using you the right way. I've re-thought. I have it now."

He waited, praying she'd give him a chance, even though he sounded slightly deranged.

"Well…" She sighed again. "Okay, I'll wait."

"Thanks." He pumped his fist, started a slow jog. "I promise you won't regret it."

"If you say so."

Jack shoved the phone back into his pocket and started running toward Come to Your Senses and his studio, confident now, no longer chased by demons. He had his shot, the right one for this model. He'd work like hell to keep his professional distance. And if he couldn't, then maybe this woman was meant to be more than an inspiration to him.

Running fast now, he laughed, buoyant with energy, not feeling the distance in his lungs or in his legs, driven by his excitement.

Jack had promised Melissa she wouldn't regret this. He'd do everything possible to make sure that stayed true.

"FOR THIS SHOT, I WANT YOU on your stomach, but half-lifted, one knee forward, reaching with your arm, as if you're trying to crawl away from something." Jack reached into the refrigerator and pulled out another of her old friends. "Guess what?"

"An apple, oh, goody, something new!" She grinned at him, still feeling the beer and trying to hide her buzz, wondering if he'd been indulging, also. He'd left the studio tight-lipped, tense, broadcasting dissatisfaction from every atom, and walked back in smooth, charming, lit by a creative energy she was instantly drawn to. Violently drawn to. Violently sexually drawn to. Worse than the way she'd been attracted to him that first day in his shop. Then he was just hot. Now he was on fire. Or maybe it was the alcohol in her system. "So you want Eve to resist temptation. I like that."

"It's time we gave the woman a little more credit."

"I bet she deserved some." Melissa stretched out on the floor, one arm forward, one knee lifted, making sure her stomach stayed sucked in. If she was going to represent the earth's very first woman, she wanted to do a good job.

It took her a second to settle into the pose, then she called on her yoga relaxation and tried desperately to channel Eve, woman of all women. First and only female in the Garden of Eden amid every delight imaginable.

To her surprise, instead of feeling stupid and awkward, the way she had in previous poses, even those that were more natural for her body, she felt right in this one, strong and purposeful. Jack had changed the lighting, making it less of a cold, harsh searchlight, more of a warm, gentle sunbeam. Or maybe she was just responding to Jack's new light, his charisma and enthusiasm.

And rock-solid shoulders and abs, and amazing chest, thighs and—

Down, Eve.

"Good. Good. Reach farther, really make an effort to get away."

She strained with her body, made frantic claws of her fingers, caught the mood right away, as if he'd injected it into her. "Like this?"

"Yes. *Yes.*" His voice was low, caressing; she could sense his excitement and his eyes on her through the camera. Total aphrodisiac even though she knew it was his art that was turning him on, not her. "Can you look more…

vulnerable? But strong and determined in your body. Yes, like that. There. Yes. God, Melissa, you're perfect. I'm going to come over and figure out how to position the scarf now. Hold on."

She held the pose, breathing steadily, trying not to betray her pleasure at his compliments.

"This will spiral around you." The soft material brushed across her naked back, across her upper thighs. The touch was sensual, the air around them turned electric. Or was that just her imagination? "Melissa."

"Yes." She could only whisper.

"If it's okay, I'd like to move your panties so more skin shows…here." He touched the side of her hip, and his fingers trailed briefly over the white cotton covering her right buttock. It was all she could do to stay in the pose. She wanted to arch up into his hand. She wanted him to flip her over and take her right there under the warm lights.

What on earth was happening? She was turning into a primal beast. *He* was turning her into one.

"Sure." She tried hard to sound as if men asked her to move her underwear out of their way so often she found it incredibly tedious. "No problem."

His warm fingers trailed again, this time moving the cotton, knuckles brushing her bare skin underneath. Impersonal to him, artist tending to his model, yet his touch set fires wherever it landed.

By some miracle Melissa stayed calm, kept her breathing yogic, slow in, slow out. Affecting her? Of course not.

"Good. Okay, let me figure out the scarf part." He walked around and looked at her head-on, hands in his pockets, scarf dangling from his hip, feet planted. His strong stance made her feel even more vulnerable half-naked on the floor in front of him. And even more turned on. "Okay, I have an idea. You okay like that?"

"Oh, sure." She smiled at him, ho-hum. "All that practice clawing myself away from snakes with apples has come in handy."

Jack snorted. "Good news. Now, for the snake, how about…"

He walked behind her again. She felt the brush of his hands on the back of her leg, the smooth soft material winding around twice, calf, thigh. Then he reached under and brought the rest up between her legs, pulling slightly.

Oh…my…

She had to close her eyes again, force herself to stay calm. She wanted him to kiss her. Her mouth, her back, her thighs, everywhere.

He splayed the end of the scarf across her back, so it hung down, covering her right shoulder and breast. The apple he put on the floor, under the material's hanging edge. "I think that will work."

Depending on what he was trying to accomplish…yes. Something was definitely working. Or getting worked up. He needed to move away from her, because she could feel the warmth of his body and the warmth of the lights, and the material pulling between her legs. He was crowding her, her feelings were crowding her, her need was crowding her. She didn't like this. She liked having freedom to move, freedom to call the shots. She needed to be in control and here she was…not.

"You sure you're okay?" He came back around, knelt by her head and brushed a lock of hair across her face.

"I'm fine," she whispered. The silence in the studio was like a black hole.

"Part your lips." He was speaking quietly, too. Melissa couldn't help it. She looked up at him, and caught his expression. Jack's eyes were dark and intense, his jaw set. Was he looking at Eve? At his picture? Or…at Melissa?

Kiss me. Please.

She parted her lips. A lock of hair caught in the corner of her mouth. Jack pulled the strands away, repositioned them. Even that practical, professional touch on her cheek traveled down between her legs. Melissa was clearly beyond help.

He stayed near her for a beat, started to speak. Stopped.

Kiss me, Jack. Touch me again. Make love to me.

He moved away.

Thank God he had sense. She was insane with lust, as if the scarf had really turned into the snakelike agent of the devil, tempting her, making her someone she had never been before, someone who didn't feel like Melissa Weber.

Deliver her from temptation...

Men had always been the physical aggressors in Melissa's past. She'd felt, rather uncomfortably, as if lovemaking was something she controlled, and doled out to the deserving few. She'd never wanted it to be like that, believed the woman should want sex as badly as the man, and though she knew that was possible for some women, too bad, so sad, it had never happened to her.

It was happening now.

Click. Click. Click. She tried hard to concentrate on the pose, on the look, on being Eve and getting away from the snake and the apple.

"Relax, Melissa. Be who you are right now. Eve. Yourself. More what you're feeling, less what you think I want you to feel."

Breaths in and out, she opened herself to Eve, new to the world, innocent to fear and betrayal, but with an inner strength that guided her toward what she wanted. She allowed herself to be Eve and to be herself, aware of her near-nakedness, her vulnerability, her power, allowed herself to feel the lust, the fear, to indulge them both, hating the snake, loving the snake, wanting the apple, afraid of it, too. She was Eve and she was Melissa.

Click. Click. Click. Picture after picture while she moved in new ways, inhabited the character to a degree she wouldn't have thought possible.

The white cotton bra felt ludicrously wrong, constraining, artificial. Eve's breasts should be bare. Jack wanted that for his picture; Melissa was bold enough now to give it to him. She secured the scarf by squeezing her legs together and sat up.

"Something wrong?"

She didn't want him to talk, didn't want to think rationally or allow her Melissa-neuroses to stop her; she unhooked her bra, let it slide off and crouched forward again. Her hair tumbled over her face, and she felt like Eve combined with Xena, combined with Lady Gaga. The air in the room was cool on her nipples; this was wild and free and right.

It took maybe two seconds to realize the camera was quiet. She turned, peering somewhat dazedly through the curtain of hair.

He was watching her. Hungrily. Frozen by his camera, hand on the tripod. Not Eve and Photographer, but Jack and Melissa. This time there was no question.

Neither moved. His dark eyes were reaching across the space between them, beckoning. She wasn't going to go, couldn't quite make herself. But oh, how she wanted to.

"Hold that." Jack broke the spell, moved back behind his camera. "Don't move anything."

She didn't think she could to save her life.

Click. Click. Click.

Her position had barely changed, only her head had turned, but the meaning and her role had clearly shifted. This time she wasn't resisting temptation, this time she *was* temptation, the snake and the apple and her bare breasts all part of an invitation to Jack to lose control.

"Perfect. It's perfect. God, you are beautiful."

The passion in his voice nearly undid her. Following an instinct she didn't understand, she reached to unwind the scarf, brought her knees up to pull off her panties and draped the scarf quickly to cover herself, then rolled to her side, tugging the rest of the material up between her breasts, stretching the hand holding the apple way over-head.

Click. Click. Click.

He'd taken the camera off the tripod, was coming closer. "Yes. Yes. Keep going. Whatever feels right, Melissa."

She was breathing hard now, afraid of what she was doing, loving what she was doing, not sure when or how she'd stop. She lay on her back, scarf between her legs, twisted her body to the right, hands flat on the floor, apple by her breast, and looked back at the camera. Looked back at her photographer. Looked back at Jack.

Come get me. I dare you.

7

JACK LOWERED HIS CAMERA, emerging from the dazed concentration of watching Melissa transform into everything he'd hoped she could be and more. A lot more.

Was he seeing what he thought he was seeing? Invitation, pure and simple, in her eyes.

Or was it in Eve's eyes? A role she was playing for the camera?

He'd wanted Melissa from the first moment he saw her in the park, arching her back in Upward Dog, face turned to the sun. Now she lay in front of him, naked, barely covered by the snake-scarf between her legs, breasts swelling free, the brilliant red of the apple contrasting with the stark white of the sheet under her and the golden hue of her shoulder. Lips parted, hair in wild disarray—she'd made him hard even without the come-on look in her eyes.

One step, two, then he lifted the camera again, moved so he was straddling her, one foot on either side of her thighs, aiming his lens at her lips.

She twisted around, lay on her back, hands cushioning her head.

To hell with the camera; this was a conquest. He lowered it again, gazed down at her long smooth legs, beautifully curving hips and narrow waist, tight nipples on round soft breasts, and at her delicate features: rosebud lips, high pink cheekbones, heavy-lidded smoldering gaze. That gaze changed as he hesitated. Her eyes grew wider, allowed in a touch of vulnerability. No more Eve. This was Melissa looking at Jack.

The seduction game he knew, had played it many times over and enjoyed it every time. He'd also seen plenty of women play the role—the sexy movements, flipping hair, exposed necks, sultry gazes—and behind them always an odd combination of anxiety, desperation and cynicism.

That wasn't what Melissa was projecting. None of it. This wasn't a knee-jerk seduction for her.

He pulled his camera strap from around his neck, lowered it safely to the floor. Knelt and put his hand flat over the notch of her collarbone, then drew it down her body in a leisurely stroke, savoring the smooth pliancy of her skin, the swells of her breasts, parentheses for his hand, the graceful spread of her rib cage, her muscled abdomen. He stopped before the slow slide into soft curls.

He stopped.

"You're beautiful, Melissa."

"Thank you." Her voice had turned shy. She couldn't meet his eyes, lowered hers so they were almost closed. She was lying there, waiting for him to make the next move.

Jack held still, watching the sweep of her eyelashes over her cheek, their shadows delicate spikes on her skin. His hand grew restless on her abdomen, wanting to explore. Yet Jack—the great seducer, the great lover, conqueror of women citywide and now kneeling next to this stunning woman who was offering herself in no uncertain terms—was holding back.

He'd never sleep with one of his models, but Melissa

wasn't a professional, and he wasn't paying her. Those ethics weren't driving his hesitation. Something else. Something that felt again very much like whatever had kept him in the trees, photographing her from that distance for so long.

Her lids rose, blue eyes gazed at him expectantly, questioningly; her beauty made Jack's breath catch in his chest. He leaned over, supported himself on one arm and brushed his lips across hers, as warm and sweet as they looked.

He tasted her again, then again, half of him on fire to take it further, the other half bogged in confusion.

She gave a soft, sweet moan and slid her arms around him, mouth hungry against his. Passion won him over; he collapsed next to her, rolling her on top of him to spare her the hard floor. Her body felt so good against his; he followed the curve of her back to the gorgeous firm ass that seemed made for his palm. She was everything he'd imagined.

Her hands went up under his shirt; her mouth explored his chest. Arousal burned through him; he cupped her buttocks and held her firmly over his straining cock, the material providing an effective barrier for now.

Barrier. Condoms. He didn't have one. He doubted she did, either.

But there were other things they could do to—

Melissa raised herself, hands braced on his chest, her hair falling forward, lips parted, two gorgeous breasts begging for his touch. He couldn't resist, took their soft weight into his hands, then made the mistake of looking up into her shining, slumberous eyes.

Something shifted, some element between them clicked into an unrecognizable place that felt as strange as it felt inevitable.

"Jack."

She bent forward; he lifted his head to meet her, cupping the nape of her neck, kissing her with passion that nearly swept him away, openmouthed kisses with tongues touching and stroking. Her breath accelerated; she gasped. They tumbled to one side; she landed hard, didn't stop kissing him, her arms around his back like bands of desperation. Emotion, thick and powerful, threatened to overwhelm him.

He left her mouth, found her neck, biting gently, down lower to her breasts, sucking hard. Better. Easier. Familiar territory. His hand sought then found the warm wet place between her legs, nearly losing his mind when she gasped. Cried out. Gasped again.

Except…his lust-clouded brain registered that something was wrong.

"No."

That got through. He moved his hand away, came up from her breast. She was staring at him, panting, looking as if she was about to cry.

"Melissa." Instinctively he tried to gather her close; she resisted, pushing against his chest. He let her go. Had he hurt her? He didn't see how. "What is it? What happened?"

"I'm sorry." Tears welled, spilled over. He felt horrible, filthy, as if he'd gone too far. "I just… I don't know what happened. I'm so sorry."

"Melissa, you have nothing to be sorry for." He wanted to touch her again, but instead took off his shirt and draped it over her shoulders. Sat next to her again, cursing himself for not listening to the instinct telling him to stay away. "Any guesses what happened?"

"Oh." She wiped her eyes. "I'm just an idiot."

"I doubt that." He wanted to help, wasn't sure how. "Try me?"

"It was just…" She waved a hand, let it drop helplessly to the now-rumpled canvas underneath them. "Intense."

"Uh-huh." He understood that. Big-time. More than she knew.

"And it sort of scared me." She laughed nervously, still not meeting his eyes. "I'm sorry."

He gave in to his need, lifted her hair so he could see her face, so lovely even sad. "Why are you sorry?"

"Because it's ridiculous. I wanted you to— I wanted it. I asked for it." She snorted. "And then, I turned chicken or something."

"Actually—" he stroked her back, let his arm rest across her shoulders, feeling her body relax against him, surprised at his pleasure when it did "—it got to me, too."

Melissa turned her tearstained face up to his. He nearly choked. What the hell had he done? All but told her she *scared* him? Come on. That wasn't part of any game he'd ever played with any woman.

"Really?"

He desperately wanted to look away, to stop the tenderness piercing his chest. But he couldn't do that to her. Even though he was about to lie again, which bothered him.

"Really." The word came out easily. And didn't feel like a lie. Which bothered him more.

"Look, Melissa. It's no big secret I'm attracted to you. And obviously I set up a charged situation with this shoot. But that doesn't mean we have to cross the line again. What happened today was probably a good clear sign that we shouldn't."

She nodded, her body drooping into obvious relief.

That bothered him, too.

"So this is good." He squeezed her in a buddy-buddy way. "We know where we stand now. We can try the photography again another day and stay away from physical contact. How does that sound?"

Uh. Had Jack Shea just suggested to a woman he wanted that they *not* become sexually involved?

"It sounds good." She managed a small brave smile at him, and he wanted to kiss her again so badly that he took his arm from around her and jumped up to get away. "Thank you, Jack."

"For attacking you?" He quirked an eyebrow so she'd know he was teasing.

"For understanding me. Both now and before, during the shoot. That was…amazing."

He nodded, sure, no problem, *de nada,* and watched her gather up her underwear and walk out of his studio, the stunning length of her legs, the sweetly vulnerable bend to her head, the stride that had lost its serene confidence, turning her from the perfect Eve to a woman who apparently could get to him in a way he'd never experienced before.

Agreeing they'd keep their distance was good, it was right. He was putting Melissa at ease and sparing himself any weirdness in the future. At the same time he was acting in a mature and responsible manner, which couldn't be a bad thing. By staying away from her physically he was saving himself from complications he had no interest in inviting into his heart.

If only he could shut away the nagging thought that at the same time he might be denying himself something vital to his soul.

BONNIE SAT AT HER COMPUTER, nursing a glass of wine poured from a bottle Seth had insisted he didn't care for, and would she please take it off his hands? Yeah, boy, gotta hate those French burgundies. She should have called him on it, but frankly, having a glass of wine at night was a luxury she really missed, and she'd gone along with his ploy, made all the more ridiculous since they both knew perfectly well what he was up to.

Ridiculous and really, really sweet.

Deep breath, another sip and she launched her browser, typed in the address: Seattledates.com.

God help her. Drinking wine given to her by the love of her life while she tried to find a new boyfriend.

She'd filled out a Seattledates profile the night before and, my God, how exhausting was it to try to sound honest and sane, caring and supportive, and sexy and funny in a few short paragraphs? She'd done okay, she thought, but hadn't had the courage to set the profile to public view just yet. One baby step at a time. Tonight, having finished her latest Bonnie Blooms' Blog, a rather irreverent size-matters story about how passionflowers could only be pollinated by really big bees, she was going to check out the male merchandise, see if there was anyone worth looking at. From what she'd heard, the free sites tended to attract as many perverts and weirdos as real, sincere men. But she couldn't afford the steep rent of the paid sites.

She pulled up the search criteria and filled in a few to narrow the list. Woman seeking man. Within five years of her age. No smoking. Thirty miles distance. Single only. With a job. At least some college. Was that enough? Not enough? Too much?

Finger held over the Enter button, she finally got up the nerve and poked it.

Good God.

Twenty pages of thumbnail summaries. How many on a page? Dozens.

Half an hour later, her glass was empty and she'd broken her rule about making the bottle last as long as possible by pouring herself more. This was nuts. What could she tell from pictures of men she'd never seen move or blink, heard speak or laugh, never smelled them or their aftershave? Complete strangers. How was she supposed to choose with any reliability?

Another half hour gone, another glass, she decided she couldn't pick sensibly, so she'd just follow her gut. Bald guy with beard, no; bald guys with beards looked upside down. Guy with picture of his mother, no. Guy whose typo-ridden profile proclaimed his love of *pubic* displays of affection, no. Guy whose picture was a close-up of his crotch, no. Guy who undoubtedly murdered someone and got away with it, no *thank* you.

She wanted nice, boy-next-door normal. Wasn't there a little field you could click for that?

Apparently not. Looking sadly at her empty glass, and longingly at the bottle, Bonnie made herself click on the next page, determined to go through the candidates thoroughly, to give everyone a chance.

No…no…no…

Ooh, how about that one?

She clicked to view his profile and additional pictures. Definitely possible. Not gorgeous, not ugly by any means. Normal. Looked like he had a decent body, too. And his introduction…

I've been out of a relationship for a year and am ready to dive in again, but fine waiting until it's right. I'm an IT geek, but I was a journalism major and write on the side. I've got good friends, am healthily close to my family, love cooking and eating, travel, conversation, working out and continuing to evolve out of the cave. I don't love writing commercials for myself. (Now how much would you pay?) On a date I am easy to talk to,

interested in who you are and am generally well behaved. I am attracted to women who are positive, confident, passionate communicators and see the humor
in everything. Infatuation doesn't last, but I believe if
both parties are determined to keep the passion in a
relationship they can.

"Ooh." Bonnie put her hand to her heart, which was
doing a pretty impressive tap dance. This one looked really
good.

Maybe she should write to him. No reason not to. It
wasn't as if she had to marry him. She didn't even have
to answer him if he wrote back. No risk.

Bonnie's cheeks flushed hot. She giggled nervously.

Well.

One click brought up a blank message screen. What the
hell was she going to say?

Dear Mercer533. Hi.

Oh, that was brilliant.

I saw your profile online, and liked it. If you think mine
looks good, too, then—

"Knock knock." Seth's voice from her foyer. None of
the tenants of Come to Your Senses bothered locking their
apartment doors unless privacy was vital. Bonnie should
have locked hers.

She scrambled to save the note, hit the wrong combination of buttons. A window popped up she'd never seen
before. What the—

"Hello?" Footsteps sounded in her living room, her
kitchen. "Bonnie?"

"Yeah, in here." She got rid of the weird window, jabbed more buttons to save the profile.

Her computer froze.

Damn it.

"Here you are." He pushed into her room as if it was his.

"Oh, hi." Bonnie shoved back from the monitor, jumped out of her chair and whirled around. "Hi, Seth."

"Uh." He looked at her curiously. "Hi?"

"Yeah, hi, how's it going?" She sounded exactly as guilty and nervous as she was feeling.

"Fine, thank you." His gorgeous gray eyes narrowed. "And what were we doing in this room just now?"

"Geez, Seth." She started to move in front of her monitor to hide it, then realized what she was doing. For heaven's sake. She was free to date anyone she wanted to date, and too bad for him if he found out. In fact, maybe it was better he did. She had nothing to feel guilty about. "It's my room. I can do what I want."

"Yes, it is. But when you jump up and give me a look as if you were plotting the illegal overthrow of the U.S. government, it's my duty as a loyal citizen to ask questions." He folded his arms over his broad chest, looking his steely-eyed sternest. "You have something to tell me, young lady?"

She grinned, couldn't help it. "Only name, rank and serial number."

"Hmm." His eyes went past her to the screen. His faux-commando pose faltered. "What the hell is that?"

"Oh. That's Seattledates.com." She tried to sound nonchalant, but only ended up sounding like someone trying to be nonchalant and failing. "I signed up."

"Yeah?" He bunched his lips together, a sure sign it bugged him but he didn't want to let on. "How's that working for you?"

She shrugged, searching his face, trying to cope with the turbulence inside her. Guilt she was angry for feeling, worry for Seth she was even angrier to be feeling, plus determination to kick this man out of her heart once and for all, plus doubt she'd ever be able to. Nice little stew. "I'm just starting."

"Yeah? What brought this on?"

She sent him a look that implied he was failing adult kindergarten. "I want to go out with someone? Have fun with a guy? Maybe get serious? I'm old enough, you know."

"Sure. Yeah." He walked over to her bookshelf, chose a book and opened it with interest he had to be faking because it was total chick lit and he wouldn't be caught dead reading it. "I'm just not sure why you picked now."

"Because now is when I'm ready. What are you getting at, Seth?"

"I just feel like…" He shrugged, leafing through the book he wasn't reading. "I don't know."

He didn't know. He never knew. And that was why she had Seattledates.com up on her screen right now. "You feel like you don't know?"

Seth blew out a breath of frustration. "I feel like you and I are getting closer again. Kind of."

"Kind of?" She wanted to slug him. Closer? To what? Mutual annihilation? Her anger got stronger, and with it her courage. "What do you mean, Seth? Exactly. Spell it out."

"Okay." He put the book down—not back where he'd found it—and faced her. "I thought you and I were heading for each other again."

"Heading for each other?" She knew what he meant. She was going to make him say it and then she was going to correct him in no uncertain terms. If he hadn't seen her profile up on Seattledates.com there was no way they'd be

having this conversation, and this "closer" they were supposedly getting would not bear anything like relationship
fruit for another century at least.

"You know what I mean, Bonnie."

"Indulge me."

"Give me a break." He shoved his hand through his
hair, then jammed it on his hip. "I'm trying. Okay? It is
hard for me to—"

"Yeah, Seth. It is. And I truly feel for you. But I have
finally figured out that while I adore you, I want someone
who isn't scared of his feelings. Who not only thinks I'm
amazing, but has the balls to tell me so, and who, without
hesitation, commits himself to figuring out what we can
have together."

There. She'd done it. All she had to do was start, and
once she did, the words rolled out as if they'd been cooped
up inside her head for years, just waiting to emerge.

Which they had been.

"Yeah. Okay." He looked stunned, his cocky confidence
deflated.

Bonnie's heart ached for him, her tears rose again, but
she also felt more powerful than she had in months, maybe
years, probably since the year they'd been together in college, starting to get serious, and she'd first sensed him
drawing away from her.

"You're right. You do deserve that." He nodded slowly,
brows drawn down, eyes shadowed, looking so unbearably
handsome she felt as if her heart was trying to rip itself
out of her chest. "I hope you find it."

Bonnie's turn to be stunned. More pain. As if after
everything she'd been through and all her new resolve, a
stupid part of her still hoped hearing that she was looking
for someone else would somehow push him to—

No. She knew better. And she also knew her heart

couldn't sink any further because it had already sunk as low as possible. Seth was turning her loose. Whether for her sake or his, it didn't matter. They were on their way to being truly over. This would hurt more later, she knew. And she also knew the pain was an important part of the healing.

"So." Seth rolled his shoulders convulsively, as if shaking off the silly inconvenience of losing her forever. "I might be able to help you."

Her eyes widened incredulously. "Help me *date?*"

"Uh, no, thanks." He shoved his hands in his jeans pockets. "Help you with your financial situation. A…friend wants to start a perfume shop. Maybe she could rent out a corner of the store. Help you out, help her out. You'd have the whole smell-good thing in common. Maybe you could do some marketing along those lines."

"Wow." Despite her misery, a ray of hope. Rent income would be fabulous. But something about the way he'd said *friend* set off alarm bells. "That is really sweet of you, Seth. Who is she?"

"She's…" He coughed uncomfortably. "I met her, uh… recently."

Bonnie grew very, very still. She knew this man way too well. He was sleeping with her. Or wanted to.

The bastard. Of course he was fine cutting Bonnie loose. Of course it was fine if she dated other people. He had someone new, someone he was trying to get in good with by giving her space in Bonnie's shop.

How effing low could he go?

"Really?" She spoke sweetly. His eyes grew wary. He knew her way too well, also. "How recently?"

"Last week. At Noc Noc." His favorite dance and pickup spot. Full to the brim with willing, nubile hotties.

"Yeah?" She kept the sweet tone going, hot rage building in her blood. "She good in bed?"

Seth's jaw dropped. "What—"

"Did it not occur to you how I would feel to have some woman you were dating set up in my shop?" She was past rage, past sanity. Grief and frustration were channeling words to her vocal cords before she had a chance to monitor them. "Were you planning to come by and make out with her every day in front of me so I could enjoy the view?"

He stepped closer, not backing down an inch. "What the hell are you talking about?"

"'Go ahead and date someone, Bonnie, really, go right ahead. Because I just happen to have this new piece of ass I can—'"

"Stop." He grabbed her shoulders. "Right there. Stop. Listen to yourself."

She was panting, struggling, out of her mind. "Let go."

"No. You think the worst of me every chance you get, Bonnie. Look at all that crap you just came up with, boom, off the top of your head. You didn't give me a chance to explain, didn't even let me finish a freaking sentence. You think I keep *you* at a distance? What's more convenient to help you do the same than telling yourself over and over that I'm the world's biggest jerk?"

Bonnie froze. His words stopped her like a sucker punch. She shook her head, unable to respond.

"Listen to me." His voice and his hold on her gentled. "I'm not involved with Matti. I have no desire to be. My only interest in her is how she can help you out of your financial situation."

Oh, Seth. Bonnie looked into his eyes, conscious that hers were probably swollen and streaming, and that she could give Rudolph nose-envy. She was dying to believe him, even knowing it couldn't change anything between them.

Seth looked back at her, direct, unwavering. He was telling the truth.

Oh, God. He was right to be angry. But look how quickly and easily she'd jumped to conclusions. Without trust, there was no chance for a relationship.

"Seth, I'm sorry."

"Okay. Thanks." He nodded once, then again, his body relaxing. "It's okay."

"No, no." She put a hand to his chest, lips twitching. This was a game they'd played before. Silly, but it had always helped them come down from tough fights, of which there had been many. "You don't understand. I'm *really sorry*."

"No, no." A small grin started on his sexy lips. "It's *really okay*."

"Seth, I'm not sure I'm making myself clear." She felt a bubble of laughter rising, the giddy relief that came after an argument was safely over. "What I'm *trying* to say is that I am so very completely and utterly sorry. Does that make more sense?"

He grinned and pulled her into his arms, a brotherly bear hug. "All forgotten."

She let herself relax, found the spot on his shoulder where her head lay so perfectly. This was goodbye and they both knew it. When he left the room, she'd finish her email to Mercer533, and, if nothing happened there, she'd try someone else. She was young, decent-looking, fun—someone would work out, at least long enough to get her heart in a better place, away from Seth, so she could finally find Mr. Right. She really needed to do this, and having Seth's blessing was an important piece of it.

His arms moved, one draped across her shoulders,

one slid across her back, fitting her to him. His body was strong and utterly familiar. They'd had quick careful hugs along the way since their breakup, but she hadn't had the chance to remember his body like this in a long, long time.

Slowly, and maybe inevitably, the embrace began to change. Had he shifted? Had she? Were their bodies taking over, sending each other the signals their brains wouldn't dare to with so much crap having passed under their bridge?

She started to pull back; his arms held her still. His chin moved to her forehead and she felt his lips at her hairline.

Seth. She was so hungry for him, for his mouth, for his body. But she couldn't do this. This was goodbye for them, hello to a fresh start, a new man, a new lease on her romantic life.

His lips moved to her cheek; he nuzzled her temple, whispered her name.

She moaned and turned her face up until their lips met, clung, once gently, again fiercely, then she pulled away and buried her head against him. "I'm doing the right thing dating, Seth."

"I know." His words rumbled through his chest; his arms tightened around her, then let go. He took a step back. "I know. I hope you…well, if any guy gives you trouble, you tell me. Okay?"

She nodded, again not trusting herself to speak.

"I'll tell Matti you're interested. We'll see if you can work something out. And she's loaded, so charge her a lot."

Bonnie came out with a laugh that sounded like small animals being stepped on. "I will."

"Okay." He backed away, cocky again, but his movements were jerky, tense. "Seeyaround."

"You bet." She waited until he was out of sight, then let her cemented-on smile crack and fall off.

But instead of collapsing completely into the pain, she felt, incredibly, some relief. She'd done the right thing. She'd stayed strong. Of course, Seth had helped. If he'd wanted to seduce her he could have, and he undoubtedly knew it. For that she was grateful. He was never quite the monster she wanted him to be. A monster would have been much easier to kick out of her heart.

She rebooted her computer, poured herself the rest of the wine, pulled up the email again, to Mercer533, worked on it until she was happy with how it sounded, with the way she came across. Then she counted out some courage: one, two, three…

And hit Send.

8

Blood Pressure: Normal

"SO YOU NEVER TOUCHED HIM." Melissa smiled indulgently at Mary Jo, wanting to do anything but smile. From the moment the woman had come into her office, Melissa's alarm bells started ringing. Nothing Mary Jo said had been particularly incriminating in the Bob Whatsisname sexual-harassment complaint. It was just her look. And she did this weird sniffing thing when she talked that made Melissa want to hand her a tissue. Or have her take a drug test.

"He was always wanting me to touch him." She sniffed, put a hand next to her burgundy mouth and made her fingers "talk" as if they were inside a sock puppet. "'Hey, Mary Jo, I spent forty minutes on my glutes today at the gym. Check 'em out.' I mean really, the guy is obsessed with his appearance."

Melissa nodded, keeping her demeanor professional when she wanted to roll her eyes. A little ironic for Mary Jo to be accusing Bob when she'd clearly had a face-lift, dyed and permed her perfectly coiffed hair, wore expensive and stylish clothes and jewelry and, judging by the impressive size of her chest, possibly had implants. "So you never touched him?"

"The guy wouldn't leave me alone!" She folded her arms, bracelets jangling. "'Check out these biceps, you can crack walnuts on them. Check out my thighs, they're ready to tear through my pants like the Hulk's.'"

"But…" Melissa made herself stay calm. Her blood pressure had been amazingly low that morning and for the past few days. She didn't want to blow that promising trend now. "Did you ever touch him?"

Mary Jo looked at her blankly. Sniffed. Melissa got the impression that behind those lifeless eyes, her brain was whirring. "Well, I mean, we work in the same office. Handing over papers, maybe our fingers touched. Walking next to him to a meeting, maybe we bumped shoulders. You know, the way you'd do with anyone. But *touch* him like 'Hey, baby, let's go do this thing now'? Ha, that's totally different."

Totally different, but…Mary Jo hadn't ruled it out.

She picked something Melissa couldn't see off her skirt and threw the invisible particle on the floor. Then sniffed.

Melissa took a deep breath to quash the groan of frustration coming into her throat, picked up her pen and wrote on Mary Jo's file: Will not answer the question.

"Guys like Bob Stoker, they're players. They always will be players and there is nothing that will ever change them. I swear he's slept with every woman in the office." A particularly vicious sniff. "I must be the only one he didn't land."

Or the only one he didn't try to land? Which was insulting enough that she might be exacting revenge?

Melissa weighed the flash of insight, trying to determine whether it felt true or grew out of her instant dislike for this woman. She had to be objective, unbiased as a judge. Barbara liked and trusted Mary Jo, and that counted for a lot.

A few more questions elicited equally rambling and unsatisfactory answers. Finally Melissa ushered Mary Jo out, not knowing what to think. Except, if someone from human resources had asked Melissa if she'd touched a guy improperly and she hadn't, she'd be yelling "No" as loudly and as often as possible. And if that same someone also happened to ask whether Melissa would rather sit down for a beer with Mary Jo or Bob, she'd pick Bob every time. Which didn't mean he was innocent. It just meant she liked him better. Which wasn't saying all that much, considering Mary Jo.

This was confusing.

Back at her desk, she glanced at her phone as she'd been doing obsessively for the past few days to see if Gretchen had called. She and Ted were taking a ridiculous and annoying amount of time getting back to Melissa about the flowers and cake. Melissa couldn't imagine why they weren't returning her calls. She had half a mind to go ahead and book Bonnie and Angela without Ted's almighty approval. He wasn't going to stand in the way of her sister's dream wedding.

She did have one new voice mail. But not from Gretchen. From Jack.

Her heart skipped. She scoffed at herself. He'd be calling to schedule the next photo session. And during it, she would not touch alcohol, nor would she go mental and offer herself like a freshly baked ham at Easter, which undoubtedly every other woman did around Jack. And maybe what Bob was doing to the women in his office?

Hmm. She couldn't quite see it.

Regardless, she was back in control of the situation with Jack, and had decided she had nothing to apologize for or worry about. She'd gotten carried away, and then found her sanity in plenty of time. Nothing so terrible about that. And he'd been sweet and understanding about it.

Really sweet.

Incredibly sweet.

She jerked herself back to reality and dialed into voice mail, annoyed when his voice came on and she got a little fluttery.

"I was wondering if you'd like to drive over to Seward Park with me after work today, walk some of the trails."

Melissa narrowed her eyes, heart positively jumping, while her brain very wisely told it to calm the hell down. She was Jack's model; he wanted to take more pictures, apparently outside this time. It wasn't as if he was asking her on a date.

She called him back, still annoyed at herself, this time for being ludicrously nervous. Hadn't she decided she had this under control? Photos taken outside would be perfect, much less intimate than in his studio. And he certainly wasn't going to make her get naked in public. "Hi, Jack. I got your message."

"Hey, there, Melissa." His voice was casual and confident. He was back in control, too. "Want to take a walk with me?"

"I'm guessing you want Eve outdoors this time?"

"If the mood hits there's no telling where I'll want her."

Melissa couldn't help smiling. Back to Jack the auto-flirter. That guy she could handle. It was the sexy artist she had trouble with, the man who'd connected with her on such an intensely personal level that she felt as if he was bringing part of her to life for the very first time.

Melissa snorted. Honestly. He was hot, she'd been tipsy and horny, that was that. "I'm in a suit right now, but can go home and get other clothes at lunch. What would you need me to wear?"

"I'm thinking…a small tree branch. Maybe two."

"Come on." Nervous laughter burst out of her. "You think I'll get naked in a public park?"

"I think you'll get naked anywhere, Melissa."

She couldn't keep back a gasp, even while simultaneously realizing he was kidding. "Be serious."

"Ah, Melissa." He chuckled. "You know I'll never make you do anything that isn't totally comfortable. Not just because I'm the world's absolute nicest guy, but also because if you're unhappy the pictures suffer."

"Right, okay. What time do you…" She almost said "want me" and decided not to feed him that line. "What time?"

"What time do you get off? Work, that is?"

She rolled her eyes. "What are you smoking today?"

"I'm taking prints of our last session to Pierre Balzac, owner of the Unko Gallery, in approximately five hours, and I'm nervous as hell."

Melissa blinked. From supremely confident player to vulnerable artist in zero point six seconds. No wonder he was giddy. She was suddenly a little anxious herself.

"How did they come out?"

"They're incredible, Melissa." His voice was low, earnest, and just like that she turned shivery and had to clench her thighs together.

"Well." She used her prissiest voice. "I hope he likes them. Do you think he will?"

"I'm too close to judge. They're not like anything I've done before, so there's no telling."

"I'll have my fingers crossed."

"Well, thank you, Miss Melissa. I'll pick you up on

Sixth Avenue, a silver Volvo sedan. Don't get into any
other cars. I don't want to lose you."

"You say that to all the models."

"None but you!"

She chuckled under her breath. When he was like this,
Jack was plain, simple fun. And most importantly, no big
threat to her sanity. "I'll be waiting outside. Five-thirty
okay?"

"I am already counting the minutes."

She hung up the phone, grinning now, feeling more
comfortable. Today would be fun. They were still on a
good track.

A text came in from Barbara. "Meeting over? Come
see me."

Melissa grabbed the file from her desk, feeling lighter
than she had in days, and strode over to Barbara's office.
"Hey, there."

"Hello, have a sit." Her usual smile was missing today.

"How are you, Barbara?"

"Fair to middling." Barbara looked up from her computer. "I'd feel better if my ex would drop dead. Or be hit
by a bus. Or two busses."

"Oh, no." She sat opposite her boss. Barbara's ex delighted in making her life as miserable as possible.

"The thing about divorce?" She closed a computer file
with a vicious stab of her finger. "It doesn't go away. At
least not as fast as love does."

Melissa's stomach gave an almost angry jolt. "Barbara,
I'm sorry."

"No, don't worry. It'll pass." She made a wry face. "Like
gas. What's up with Mary Jo? Did she help nail Bob?"

"Not exactly." Melissa summarized the meeting, trying
to stay neutral, sticking to the facts.

"Hmm." Barbara frowned. "You sure you asked the right questions?"

Melissa's gut jolted again. Uh…not like she was new at this. "I asked three times if she'd touched him inappropriately. She avoided the question, kept zooming off on tangents."

"Oh, yeah, she's like that." Barbara opened her desk drawer, poked around looking for something. "I wouldn't worry."

Not worry? What did that mean? Melissa started feeling restless, wanted to get up and start pacing, tried to do her yoga breathing to calm her heart. "I can't help thinking there's something strange about this."

"Ya think?" Barbara rolled her eyes. "Something strange that this is Bob's *third* claim? Once we clear Mary Jo I think it might be time to ask him to leave the company. Or find him work in the mailroom or stockroom or driving trucks or somewhere it's all men."

Melissa's leg started jiggling. Barbara had misunderstood her, coming down clearly on Mary Jo's side, just when Melissa was starting to wonder if Bob might be telling the truth. Maybe he always had been.

"So what's new with you? What's happening with that photographer?"

"It's going fine." She forced herself to speak naturally, and not blush. "Not what I expected, but fine."

"Hmm." Barbara was watching her shrewdly. "Is he behaving?"

"Oh. Yes. It's totally professional." At least it would be from now on.

Barbara frowned and closed her drawer. "Something happened."

"No, no, nothing. Well, nothing bad." She couldn't stand lying to her boss and friend, but she didn't want Barbara seeing this in her black-and-white way and condemning Jack for what was essentially Melissa's mistake. "It almost did, but no, nothing. We talked about it and it won't happen again."

"Really."

Melissa got up and almost started pacing, then realized what she was doing and forced herself to stand still, to take a breath and slow her speech. "Yup. In fact he wants to shoot outside after work today, in public, at Seward Park. Can't get more innocent than that."

"Uh-huh." Barbara was clearly skeptical. "The guy got a taste of you. He's not going to stop until you're in bed with him, Melissa."

Melissa scratched the back of her neck even though it wasn't itchy. "I really don't think so. He seems like a good—"

"Let me give you a piece of advice, my dear." Barbara leaned her elbows on the desk; Melissa was absolutely sure she did not want to hear whatever was about to come out of her boss's mouth. "Guys will say anything to get laid. Anything from 'I won't touch you, really' to 'I love you.' If you're smart, you will not take any of it seriously. Actions are the only things that count. And if what I think happened did happen, then he's figuring he's already laid the groundwork and can proceed as planned. Guys like that, like Bob, like my ex, they have the whole grand plan figured out down to the last detail. Different plans for different types of women. It's an effing science."

Melissa went back to her chair. Her heart was pounding, her face red, she was light-headed. So much for lowering her blood pressure.

Women the world over had fallen for jerks throughout time, and would continue to. But they weren't Melissa. She wasn't some weakling at the mercy of her hormones.

The session in the studio had been unexpected, yes. She couldn't shake the memory of how wild and freeing it had felt to subject herself completely to Jack's vision. But that passion had been about art, about discovering a new part of herself, not about being sexually vulnerable. It was not about Jack. "Thanks, Barbara. I'll be careful. But I really do have it under control."

"Yeah." She laughed bitterly, shaking her head. "You think you do. Every woman thinks she does. Trust me, Melissa, that's when they can hurt you the most."

Blood Pressure: Normal

MELISSA STOOD ON THE SIDEWALK outside Au Bon Repas, waiting for Jack. It was ten minutes before he was supposed to show up, but this way she could take a little time to prepare for his arrival, perform a few exercises for mental clarity, make sure her body was calm and her breathing uninhibited. Then when Jack did show up, she'd be the big ball of tranquility he counted on.

For a moment she let herself wonder what type of woman would get Jack in the end, more of a sweet, placid beauty or a dynamic go-getter hottie? Would he keep to his vow of faithful until death or not be able to put his old habits to rest? She couldn't imagine him drifting along forever the way he was now. He had a solid core she'd bet would keep him from the eternal bachelor fate—middle and old age spent reveling in past sexploits, dressing too young, drinking too young, approaching too-young women with a gut hanging over his belt as far as his hairline was receding.

Melissa giggled, not able to imagine Jack as anything but devastating up until his death at age ninety-nine.

Oops. She shouldn't be imagining anything right now, she should be concentrating on clearing her mind…

Her phone rang. She dug it out of her bag and peered at it, frowning. Was Jack cancelling? Going to be late?

It was finally Gretchen. Thank goodness.

"Hey, stranger, where have you been?" She covered her free ear as a motorcycle roared by. "I've been calling forever."

"I know, I know. I'm sorry."

"Everything okay?"

"Sure, yes, of course." Her sister sounded different. Not herself.

"You're sure?"

"*Yes,* everything is fine. Which, coincidentally, is why I said everything was fine."

"Okay, okay." Melissa was worried, but what could she do? Gretchen was a grown-up, and if she didn't want to confide in her sister, that was her business.

Yes, okay, it hurt and she was pouting just a bit. "Did you talk to Ted?"

"I did. We'd be happy to accept your gift of the cake and flowers and the photographer at our wedding, Melissa. Thank you so much."

Melissa blinked. Who was she talking to? Her sister sounded as if she were responding to some loathed relative, *Yes, please, I'd love a tongue-and-headcheese sandwich, Aunt Flossie.* "Okay. Good. I'll let Bonnie and Angela know."

Silence. There was never silence between the sisters, not even for a second, unless they were furious with each other, and, as far as Melissa knew, they weren't.

"So…how's the modeling going?" More politeness.

Melissa sighed. She hated this. For whatever reason, her sister suddenly didn't want to talk about the wedding she'd done nothing but talk about since she got engaged. So, okay, they wouldn't. "It's going well."

"Has he shown you any of the pictures? I can't wait to see them."

Melissa bit her lip. When she'd been posing for Jack, it hadn't really sunk in that her sister and probably her father and her colleagues and many, many other people she knew or didn't know would be standing in the Unko, staring at her naked. "Well. Yes. You will. I guess. I mean if the gallery…likes them enough to show."

"Why shouldn't they? What are they like? How did he have you pose?"

Melissa took a deep breath and told her, because she told her sister everything, then held the phone away from her ear while Gretchen shrieked in delight.

"You were *naked?* And the scarf was— Oh, my *God.*" Then a horrified gasp. "Dad is going to have a *fit.*"

"I know, I know." She was laughing, partly at the thought and partly at the relief of talking to her sister in a normal way again.

"Was it weird being naked in front of this guy? How old is he anyway?"

"Oh…about my age." Her attempt to sound matter-of-fact was laughable.

"Oh, *re*-ealy. Cute?"

Melissa actually giggled, as if she were twelve. "You might say that."

Another gasp. "Melissa! I knew it. What is going on between you two?"

A gust of wind blew down the street, giving a ride to a piece of crumpled paper. How would Melissa describe what was—or wasn't—going on between her and Jack?

She did her best. Held nothing back. The attraction, the sexual contact and her immediate pullback, her confusion and their mutual resolution, Barbara's reaction... If nothing else, if she spilled her guts wide-open, it might inspire Gretchen to do the same.

"Wow. Melissa."

"I know." She laughed, gesturing at nothing. "Crazy, huh?"

"I've never heard you talk this way about a guy before."

"Yeah, well, I've never met a guy like this before." To her horror what she meant as a playful statement sounded throbbingly earnest. She cleared her throat frantically. "I mean a guy this, uh, complicated. And interesting. You know, artistically."

"Uh-huh." Gretchen was enjoying herself way too much. "I think maybe you're a little in love with the guy."

"In *love*? With *Jack*? Ha!" She snorted, then for good measure did it again. "Not a chance. He eats women and spits out only high heels and accessories."

"Okay, not in love yet, but certainly a crush." She snickered. "A bi-i-ig one."

"Barbara put it better. She said I should stay far away from this guy because he—"

"Melissa?" Her sister's voice was uncharacteristically sharp. "I've never said this to you, and I have no idea how I have the guts to do it now, but I'm going to. I know Barbara has helped you out and you've relied on her for advice and direction over the past few years, but Ted thinks the woman is a bitter mess."

Melissa took a step back, as if her sister's words would have knocked her off balance otherwise. "Well, of course *Ted* would. He's—"

"I think so, too, Mel. She's an angry, sad woman. You're young and gorgeous and you've closed yourself off to love for some reason I have never been able to understand, but

I suspect she has something to do with helping you validate that mistake."

Melissa's mouth had to close about three inches before she could speak. "I have *not*—"

"Then why were you freaking when kissing Jack got so intense?"

"I… Because it was…" Because it felt as if she was going to get sucked into him and never be whole and herself again. "Because a relationship right now would interfere with my life plan, with the woman I want to be—"

"Interfere with your *what?* Excuse me, Barbara, can you put Melissa back on?"

"Okay, okay." Melissa glowered at a passing pedestrian. "Because to a guy like Jack, kissing is just a recreational activity."

"Barbara again. Jack told you the kissing was intense for him, too. If you were just the next chick in line he never would have admitted that." She made a noise of true exasperation. "Barbara has you all messed up. Being strong does not mean becoming hard. There's nothing weak or shameful about loving someone."

Melissa backed up again, this time until she had cool, solid concrete to lean against. Gretchen had never spoken to her like that before. No one had ever spoken to her like that before. Worse, everything Gretchen said was terrifying, and Melissa knew enough about psychology to know that meant Gretchen was hitting her mark.

"Just think about it." Silence again, while Melissa writhed in agony. "Oh, how is your blood pressure these days?"

"Better and better."

"Since you met Jack?"

Melissa groaned. "Come on, I thought I was getting a change of subject here. What does *he* have to do with it?"

"Well? Is it lower since you met him?"

"*Purely* coincidentally, yes."

"Uh-huh. I have a theory about that, too."

"Having theories is *my* job, Gretchen."

"I know, and this one you won't like, either."

Melissa stiffened. "I think I've had enough, but thanks."

"For whatever reason, honey, you have a terrible fear of just being you. And trying to be someone you're not is really stressful. I was just reading a book on this very subject."

"Give me a break." Melissa was vastly relieved. This theory had nothing to do with her. Gretchen's psychological focus changed along with her nighttime self-help reading. "Jack is entirely unrelated to my blood pressure."

"What else has changed since it went down?"

Melissa opened her mouth to proclaim, very loudly, what exactly had, besides meeting Jack.

Nothing. Cutting out the classes, taking up yoga—they'd helped some, but hadn't made her numbers plunge the way they had lately. "I don't know, the stars, the global economy, my hormones. Maybe it was a delayed reaction to something else."

"Melissa, Jack seems really cool. It sounds as if you have something good between you, and the promise of something better. You're not the type to fall for a real player. Your instinct would warn you off."

Melissa's heart was pounding. But she didn't feel hot and light-headed and as if she was going to explode from restless energy as she had in Barbara's office. She felt… alive. And really, really scared. "I think you're jumping to a very large and dangerous conclusion."

"Not dangerous! Attraction is completely natural, Melissa. This is what being human is about. You meet someone, you check him out and see how you fit. You don't run screaming for the nearest guru to tell you that what every man, woman and child was born for is wrong and weak."

Melissa was flabbergasted. This was not like her sister at all. "What the hell have you been smoking, Gretchen?"

"Sense-weed, I don't know. You want to kiss the guy? Kiss him. You want to make love with him? Do it. You want to see him over and over again? Go ahead. How else are you going to find out who's right for you if you never find out who's wrong?"

"I'm not…" She stopped in frustration, utterly disoriented. Melissa was the one who gave Gretchen advice. Melissa was the together one, the substitute mom, the caretaker who'd helped raise her sister when their father had all but abandoned them to grief.

"In short, what the hell is stopping you from doing this guy except that you're a nanny-goat chicken-wattle scaredy-pants?"

"Say *what?*" Melissa bristled at their ultimate childhood insult. "You are fighting dirty now, girl."

"I know, I know." Gretchen chuckled. "I'm done, I promise. But think about what I said. You owe me that because you can't imagine what I went through to get up the nerve to say this stuff to you. I have to shower now because I've been sweating like a marathoner."

"Ewww." She giggled, glad they were back on familiar ground. Melissa could run a marathon and sweat maybe half a teaspoon, while Gretchen would fill a quart bottle.

"I know. But if I didn't think there was something really worth exploring there, I wouldn't have put myself through this. Give Jack a chance, Melissa. Or more to the point, give yourself one."

She hung up, leaving Melissa on the sidewalk, clutching the phone to her ear, listening to the dial tone. Then suddenly she laughed. And laughed some more. She had no idea what had happened to Gretchen, but her sister was glorious, and Melissa was wildly and deeply proud of her, though she wished Gretchen had gone postal on someone else.

But she did have a point. Melissa wasn't going to lose herself to Jack. She wasn't the type to be happy disappearing into a man, she wasn't Gretchen or her mother.

Maybe if Jack—

"Melissa."

She started. A silver Volvo had pulled up to the curb, with a hot-as-hell driver wearing sunglasses that made him look even hotter. Smiling. Beckoning. They'd get in the car together, drive to the park, take more pictures. Would their chemistry explode again?

Attraction is completely natural, Melissa. This is what being human is about…. You want to kiss the guy? Kiss him. You want to make love with him? Do it…what the hell is stopping you?

Right now, finding herself with a grin the size of Kansas on her face and feet that were nearly running toward the car, she wasn't sure anything could.

9

JACK WAS FIDGETING. Jack never fidgeted. He might on the inside, no one was cool in every situation, but he prided himself on at least giving that impression. Dumb macho thing maybe, but hey, guys did that stuff and he was a guy.

"Hmm." Pierre Balzac was poring over the shots Jack had taken of Melissa. Every now and then he'd shake his graying head or chuckle quietly. Those were the only reactions so far.

Jack wanted to grab him by the shoulders and demand, "What? *What?*"

Instead he paced a couple of steps, scratched his shoulder, picked up one of the gallery business cards on Pierre's worktable and put it back.

He was stunned at how the pictures of Melissa had come out. No, this wasn't the series he'd envisioned. His concept after coming back from the park had been relatively simple: Eve working to overcome temptation. But Melissa had taken his idea and turned the Eve-snake encounter into an epic battle that Eve had won, outmaneuvering the snake, practically feeding the apple back to him.

She glowed in the photos. She took over Jack's art and

became the ultimate celebration of womanhood: beauty, sexuality and power.

"Well." Pierre turned over the next picture, the one where Melissa's sensuality erupted from the flat surface of the print with a force Jack could only describe as torrential.

Well, what? This work was unlike anything Jack had done before; he felt as if his old familiar artist-self was being dismantled and reconstructed. Maybe his whole self. A difficult process. His photography mentor in college, Arliss Hunter, had always said artistic growth was painful. Jack hadn't understood until now, when he felt like a snake himself, his old, comfortable skin suddenly itchy and strange, needing to be shed, so he could emerge larger, stronger, better.

But it sucked in the meantime.

"Huh." Pierre turned the last page, fixed his eyes on Jack over the tops of his reading glasses then took the glasses off with a dramatic flourish. "This is not what I expected."

"That makes two of us."

"Really." Balzac folded one arm across his chest. "Who is she?"

Jack shrugged. "A woman I saw in the park."

One of Pierre's bushy eyebrows went up. "Who is she to you?"

"A model. A friend."

"A lover."

"No."

"Hmm." Pierre watched him for an uncomfortably long moment, then nodded smartly and closed the album. "These pictures have more humanity, more warmth and passion than any I've seen from you. You are no longer holding back. They are a real style breakthrough. I want to see more."

"Okay." Jack's heart gave a jump. He was meeting Melissa in half an hour to drive out to Seward Park. He'd planned to get some shots, but wanted mostly to talk to her, try to figure out how and why she'd turned the tables on him during the shoot, what she'd been thinking, how she'd gotten this new style out of him. How she'd seduced the snake…and him.

Pierre handed back the portfolio. "I have a show in two months which just cancelled. The artist is ill and can't finish. You interested?"

Holy… Two months. He stared at Pierre, calculating. If Melissa could give him a lot of time over the next few weeks, he might be able to do it. If he managed to shuffle some of his other appointments.

If…

"Sure." He nodded firmly, as if he had all the confidence in the world. "I could do that."

"*Très bien.* We'll be in touch."

"Absolutely." Jack tucked the book of photographs under his arm and left the gallery, the picture of cool until he was around the corner on the sidewalk opposite his car. What the hell had he just promised? For a second he was tempted to go back in and tell Pierre he'd been insane, that there was no way he could deliver an entire exhibit in that short a time. Especially because this new artistic self he was developing was still strange to him. No telling whether he'd be able to recapture the magic he'd found three days earlier with Melissa.

And yet the challenge was irresistible. If he could clear his schedule, if Melissa could give him enough time…

If.

He got into his car, sat gripping the steering wheel. Two

months. At UW Seattle he'd put together an exhibit in a crazy short amount of time, skipping most of his classes and for a week immersing himself in nothing but the project. He'd emerged exhausted, undernourished and half-nuts, but having produced some of his best work. Being able to clear away life's extraneous crap and concentrate on his art—it had been torture and a privilege at the same time.

Of course, that was college. As an adult it wasn't nearly as easy to push the rest of life away.

The beep of a car horn next to him brought back reality. He acknowledged the woman hoping for his parking place, started his engine and pulled out into traffic, headed to Sixth Avenue and the Au Bon Repas corporate headquarters where Melissa had said she'd be waiting.

She was. She'd changed out of the suit into a pair of blue slim-fitting pants with blue tennis shoes and a white top that had blue and black robotic figures scrawled on it. She leaned against the building, gazing at nothing, phone to her ear. Jack itched to photograph her right there: the perfect combination of sex and innocence.

That wasn't all he itched to do, but he wasn't going there again.

"Melissa."

She started, then her face broke into a huge grin, which made the same thing happen to his, and she hurried to the car as if she couldn't wait to see him, which gave him the absurd idea of getting out and meeting her in a swing-around bear hug as if they were starring in some sappy chick flick.

He stayed where he was.

"Hi, Jack." She climbed in, bringing her fresh scent into his beloved Volvo.

"Hey." He made himself look away because if he didn't,

he was going to sit there like an idiot, staring. Somehow when Melissa wasn't around, it had been easy to convince himself his attraction was all about art. Faced with her in person, remembering the way she'd taken over in the studio, he wasn't so sure anymore.

Come on. He had to be overreacting, complicating the simple fact of a perfectly ordinary attraction. Silly to act as if Melissa had some kind of superpower. "How's it going?"

"Not bad. Long day." Melissa pulled her seatbelt across her slender body. She was different today, energized. "How did Pierre like the prints?"

"He liked them." He tried to keep the excitement out of his voice as he pulled out from the curb and merged with traffic. "A lot. In fact, he wants more."

"Hey, good for you. Congratulations!" She turned to him, face alight. He had to force himself to look back at the road.

"Thanks. There is a catch. I'm not sure you'll like it."

"He wants you to use a different model?"

"God, no." His vehemence surprised them both. "You totally make the pictures, Melissa. Pierre loved you."

"Ah." She turned casually toward the window, but he saw her grinning and felt pleased. "Then what's the catch?"

"One of his artists cancelled out of a show." He pulled up to a red light. "He needs the series soon."

"How soon?"

"It doesn't sound soon, two months, but in terms of putting together an exhibit, it's an eyeblink."

Melissa rubbed her hand across her chin. "What would that mean?"

"For the next week or so, if you're willing…" Jack hesitated, not sure why the next words were difficult to say. "We'd, uh, spend a lot of time together."

She glanced at him sharply. "How much time?"

"As much as possible. Evenings, weekends, late nights if you can manage it, all night if necessary." He waggled his eyebrows playfully, feeling dead serious inside. "Whatever we have to do to get it done."

"Hmm."

He waited, but that was apparently the extent of her comments.

For the second time that day, Jack was fidgeting.

He took the ramp onto I-5 heading south. "What, you're not panting at the chance to spend the night with me?" He pushed, deliberately, loving the way she'd exit her placid state and bristle at him when he flirted.

"Oh, please." She didn't disappoint. "I'm sure you have a lo-o-ong line of women to call on for that."

"You are, huh?" He was uncomfortably aware that he wasn't taking his usual pride in his reputation. "What makes you think so?"

"Bonnie and Angela implied as much. And the way you act…"

"How do I act?"

She lifted an eyebrow. "'What, you're not panting at the chance to spend the night with me'?"

"Oh, that." He made a dismissive sound. "That's flirtation."

"Reflexive and meaningless flirtation."

"You think so?" He sent her a look. "I wouldn't be so sure, Melissa."

She snorted, which made him laugh, which made him nearly miss the exit onto I-90.

"So you have me pegged, huh?" He kept his voice light, but his chest was oddly tight. "A player who scores as often and as randomly as possible?"

"Let's put it this way." She matched his tone, but her eyes were serious. "Yes."

He had to work to keep his smile going. For the first time in his life, Jack felt compelled to explain himself. "I'm not a player the way you think, Melissa. I'm not into one-night stands unless that's all she wants. I've genuinely liked and respected every woman I've been with. I don't keep score and I don't use people."

"And you don't bring them home to meet your mother, either."

"Are you kidding? And give her a heart attack from the shock?" He had to yank the wheel back to stay on course. Bad idea to stare at a laughing, beautiful woman while driving. "How many guys have you brought home to meet Dad?"

"Let's see." She brought up her hand to count on her fingers. "One. Two. Three…none."

He sent her a grin, pleased she'd lightened up. Maybe she'd really understood. "No one worth it?"

"Nope." She settled back into the seat, broadcasting Subject Closed. Jack turned onto Rainier Avenue, heading southeast. "So, besides being considerate of her nerves, are you close to your mother?"

Jack tightened his lips, wanting to share at least part of the story of his life, not sure what the consequences would be. "Not during childhood, though I am now. Not her fault. Dad took off when I was about the age you lost your mom. I didn't react well."

"Oh, Jack, I'm sorry." She spoke with sympathy that warmed him. "Though I don't know what constitutes reacting well to the loss of a parent."

"Good point. I ran pretty wild. It was hard on her."

"I did the opposite." She laughed disparagingly. "Stayed home every night, mothered my sister, took care of Dad and basically became Little Miss Responsible."

"Hard at a young age."

"So is spinning out of control."

He gripped the steering wheel. He didn't regret telling Melissa about his father's desertion, but he knew what the consequences were now. Her understanding and empathy disconcerted him, made him want to withdraw into a nice heavy suit of man-armor she couldn't penetrate.

It was a relief to enter the park and pull into a lot near the beginning of his favorite trail, one that wound through an old-growth forest of fir, cedar, maple and orange-trunked madrone trees, a color he'd love to photograph Melissa against.

They got out into the cool air. The piney smell of the park combined with the picturesque lake to make it one of the most evocative places around. The light was perfect, softening into evening; the sun would soon cast a faintly pinkish glow that would only intensify as the evening wore on and would bathe Melissa's skin with gorgeous tones.

Jack inhaled deeply, then grabbed his camera bag out of the trunk. "Ready to walk? I'll see if any of the vistas inspire me."

"Sure." Melissa was looking around blissfully. "It's beautiful here."

"We'll get you posing and it will be even more beautiful."

"In my tree-branch outfit?" She was teasing him, but all he took in was the way she carried herself, large eyes bright with mischief and intelligence, breeze lifting hair away from her cheeks, tinted pink in the soft sunlight. He pulled up his camera, aimed and got her, which made her go stiff with self-conscious laughter. "Shouldn't I have snakes?"

"Done that." He took another picture. "Something about your face begs to be photographed."

"Ha! Photograph this." She crossed her eyes, stuck out her tongue, pulled up the tip of her nose.

"Ooh, so *hot*." *Click.* He aimed again, chuckling, feeling free in the great outdoors, giddy with the fresh air. "I'm hanging this one in the men's room at Safeco Field. 'For a good time, call Mel-*lis*-sa at—'"

"Uh, no. That one gets deleted ASAP."

"But it has such good blackmail potential."

"You've got plenty on me already." She plunked her hands on her hips. "Snakes and apples and God knows what else you'll do to me today."

"True." He grinned, she was grinning. The breeze died. The stillness around them was broken only by the nearby gentle lapping of waves. Melissa looked away, out over the water, down at her feet, then over to the trees, as if she had no idea where her gaze should go. He had an almost violent urge to kiss her, to feel those warm lips softening against his.

A car full of yelling kids pulled into the parking lot. Jack turned away. "Let's walk."

She matched his stride as they trudged along the nearly empty trail, Jack scanning the woods for likely settings. Half his mind was on today's shoot—he envisioned Melissa among trees veiled in black and white, both widow and bride—and half on the woman beside him.

"How go the plans for your sister's wedding?"

"Oh. They're going." She sounded dispirited, first time tonight. "I had a strange conversation with her right before you picked me up."

"Yeah?" Their shoulders bumped; he wanted to grab her hand. It occurred to him their conversation tonight felt more friend to friend than photographer to model. He liked that; it felt easy and right.

"I got Angela, Bonnie and your services, all paid for

by me, so she could have a really beautiful wedding. The kind my mom always talked about us having. Gretchen acted as if she was being forced to accept them."

"Hmm." He bumped into her again and deliberately used his next few steps to put more space between them. "Maybe she doesn't want them."

"How could she not?"

"Don't ask me. But maybe she doesn't. Maybe she and her fiancé want nothing to do with a traditional wedding. Not everyone does."

"But that's crazy." Her voice was rising, but she looked thoughtful, as if she were considering his words.

"Hadn't they made plans already?"

"Well…sort of. More like whatever they could throw together."

"Maybe that's how they wanted it. Not too planned, not too formal. Is that what they're like?" He took a few more steps toward a clearing he could barely see deep in the woods, then noticed Melissa had stopped. She was standing frozen in the road, looking stricken. He walked back to her. "Hey, what's wrong?"

"I bet you're right, Jack." She could barely make sound. "I bet you're right. I wanted Gretchen's wedding to be the way *I* wanted it, not the way she did. I couldn't even see that."

He laughed without amusement. "Yeah, um, none of us are really experts at seeing our own flaws."

"Flaws?" She glared at him in outrage. "You think I have *flaws*?"

He stared for a second, then cracked up a split second before her glare collapsed into laughter. Except hers had a few tears along with it.

"She tried to tell me. It's obvious now. But she's so sweet, she didn't want to hurt me. God, Jack." She shook her head, sniffling. "She was willing to have the wrong wedding to make *me* happy."

"It's not too late. You haven't made anything go wrong."

"No." She wiped at her eyes. "No, you're right. I haven't. I'll call her when I get home."

"Good plan."

"Jack." Melissa stepped forward and laid her hand on his forearm, looking up at him with a sad brave smile that nearly gutted him. "You've done something really wonderful for me tonight."

He had no idea what, but he felt a weird combination of proud pleasure and strangulation. "Aw, c'mon. It wasn't really—"

"No, it was really important." Her fingers tightened. "Tonight you've given me a gift by showing me that I'm an intolerant self-centered bulldozer of a person, and I don't know *how* to thank—"

She was in his arms before he had time to realize he'd grabbed her to him, grinning like a fool, feeling her giggle helplessly against him.

Somehow he managed not to press his lips to her hair, her temple, her cheek. Melissa made him feel strangely powerful. Not like he felt when he'd seduced a woman. That was vanity, at best a very primitive power. This was different. He didn't have words for it, but it was sweet. And also terrifying.

"Let's find our photo spot, Ms. Bulldozer." He let go of her reluctantly, keeping his voice nonchalant, and pointed to the clearing he'd been eyeing. "We should check that out. It's calling my name."

"Okay." She wiped her eyes carefully again. "Oof. I should have brought more makeup."

"You're gorgeous." He touched her cheek, golden and

smooth pink in the softening light, as he'd anticipated. "Come on."

He led the way to the clearing, bright enough for natural-light shots at a low speed. At the edge stood a madrone tree, its deep orangey-red bark covering a smooth, muscular trunk. Next to it, the weathered gray of an enormous red cedar made a perfect contrast. "Stand between those trees."

Melissa stood obediently, dwarfed by the old-growth cedar, set off beautifully by the smaller madrone. Jack unpacked the veils from his bag and gave them to her to experiment with while he set up his equipment.

"Am I bride or widow first?"

"Whichever you want."

"Widow, then."

"Kill off the guy, huh?" He set up his tripod, checking the distance, making sure the ground was firm under his equipment. Then he took a few shots, testing the light. Her features were still visible under the loose-weave netting, just the way he'd hoped.

"Put your hands out to the side, pushing against both trees. Yes, like that. Like Samson. Pretend that you're trying to change the world. Your world."

She pushed. "Like this?"

He looked through the lens, pressed the shutter release once, then again.

No. Not like that.

"Try…both arms on one tree." He checked again, took more shots. Tried a few more of the poses he'd envisioned. Then tried them spontaneously without the veils. She was lovely, the light hit her perfectly, the composition was outstanding; his instinct hadn't failed him. But the pictures lacked…something.

Really? Or did they only seem that way in comparison

to their last session on Sunday? He didn't know, felt cut adrift again from his art. But this time he wouldn't panic. This time he'd trust that they'd be able to find their way together to a solution.

Half an hour later he called a break, took a deep breath, worrying about the light, which would move and fade all too soon. The shoot was still not going well. The pictures were exquisite, but cold. They felt too familiar, too easy, and were missing whatever Pierre had seen in the ones Jack had shown him. This exhibit was supposed to be taking a new direction. It was possible Jack was too pressured by the deadline, feeling he had to come up with something brilliant immediately. Or pressured by Pierre's compliments for the Eve pictures. Or too distracted by Melissa to get what he really wanted.

When he most needed his muse to work for him, she'd deserted him. Why always with Melissa? Last time it was because he hadn't let her take the lead and spark his creativity, show him where his art wanted to go. Maybe he needed to let go again.

"Forget the veils. Try something else."

"Me?" She pointed to herself incredulously.

"Yeah. What do the woods say to you? To your body? What do they suggest?"

"That only I can prevent forest fires?"

Jack rolled his eyes. "Got a bear suit?"

"Sadly, no." She thought for a moment. "How about I'm a leprechaun trying to keep my marshmallowy cereal away from pesky kids?"

He stifled a burst of laughter. "Next…"

"I know!" Melissa snuck behind a hemlock and peeked out, holding fingers up by her head to suggest horns. "Weird woodland creature prowls Seward Park and terrorizes the tourists."

Jack's smile faded. The greenery made a fresh frame
for her face, the light threw dappled shadows on her shoulders and lit her eyes.

That was it. Right there. So simple. Behind the tree
she looked ethereally beautiful, like a wood nymph, like
a sprite...

"Hold there." He got to a crouch, aimed his camera. *Yes.*

"You're kidding." She giggled. "You want me like this?"

"Without the horns. A tree nymph. Perfect." He lowered
the camera. Almost perfect. She was not going to like this.
"Except...those clothes don't really say nymph."

"What?" She looked down at them, then back at him
warily. "Don't tell me."

"You'd be perfect naked."

"I said not to tell me." She shook her head. "You are a
pervert, you know that?"

"How many nymphs do you know who wear tennis
shoes?"

"How many nymphs do you know, period?"

He grinned and caught her exasperation on camera. He
was feeling back in control now, excited, sure of what he
wanted, pleased he'd been able to trust the process—*their*
process—this time. "C'mon, off with it."

"You don't pay me enough for this." She pulled her
T-shirt up and over her head, reached behind to unhook
her bra then caught him watching. "Do you have to stare?"

"Do you blame me?"

She made a face, slid off her bra, balled it up and hurled
it at him.

He ducked, laughing, and aimed the camera again.
"Okay, nymph. You're there in the tree, shy and timid.
You hear someone, a hunter, maybe. You're curious, and
also afraid. You're peeking out and at the first sight of him
you're smitten."

"Right." She rolled her eyes, making him grin again. Then she stood concentrating for a moment. Her expression grew anxious, her head tipped so that a needled branch touched her cheek, leaving an intriguing shadow. *Click.*

"Actually…" She tipped her head the other way. *Click.* "In mythology, nymphs were not that timid. They were in charge of what they wanted sexually and when. Males, females, whatever, whenever."

"Really?"

"Really." Her expression became more provocative. Her lips pouted slightly. *Click.* "Their sexuality was entirely outside male control. I like that about them."

Click. "So do I. Very hot."

Melissa arched her back. The dappled light coming through the green caught her breast, made the skin more golden, the nipple rosier. He was not going to survive this. And yet…yes, now she was perfect.

"Your problem here, Jack—" she kicked off her sneakers, shimmied out of her pants and underpants, flung them at him "—is that you need to let your women have more power."

Click. "Tell me more."

She turned, positioned herself so that her gorgeous peaches-and-cream ass curved out from the branches; her face in profile showed over the slope of her shoulder. "You and I are both strong people, who need to be in control. It's how we manage our love lives. You have lots of women. I have no men. That way we're both in charge, nothing can touch us."

She put her hands to her breasts, barely visible through the feathery branches, but enough to make him swallow.

"But I'm thinking now that one of us will have to give up control, Jack."

Click.

She had no idea how close he was to doing just that.

"Nymphs have power." Her arms stretched over to grasp the smooth reddish trunk of the madrone; she stepped close and pressed herself against it, cheek, breast, stomach, thighs parted around the trunk, knees slightly bent.

Click. Lucky tree. He was getting a hard-on.

"Sexual power." She arched back, holding the tree with the tips of her fingers and the strength in her thighs. "You need to let the women in your life indulge that power."

Click.

The sun went under a cloud; her color and the tree color got lost in the encroaching evening, which came early in the woods. Over the water daylight still reigned, but here it was harder to tell where the tree ended, where she began.

Click.

"So tell me…" She let her head drop back, hair cascading down and away. "Jack."

Click.

"Are you the hunter?" His magnificent naked nymph let go of the tree, stepped in front of it and leaned back provocatively against its slanted trunk. She smiled, lips parted, eyelids heavy. "Or am I?"

A breeze swept through the clearing, fluttering her hair as if it were leaves.

Melissa.

He put the camera down, and reached her in two strides.

10

MELISSA WATCHED JACK APPROACH, covering ground so fast he seemed to be flying. She braced herself against the tree, forcing herself not to reach for him, feverish for his arrival.

He stopped inches away; his deep brown eyes connected with hers in that way that left her breathless. "You know what you're inviting?"

"Yes," she whispered. "Yes, I do."

She hoped.

"You want this."

"Oh." Her body was trembling. She craved his touch as much as she was afraid of it. But yes, Gretchen, she was going to take this chance. "You have no idea."

"Actually, I think I do." He leaned his arms on the trunk above her head, biceps bulging under his sleeves, his lean body taut. "No turning back this time?"

"None." She pulled him to fit against her, solid, warm, the tree bent at the perfect angle so she was underneath him without taking on his whole weight.

Instead of the attack she expected, Jack rested his forehead against hers, mouth so close her lips tingled with need. "It will be intense between us, Melissa."

"I know." She lifted her face; their lips met and the hunger was unleashed, the passion revived. All polite talk, thoughtful exchanges and civilized trappings were blown away, replaced by pure, primitive instinct.

Melissa closed her eyes and concentrated on the warmth of Jack's mouth, the heat of his hands on her skin, trying to ignore the fear that this flood of feeling would submerge her, drown her then toss her up on some shore, a bloated shade of her former self.

No fear. She forced herself to stay in the moment, to breathe him in, simply to feel, not think.

No thinking.

Jack's mouth left hers, journeyed to her collarbone, kissing a line across the bones, then lower, engulfing her nipple with pressure so firm and sweet that she gasped. Opening her eyes, she watched him suckle, the familiar strong stubbled lines of his jaw contrasting with her paler skin.

The sight drove her panic up further. He was real. He was here. The more he touched her, the more she'd feel, the farther she'd sink into him and the harder it would be to save herself.

She could still escape.

No. This was what she wanted. What she'd invited. What she'd both desired and avoided her whole life.

She closed her eyes again, tangled her fingers in his hair, urged his mouth along, using the panic to fuel her passion and arousal, finding the combination of fear and desire extra-potent.

A new sensation enhanced the touch of his mouth on her breast. Jack's fingers encircled her ankle, his palm rising slowly up her shin, over her knee, along her thigh in an unhesitating, unapologetic exploration, which stopped between her legs, just shy of heaven, making her hold her breath with anticipation, body shaking.

Please, Jack...

His mouth moved to her other breast, leaving the first to cool and dry in the breeze.

Slowly, tantalizingly, his thumb slid up her inner thigh. Closer. Closer.

Oh. Melissa's breath exploded. She couldn't do this. The sensations were too intense, the emotions were too, too intense.

"Jack." She could barely say his name. He found her clitoris, started rubbing a lazy circle.

"Mmm?" His lips kissed a hot trail down her stomach. And down. And down…

Oh, no.

Oh, yes.

His tongue found the spot his thumb had abandoned, firm, wet and so warm in the cooling air. Melissa nearly came apart, could barely stand, even with most of her weight leaning on the tree. She spread her legs wider. Her head lifted and fell back on the smooth bark. Jack opened her with his fingers and entered with his tongue, thrusting inside her while his fingers played outside.

If she thought she'd been lost before, it was double now, with this man's mouth and fingers working her. She was defenseless, at his mercy, moaning louder than she should be, hips straining toward him, wanting him deeper, wanting, wanting…

The orgasm came on slowly, inevitably, taunting her, just out of reach, then hitting full-force, a hot intense wave that seemed to stop time. She muffled her cry and rode it, letting it take her, contracting, pulsing, aware of Jack as intensely as she was of her body's ecstasy.

Her legs turned to mush; she started to slide down, realizing and not caring that her back would be scratched to ribbons.

Jack's strong hands stopped her. He gently kissed her

still-swollen clitoris, her abdomen, then looked up at her
with something like awe.

"Melissa," he whispered. "That was the sexiest thing
I've ever seen."

"It was…oh." She laughed, breathlessly. "You really—"
Know what you're doing.

The sentence died. Yes, he did. Because he'd done this
dozens of times before to dozens of women. Whereas Melissa had come in less time than it took her to get mildly
aroused by other men.

He stood, gathered her in his arms, turned them so his
back was to the tree and probed her spine with light, stroking touches. "Any scratches?"

"No, no. I'm fine." She was sort of fine. His erection
lay long and hard against her abdomen. She desperately
wanted to give Jack as much pleasure as he'd just given
her, but she didn't have either his experience or confidence.

Ah, but today, in this park, she was a tree nymph, right?
Out of the control of men? Totally confident in her sexuality?

Maybe.

As she wavered, Jack, using his strong hands in the
gentle way that gave her goose bumps, stroked up her neck
to guide her head toward his, enveloped her in his arms,
and kissed her, sweetly at first, then with such passion that
hers flared again. She pressed her still-sensitive sex against
his erection, rebuilding her hunger, building his higher.

"You are so beautiful." He looked down at her, cradling her head in his arm, his expression slightly bewildered. "Making you come, watching you, I don't think
I've ever… I've never…"

He laughed self-consciously.

Ever? Never?

Whatever Jack was too nervous to say meant something

between them had been new to him. New with her. Maybe she was really more than just his next lay.

The thought was all she needed. Melissa slid down his body—Melissa, not some stupid nymph—and poised her mouth over the straining fly of his shorts. Jack stilled, frozen, until she pressed her lips against him and began his thaw.

His groan made her smile with satisfaction. She undid his fly, unzipped and reached in for the smooth hot erection that sprang eagerly toward her lips—then inside them. She slid her mouth toward the base of his cock, banishing fears and insecurity, letting herself tune in to Jack, to the signals his body was sending.

She learned he liked it when she stretched the skin at the base of his penis.

She learned he liked it when she circled his tip with her tongue, gently, carefully, then abruptly deep-throated him.

She learned he loved it when she fondled the soft bundles of his testicles at the same time as she sucked him in deep.

"Melissa." He let out a sound of frustration and grabbed her shoulders. "You're making me crazy. If you keep doing that…"

She was making him crazy.

Something snapped inside her then, a final thread tethering her to Old Nervous Melissa. A sweet, beautiful relaxation came over her, more profound than any she'd known, a certainty about who she was and what she wanted. She pulled Jack's shirt up and off, laid it carefully on the ground, found hers where she'd hurled it, and spread it beside his so they formed a roughly body-shaped covering for the dry earth.

He was watching her, hands on his hips, erection magnificent and proud.

"There." She backed up to survey their love nest. Warm arms encircled her immediately; his hand found her breasts. "Are you going to let me make love to you on the forest floor in the middle of a public park?"

She arched back so her bottom pressed against him. "I'm going to require you to. As long as you have a—"

"Condom?" He held one up, magically produced from thin air.

"Just in case?" She sent him an acerbic look with enough humor that he'd know she was teasing.

"A guy can always hope." He moved them to the shirt-bed, knelt with her, lowered her gently to the ground and rolled on the condom. "In your case, it was less hope than desperation."

"Really." Melissa welcomed his weight on hers, no fear this time, no sense of shame, no inkling of inner protest that this was too much, too soon, that she was being un-wisely risky with her body and heart. So new. So wonder-ful. Everything about this moment felt natural and right. She traced his lips with her forefinger. "I think I've expe-rienced some of that desperation, too."

"Yeah?" He returned her smile, then his faded slowly; a small frown creased a line between his brows. One soft, sweet kiss, then he pulled back just until their lips came apart. "You are a remarkable woman, Melissa."

She stared into his dark eyes, feeling a glow of some-thing she barely understood. A ray of sun made its way through the trees and lit his face, touching his black-coffee hair with glints of auburn, lighting his skin, making him look positively godlike. "You certainly make me feel that way, Jack. And you are—"

"No, shhh." Her personal god put a finger to her lips. "This is your compliment session. Mine comes later. When we have a *lot* more time."

She burst out laughing, then stopped abruptly when he kissed her, a serious, sensual kiss that left no question what was on his mind.

Her mouth responded, her arms crept around him, her brain sent signals that this man was getting deeper and deeper into her heart and mind, places unused for so long that they'd been in danger of atrophying. That was a good thing, no matter how or when or whether she and Jack ended.

His erection nudged at her; she opened her legs eagerly, reached down to help guide him.

An inch at a time, pushing in, pulling back, he went inside her, watching her, closing his eyes in pleasure for brief moments, then opening them again. It was too much, but it wasn't fear she felt this time. It was an emotion Melissa couldn't name. She had to look away, could only manage glances back up at him.

Then he was all the way in and slowly, gently, he began to move. As it seemed with everything between them, the sex was more. More feeling, more friction, more awareness of the contact between their bodies, of the stunning intimacy, of the breeze washing over them, of the forest whispers, of their natural place lying on the earth, tree and freshwater smells surrounding them.

Melissa never wanted it to end. The push and pull of his hips, the touch of his broad firm chest against hers, the wide, smooth planes of his back under her fingers, the sweet murmurs in her ear. She'd never had a lover like this. Jack was skilled, yes, but he was also *there,* in every sense, acknowledging and indulging each sensation along with her, a connection she'd never experienced to this degree.

Gradually, urgency crept into their movements; their breaths became shallower, shorter.

"Melissa." Jack kissed her shoulder, her cheek then her

mouth, hot and hard, on and on while their bodies reached higher and more frantically for release.

His approached first, his body tensing. A groan ripped from him that was so sexy it pushed her over the edge and she burst into a second orgasm, barely keeping herself from shouting at the power of it, clinging to him helplessly as their bodies pulsed together…and came down.

Then all was quiet and calm, the earth still turning, birds flying home to roost, sun on its way to ending its daily appointed round. Jack lifted his head, breath coming fast, face flushed, eyes bright with pleasure.

"That was…" He laughed and shook his head.

"Yes." She grinned at him, drew a line down from his temple to his strong chin. "It was."

"Can we do that again sometime?"

Melissa pretended to consider. "Well, I suppose if—"

"Hey, Dad! Come look at this!"

Melissa was pretty sure neither of them had ever moved quite so fast in their lives as they lunged for their clothes.

"Good lord." She crouched, peering through the trees, fumbling with her bra. "That's all we need, to scar a small child for life. What were we thinking?"

"We weren't." Jack stepped into his shorts. "He's run back to his family. I don't think he was talking about us."

"I hope not." She pulled her shirt over her head. "That would have been horrible."

"Would have been." He bent to kiss her as she struggled into her pants. "But wasn't."

"Next time we do this—"

"Inside. In bed, behind a locked door. Yours, mine, doesn't matter."

She nodded as if they were discussing business, while inside she was celebrating. They would get to do this again, go to that amazing place together again. "Good plan."

He grinned and pushed back the hair that had fallen into her eyes. "You know, you look adorable when you're in danger of being arrested for indecent exposure."

"Aw, thanks." She beamed at him. "And you look gorgeous when you're guilty of lewd conduct."

He brushed something off her shirt. "Would you like to go sit on the beach and watch the sunset with me? We got cheated out of our afterglow here."

More beaming. She wasn't ready to let this day with him end yet. "I would love to."

"I've got sandwiches and a bottle of decent wine."

"That sounds really nice, Jack." She was touched, very touched. He'd planned, organized, prepared for their time together. Not what she expected from a player.

Yeah, well, maybe she needed to worry less about what she expected from his "type" and concentrate more on who he really was. *Ya think, Melissa?* It might feel safer to cram Jack into a neat little box, but it wasn't fair and it wasn't right, and it wasn't nearly as much fun.

Barbara would say Melissa was being naive. Surprisingly, she didn't care.

They found a beautiful spot near the entrance to the park on a just-abandoned bench—debatable whether the thin stretch of muddy rocks deserved the term *beach*— with a stunning view of Lake Washington. Off in the distance Mount Rainier's snowy top poked through the cloud line. Jack had retrieved a cooler from his car containing thick roast beef sandwiches, chips and a nice Washington State sauvignon blanc.

They sat eating and sipping, watching the sky, lake and mountain colors change as the sun dipped lower.

"This is wonderful, Jack." Melissa sighed contentedly. "I feel so relaxed."

"Good sex will do that."

She threw him a smile, and almost couldn't look away. The man was stunning, the breeze occasionally lifting a tousled lock off his smooth forehead. She wanted to photograph him, be able to look at him this way whenever she wanted. Which would be embarrassingly often. More than just looking, she also wanted to tell him everything about herself, and to learn everything about him.

"I've been lying to you, Jack."

"Uh-oh. You're really a man?"

She laughed. "I'm not really calm. I have hypertension. I've been fighting it for months. That's why I'm taking yoga. When you said you picked me to model because I was serene, I nearly died laughing."

"But you are." He looked genuinely surprised. "You're very centered, very solid."

"Recently, yes. Right now my blood pressure is so low I bet if I stood up I'd pass out."

"Good sex will do that."

She giggled. "Where have I heard that before?"

"No idea." He reached into the cooler, brought out the bottle of wine. "Sex and yoga, but I bet posing for me also helps. In front of the camera, you're not involved in real life or ordinary stresses. You're just being, down to your most elemental."

"As Eve."

"Sure. Or a nymph. Or Venus. Or whoever. Ironic, isn't it?" He offered her more wine, poured carefully as she held out her glass. "In trying to be someone else you've probably come closer to being yourself."

"Hmm. My sister said my blood pressure was up because I've been trying to be someone I'm not."

"Your sister sounds like a wise woman." He put the bottle back in the cooler.

"What about you?" She raised her glass to him. "You're more yourself behind a camera, too, you know."

"Me?" He looked at her in pretend astonishment, then his face cleared. "Oh, you mean I'm even *more* amazing?"

"You have two distinct personalities." She put her drink down and curled up on the bench, hugging her knees. "No, three. One, the glib charmer."

"Glib!" He put a hand to his chest and addressed a nearby seagull. "She thinks I'm glib. Can you believe that?"

Melissa looked at him speculatively. "I'm guessing that's your way of hiding your real self while staying invulnerable to—"

"Oh, no." He shook his head, waggled his finger at her. "Not the I-know-you-better-than-you-know-yourself speech."

Her eyebrows shot up. "I'm sorry. Wasn't that you telling me just now I'm more Eve the Tree Nymph than Melissa?"

"D'oh." He winced. "You got me."

"Personality number two." She held up two fingers. "The grumpy old man. Or toddler. Cranky when you're frustrated."

"Not cranky. When I'm frustrated I get frustrated. In a very masculine and mature way."

"And three." She sent him a provocative smile. "My favorite. The intense sexy artist."

"Speaking of sexy." He leaned over and kissed her. Then again. And another. "You know, most women think I'm sexy when I'm being the charmer."

"Ha! I am not most women." She meant the words playfully, but he didn't smile.

"I'm beginning to realize that."

"No, no." She felt her cheeks flame and hoped he'd mistake the blush for sunlight. "I was kidding."

"I know. But it's true." He picked up his glass again, draped an arm around her. She didn't know when she'd felt this happy and deliciously out of worries. Probably not since her mother had been alive. "You have three personalities, too."

She grimaced comically. "I was afraid of this."

"One, the chilly office lady." He shuddered.

"Brisk as the north wind?"

"And twice as frigid."

"Hey."

He gave her a kiss her glare had no chance of surviving. "Two, the lost and uncertain child."

"Child? You just made love to a child?"

"Oh, no." He leaned over and pressed another kiss to the back of her neck, one of her favorite spots. "That was the sexual goddess."

"Mmm, thank you. I like that third one." She made herself frown thoughtfully, bursting inside with happiness at the label. With Jack she felt exactly like a goddess. He brought out parts of her she didn't know she had. "But wait, wasn't this supposed to be *your* compliment hour?"

"You've given me plenty." He put their wine down, reached over and lifted her onto his lap. "We should go soon, but come here."

She wrapped her arms around him, leaned her head against his shoulder, inhaling the sweet lake air, thinking about what had happened in the woods. To him. To her. To them. "Tell me something, Jack."

"Mmm?"

"What made you become a photographer? Was it something you were born to do? Or something outside you that drew you in?"

"Hmm, good question." She felt his body tense under hers and held still, wondering what demons he was wrestling with and whether he'd tell her. "Best I can come up with is that having grown up in a fairly dysfunctional family, I took on the role of observer."

"Safer than being part of the mess?"

"Yup." He spoke haltingly, not in his usual smooth way. Melissa's heart added a new sensation: pain on his behalf. "It was mostly my dad. He felt saddled with my brother and me, never wanted a family, never loved my mother. All of which would have been sad but okay if he'd either shut up about it and accepted his responsibilities, or exited gracefully at the beginning. Instead he hung around for a decade or so making sure we all knew we were the source of his very loud and very bitter unhappiness."

"Oh, my God, Jack. What a burden on you."

"It was not the most fun." His arms tightened around her; she wasn't sure he realized he was doing it. "He left right after my mom got laid off. Disappeared while we were at school and she was out on an interview. He took as much as he could fit in his car. We never heard from him again, not that any of us wanted to. Asshole to the very end."

"I'm so sorry."

He shrugged. "Me, too, sometimes. Other times I think, okay, it could have been better, but it also could have been worse. I'm not the only one with problems. You lost your mom. That was hard, too."

"It was." Her voice thickened. Even after all this time it was rough talking about her mother. "She was the heart of our family. Her death changed everything. You know what that's like. It's hard to learn so young that bad things happen. I used to hear my girlfriends complaining about their mothers not letting them buy this or that, or go here or there, and it just about killed me. I would have *loved* to have a mom to hate."

He stroked her hair. "I guess we both had to grow up too fast. Probably why you try to mother your sister."

"Nah." She wrinkled her nose. "I'm just a bossy control freak."

He chuckled. "A very sexy, very beautiful bossy control freak."

Probably ten of the most glorious minutes happened next, spent kissing, kissing more and then kissing again. Kissing Jack Shea during a sunset on a lovely summer evening would go down in the record books as the very, very best way possible to spend time.

"This has been a…perfect evening, Jack." She leaned against his shoulder to hide the emotion threatening to hijack her cool. "Thank you."

"We'll do it again." He pressed his cheek to her hair, which made her heart go soft and melty. "Remember, we're going to have to spend a *lot* of time together."

She lifted her face to show him how big her smile was at that thought. Gretchen had said Melissa was a little bit in love with Jack. At the time she'd scoffed. How could that be true? Tonight, here, it felt as if it was. As if she were truly a little bit in love with him. Only a little.

But in very big danger of falling the rest of the way.

11

"WELL, LOOK WHO'S HERE." Seth hoisted his beer to Jack, smirking.

"Coming up for air?" Angela smiled sweetly, fingers laced with Daniel's as they sat pressed together on the futuristic black-and-white love seat in the Come to Your Senses common room.

"Jack, right? Jack Shea?" Bonnie pointed to him triumphantly. "I knew you looked familiar."

Jack rolled his eyes good-naturedly, heading for the refrigerator. He'd been working every spare second with Melissa for the past two weeks, and had had a feeling he'd be in for this when he finally met up with his friends. "You are looking at an artist who's been hard at work."

"An artist who's been hard at something."

"Seth!" Angela shook her head at him, giggling. "How's the series coming, Jack?"

"How is your *model* coming, Jack?"

"Seth!" Bonnie could barely hold back her laughter. "You need to behave or leave the room."

"Sorry, Mom." He put the bottle to his lips, cocky grin in place as usual. "Seriously, Jack, tell us. Are you shooting well?"

Bonnie socked him on the shoulder and pointed to the exit. "Go."

"What?" He feigned innocence as only Seth could. "I'm interested in his work."

"Honestly." Bonnie pretended utter disgust, but was unable to hide a rogue giggle. "The man puts a love song up on YouTube and he thinks he owns the world."

"Don't tell them that." Seth looked mortified.

"Oh, why, because YouTube is so private?" She socked him again, with affection this time. "I think it's great."

"Seth, that *is* great." Angela gave him a virtual high five from her seat across the room. "We should bring in someone's laptop and listen."

"I think we were talking about *Jack*." Seth gestured toward him. "Right, Jack? Your work?"

"It's going well." That was a classic understatement. The sessions with Melissa had been an emotional, physical and mental workout, but supremely satisfying on all counts. Jack had gone deeper than he ever had on all three levels, and yeah, Seth would have a field day with that one, too. "Though not the way I expected."

"No?" Angela turned from gazing at Daniel. Jack yanked out a beer. The way Angela adored her boyfriend made Jack miss Melissa, and he didn't like missing women. Loving them when he was with them, getting on with life when he wasn't: that had always worked for him.

It wasn't working so well now.

"How has it been unexpected?" Bonnie asked.

"More of a collaboration instead of just my ideas." He made sure he looked casual, no stars in his eyes, no telltale bulge in his shorts. Truth was, Jack was high on pretty much everything, and he wasn't talking about drugs. He hadn't realized how much of his father's life-sucks-then-you-die philosophy he'd internalized until Melissa offered him all this plain old fun. "Melissa's my muse as well as my model."

"How great that you two work so well together." Angela smiled too sweetly. "And are you…getting along otherwise?"

Beside her, Daniel chuckled. "Was that too subtle, Jack?"

"What?" Angela pretended to be mystified. "I just asked if they were enjoying each other's company."

"We know what you were asking." Daniel soothed her with a brief kiss.

"We all wanted to ask the same thing." Bonnie patted the couch next to her. "So, Jack, if it's not too personal, tell us something of what's happening. And if it *is* too personal, then tell us absolutely everything."

He took his time settling onto the couch. "You think that's any of your business?"

"Yes." The entire room answered his question.

He cracked up, popped the top off his beer and took a long, refreshing swig. "I think we should hear a few Seattledates stories first."

"Oh, *what* a good idea." Seth looked viciously triumphant. "Why should we be the only ones publicly disemboweled?"

"Let's see." Bonnie put a finger to her cheek, looking prim. "Would you like to hear about the guy who sent me the twenty-nine-page story of his life? Or the one who asked me out and then when I said yes, disappeared? Or, no, how about the guy who in his second email described seeing his father naked in the hospital?"

"Oh, no, Bonnie." Angela nudged herself closer to Daniel, clutching his arm. "They can't *all* be that bad."

"Or maybe they can." Seth waggled his eyebrows.

"So far they are, but I'm still *very* optimistic." Bonnie

spoke pointedly, glancing at Seth, then turned to Jack. "That was my gut-spilling duty. Your turn, Jack, and no backing out."

"You were about to tell us how it's going with Melissa," Angela prompted.

"Melissa…is a great person, a good friend, and we are getting along fine."

Silence, while his friends exchanged glances.

"He's getting some," Seth said.

"Dude." Daniel nodded. "Is he ever."

"We're happy for you both," Angela added primly. "And we want detailed pictures of every position."

Jack shook his head, laughing with the rest of them. His friends might resort to comedy routines to express support, but their affection was sincere, and he was grateful.

"So, old man, now that you're hooked, when's the wedding?" Seth toasted him with his beer. "You'd better hire a photographer soon. I hear those guys book up quickly."

"Oh, Melissa would make a gorgeous bride. She's so beautiful alread—*ow*." Angela glared at Daniel, who removed his hand from her neck, shaking his head.

"She'd be a stunning bride." Bonnie gazed dreamily off into space. "I can see her with pink sweetheart roses. Maybe one in her hair. We can put a picture of her on my website. I can blog about—"

"Yeah, I think you can save those fantasies for another millennium." Jack rubbed his jaw impatiently. This time the teasing was getting to him.

He looked forward equally to the art he and Melissa collaborated on, the passionate lovemaking and the quiet times when they sat or lay together and talked, got a bite to eat or went for a walk when they needed a break from the sessions. He'd never realized how many barriers existed between him and the women he was with until he'd found one who didn't put any up.

Melissa was tearing his down, too, and he didn't like it. She was incredibly fun to be with. Intelligent, thoughtful, sweet, sassy, but no part of his life felt like his own anymore. She'd sneaked into every corner, like wafts of some fragrance that enters your house and ends up taking such deep root in your olfactory system that you smell it even when the source is gone.

Doubtless his emotions for Melissa were intensified by the way she'd become so tangled in his art and in his creative process. But that was a hell of a long way from worrying about a life commitment. He wasn't even comfortable going to her sister's wedding. Something about the occasion brought out the romantic in women. All you had to do was look at the dreamy look on Bonnie and Angela's faces to prove his point. Who knew how Melissa would react? Jack had made it clear he was working the wedding in return for her contribution to his series, period. Just because Melissa would be there and he would be there didn't mean the event had turned into anything other than his next job.

"Can I join you guys?" Demi walked into the room, arms folded.

"Only if you take my side against these vultures." Jack stood. "Can I get you a beer?"

"Thanks, Jack." She sat in the rocking chair, looking ill at ease.

Jack squeezed Bonnie's shoulder in a pointed message to stop scowling at their least social business partner.

"How's the new table working out?" Seth asked.

"Oh, fine." She smiled faintly at him. "The old one was secondhand, in sad shape. It was my first table."

"When did you start massage therapy?" Jack broke the

few seconds of awkward silence on his way to the fridge. The last thing Demi needed was to feel as if her presence inhibited the rest of them. She'd never show up again.

"In college. That table's seen a lot of use."

"Okay, *I* want to know who that guy is who went to see you yesterday, at about ten." Angela fanned herself. "And what body part did you get to work on?"

"Hey." Daniel pretended to be hurt. "You're not supposed to notice other men anymore."

"Oh, right. And you'll stop watching Jessica Alba movies now?"

"Oh." He looked comically crushed. "Well, uh…"

"Case rested." Angela kissed his cheek. "Demi?"

"You must mean Colin."

"Firth? Farrell?" Seth asked.

"Even hotter." Angela patted her fiancé's knee. "Though of course he's not nearly as hot as you are, Daniel."

Daniel rolled his eyes. "Right."

"He has disk issues in his back." Demi accepted her beer from Jack with a smile. "A really talented Ironman triathlete. Very hard for him to have to give it up."

Jack was surprised to notice Demi blushing faintly. So the ultracool woman had feelings after all. He'd suspected as much. Still waters ran deep. He'd often been surprised how many women like her turned out to be wild animals in bed.

Like Melissa. Their lovemaking over the past couple of weeks had become more and more exciting as they became familiar with each other's bodies and preferences and needs. She constantly surprised him with how real she was. In bed together they communicated at a totally honest level. When a sexual idea worked, they went for it; he never got the feeling her noises and movements were put on for his benefit, but was sure they came from a deep and natural place. When something didn't work, there was no embarrassment, no awkward apology, just laughter and joking and on to the next. Sometimes in the middle of love-making they'd talk about whatever was on their minds, until one of them changed positions and they'd be lost to the process again.

"Well, you'll be seeing Mr. Colin again, then," Seth said. "Disk injuries are tricky."

Demi nodded. "They can be."

"No kidding." Daniel said. "I was—"

"I'm hoping I can help him," Demi blurted out.

"I'm sure you can." Angela smiled supportively. "So what do—"

"He'll probably have to be in therapy for a long, long time." Demi sighed, eyes downcast. "Weeks if not months."

"That is so terrible." Angela, tenderhearted as usual. The rest of them were exchanging o-kay-Demi glances.

"Terrible? Really? You think so?" Demi drank her beer, but her eyes were dancing and a dimple appeared in her right cheek.

Angela nearly spat out her beer, then Demi's joke hit the rest of them and the laughter spread. Even Bonnie smiled. Jack was glad Demi was relaxing with them. She should come by more often.

His cell buzzed in his pocket; he dug it out to look at the display, annoyed that he was hoping it was Melissa. He got plenty of calls all day long, clients and friends.

It wasn't Melissa. It was Tammy.

Oh, man.

Tammy was a management consultant he'd met at a downtown bar one night a few years back—how many now? Three? Four? Jack didn't remember. Whenever she was going to be in town—several times a year—she'd call him and they'd hook up, whether either of them was dating other people or not. She was the closest thing he'd ever had to a long-term relationship. And yet for both of them it was out of sight, out of mind until they got together the next time. In her early- or mid-thirties—he knew better than to ask—Tammy was beautiful, smart, funny and uninhibited. Beyond that, he didn't much care about anything else, just enjoyed her a hell of a lot.

And hadn't even thought about her in weeks. No, months. Not since he'd first seen Melissa in the park.

The phone kept ringing. Jack should answer. He always answered. He and Tammy had an understanding.

He strode out of the apartment and down the hall. By the time he got back to his apartment at the other, the voice-mail notifier had appeared. He should call back right away and make plans with her.

Instead he dialed into his voice mail.

"Hey, hey, Mr. Shea." Tammy's familiar sexy voice filled his ears, bringing with it a mental picture of her: tall, slender, well muscled, frosted blond hair, expert makeup and stylish clothes, ultraconfident. "I'll be in town next week Tuesday for three nights and I am having a serious Jack-attack. I'm not traveling as much these days and it's been way too many months. Where shall we meet?"

He had nothing on his schedule any of the three nights she'd be in town. She knew better than to bother asking if he was busy. For her, he never was.

Jack closed his eyes, leaned back against the wall.

This was bad.

This was really bad.

Even with nothing on his calendar, Jack no longer felt free.

Blood Pressure: Normal

"SO THEN HE HAD ME pose as Venus, goddess of beauty, on this hilarious plastic clamshell like the Botticelli painting." Melissa placed a small handful of silver and white Jordan almonds onto a square of white netting. She and Gretchen were putting together party favors for guests. The wedding day was coming together beautifully now that Melissa was no longer trying to have it all her way—and she still cringed when she thought of what she'd nearly done to her sister, though Gretchen had been totally wonderful when she'd apologized. "Only instead of covering myself up, I was holding a mirror, as if I was saying, 'Don't look at me to see beauty, look at yourself.' Isn't that cool?"

"Yes, wow, that is a really clever idea." Gretchen glanced up from tying a silver ribbon around her package of almonds, beaming her approval. "Sounds like you've been having so-o-o much fun with this guy."

"I have." Melissa giggled like a complete moron. She hadn't stopped smiling for the past couple of weeks, ever since the shoot with Jack in Seward Park. Why should she stop now? "It's been really great. He's really great. The photography is really great. The hanging-out time together is really great. The sex is *really* great."

"So if you could think of one phrase to sum up what it's like with Jack…I don't know, maybe you'd pick *really great?*" Gretchen snorted.

"Nah. I'd say *average.*"

"Uh-huh." Gretchen rolled her eyes. "I knew you liked this guy. You've been different since you met him."

Melissa heard herself sigh blissfully. She was really nauseating these days. "I feel different."

"Tell me how." Gretchen put a finished favor into the

box holding the others. "I'm curious whether it's the same
as what I've noticed."

Melissa stopped to think. It wasn't an exaggeration to
say that posing for Jack had changed her life. She was seeing herself the way he saw her, discovering to her surprise
that she was a highly sensual and sexual person after all,
and that she had creativity in her soul she'd never dreamed
was there. Throughout school and for the past three years
she'd been absorbing facts and skills other people handed
out, neglecting to look inside herself for what Melissa
might be about. The more she blossomed, the more her
self-confidence rose, and, ironically, the more tolerant she
grew of others.

She was even allowing herself to wonder if Barbara
was less of a good influence than she'd thought. Growth,
personal enrichment, all those were important, sure, but
how about happiness? Waking up next to someone—or
alone—feeling luxurious and relaxed, not worrying that
every second of downtime was a curse. Getting the chance
to laugh to tears with someone every other day. Enjoying
lazy hours outside, strolls along the water. In her prescription for the right way to live, Barbara must have forgotten
happiness, forgotten that a man could bring that as well
as pain to a woman. Jack made Melissa happier than anything she'd been able to accomplish on her own. Was that
weakness? Or was it simply part of being human?

"I'm more relaxed for sure, and my blood pressure
shows it. But also… I don't know. Things don't bother
me as much. I feel more on top of my life. Less like everything I do must be so important to developing who I
am. More as if I've discovered I existed on some deeper
level I wasn't aware of." She laughed self-consciously. "I'm
sounding like an idiot."

"No, you're not. You sounded like an idiot when you

were spouting Barbara-speak. These are your words and they make total sense to me. Falling for the right person brings us in touch with the best parts of ourselves." Her sister's face went soft and dreamy. She was clearly thinking of Ted. "And having that support in your life does make it seem as if fewer burdens are sitting on your shoulders alone."

"Yes." Melissa's heart swelled with emotion. "That's it, exactly."

Gretchen shrugged. "Though to be honest, Ted and I have been together so long I hardly remember what it was like not to be with him. I mostly remember being sad."

"We grew up in a sad house." Melissa shook a square of netting to free it from its clinging cousins. She found herself grieving her mother harder and more often these days than she had in years, making her suspect that she'd cheated herself out of some of the process as a child by diving in to take her mom's place.

"Speaking of sad, I called Dad the other day." Melissa cut several more lengths of ribbon. "I told him it was time to get off his butt and start dating again."

"Melissa!" Gretchen froze with her hand in the tin of almonds. "You didn't."

"I did. Sure. Why not?" Melissa grinned. "Okay, okay, I didn't use those actual words. I told him I was worried about him and made him promise to get a physical and mention his depression. And then I sent him an email with the link to a seniors' dating website."

"Oh, dear God." Gretchen's eyes were wide with curiosity. "What did he say?"

"Believe it or not, he said he'd been thinking about it for a while."

"Wow." Gretchen put her hands in her lap, apparently

stunned. "Wow. Good for you, Melissa, that was really brave."

"I don't know about that." It would have been much braver to have done that a long time ago, instead of sitting in judgment on his lifestyle. "Overdue I'd say."

"Do you think he can be happy again after what he and Mom shared the first time around?"

"Uh." Melissa gave her a look. "Happier than staying home watching TV every night?"

"I *meant* in the relationship."

"I know. I was trying to say that isn't really the point. The point is he should be happier than he is now."

Gretchen was beaming. "And your prescription for happiness suddenly includes a romance."

"I'm just saying…" Melissa piled up more silver and white almonds. "I don't think there's only one person for each of us. But I do think some matches are better than others. Like Dad's and Mom's and yours and Ted's. Still, there has to be someone out there who could make Dad's life better and vice versa."

"You think Jack could be a really good forever match for you?"

The question startled Melissa so much she couldn't even come up with a flip response. She managed a shrug, then horrified herself by having to swallow hard and blink harder.

"Oooh, Melissa!" Gretchen had stopped all pretense of making favors.

"Don't say it." Melissa held up her hand. "Not one damn word. We are going to talk about your wedding."

"No, let's talk about yours."

"Not going to be one."

"What makes you so sure?"

"Jack is not the settle-down kind." Her voice broke.

"Pthhpt." Gretchen effectively dismissed that comment. 'Three weeks ago you weren't, either. If he's right for you, he'll become the settle-down kind. You might have to be patient, but it will happen, you watch. And if you even *think* of—"

"When are you picking up the cake from Angela?" Melissa asked pointedly.

"Okay, okay." Gretchen sighed her disappointment. 'End of the week. I'll decorate it over the weekend. Bonnie's giving me flowers for the cake then, too. I'll get the bouquet and table decorations the day before the ceremony. I also have the disposable cameras for friends to use at the reception."

"I'm glad you're having Jack do the formal portraits." She batted her eyes ridiculously. "Because it frees him up to be my date after the ceremony."

"Well, you know, sister dear, weddings are *great* places to cement relationships…"

"Don't start with me." Melissa sent her sister a warning glare, stomach-butterflies fluttering away.

"Hey." Gretchen reached across the table to squeeze Melissa's arm. "You know what's also different? It's not like you're trying to be my mom anymore. It's like you're really my sister now."

There was no way Melissa could hold back tears after that one. "Gretchen, what are you trying to do to me?"

"Ha! Look at you." She squeezed harder. "Leaky waterworks are the final proof. Melissa, girl, you are in love. If you blow it with this guy, I will never forgive you. And if he screws it up, give me his address, because I'll personally—"

"Hey, you girls need help?" To Melissa's relief, Ted walked in from the other room and kissed Gretchen as if he hadn't seen her in three months when their separation had probably been all of an hour. Usually Melissa wanted to gag when she saw them together like that. Usually she started thinking unkind thoughts about codependency.

Now, what she felt wasn't nausea, it was wistfulness for that kind of commitment and mutual adoration.

Gretchen was right. A month ago the idea of being coupled with the same person for the rest of her life had practically given her an allergic reaction. Jack had her envisioning a different kind of partnership, not the breathe-in-sync variety that Mom and Dad had had and that Gretchen and Ted had. That would drive Melissa nuts. She wanted a different type. A deep bond between two strong, independent individuals passionate about living life to its fullest who challenged each other, disagreed vehemently about some things, came together as a powerhouse on others and spent as much time together naked as possible.

That kind of relationship.

Which, totally coincidentally, Melissa could envision herself having with Jack.

12

"I LOVE HOW THIS ONE came out."

Jack nodded and nudged Melissa's shoulder next to his on his couch. He was particularly pleased with the way the print had worked, too, the one of Melissa on the clamshell as Venus. On the "mirror" she held outward, he'd merged in a face, indistinct, androgynous, Anyman or Anywoman. Melissa's hair blew in sexy disarray around her face, and her blue eyes shot out of her fine-boned features with particular intensity, lips curved in a sensual smile, broadcasting a welcome, urging the viewer to consider his or her own reflection as the embodiment of beauty.

This picture had been his idea, but Melissa had imbued it with such life and emotion—beyond what he would have known to demand. The way she internalized his concepts then communicated them back out to his lens…she was remarkable. The most intelligent, versatile and talented model he'd ever worked with.

Not that he was biased.

"I'm pleased with that one." Pleased, hell, he was strutting like a rooster over it and all the other shots they'd done together. The initial discomfort, the feeling that he was stretching himself into something that didn't quite fit yet had passed almost entirely. These images weren't the final versions, they were the raw materials for what he'd hoped to convey: female power, pride, independence co existing with sexuality that didn't need to be hidden or shamed. Jack was content, an emotion he rarely felt when it came to his work, and he was confident Pierre Balzac would be, too.

He and Melissa were sharing the album and a bottle of wine after another photography session, their last. When they finished, he'd find something for them to eat in the kitchen or they'd go out to dinner. They'd come back and make love again, maybe spend the night together.

It was starting to feel natural to spend so much time together. Jack had never shared more than a night or two a week with whomever he was seeing, maybe more at the beginning when passion burned brightest. Making sure he kept plenty of time for himself and his other friends and passions kept him from ever feeling he was being swal lowed up by any one woman.

Right now he was being swallowed up by this one. Half of him wanted to crawl deep into Melissa and merge them completely. The other half wanted to run screaming and not look back.

Since he was pretty sure he couldn't split himself down the middle, Jack was left in a painful, tug-of-war stalemate that was making him irritable and anxious. Which was probably making Melissa anxious, though she was trying hard not to show it.

Something had to give.

"More wine?" His voice came out harshly; Melissa turned questioningly from one of the Eve photos he'd taken their second day in the studio, then smiled and kissed his cheek.

"Sure." She held out her glass. Jack poured carefully,

then more for himself. He was drinking the stuff too quickly. "It's good, this Malbec. I like it."

"Same." He clinked glasses with her, holding her gaze, indulging the push-pull emotion that was starting to be familiar. Pull her close. Push her away.

She settled back against him, nestled under his arm where she fitted so perfectly. Their bodies seemed made for each other—rarely did they have to adjust sleeping positions. Was that significant? Hardly. But it was one more of what were starting to feel like signs pointing ahead in a smooth dark tunnel to forever, when he wanted to be sure there was an exit at every step.

"So what are we going to do together now that the shoots are over? It's going to feel weird being naked around you only for sex."

"Yeah." He drank, then drank again. The shoots were over. Goodbye sexy model and virile photographer having a torrid affair. Hello Jack and Melissa, boyfriend and girlfriend. The former sounded so hot and exciting. The latter…he could not feel enthusiastic.

"I think we'll be able to handle it." She put her wine on his coffee table, then placed his beside it. His and Hers glasses. "Don't you?"

He didn't know. But he did know he had no problem with Melissa moving to sit across his lap, no problem putting his arms around her beautiful body, holding it close, kissing her, feeling his penis stirring just from the way she used her mouth against his.

This woman had drawn him physically from the first moment he saw her. That hadn't changed. But Tammy's call the night before had clearly brought to his attention the fact that everything else about his life was changing, and he didn't want it to. Not yet. Maybe not ever. Change meant pain, risk, danger—and what was a bigger change than losing your heart to someone? Maybe having a kid, but, ha, that was so far off his radar, it wasn't worth including.

Except... He imagined Melissa pregnant with a junior version of Jack, or a junior version of herself, a beautiful blond baby girl with her mother's blue eyes. Even while his heart softened, his body started to sweat. This had to stop.

"I have something to tell you." She drew a line down his chest with a slender finger.

"What's that?" Even though her playful tone told him nothing serious was coming, his gut tensed.

"I've been naughty, Jack." She turned to straddle him on her knees, her black knit miniskirt stretching and lifting to give him a cock-hardening view of her long, smooth thighs.

He hid a grin under a pretend scowl. In this arena, he had no complaints about his feelings for Melissa. His desire for her was pure, simple and incredibly strong. "What have you done?"

Melissa put her mouth next to his ear to whisper, "I never put my underpants back on."

Jack groaned and swept his hands up her thighs, bare all the way to that gorgeous firm ass that drove him wild. "No, you didn't."

With a tug she pulled off her shirt, unhooked her bra and tossed it over her shoulder. Topless, with the skirt barely covering her, she was every man's fantasy. He wanted to pull her close, hold her, feel the soft warmth of her breasts against him. He wanted it too much. Too possessively.

"Do you think I need punishment, Jack?"

"Yes." He lifted her leg, slid out from under her and turned her so she was on her hands and knees facing away from him, relieved to have this game to play. With flying fingers, he unsnapped and unzipped his pants, pulled his erection free. "I think you do."

"Oh, goody." She giggled, and sent him a sultry look over her shoulder. "I was hoping."

"No laughing. This punishment is serious business." He took a moment just to look at her strong thighs, at the black horizontal hem of her skirt, which clung to her hips and buttocks as if it was as infatuated with them as he was. He placed both hands on her thighs just under the hem and slowly pushed upwards, exposing her to him, the beautiful rounded slope of her bottom.

Mine.

The word came without his permission. He didn't question it now, that would come later. He simply bent forward, inhaling her light feminine scent, relishing her gasp of surprise and pleasure.

"Oh, Jack."

Oh, Melissa.

He covered her bottom with his palms, then lightened his touch with one hand to nearly nothing, traveling in lazy tickling circles.

A small gasp, then she grew statue-still. "I've never… mmm." Her breath came out in a sigh of ecstasy. "That is really…nice, Jack."

"Good." He felt pride, caveman ownership, in showing her this new source of pleasure. And with that pride came a fierce, deep tenderness he didn't want to feel.

"I'd like something else now." Her voice was breathlessly sexy.

"Mmm?"

"You. Inside me." Her body tensed. "I mean the old-fashioned way."

He chuckled and kissed both of her beautiful rounded cheeks. "I can do that."

"Oh, *thank* you, Jack." She twisted to give him a mock humble look. "I *so* appreciate it."

He laughed and got on his knees, put on one of the condoms he had stashed around the apartment for convenience and laid an affectionate hand on her back. He loved that they could be like this, that sex wasn't all earnest and animal between them, but had moods and rhythms that were constantly changing.

"Wait, did you mean now?" He took hold of his penis, rubbed its hard tip against the part of her he'd left warm and wet. "You wanted me inside you now?"

"Yes." She arched, pushed her hips back toward him. "Now. Please."

"You're sure?" He spread her labia with his free hand, loving the pink winged look they took on, and pushed himself slowly in. He pulled back when he needed to, then continued, closing his eyes, concentrating on the sensation of her warmth gripping him, taking in her gasps and moans of pleasure. For a second he held still, inside her to the hilt, lightly holding her hips.

Melissa.

She waited, head tipped up, hair cascading over her shoulders. Then turned. Their eyes met. He wanted to pull out, take her face in his hands and kiss her mouth, turn her so they lay face to face, make love to her, watch her eyes change, darken, her head moving from side to side, her lips parting with the pleasure he was giving her. He wanted to be there, joined to her when she came. He wanted to catch her breath in his mouth, hear her cry out as the orgasm peaked, be there to support her as she came down, hold her in his arms and keep her safe, keep her his for the rest of their—

No.

He pulled halfway out, tightened his grip on her skin and pushed home, hard. He heard her grunt in what might have been pain, pleasure or both, his fingers digging into her flesh as he moved inside her with powerful, angry thrusts, skin slapping skin, his jaw tight, teeth clenched, breath hissing through them. Over and over, he buried himself in her body, blocking out emotions, blocking out thoughts, just feeling, just being.

Melissa braced herself against the armrest of the couch, lowered her head, shoulder muscles straining, breasts bouncing forward and back as she absorbed the impact.

He closed his mind to her, to her vulnerability, to what she must be thinking of his virtual attack on her. He thought only of what his body wanted, to dominate, to subjugate—not her, but the demons inside him that would only be satisfied when she totally and thoroughly belonged to him.

Nature took over, brought him to the brink much faster than he usually allowed it to. He pushed on, quickening his pace, sofa scraping the floor, guttural sounds escaping his throat, dimly aware that Melissa was twisting oddly, supporting herself only on one arm now.

He should stop.

He had to stop. If he was hurting her…

She was so tight, so hot, he was so close.

One push, another, and the wave caught up with him, pulled him under, tumbled him over and over and over; he was barely aware of Melissa yelling, then the wave receded, left him washed up, panting, bent over her rigid, trembling body.

What had he done to her?

"Melissa."

"Yes." She was out of breath, shaking now, muscles still locked as if she thought he'd be slamming into her again at any moment.

Shame set in. "Are you all right? What happened?"

"Yes. Yes. I'm fine." She straightened painfully, rotated her left shoulder.

Jack pulled out of her, sank back onto the couch, yanked his pants the rest of the way off, grabbed a tissue and took care of the condom without looking at her face. Without being able to. "Come here."

She waddled over awkwardly on her knees, sank onto his lap, laid her head on his chest. He wrapped his arms around her, rocked her gently. "I'm sorry I was so—"

What could he say. Brutal? Punishing?

"Hot?" She turned her face up to his, looking a bit dazed, but smiling sweetly. "Sexy? I don't think I've come that hard ever. I hope your neighbors didn't call the police. Talk about yelling bloody murder."

He blinked. Stared at her.

Then realization struck. When he thought she was twisting in pain, she was straining down to touch herself, to bring herself off.

"You came?"

"Uh…yeah? You didn't hear me?" She laughed, flushed, glowing, the most beautiful woman he'd ever seen. "I'm surprised your windows are intact."

Jack moved without knowing he was going to, kissed her over and over, grabbed another condom from the coffee-table drawer, tumbled her back onto the couch, covering her body with his, matching her—face, chest, groin, thigh, toe—the way he'd wanted to before and didn't have the nerve. She opened her legs and he was between them, hard again already.

This time, no banging, no assault. He was gentle, sweet, kissing her leisurely, making love to her slowly, experiencing her, eyes, lips, hair, skin, taking his own pleasure, aware of her response as much as his own every time he moved inside her. No hurry, no urgency, they had all the time in the world alone with each other.

He loved her.

The certainty made him close his eyes, started his body tensing.

"Jack," she whispered. She touched his face, stroked his cheek, ran a sweet fingertip over his forehead.

He opened his eyes to the truth in hers.

She loved him.

Fear warred with passion; he tunneled his arms underneath her, pulled her closer still, and brought them both slowly to climaxes that were torn from them, that shot them up and held them together, then let them down gently, a bit at a time.

Fear pushed hard. Was that love? Shooting you to heights then letting you down?

He buried his face in her neck, inhaling her scent, telling himself to stay calm, not to go mental. Telling himself to have the balls to stay with her, to find out if this would last, when an increasingly large part of him was yelling, "Ditch her, run, stay safe." The same emotions his father must have felt. The same claustrophobia: both loving and hating his emotions, rejecting and embracing them. No wonder his dad drank. No wonder he self-destructed. No wonder he ran.

Jack rolled to the side, pulled Melissa against him, rested his hand over his eyes. He'd thought he could put her in a photographic box and she'd busted it wide-open, changing his pictures and him. He'd thought he could control his emotions, keep them stuffed down and unthreatening, and she'd turned them loose to a degree he hadn't believed himself capable of.

"Mmm. That was so nice, Jack." She stretched luxuriously. "It was different. So slow and lovely."

He raised her hand to his lips, kissed it, laced their fingers. "You hungry?"

"Almost." She smiled dreamily at him. "A few more minutes. I'm so relaxed."

"How's the blood pressure these days?"

"Perfectly normal. You've been so good for me." She squeezed his hand, nestled her head more comfortably on his chest and yawned. "My sister says I'm unrecognizable."

"And…that's good?"

Melissa giggled. "She thinks so. By the way, Dad won't dance, so at her wedding, Gretchen wants us to come onto the floor after she and Ted start their first dance, to get everyone else to join in."

"Uh…" Jack wasn't sure he'd processed that correctly. "I'm working her wedding."

"Right. But just the ceremony and formal photos."

"I know, but it's not like I'm going." He watched her beaming expression fade into bemusement. This was exactly what he'd worried about. His mistake for not bringing it up sooner and making sure their roles at this event were clearly defined.

"Not going?" She lifted her head. "What are you talking about?"

"I'm not going as a guest. We agreed I'd work, and that was it."

"Jack." Obviously he was making as much sense to her as she was to him. "We're both invited. We're sitting at the head table. And we'll be the first ones out dancing after Gretchen and Ted. What did you think—I'd make you eat in the kitchen?"

He stared at her, feeling his own blood pressure rising. "Melissa, we only agreed that I'd work this wedding."

"You said that, Jack." She struggled to sit up. He followed suit. "This is about something else, isn't it?"

She was no dummy. He owed her an explanation. Something besides *I love you and it scares the crap out of me.* "Melissa, I'm sorry, I don't see that we have a go-to-weddings-together relationship."

Melissa looked around as if trying to find the spaceship he'd flown in on. He didn't blame her. He was talking like an idiot. "Jack, what the hell is a go-to-weddings relationship?"

"Uh…" He attacked his hair again. "You know, a boyfriend-and-girlfriend relationship. The whole marriage track."

God, what was he saying? Wasn't that what he felt for her?

Yes, but only half of him. A half that was rapidly shrinking in the face of panic.

"Jack." She was looking at him as if he'd just told her he could see dead people. "In case you haven't noticed, we've been having sex pretty constantly for the past few weeks. I don't think it was really weird of me to assume we'd hang out at the wedding together when you've finished shooting. And I don't see what is so threatening about eating lasagna next to me and swaying on the dance floor for five minutes to help out my sister."

Christ. This was getting worse and worse. She was making perfect sense. All he had to counter with was his fear and his gut certainty that he couldn't put on a suit and sit through a wedding reception as her date with all of Melissa's family and friends there. Rational? No, not entirely. But there was no way.

"I'm sorry, Melissa." He hated how he sounded, hated the hurt on her face, but if he said he'd be happy to go with her, he'd be lying to them both. "It's just not something I can do."

Her breath caught. She rolled off the couch and stood

to face him, arms folded across her chest. "What are you
really saying here, Jack? That I'm not your girlfriend or
going to be your girlfriend? That I don't belong with you?
After we just made love the way we did, you can say that?"

She didn't understand. "We've had a lot of fun. A lot.
But I'm not ready to play husband to you at some formal
function like it's our—"

"Husband?" She was incredulous. "I'm sorry, did I ask
you to marry me? Because I don't remember that at all."

He got off the couch, strode to the other side of the
room, took deep breaths to cool off. "Look, Melissa. Here's
what it is. We're at this point where you're starting to want
more and I'm starting to want less. I've been at this point
many times, and I know—"

"Oh, for God's sake, spare me the you're-just-like-all-
the-others bullshit. That isn't true and you know it." She
unfolded her arms, stalked across the room and got right
into his face, topless and sexy as hell in the black miniskirt
with fire shooting out of her eyes. Even now he wanted
to back her against the wall and take her again. "There is
something special between us, which I am no longer afraid
of. If you are, there's nothing I can do about that. If you
won't go to the wedding with me, fine, but don't you *dare*
start acting like some big sex god who made yet another
girl fall out of her depth with him."

Jack clenched his jaw hard. Closed his eyes, trying to
control his temper, collect his thoughts. Breathing. Thinking. Controlling.

He opened them. Melissa hadn't moved. "You're right.
What we have is special. And you're also right that I'm
afraid of it. But that isn't going to change. So I leave it
to you. Either you take me as I am, one day at a time, no
guarantees, no commitment, or we quit now. I'll photograph your sister's wedding because I said I would and

because I want to. But I'm leaving the suit at home, and I'm checking out after the pictures are done. If you want to see me after that, you can call me anytime and I'll be really happy to hear from you."

He could swear she'd stopped breathing, seemed about to collapse in on herself. It was agony.

Then she straightened, swallowed and nodded. "Fair enough, Jack. I don't see the point of me pretending I'm not falling in love with you. So if you can't handle that I will go find someone who can."

She grabbed her bra, flung her shirt back over her head, stepped into her sandals…

And was gone.

13

Blood Pressure: High Normal

"Hi, I'm Georgina, from the sales office downstairs. Can I talk to you for a second?"

Melissa looked up from the file of a new hire in Chicago. She remembered Georgina, administrative assistant for the department. A tall slender woman with short side-parted hair and a tattooed bracelet on her upper arm. "Hi, Georgina, good to see you. Come on in."

"Thanks." She walked in rather furtively, and shut the door behind her, took a seat and trapped her hands between her knees. "Um. I'm here about Bob. Bob Stoker."

"Right." Melissa closed the file and pushed her chair back. Uh-oh. She hoped this wouldn't end up looking bad for Bob and good for Mary Jo. The more she thought about the duo, neither whom she'd want for best friends, the more she suspected Mary Jo and the less she suspected Bob. "How can I help?"

"Thing is, I've worked with Bob here for about a year. One of my girlfriends, Patty, used to work in the Minneapolis office with him."

"Oh, yes, I think I met her when I was on a trip out there."

last summer." Melissa forced her voice and manner to be calm, but her heart rate and no doubt her blood pressure were high and climbing. She'd barely made it into work that morning after a night spent productively curled into a ball either crying or staring at the wall.

"Patty and I were talking last night. And we agreed I should come in today and talk to you. About Bob."

"Okay." Melissa folded her hands on the desk, looking as friendly and approachable as she knew how. Not as if her life was burying her in an avalanche of goat poo. "Go ahead."

Georgina laughed nervously. "Actually this is kind of scary. We're a little afraid for our jobs."

"You have nothing to be afraid of. You can't be fired for telling the truth." She wished that were true. Melissa wouldn't be doing the firing, but sometimes the truth could piss people off in positions higher up than hers.

"Well, I don't know about that. Because *we* know it's the truth, but we might not be able to convince other people."

Melissa's knee started jiggling. *Just say it.* "Please go ahead. Hearing the truth is very important to me. And I'm sure it's important for Bob that this situation gets cleared up."

"Okay." She scratched her cheek, looking more fourteen that twenty-something. "Well, Bob is a really great guy. But he…he's sort of into himself."

"Go on."

"And he's gorgeous, and he's kind of a character. So he gets into these situations where because of his ego and his way of…I don't know, I guess putting himself out there, women think…they think he's sort of inviting something, and so the more aggressive ones get him in trouble. Because, really, he wouldn't want to do anything with any of them. I can promise you that."

"You know this because…"

She lifted her eyes, so dark brown they were nearly black, with long lashes. "Because Bob is gay."

Melissa couldn't move. She wanted to laugh, not because it was funny, but because the solution could be just that simple, and she rather viciously hoped it was. Serve Mary Jo right. Not nice of Melissa, maybe, but she was in the mood to be vicious. "How do you know this?"

"He told me." She made a face. "Though a few of us had already figured it out. I'm a lesbian and I'm out in the office, but he's not. He's too scared of what people might think. So he kind of goes overboard with the I-like-women thing. I guess to compensate. And some women, especially the older ones, I guess they think he's fair game. And they really come after him. Mary Jo has been the worst. She won't leave him alone."

"Okay." Ha! Gotcha, Mary Jo. Oh, this felt good.

"I heard them arguing once." Georgina wrinkled her nose. "Well, I could have moved out of earshot, but…"

"Too good to miss, huh?"

"I guess, but also I knew she'd been bugging him and he needed a witness. Anyway, Bob really did ask Mary Jo to leave him alone in a really nice way. He complimented her, said she was great, but that he wasn't interested, something like that. *Then…*" Georgina slapped the arm of her chair. "Mary Jo said he'd change his mind if he ever had her, and when he said he didn't think so, she threatened to fire him and then apparently she started undressing."

"Good lord."

Georgina choked a little, put a fist in front of her mouth and swallowed a few times, holding herself rigid. It took a minute for Melissa to realize she was trying not to giggle. "He came running out of there and into my office, looking white as a sheet."

Having seen Mary Jo, Melissa wasn't surprised. And if she hadn't spent such a miserable night, she'd be giggling, too.

A final snort escaped Georgina; she put a hand to her chest. "I'm sorry. I know it's disrespectful to laugh, and that this is a serious situation. But it was also...well, it was hilarious. The poor guy. I thought he was going to throw up, he was so upset. He kept saying, 'Why does this keep happening to me?' So we talked about it for a while, how he was behaving and maybe sending out signals he wasn't aware of. Maybe he does get it now. I hope he does. The poor guy."

Yes. Poor Bob. Everything about Georgina's explanation made instant sense and felt true and right. Melissa's confusion over whom to believe was magically erased, just like that. If only she had a solution that easy for her mess with Jack. "Georgina, I am so glad you decided to talk to me."

"I hope it helps him." She stood, smiling with relief. "He's a good guy. Sort of a mess, but..."

"Who isn't?" Melissa offered her hand, bursting with eagerness to tell Barbara. Case closed! Or it would be after the proper channels were gone through. It would have made Melissa very uncomfortable if Barbara had insisted they take Mary Jo's side.

The second her office door closed behind Georgina, Melissa picked up the phone and called Barbara. "You busy?"

"Always am." She sounded terse, crabby, as she'd increasingly been over the past couple of weeks. "What's up?"

"Just had a break in the Bob Stoker case."

"You mean Bob Whatsisname?"

"Yeah, that one."

"Oh, good. A castration would brighten my morning. Come on over."

Melissa hung up the phone, wincing. Ted thought Barbara was bitter, and so did Gretchen. Rather agonizingly, Melissa was starting to wonder, too. Had she been listening to the wrong person all these years? Hearing what she wanted to hear to protect herself from getting hurt?

If she'd listened to Barbara, she wouldn't have met Jack. She wouldn't have agreed to be photographed, she wouldn't have let him touch her. She wouldn't have fallen at least some of the way in love with him, and she wouldn't now be horribly miserably hurt and looking at the rest of her life as one big mess of time without him.

But she could say the same thing again and mean something completely different. She wouldn't have met Jack. She wouldn't have fallen in love with him. And she wouldn't now be looking at the rest of her life realizing how much she wanted him in it. If she couldn't have him, then she would find another man, though she couldn't even fathom that right now, because her brain and her heart and her soul were so full of Jack and the promise of what she believed they could have. But people got over devastating losses. They moved on. They found new happiness. Sitting in one self-improvement class after another, while useful, important and enriching, hadn't brought her anything like the beautiful richness she found in him and in herself when they were together.

She found Barbara typing at her computer, tight-lipped, banging on the keys with such force Melissa was surprised they could still pop back up.

"Hi." She walked in with all the enthusiasm of someone approaching a firing squad. "Another tough day?"

"Are there any other kind?"

Melissa couldn't bring herself to laugh, which she usu-

lly did. Then she'd feel bonded to Barbara, the solidar-
ty of head-in-the-sand cynicism. Given that Melissa had
ived through a few moments in the past nearly twenty-four
ours when poking herself with darts seemed like a vaca-
ion compared to her pain, she wasn't willing to go back
o the Land of Negativity right now. Especially because
3arbara had so many chances to move beyond the misery
nd get on with her new single life, instead of clinging to
er husband's betrayal.

"Sorry to hear that. I just had a talk with Georgina, the
ecretary in—"

"Oh, yes, I know Georgina." She smiled tightly, folded
er hands on her empty desk. "She's a great worker, a very
mart woman."

Melissa prepared herself to drop the bomb, trying not
o look pleased. "Mary Jo is the problem."

Barbara's smile did a rapid vanishing act. "I sincerely
loubt that."

"Why?"

"Because she's a friend of mine, she's a good person
nd—"

"A woman?"

Barbara's mouth was still open for her next word, which
lidn't come. Melissa had never ever spoken to her like
hat. She wasn't even sure she should have this time, but
vhatever was bothering Barbara, it wasn't fair of her to
ake it out on Bob.

Still no response. Melissa clenched her fist, waiting for
er heart to start pumping, her head to feel as if it wanted
o explode off her body and soar into space.

It didn't.

"Okay." The smile was back, but it wasn't a particu-
arly friendly one. "Maybe you need to tell me what you
nean by that."

Maybe she'd better stick to the case. "Georgina only confirmed what I already knew, Barbara. I spoke to Mary Jo and to Bob, as you know. The more I thought about it, the more convinced I was that Bob was telling the truth and Mary Jo was lying."

"There is no way Mary Jo is lying." Barbara banged on her desk for emphasis. "That guy has caused one too many problems for this company."

"I'm sorry if this isn't what you want to hear, but Bob did not harass Mary Jo, it was the other way around." Melissa found herself speaking quietly but with an authority and force she didn't know she could muster. "I have a witness, who also told me that Bob is gay."

Barbara blinked. Melissa allowed herself to hope her boss would realize her mistake and this whole weird nightmare of having to accept that her most trusted advisor might be full of hot air would end. "How does Georgina know he's— Oh, right, takes one to know one."

Takes one to know one? Were they still in grade school?

She summoned her patience and tried another tack. "Barbara, what's going on? You seem really upset."

"I am upset." She opened a drawer and shut it, then did it again with another one. "I haven't told you, but I'm being unfairly accused by the men who run this company. They've been snooping into my business, trying to find a reason to get rid of me. They can't stand powerful women. None of them."

Melissa's stomach muscles were nearly cramping with tension, but she forced herself to sit quietly. Usually she'd jump to her boss's defense with an oh-how-could-they rant. But today she was seeing her through radically different eyes. Maybe the higher-ups were investigating because they had a good reason to.

"Barbara, I'm so sorry. That must feel terrible."

Barbara put her head between her hands. "Oh, it's way beyond terrible. It's outrageous."

"But if you haven't done anything, how can they get rid of—" She stopped. Bob hadn't done anything, either, and that hadn't stopped Barbara from wanting him out.

"Child." Barbara shook her head, hands still at her temples. "This is men we're talking about. Have I taught you *nothing?*"

Melissa got to her feet. Her patience had run out, along with the time she wanted to spend in this office. Bob would stay, she'd see to it. Mary Jo would suffer the consequences of her actions.

At Barbara's door, Melissa turned. "Pretty much, yeah."

She left before Barbara could figure out what she'd just said.

BONNIE KNOCKED ON SETH'S door. Her turn to pester him for a change. She had no idea if he knew what was happening to his song on YouTube. If he didn't, she was planning to tell him. If he did, she was going to help him celebrate.

And she would ask him about the perfume chick, Matti, and whether she was still interested in renting space at Bonnie Blooms. A few more weddings had come through recently—Melissa's sister, Gretchen's, on the twenty-ninth, though it wasn't a huge job, and a couple of others. One was the friend of a bride whose wedding Bonnie had designed the previous year. That was encouraging. Word of mouth could snowball and friends of friends of friends would start calling. She kept praying like mad it would happen. In the meantime, she was cultivating relationships on Facebook, introducing herself to hotel managers, restaurateurs, ministers, rabbis, funeral home directors, wherever she could imagine flowers being used. Exhausting, but at least she felt as if she were doing something. Much better than sitting home feeling herself failing bit by bit.

Something would happen.

"Hey, come in." Seth stood at the door, gaze vacant, motioned her in robotically, then strode off in the direction of his studio. Bonnie followed, smiling. Weird dudes, those composers, lost in their alternative worlds of creation, their brains staying there sometimes even when real life intruded.

Notes sounded from the studio—guitar this time. Seth would be working out some passage he nearly had right. If he was in a total impasse he would have ditched the music and hung out with Bonnie until his muse was ready to cooperate.

She went into the studio, surprised to find a fast-food bag on the piano, and papers on the floor that looked as if they'd fallen and been left there. Very unusual. This room never had a dust mote out of place.

While Seth worked, she threw out the garbage, piled the papers neatly and put them back on one of his nearby music stands.

"Thanks, sorry." Seth made a final notation on his music paper and put the guitar back in its case. He looked tired and a little down. He must not know about YouTube yet. How like him to post a video and then forget about it while he went off in a new direction. "Just had a breakthrough."

"I figured." She gave him a quick peck on the cheek. "You look like hell."

"Hey, thanks again." He stretched, groaning. "Haven't been sleeping."

"No?" She was troubled. Seth could sleep during a bear attack. "What's going on?

"I dunno." He got up and sat at the piano, a place he always retreated to when he felt uneasy. "Just not sleeping."

"Seth." She was beyond exasperated. "You have the emotional consciousness of a flea. Something must be bothering you."

"Something is." He tried out a few dissonant chords. "I don't want to talk about it, okay?"

"Yes. Okay. I'm sorry." Bonnie held up both hands in surrender. She was not here to argue with him yet again. Seemed as if the only way they'd been able to interact lately was to get on each other's nerves. "So…"

She waited until he looked over at her, his gray eyes vibrant and magnetic, even swollen with fatigue. "So… what?"

Bonnie nonchalantly ran her hands over the black varnished wood of his piano. "So have you looked at your YouTube video lately?"

"Why would I look at it? It's me."

"I mean to see how many people have watched it."

"Why would I?"

"Seth!" She wanted to bang the piano lid down on his hands. "You went viral. Big-time."

His hands froze on the keys. "No way."

"Total way. Guess how many hits."

A smile bloomed across his features, turning him sweet and endearingly boyish. He stood up. "I have no idea. Tell me."

"Nope." She lifted her chin, taunting him. "Guess."

"Tell me." He lunged for her, spun her toward him and pinned her against the piano, holding her hands behind her back. "Now."

"If I don't?" She gave him a saucy look, like a little sister or a pal. But it was damn hard to pretend that's what she was feeling when he was so close. He hadn't grabbed her playfully like that in a long time, and invariably when he used to…stuff happened. "What'll you do about it?"

A beat passed. "I'll kiss you until you can't breathe anymore."

Bonnie gasped, then made a sound halfway between a plea for mercy and one for him to do exactly that. Color flooded her cheeks, her body woke fully from its sexual hibernation. Seth's eyes darkened; his gaze fell to her mouth.

No. "Okay, I'll tell you. Three hundred twenty-five thousand—"

"Too late." His mouth came down, hard, possessive and full of erotic promise. She responded full-throttle, her body reacting without her permission.

She and Seth had always been good. In bed, on tables, chairs, floors, sofas, window ledges, beaches, bathrooms, vehicles…anywhere they wouldn't get caught. Together they'd been wild, uninhibited, extremely flexible and willing to try anything anywhere anytime. All those memories started pouring back as she clutched his broad shoulders, unsure whether she was trying to pull him closer or push him away. She'd never been with a lover like him, never had this instant fiery attraction with anyone else. Not even close.

His tongue entered her mouth, the bulge of his erection pressed insistently between her legs. Her longing for sex became desperate, overwhelming. To have a man inside her, to touch a male body, stroke his skin, feel hard muscle and flesh against and in possession of hers.

She wanted that. And here was Seth…

Just this one time, animal and satisfying and purely physical. He'd expect nothing more afterward and neither would she. She had three dates lined up for the following week. Three promising guys. It was her one chance to do this again with Seth before she belonged to somebody else.

His hands lifted her shirt, yanked it off. She pulled his off, too, devoured his mouth hungrily again, shoving down her skirt and panties, loving his moan of appreciation as her body emerged from its cover. He'd always made her feel so female, so sexy…

Except when he made her feel like dirt on his boot. She wasn't going to forget that.

His pants hit the floor and it was her turn to moan, her hands reaching for his already erect cock. He was so beautiful, thick and smooth, faintly pink at the tip.

He took her hips, swung her around and turned her away from him. Bonnie understood. He wanted this the same way she did, urgent and with a quick release, no chance of emotional overload.

She bent forward over the arm of the couch and offered herself, heard his quick intake of breath and then felt him thrusting, searching for entrance. She reached back and guided him; they both went still with pleasure as he found what he was looking for, then pushed in and started pumping, aggressive, the way she loved it from him, hard and no-nonsense, building up heat and friction.

She moved forward onto her elbows, sinking slightly into the cushion, balanced her abdomen on the sofa arm and locked her legs behind her around his waist. He moved her up high enough that he could stroke her clitoris while he thrust. Bonnie gave a cry that was almost a shout, getting so hot, then so much hotter, burning, building to her climax fast and easily, then coming in a huge rush of ecstasy, yelling his name. He drove into her and she heard the familiar burst of air between his teeth that meant he was coming, too.

They came down together, and then it was over…and Bonnie was okay. Intact. Blissful even, triumphant. She disentangled her legs from his waist; Seth lowered her gently. She stood up, smiled at him. "That was awesome, thanks."

He reached for her, but she kissed his cheek and went to find her clothes, checking in with herself to make sure she wasn't just being dim or suppressing. That she really had survived sex with Seth exactly the way she thought she could.

Yes. Bonnie Fortuna was okay. She shook her hair back, grinning widely. Really okay. Next week she'd go on her new dates, and think fondly of this last time with Seth, but there would be no more pain.

Wow. *Wow.*

"Oh, Seth." She crawled to retrieve her panties from under the piano. "I meant to ask about Matti, the renter. Is that going to—"

"Bonnie."

She turned to face Seth, her smile fading. She'd never heard him use that tone. "You called?"

"Didn't we just have incredible sex here?" His hands were on his hips. He was still naked, straight and tall, a thing of godlike beauty, gray eyes somber.

Uh-oh. Keep it light, Bonnie. Don't let him drag you into this again.

"We did. Incredible sex." She stepped into her panties, pulled them up. "But when have we ever had any other kind?"

"It didn't change anything?"

Change anything?

"No, of course not." She pretended not to be furious. Pigheaded idiot. How many chances had she given him over the years? How often had she pined for him? How often had she been rejected exactly the way she was doing to him now, only ten times worse because they'd suppos-edly been serious about each other? Now that she was declaring them completely over, had told him about the men she was meeting the next week, he was expecting her to come running back because they'd screwed each other. "It changes nothing."

"I'm going to start therapy."

Bonnie gaped at him, her skirt halfway up her thighs. She couldn't have heard that right. "Therapy? Why?"

"Because I need to find out…" He pressed his lips together, making an obvious effort to finish the sentence. "Why I can't be with you."

She pulled her skirt the rest of the way up and stood for a moment, monitoring her emotions. The old Bonnie would have thought, "Oh, gosh, he really does love me," and she would have melted back to him, her battered hope alive once again.

The new Bonnie was beginning to understand that Seth was like a bacteria or virus, which kept mutating so it could still infect and/or damage its target host no matter what medications were invented to wipe it out.

"Seth, why hasn't it bothered you for the past several years that you couldn't be with me?"

He hung his head, gave her a sheepish smile. "Bon, if I knew that I wouldn't need therapy."

She sighed, then gave in and laughed. "Okay. Well, good. I'm proud of you. I know that's a huge step."

"Thanks."

Deep breath. She had to make sure he understood. "But nothing changes for me. I'm still dating and still trying to find a man who wants me right now. If you get your shit together, fine, we can talk. But until then…"

Seth gave a single nod. "Fair enough."

"Good." She gave his body a wistful once-over. "Put some clothes on, would you? A woman can only take so much perfection."

His grin spread again. He picked up his jeans and dragged them on. "Yes, ma'am. And I'll double check with Matti, but she sounded enthusiastic when we first talked."

"Thank you." Bonnie stepped toward him, kissed him quickly, squeezing his arm. She hadn't felt on such an even keel with Seth since they'd been dating and happy together in college, before Seth freaked and moved on. She liked this about herself. She liked it a lot.

And if she had anything to say about it, she wouldn't ever go back to the way things used to be.

14

JACK WALKED INTO THE Come to Your Senses common area and headed for the refrigerator, feeling as if he were hauling around giant blocks of lead in his chest. He was out of beer in his apartment and didn't have the energy to go and get more.

Seth sat on the worn green couch, elbows resting on his knees, the brown glass top of a beer bottle visible in his right hand. "Hey, how's it going?"

"Good." Jack scanned the contents of the refrigerator. Apparently it was going to be a Miller Genuine Draft day. Seth must have finished the other brands. "You?"

"Good."

Jack sank sideways into his favorite chair, draped his legs over the worn armrest. "Long day."

"Same here."

They drank in silence.

"Wanna listen to tunes?" Jack asked.

"Machine's busted."

"Oh."

More silence, except for the glug of swallowed beer. Amazing how much guys could say without words. Jack knew exactly what was bugging Seth. "Trouble with Bonnie, huh?"

Seth laughed bitterly. "Is there ever not?"

"I guess no."

"It's my fault. I'm not…" He blew a raspberry. "Whatever. Trouble with Melissa?"

"Yeah. My fault, too. I'm not—" Jack imitated Seth's raspberry "—either."

Silence. An apartment door opened, then closed down the hall. Footsteps headed away from them, toward the elevator.

"We should go out," Seth said. "Hear some music."

"Yeah. This is bullshit."

"It is."

Neither of them moved. Their beers were dutifully consumed.

"Where's Bonnie tonight?" Jack asked. "I saw her leaving a few hours ago, all dressed up."

Seth shrugged as if he didn't care. "She's got a date."

"A date with a guy?"

Seth gave him a withering glare. "No, a date with a gerbil. Geez, Jack."

"Right, sorry." He was torn in half, proud of Bonnie and sick for Seth. And for himself. Melissa would start dating again, too. Probably soon. She'd be snapped up in half an hour. Maybe less. Undoubtedly less.

It would kill him.

"Where's Melissa?"

Jack shrugged as if he didn't care. "Probably helping set up for the wedding tomorrow. Rehearsal dinner, something like that."

"You going tomorrow?"

"I'm working it."

"Ooh." Seth winced. "That's not going to be fun."

"About as much as you waiting for Bonnie to come home tonight."

"Uh-huh." Seth tossed his empty bottle into the re-cycling bin, got up and got himself and Jack new ones. "Sometimes I wonder what the hell I'm doing, you know? What is wrong with me? Why can't I just say 'yeah, okay, she's what I want and let's go'?"

"Because you're a moron?"

Seth's eyebrows rose. "Dude, I'd like to think it's a little more complicated than that."

"It has to be." Jack tossed his beer toward the bin the way Seth had. Only he missed. "Or I'm a moron, too."

"Yeah? Let me guess. She wants more than you can give her. Am I right?"

"Not that simple, either." Melissa had never pressed him for anything more than naming what was already happening between them. She'd been right that Gretchen's wedding was just a party. It even made sense that she'd expected him to be her date. "The irony is that she wants exactly what I want. But it's like I don't know how to let myself have it."

Seth lifted his head. "Yeah. Yeah, exactly."

"How do you explain that to someone when it doesn't make sense?"

"Dude." Seth shook his head mournfully. "You can't. Or we would have."

They subsided back into silence.

"So, um." Seth fidgeted on the sofa. "I'm, uh, thinking of going to talk to someone."

"Bonnie?"

"Professionally."

"A shrink?" Jack stared at him. This was like a vegan applying for a job at a slaughterhouse.

"Yeah. Yeah, maybe someone can figure this out. Like

it all stems from not getting breast-fed or wanting to kill my father or something."

Jack snorted. "Yeah, I can think of a few times in my family when that last one seemed like a good option."

"No kidding." Seth hunched his shoulders. "That piece probably has something to do with it. Men and their fathers, all that stuff."

"Probably does. So you're going to dig up all that crap again?"

"I don't want him to win." Seth's voice rose. "My whole life he had all the power in the house, over all of us. His moods, his behavior, everything was up to him. Whether we were happy, sad, safe, every freaking thing."

Jack had to try twice to produce sound. "Dude, I hear you."

"I left as soon as I could, but he's still effing me up, even this far from him, across the whole country. It pisses me off. I can't let him win, Jack. I can't let the son of a bitch win. Especially if it means hurting someone I love over and over." He laughed bitterly. "Then I'm no freaking better than him."

Jack's blood went cold. He put down his beer. Hurting people he loved. Not being there for them, withholding affection, withholding time and any sense of security. All relationships conducted on the bare surface of what there could be.

Just like dear old Dad.

Jesus. While Jack was busy swearing he'd never be anything like his father, he'd turned right into the bastard.

"I don't know about you, Bonnie, but this looks like the most depressing party I've ever been to."

Jack and Seth jumped and turned. Angela and Bonnie were standing in the doorway, Dèmi behind them.

"Seriously." Bonnie flounced into the room, looking

beautiful in a green draped minidress that was making poor Seth grit his teeth. "Who died and where are our beers?"

"Whew." Angela flopped onto the black-and-white couch. "I'm beat."

"Where have you been?" Jack asked.

"We went dancing." Angela fanned herself. "Serious dancing."

Seth glanced at Bonnie. "We who?"

"Well." Angela lifted her hand and let it smack down. Unless Jack's intuition was malfunctioning, she was feeling no pain. "I was coming back from Daniel's early because he has to get up at the crack of dawn for some meeting and I bumped into Bonnie, who'd just escaped her date from hell. We both bumped into Demi and dragged her with us. However, we wish we hadn't because she totally showed us up on the dance floor."

"Oh, come on." Demi had color in her face, was laughing, animated. What a difference.

"You did. Don't deny it." Bonnie, while not exactly oozing affection, at least wasn't sneering at her.

"Let the party begin." Seth tossed his empty beer bottle over his head. Incredibly, it went bang, without breaking, into the recycling bin to cheers from the crowd. He jumped up, grinning, and ran to the refrigerator to dole out more. Funny how the phrase *date from hell* had revived him.

"We were waiting for you." Jack swung his legs to the front of the chair. "It's tough being men alone."

"Yeah." Seth handed Bonnie a beer. "We don't know what to say after, 'How about them Seahawks?'"

Jack caught the bottle Seth tossed him. "Now we can just sit back and listen to you."

"Bonnie, we especially want to hear all about your

date." Seth popped the top off his beer and toasted her smugly.

"Bastard." She sent him a well-deserved glare, but because Bonnie was Bonnie, she grabbed center stage and started in.

Jack heard something about breath she could smell across the table, and OBG—which she defined as Obsessive Golf Disease—before his thoughts drifted, his mood further buoyed by the laughter and camaraderie around him. Good friends. Good people.

Tomorrow afternoon he'd show up at Gretchen's wedding, ready to take pictures. He'd also be wearing a suit and be ready to dance that first dance. Ready to tell Melissa they belonged together, and that even though she might need to be patient with him, he'd do everything in his power to prove he believed it.

His gaze landed on Angela, shrieking with laughter next to Demi, who wasn't shrieking, but smiling widely. Something was kicking in the back of his mind. Something about Angela and Daniel, and how they'd initially committed to each other.

Yes. There it was.

Tomorrow afternoon he'd show up at Gretchen's wedding with his photographer's hat on.

Tomorrow morning he'd be doing something else entirely.

MELISSA STOOD NEXT to her sister, Ted on the other side of Gretchen, their dad on the other side of Ted. They were all smiling. At Jack.

Before this she'd been standing next to her sister and Ted and Ted's best man. And she'd also been smiling. At Jack.

Before that there had been other pictures. In all of them

she'd had to stand there, her emotional guts being hauled out of her body with giant grappling hooks as she smiled at Jack.

The ceremony had been a beautiful, simple service held in her father's backyard on this absolutely perfect day, breezy, sunny and warm, but not too warm. Gretchen was the perfect bride, stunning in the dress she'd made, baby's breath and cream-colored sweetheart roses tucked into her hair. Her bouquet was more sweetheart roses, some of which matched the pale pink dress Melissa wore.

Bonnie was a genius.

Angela's tiers of cream- and pink-frosted chocolate cupcakes stood ready, as did the butter cake she'd made for Gretchen to decorate with swirls of subtly colored frosting that matched the embroidery on her dress and more of Bonnie's roses. On the table were pans of lasagna, bowls of salad and loaves of French bread that Gretchen, Bonnie and her friends had pitched in to make. Chilling in ice-filled tubs were bottles of reasonably priced French sparkling wine—Seth had recommended the brand, and he knew his stuff—beer, regular wine and sodas.

Everything about the occasion had turned out ideally. And Melissa had never been so torn. On the one hand, she was deliriously happy for her sister. Gretchen and Ted's love for each other was so powerful it was palpable, infecting the party with the type of joy that only came from a match everyone was thrilled about.

On the other hand...

She missed Jack. Terribly. Watching a man commit the rest of his life to a woman with such ease and certainty made it pretty hard to swallow that Jack couldn't commit to so much as a dance.

And yet. If he couldn't, then he wasn't the right man for her. And when the bleeding stopped from the gaping wound in her heart, she'd try again. Because she knew now what she really wanted and needed in her life. Not what Barbara said she wanted. Barbara, who was now her ex-boss, fired for routinely informing female hires of the salary gap between them and their male counterparts.

Melissa still wanted to be strong and independent, but thanks to having met Jack, she realized she could be strong and independent alongside a man. She and her future mate didn't have to turn into Gretchen and Ted, or her mother and father. There were other ways.

Obvious, maybe, but sometimes when your heart was so close to a truth it was very, very hard to see it. A little part of her still hoped Jack would realize that in time.

"Okay, that's it, thank you. Enjoy the party, and congratulations again." Jack stepped back from the tripod and sent Melissa an intense glance that seemed to say *this isn't over.*

Or maybe it said, *bye, babe, thanks for the sex.* She wasn't that great at reading intense glances. Since he'd already started packing up his gear, it seemed to mean he was leaving.

She drifted toward the party, then without meaning to, she looked back and found herself standing there watching Jack stride away, taking a piece of her heart with him. She'd grow it whole again, yes, but Jack Shea would always have that piece.

He turned down the driveway and she eventually lost him behind the cars lining the hilly street.

Gone.

Melissa joined the crowd already enjoying assorted beverages and the informal hors d'oeuvres they'd supplied—pretzels, chips, cut-up vegetables and Gretchen's beloved blue cheese dip. More of Bonnie's stunning flowers graced the buffet table and the five tables set up on the lawn. Even though Jack was no longer here, everywhere she looked,

he contributions of his Come to Your Senses friends reminded her of him.

Come on. Melissa shook herself out of her mood. This
was her sister's wedding. She'd managed not to break down
so far; this wasn't the time to start.

Holding a glass of ginger ale she hoped would look like
champagne, she tried to decide where to begin mingling.
The champagne looked delicious, but she didn't trust her
emotions if she got tipsy. And she refused to be the relative crying into the potato chips at the end of the wedding.

Unfortunately the sensible plan backfired. She'd gotten
stuck talking to—er, listening to—a childhood friend of
Ted's named Ned, who had finished making jokes about
Ted and Ned's Excellent Adventures in elementary school
and was now telling her every grisly detail of the death
of his marriage and his divorce, both of which had been
totally his ex-wife's fault. Alcohol would have made him
easier to tolerate or easier to be rude to. Either would help.

"So then, while I was out one night, working the same
job, earning the *same* salary that paid for her to stay home
and do nothing all day long but spend it, *she* goes out
and—"

"Excuse me."

Melissa's heart went into overdrive at the deep voice behind her. *Jack.* She'd thought he was long gone. Had he forgotten something? She turned, trying not to look too eager.

Oh, my God.

He'd changed. Into a suit. In which he looked good
enough to dip in blue cheese and eat.

"Hi." Ned stuck out his pudgy hand. "I'm Ned, friend
of Ted."

Jack shook his hand, taking Melissa's arm. "I'm Jack,
we'll be back."

He strode across the patio and into the yard, past the

tables, dragging Melissa with him, leaving Ned ha-ha-ing madly over the joke.

"Why are you dressed like that? Where are you taking me?" She pulled free and faced him. "What is going on?"

"You looked like you needed rescuing from Ned who is friends with Ted."

"Before he bored me dead." She gestured to his suit, laughing along with him, missing him so violently retroactively that she nearly cried while cracking up. "So this is your superhero costume?"

"This is my wedding guest costume."

"Oh." She folded her arms across her chest, not because she was angry, but because hope was making her unbearably vulnerable. "I see. So you are…"

She didn't know what he was, but she was too nanny goat chicken-wattle scaredy-pants to finish the sentence. She wanted him to say it.

"I'm here as your date."

Melissa swallowed. Okay. This was good. No, this was wonderful. But…what else did it mean? That he'd shown up today for her, but then he'd disappear? Or that they were a couple?

Ha! As if.

"My date for the wedding?"

"Right." He gave her a look. "This wedding right here. The one we're at. I'm your date."

"No, I know, but then…" She broke off helplessly, not sure she wanted the answer to her question.

"And I was thinking, if you want to do something tomorrow, I could be your date then, too." He moved a step closer, smiling his unbearably sexy smile, brown eyes warm enough to melt ice. "The day after that might work as well. And hey, you know, I hear the day after that is an excellent date day, and I'm pretty sure the following week s full of possible nights I'd like to be part of, also. After hat, let's keep at it."

She simply stared at him, unable to take in all his words yet. Her date. Today. And the next day and the next day and… *Oh, my gosh.*

A giggle started in her belly. Her subconscious must have figured it out before she did because she was already smiling at him. "That sounds pretty great."

"Good. I'm glad that's settled. Did you want to go back to Ned now?" He pointed, breeze lifting the curls off his forehead and, oh, my lord, he was the most gorgeous man in the entire world and she was madly in love with him and now she wouldn't have to spend the rest of the wedding bleeding.

"You know, I think I can give Ned a pass. Now that I have a date and all."

"Nice dress, by the way." He moved in another step, grinning at her. "You're pretty hot."

"You like it?" She smoothed her hands down her waist and hips, following the lines of the dress, which pretty closely followed the lines of her body. "Would you be upset if something happened to it?"

He frowned, not quite understanding. "What…? I guess, yeah, sure. It's beautiful."

"Like, I don't know, if it got torn somehow?" She tipped her head, sending him a look through her lashes.

"That would be too bad." He narrowed his eyes, still unsure what she was getting at. "It's a great dress."

"Like maybe…" She put her hand on his arm, smiling peacefully as if they were chatting about the weather. "If you ripped it off me?"

"Ohhh, I see." His voice was low and intimate, but he nodded emphatically, keeping up with her pretense of polite conversation. "I can't wait to rip it off you, Melissa. I can't wait to get my hands over every part of you."

"Me, neither." She threw back her head and laughed as if he'd just told her a super-duper-funny knock-knock joke. "I want to feel you touching me everywhere. I want you inside me until I'm screaming for mercy."

"God, Melissa." Jack dropped all pretense at the small talk. Maybe she'd just made it impossible for his brain to handle anything that complicated. She wasn't sure she could last much longer, either. "How long until dinner starts?"

"Half an hour." Melissa took his hand and pitched her voice up to social levels. "Have I ever told you about my antique doll collection, Jack? It's up in my old room."

"Why, there's nothing I love more than antique dolls. My mother had quite the collection." He squeezed her hand and bent closer as they walked. "Uh…in your father's house?"

"Hey, it's my bedroom."

"I know, but it's his house. You're his little girl. Does he own guns?"

She smiled sweetly, brought his hand to her mouth for a kiss then guided it down slowly, letting it ride her curves on the way.

Jack sucked in a breath. "Okay, you convinced me."

"Come on." She pulled him into the house and they raced up the stairs, giggling like naughty teenagers. Melissa led him into her bedroom and closed the door as swiftly and as softly as she could. Everyone was outside. Guests were using either the downstairs bathroom or one of the portable toilets set up in the back. They'd be okay here.

"So this is little Melissa's room." Jack stood with his hands on his hips, peering at some pictures on the wall. "You were a beautiful little girl. Not that I'm surprised."

"Thanks." She reached to the back of her neck, took hold of the zipper and eased it down as quietly as possible, amused that they were alone in a bedroom about to have explosive makeup sex and he'd decided to look at pictures. He must be uncomfortable. Maybe she should tell him her father didn't own guns, and his kitchen knives were appallingly dull. "That's me at summer camp, with the horse."

"Right." He moved to the next frame. "This one?"

She got the zipper down, let the dress fall silently and stepped out of it. "That's on our one big family trip, a cruise to Alaska."

"Your mom is as beautiful as you are. And this one?"

Melissa stifled a giggle and eased her panties down. She was going to tease him about this someday. The man who would rather stare at photos than make love. But his nerves were giving her the time she needed. Her bra was off. Luckily she'd worn thigh-high stockings in case it was hot.

"This looks like—" He turned and froze, his finger still on the glass.

Melissa lifted her chin, let her body relax. Wearing only her stockings and rose-colored heels, which had been dyed to match the dress, she was grateful she hadn't styled her hair in any fancy flower-strewn upsweep, because it would not survive what was to come.

Bring it on.

"This looks like what?" she asked sweetly.

"This looks like…naked." His hand went into his jacket pocket—putting something in? She didn't care because his fingers grabbed for his tie next. Seconds later, it flew over the back of the chair next to the bed.

His jacket did the same.

Shirt.

Trousers.

Underpants.

Shoes and socks were flung off, and then she was held against his gorgeous, naked body and wrapping her arms around him, her heart finally allowing itself to realize that this was Melissa and Jack together, that it was going to be this way not just now, but for…well, who knew. Maybe Jack would panic again tomorrow. But he was worth that risk.

She hoped.

Oh, God, what if…

No, no fear. Jack had made a big stride toward her, and she would meet him there. The future would turn out the way it would.

"Melissa." His arms were around her, hands stroking her, and—

Ouch. Her body jerked. "Something scratched me."

"Oh, I'm sorry."

"What was that?" She twisted to look behind her, touched the sore spot tentatively. No blood. They wouldn't have to worry about bandages. "Are you wearing a ring or something?"

"Oh." He looked startled, then his face cleared. "As a matter of fact, yes."

"Really?" She looked at him in surprise. "I've never seen you wear one."

His eyebrows went up; he seemed horribly nervous. "I don't usually."

"Oh." Why was he acting so strangely? Had she misinterpreted something he'd said? Was he panicking already? Regretting coming to the wedding? Or being up here with her? "What is it, like a class ring?"

"No. It's yours."

Melissa laughed uncertainly. She only owned one ring.

which had belonged to her grandmother, and that was back at her apartment. "What do you mean?"

"It's your ring, Melissa." He pulled his hand out from behind her. On the end of his pinky something sparkled. "A promise ring."

"Jack." She stared at him while he slipped it on her ring finger, right hand. His eyes were dark and serious, his skin golden. The ring would be lovely, but nothing could hold a candle to this man and how he made her feel.

"Do you like it?"

She dragged her gaze down. It was beautiful, two tiny hearts linked together, one with a sapphire in its center, one with a garnet. "Jack, this is so amazing, so unexpected."

"You'll wear it?"

Melissa's gaze shot back up to his. "Oh, yes. Of course. Yes."

He kissed her, over and over, and she clung to him, trying to take in the huge twist her life had taken in the past few minutes.

"I'm not ready for an engagement yet, Melissa. But there will be no one else in my life from now on. You can even call me your b...bo...boy—" he worked his mouth, comically "—boy... Uh, you can call me the *b*-word."

Melissa burst out laughing. This man gave her so much joy. He was willing to do this for her, to put his fear aside, and she'd done the same to be with him.

"Jack, I would love to have you as my *b*-word. In return, I will give you whatever space you need when you need it, because you *will* need it from time to time, and so will I."

He took her hands and pressed them to his wonderful mouth. "And I will make sure we continue to have the most outrageously fabulous sex either of us has ever had in our lives."

"Ooh." She giggled. "Starting now?"

"Absolutely." He got up and kissed her, moved them back toward the bed.

"Melissa? Are you up there?"

Dad. Jack and Melissa exploded apart and grabbed for their clothes.

"Yes, we're here," Melissa shouted. *"I'm showing Jack my old room."*

"I'll just bet you are." Gretchen, laughter in her voice.

"We're ready to serve dinner and need the bridal party assembled," her dad called.

"Sure! Yes. Okay! Be right down!" She had her dressed zipped a few seconds later and yanked open the door. "Coming!"

"Wait." Jack, still only half-dressed, caught her and drew her to him. "I forgot to tell you something."

Melissa glanced nervously down the hall toward the stairs, tense and agitated. She didn't want to do anything to ruin what had been a perfect wedding. "What's that?"

"I love you."

Her body relaxed into total bliss. She couldn't believe she'd heard those wonderful words from his mouth. Or that she was about to whisper them back, without the slightest glimmer of panic. "I love you, too, Jack."

She put her arms around him and kissed him until they both started pressing into each other in ways that would soon have them back in the little room with the door locked and to heck with—

The wedding!

She broke the kiss. "We need to go."

"Okay." He kissed her again, hands traveling down to her bottom, pressing it firmly toward him. "But later I want to do everything we didn't get to do just now. And then more."

"That is a very good plan." She moved her hips against

him, teasing and being teased. "How about we start out in your bed?"

"Then how about the living room?"

"And on the kitchen table?"

"As long as we end up in the studio. I'm thinking of a new series, sensual man-woman stuff." He kissed her, drew his tongue leisurely across her bottom lip. "Maybe you'd like to be my model? And best friend and partner and lover…stretching into the distant future?"

"I'd like that very much." She pulled away just far enough that she could gaze into his gorgeous brown eyes, the ones that had always seen her so clearly. "It took me a while to realize, but in fact, Jack, that's what I've always wanted."

* * * * *